PRAISE FOR

SQUEAKY CLEAN

**Winner of the McIlvanney Prize
for Scottish Crime Book of the Year**

***The Times* Crime Book of the Month**

'An astonishingly good debut. Wonderfully rounded characters, misfits all, who we really care about, in a compelling story laced with humour and humanity. Callum McSorley is an outstanding new writer who is destined to become a very big name in the genre'

Peter James

'A manic tale of blood and suds told with laconic humour and warmly engaging characterisation. McSorley is definitely a talent to watch. I knew within a page that I was in good hands'

Chris Brookmyre

'An absolute knockout of a debut! Pitch-dark and yet dripping with warmth. Packed with brilliantly drawn characters, laugh-out-loud humour, and lots of blood'

Caz Frear, author of *Sweet Little Lies*

'Formidable… The mayhem in *Squeaky Clean* is tempered by the mean-eyed humor of its underdog protagonist, and by the rapid-fire dialogue delivered through the burr of Scots dialect… With its wit, terror, guts and gumption, Mr. McSorley's first novel is a smash'

Wall Street Journal

'Shattered from staying up until the daft hours finishing this. Loved it... A serious talent'

Kevin Bridges, author of *The Black Dog*

'An uproarious, sardonic noir thriller from the Glasgow depths... Brutal, wonderfully humorous and a great addition to Tartan Noir, this novel unveils a terrific new talent'

Crime Time

'McSorley writes with a wonderfully light touch... There is humour on every page, too – this really is a very funny book despite the dark material. Both main characters are works of genius, and I very much hope there will be a sequel'

Scotsman

'A fast-paced thriller with a dark sense of humour, a grisly crime caper in the vein of *Breaking Bad* and *Guilt*'

Sunday Mail

'An absolute blast... reads like a brilliant mash-up of Irvine Welsh and Alan Parks... I can't recommend this one highly enough'

Raven Crime Reads

'Gritty, bloody and oozing with the menace of the underworld... McSorley has crafted an accomplished novel that is already being hailed as a classic of the Tartan Noir genre... The sort of page-turner which ensures that once you've started, you'll keep going until the final, gripping denouement'

Scottish Field

'As gritty as a winter pavement and as dangerous as the ice before the grit goes down. I love its two brave but burnt-out heroes, and McSorley's mixture of wit, tenderness and brutality'

Sofia Slater, author of *Auld Acquaintance*

PAPERBOY

CALLUM McSORLEY

PUSHKIN
VERTIGO

Pushkin Press
Somerset House, Strand
London WC2R 1LA

Paperboy was first published by Pushkin Press in 2025

ISBN 13: 978-1-80533-545-0

Designed and typeset by Tetragon, London
Printed and bound in the United Kingdom by Clays Ltd, Elcograf S.p.A.

EU RP (for authorities only): eucomply OÜ, Pärnu mnt. 139b-14, 11317,
Tallinn, Estonia, hello@eucompliancepartner.com, +33757690241

Pushkin Press is committed to a sustainable future for our
business, our readers and our planet. This book is made from
paper from forests that support responsible forestry.

www.pushkinpress.com

1 3 5 7 9 8 6 4 2

To my Mumber one fan

PROLOGUE

The king is dead.

Paul McGuinn, Paulo to his friends and enemies, his slave girls and lieutenants and errand boys. Fraudster, drug runner, people smuggler, murderer. His wife stood at the head of the stone in an expensive black dress, holding her daughters' hands. The crowd around them was thick with black suits and Rangers scarves.

Two polis in high-vis hovered near the cemetery gate, tense, as welcome as a fart in a sleeping bag. A woman in office drabs turned her nose up at the hearse parked at the kerb, appraising the floral tributes in the back which spelt out PAUL on one side and DAD on the other. "Tasteful," she said, as she passed the uniforms into the stone-lined path. One of them recognised her and murmured "Ma'am" with a slight bow of the head.

McCoist was attending because it was her duty—she was the DCI investigating the gangster's murder, and she was the one who'd put the cunt in the ground.

She could still feel the moment, the screaming rush, then the shocking silence following the thunderclap of the gunshot. Dead ears—a dentist-drill whine and a waterfall of white noise. Squeeze of the trigger, flash of the explosion, so fast it seemed to precede the movement, like it wasn't even her who did it. Inevitable. A slap in the face with warm blood spray. A black hole in the head, punching through hair gel, skin, bone and brain. In and out the other side. The Clyde Tunnel.

Case closed.

Not that McCoist could let anyone know it was that simple.

She watched from a distance as the Rolls-Royce of a coffin was lowered into the earth. The reverend was saying something but she couldn't hear him. What do you say when you believe the deceased is going straight to hell? *Bury him deep, boays, save him the taxi fare.*

The wife threw something into the hole. Folded paper. A letter, maybe. The daughters, both of them taller than their mother in bigger heels, did the same. Surrounding them, a who's who of Glesga's criminal underworld bowed their heads and clasped their hands like schoolchildren. The impression wasn't of praying though. It looked more like they were waiting for something. A sign.

Long live the king.

She had only been able to think of two words to write to her husband:

Fuck You

And she'd written them over and over and over again until the page was full. Lottie was never much of a writer. Not her chosen method of expressing herself.

The letters had been Gemma's idea, and she was so sincere when she came out with it that Lottie had to go along with her. Her elder daughter, Ari, had agreed it was a "*wonderful*" thought, but her eyes betrayed something, maybe envy, like she wished she'd come up with it. The floral letter tributes had been her suggestion—her little sister's paper letters were both more heartfelt and cheaper. Paulo would have appreciated that. Rich men are cheap. Never spend when you can steal. Lottie had a fleet of Mulberry handbags in her wardrobe she'd always known better than to ask the provenance of. A lot of lorries turning carelessly.

Ari stepped forward and dropped hers in—God knew what she'd written—then returned to squeeze between her mother and sister, taking one of their hands in each of hers. Gemma had read her letter out to them in the morning, tears in her eyes. Beautiful in that moment, though if Lottie was honest her youngest had too many of her father's genes to ever be considered so in the conventional way. Ari, however, was her mother's spit. An unsettling double.

The reverend was droning and the dirt was sprinkled in—a handful at a time at first, later to be finished by the excavator, reversing its earlier work.

The men didn't know what to say. Not yet. They'd find the words later on, down at the pub after a good scoop. Pints and whiskies, drinking the money she put behind the bar although she didn't plan on attending. Hoovering up something stronger off the toilet cisterns. Paulo wouldn't have minded. It's not disrespectful, it's what he would have wanted. A night out in his honour. Maybe even a club later. Or the casino. Girls. Violence.

She wondered if talk would turn to revenge. There was no way any of them believed her eejit nephew Colin had killed him as the polis claimed—put a bullet through his uncle's head after being caught making deals behind his back in a brass-bawed attempt at taking over the firm. No, the only coup young Colin could ever conceive of ate grass and said "Moo". Though maybe it would be easier for them if they pretended to believe it. Less trouble. She could understand that. She'd had to ask her own sister not to come to the funeral. Appearances needed to be kept up.

For now.

Fuck You Fuck You Fuck You Fuck You Fuck You Fuck You Fuck
You Fuck You Fuck You Fuck You Fuck You Fuck You Fuck You
Fuck You Fuck You Fuck You Fuck You Fuck You Fuck You Fuck
You Fuck You Fuck You Fuck You Fuck You Fuck You Fuck You
Fuck You Fuck You Fuck You Fuck You Fuck You Fuck You Fuck
You Fuck You Fuck You Fuck You Fuck You Fuck You Fuck You
Fuck You Fuck You Fuck You Fuck You Fuck You Fuck You Fuck
You Fuck You Fuck You Fuck You Fuck You Fuck You Fuck You
Fuck You Fuck You Fuck You Fuck You Fuck You Fuck You Fuck
You Fuck You Fuck You Fuck You Fuck You Fuck You Fuck You
Fuck You Fuck You Fuck You Fuck You Fuck You Fuck You Fuck
You Fuck You Fuck You Fuck You Fuck You Fuck You Fuck You
Fuck You Fuck You Fuck You Fuck You Fuck You Fuck You Fuck
You Fuck You Fuck You Fuck You Fuck You Fuck You Fuck You
Fuck You Fuck You Fuck You Fuck You Fuck You Fuck You Fuck
You Fuck You Fuck You Fuck You Fuck You Fuck You Fuck You
Fuck You Fuck You Fuck You Fuck You Fuck You Fuck You Fuck
You Fuck You Fuck You Fuck You Fuck You Fuck You Fuck You
Fuck You Fuck You Fuck You Fuck You Fuck You Fuck You Fuck
You Fuck You Fuck You Fuck You Fuck You Fuck You Fuck You
Fuck You Fuck You Fuck You Fuck You Fuck You Fuck You Fuck
You Fuck You Fuck You Fuck You Fuck You Fuck You Fuck You
Fuck You Fuck You Fuck You Fuck You Fuck You Fuck You Fuck
You Fuck You Fuck You Fuck You Fuck You Fuck You Fuck You

The best part of a year later…

1

"TRNSMT?! I wonder what else gets transmitted there that isn't just music."

"Gads, Alison. She's only—"

"She's a teenager. You'll have to accept that soon."

"She's our daughter. We can trust her to be sensible."

"I can't trust her to do her own washing or bring the mugs down from her room. Who are *you* talking about?"

"She's not silly, when it comes to the big things—"

"Like her exams?"

"Here we go…" McCoist was on the phone to her ex, arguing about the twins again. Not the twins, really, just Tess. Her Nat 5 results had been unexpected. Unexpectedly shite. A good slip down from the prelim results. A sign of trouble, they both knew, but what to do about it they couldn't agree on. And now she was whingeing about going to TRNSMT Festival with her pals next week and the tickets cost a lung and a pair of kidneys, so McCoist wanted to say no, but Mark questioned if that would seem like they were punishing her and could risk further alienating… and so on and on. Soft touch.

"And you know what else there is at music festivals to go with the sex and rock 'n' roll?"

"Don't say it."

"Drugs."

"Stop."

"Mountains of the stuff. There are more dodgy pills floating round a music festival than fucking bucket hats. Plus the dodgy geezers who sell them."

"Hats or drugs?"

"Shut up."

"Could you switch off your polis-brain for a minute?"

"That's not polis-brain, it's parent-brain, you should get one."

"Nice. Very clever. Very grown up."

The sight of the corpse stopped McCoist from saying something she might have regretted. "I have to go," she said instead, hanging up although she could still hear Mark speaking. He was used to it. One of the reasons for the divorce, probably.

The body was on its back, lying in a gulch between the wall of a motorway slip road and the overgrown embankment beside it. A strip of torn fencing separated the two. Beyond a flapping hole in the fence, a path had been trod up the embankment over time.

She almost whistled. "Rats?"

The photographer nodded. The thing that had once been a person had no eyes or face left. The cheeks were hollow in the literal sense, not the sickly avant-garde film-star sense. The sinews had been chewed through, clean to the bone in some places. Stripped of everything else, the former face's main feature was its lipless teeth. Large, yellow and animal-like in black, receding gums. Quite the smile. Wriggling things were living in it.

"I heard on this podcast—"

"Every time you start a sentence with that it costs me a thousand brain cells," McCoist said.

The DC tagging along as her gofer, Gaz Travis, grinned, undeterred by the practised weariness in his boss's voice. "I heard on this podcast, right, that there's so much coke floating about down there in the sewers in Glasgow—in people's pish and getting flushed down or poured out and that—that the rats are more geared up than Maradona. Makes them super aggressive."

The photographer was staring at DC Travis now, eyes narrowed. "Rats on gak..." he murmured, cogs visibly turning in his brain.

"And polis on acid, apparently," McCoist snapped. "Can I speak to someone sensible about this?" She motioned to the decaying, feasted-upon body. It was in a suit, as if ready for the funeral. Long overdue for it, actually. The suit too—past its fashion sell-by at some point in the eighties.

It reeked and she had to try hard not to pinch her nose. More than just disrespectful, it was amateur, and McCoist would not allow herself to be seen that way. There were enough rumours around her promotion to DCI already. Plenty of sniping and whispered accusations of affirmative action. A leaked WhatsApp chat had recently embarrassed Police Scotland and led to a good number of polis—bicycle bobby and senior detective alike—getting the boot or made to take early retirement, including her former boss, DCI Robson. She wasn't surprised that fat, baldy shitehawk had been involved—his contributions to the group chat had been racist, sexist and poorly spelt—and she wasn't sad to see him go, but the truth of her ascension was more complicated than convenient optics. The cost to her had been great too.

A SOCO detached herself from a group of paper-suited colleagues scouring the surrounds—the graffitied concrete temple under the slip road littered with broken bottles, empty baggies, cigarette butts, needles, crisp packets, clues—and pulled her mask down to speak, a glove off to shake. "Amy Caruso."

"DCI Alison McCoist." She held out her warrant card.

"I've heard of you…" Caruso's eyes went scary wide, a smile pulling her face apart.

McCoist gave the woman a look that said the next words out her mouth better not include a reference to a particular ex-Rangers striker.

"…You worked the Car Wash Case!"

Caruso was impressed, as if this other McCoist in front of her was also a legend.

"What little work there was to do. The lad was found at the scene of the crime."

Three dead bodies, including his uncle Paulo McGuinn, in bits on the floor of a grotty wee car wash in the east end. Poor, thick Colin, just in the right place and time to take the fall. McCoist had railroaded the boy straight to Barlinnie. Her guts knotted at the thought. She'd been bouncing between Imodium and lactulose ever since it happened. Fear, guilt and anxiety were hellish on the bowels. The Car Wash Case. Car Wash Catastrophe, more like. McCoist had really cunted it this time, worse than all her previous mistakes combined, and there were a lot of those.

"I know, but scary people to deal with, eh?" Caruso's voice lowered to a conspiratorial stage whisper.

"None as scary as DCI McCoist," Travis chipped in with a grin, fully expecting the withering look McCoist slapped him with. It had no effect; nothing did with him, he was fully assured his puppyish charm would let him get away with it. After all, the gaffer was a dog person.

"Speaking of scary, your man here with his Hallowe'en mask on too early." McCoist shifted the subject. "What can you tell us?"

You could almost hear the switch as Caruso went from star-struck to professional. "He's been here about twenty-four hours. Strangled, from what I can see *in situ*. Reckon he was dumped off the side of the ramp. Bit of blood pooling behind the head there. Impact."

"Not dragged through the hole in the fence?"

"Not likely—no obvious evidence of that but we'll take a closer look. The PM will confirm if he was dropped down but we're searching the road above anyway."

"Good." A couple of uniforms and a van were waiting to bag him up once the photographer was finished with him. "Is that a footprint?" McCoist pointed to a small patch of criss-crossing lines stamped in what was probably blood near the corpse's head, flagged by the SOCOs.

"Partial—sure we can work out the size and brand from it."

"Why drop him over, then come down?"

"Forgotten something maybe? Wallet, phone, birth certificate? Or it might not be the killer's. I'll let you work that out."

"Fair enough. Anything interesting around here?"

"Not unless you're keen on outsider art." Caruso jabbed a thumb at Travis, who was taking in the graffitied pillars as if he were in a gallery. "This is a dumpsite. He was killed somewhere else."

"All yours." The photographer stepped away from his subject and the two uniforms sucked foetid air in through their teeth before approaching with the black bag, neither one of them thrilled to be het for this task. "Rigor's still in effect, and he's nice and flat for you, shouldn't be too bad."

"That right, aye? Ye offerin a hawn then?" one of the constables said.

"Sorry, pal, bad back." The photographer smiled.

They took up a position at each end. "Wan, two, three—" They lifted. "—Fuck!" Congealed blood, stained fluids and rotted brain matter slopped out a hole in the back of the corpse's head and splattered onto the constable's shoes.

Caruso nodded in approval. "Definitely dropped."

2

Everybody called him Chuck though his name wasn't Charles. He had curly ginger hair and wore corrective NHS specs throughout his school years, and his pals were wee pricks. Despite him now having a shaved, balding dome and favouring contacts, the nickname had stuck. He didn't hate it any more though. He was nearly thirty now. He was at peace with it. It was a fact of life. It was his name. Secretly, he liked it better than "Stuart" and its attendant nicknames: Stu, Stewie, Stu Pot, Stupac Shakur. When anyone asked his name he said, "Evrybdy caws me Chuck."

"Because that's your name?" replied the old boy with a quizzical eyebrow tick.

"Because ae *Rugrats*. Ye mind that? Chuckie wae the glesses, ginger hair?"

The man shook his grey head and let Chuck into the house—not a place where children had ever lived judging by the furniture and decoration and complete lack of photographs, so it's no wonder he'd never heard of the kids' cartoon. They went through the kitchen—Chuck had been asked to come to the back door—and into the hall. "The stairs shouldn't be a problem for a strapping lad like you," the man said, creaking his way up the staircase, a brown, threadbare carpet runner covering chipped, white-glossed steps.

"Depends how many trips it takes." Five years of hauling towers of confidential waste papers and the shredded hay bales his machines turned them into had taken its toll on Chuck's knees and back.

"Just a few boxes for you. Having a clear-out." They entered a bedroom which smelt of Eau de Auld Geezer and astringent bar soap. The room was spartan: a wicker chair coming to bits in one corner; a night table at the side of the yellowing bed with a few well-read paperbacks and the Bible; net curtains which gave the place a sepia filter, as if glimpsed through a brown medicine bottle.

A fitted wardrobe the length of one side of the room was open. The clothes hanging on the rail were divided in the middle into black vestments and civvies. The large, cardboard boxes were on the floor of the wardrobe. There were five, each one marked with a decade, sixties to noughties. "Just these, cheers," the minister said. "Would you like a cup of tea? Coffee?"

"Nae thanks, pal, this willnae take lang."

The first box was heavier than expected. Bad things twitched in the small of his back as he huffed it up to his chest. The stairs were precarious. He couldn't see over the box, had to come down sideways to watch his steps, caught his knuckles against the wall—*bastart!*—as he turned at the bottom to head back out through the kitchen.

His van was parked at the garden gate, the decal on the side reading:

SIMPLY SHRED

SECURE DOCUMENT DESTRUCTION
MOBILE ON-SITE SHREDDING

He opened the side door and fired up the machine inside. The rolling blades at the bottom of the hopper churned together with relentless force, a gnawing, savage hunger. Chuck often thought of himself as a zookeeper, and it was feeding time. He hefted the box up and tipped it in.

Fifty pounds of glossy pornography tumbled into the hopper. Naked women being stuffed from all angles were chewed and swallowed by the shredder, its appetite as apparently insatiable as their own. Among the churning, ripping flesh were disembodied organs: shining nipples, a probing tongue, a cock as big as a baguette with rippling veins, dripping at the tip.

Chuck looked again at the writing on the box: *'60s.* Vintage. Lifting his jaw back into place, he went back upstairs. Seventies next. He almost wanted to lift the flap a little, take a keek at what a fifty-year-old scud book was like, but resisted. Confidentiality was the name of the game after all. Discretion. Legally binding discretion. And would he really want to touch any of these stiff, old jazz mags which had been kept by the minister for half a century? *Should probly gee the machine a good rinse oot eftir,* he thought.

A few more jaunts up and down the stairs and he'd caught up to the contemporary filth. Job done.

Almost.

"These too, son." The minster held two laptops. One old, based on how thick it was, one a bit newer.

Chuck felt something cold trickle in his stomach, his world shift a little off kilter. He had a special hard-drive shredder in the van, it was part of his services, but it was usually only businesses that asked for it. One-off Joe Public punters like this were rarely in need of it. It was the smart thing to do, considering all the things Chuck had learnt about identity theft since getting into the shredding game, but most people just left their old laptops in a cupboard to gather dust. Chuck had a healthy prejudice against the holy professions to start with. Throw in the dirty-book archive and the question of shredding the computers, along with whatever was on them, raised the hairs on the back of his neck.

He almost asked why. But he didn't. Because not asking was part of his job, and reliability was everything. He knew another guy in the game once—Harvey MacNeil, a small business solo operator like himself—who let slip a few quiet words about a customer he thought might be a nonce. And this boy, this wrong yin, found himself strung up by a vigilante mob, who battered his maw's door down and dragged him into the street in the middle of the night, kicked every Dulux sample of shite out him and put him in a coma before the polis could show up. Justice done, maybe, but Harvey was out of business by the end of the year. Nobody could trust him any more. He ran a leaky ship and everybody knew it now, even if they felt he'd done the right thing.

Chuck was running enough risks as it was through his deal with Mr Jamieson, so he took the laptops without comment.

"Cheers, son."

He held his phone under the wheel and flicked to refresh over and over, quick look up as he joined the expressway back towards town, then a glance back down. *Moan tae fuck, moan tae fuck.* Three minutes of stoppage time coming to an end. *Fucksake. Fuckin bastarts.* He prayed for a miracle. *Please.* Final whistle.

"Fuck!"

He slammed the wheel, causing the horn to blare and the driver in front to swerve slightly. *Shower ae useless pricks!* Fucking nil–nil. Hundred quid down the Tommy Crapper. He threw his phone into the stack of paperwork on the passenger seat, causing an avalanche on Mt Admin. Heart pounding, he crushed his teeth together and made growling animal noises, dredged up from his queasy stomach. Punched the horn again. The driver in front flashed their hazards and pulled onto the hard shoulder. A wee face in Chuck's passenger-side wing mirror screamed, "Wit the fuck?!"

Chuck signalled left and the wee face shat itself, thinking he was stopping to have a word. Instead, he pulled back off the expressway at the upcoming exit, headed to the petrol station at the nearby retail park.

He filled up and stomped inside to pay. It wasn't much because the tank was three-quarters full. He also bought a ten-quid scratch card. He had a green penny which lived in the dookit of the dashboard which had once proved itself lucky.

Not today.

The scratch card was tossed on the pile of paperwork. The silver rubbings lay dead in his lap. The coin went back to its home. He took slow breaths, feeling calmer. What was ten quid anyway? *Couple ae pints. Didnae need those anyway, bad fir ye.* There were other bets ready to pay out anyway. Ones that would eclipse the ton he just dropped. (Plus the ten spot.) And if all else failed, there was the Great Accumulator. A pension pot. A take-the-wife-and-fuck-off-to-Cancún pot. He had *the feeling* about this one, bubbling away in the background.

A horn peeped from behind. "Awright, awright." He raised his hand, saluting with every finger rather than just two. Back in control. He'd need it to get through his last appointment of the day.

"Ye winnin, Chuck?" Not a greeting, and not meant as a joke. Jamieson was flatly serious. Always was. He was the only man Chuck had ever met who didn't consider himself to be funny. Easily mistaken for a lack of ego, but it certainly wasn't that. No, it was something else that was missing, something more vital.

"No yet, Mr Jamieson, but there's always hope." Chuck licked dry lips, forced a smile which was not returned. Jamieson's face was a slowly rotting tumshie lantern carved with a blunt knife.

Jamieson's secretary, a Michelangelo's *David* with the added bulk of a stab-proof vest under his suit, pushed Chuck down into a seat across a busy desk from the boss man, who gave a hint of a sigh. "Useful as ye can be, Chuck, av come tae hate seein ye here."

Chuck didn't know what to say to that, so he adjusted and readjusted himself in the chair, making the leather squeak like a sneaky fart, comfort impossible. Marble loomed over his shoulder, apparently with no seat or desk of his own to do his admin on.

"Ye goat somethin fir me?"

"Aye, slipped some bits an pieces fae that new rehab place oot Bearsden way—thoat ye might find somethin interestin, a hear they've goat politicians' weans an fitbaw players' wives an aw sorts bein banged up there." Chuck held out the paperwork to Jamieson but it was intercepted by Marble, who then passed it on. Checking for paper-cut potential, maybe.

Jamieson leafed through, nothing to read on his face. As ever. Chuck had only managed to scrounge some random papers while the bloke who was supposed to be supervising the shredding fiddled around with his fags and lighter, so likely it was all useless shite, nothing to further Jamieson's cause of acquiring information about everyone and everything which made Glesga turn. "Security & Investigations" was printed on Jamieson's business cards. Rumour said before he became the business-card-carrying type he was in import and export: drugs, guns, women, anything to turn a profit. Now he dealt purely in information. His taxes were on the legal side of creative. He had an office with a listed address in the Merchant City where Chuck sat sweating.

He found himself speaking without meaning to. "There wis also this auld boay…" Desperate to break the silence, to give Jamieson something of worth. Because that was Chuck's end of the bargain. Jamieson's end—well, that hundred quid Chuck had lost on the fitbaw was just a scrap, arse-wiping money really, to what he owed to the various jackals Jamieson kept in line for him.

Jamieson was Chuck's customer when they met—investigations created heaps of confidential material that needed to be disposed of properly—then he saw the opportunity to do Chuck a wee favour. A favour to be returned. Not a favour. A deal. One that could not be reneged upon unless Chuck won big soon or decided he didn't really need thumbs any more.

So despite Harvey MacNeil crying a warning in his head, Chuck told them about the minister, the boxes of smut and the laptops.

"So?" Jamieson said.

"Wit if he's a paedo? Wit if the Church know awready? Could be somethin." Chuck was warming up to it now that he'd started. Fuck the old man. *Pervy bastart.* He deserved whatever he got. And Chuck deserved to have thumbs. "Maybe they're makin him get rid ae it. The big heed yins wantin tae cover it up."

"Maybe he's just auld an depressed," Jamieson suggested.

"How?"

"Ye know wit they say."

Marble answered for his boss: "Tired ae wankin, tired ae life."

Chuck had never heard anyone say this and looked, puzzled, between the two men: Marble as sure and solid as his nickname, Jamieson nodding sagely in agreement.

"Wit?"

"Did ye save the laptoaps?"

Chuck felt his cheeks getting hot, taking a beamer, his pale ginger's skin so easily flushed. "Naw. He wis right there next tae me."

Another sigh from Jamieson. "Al huv a hink aboot it. If that's aw?…"

Chuck made to stand up. Marble halted him at first, then let him go. He was just into the waiting room when Jamieson called: "Best ae luck." He wasn't joking.

3

Apparently, the food in the prison cafeteria was shite, but Colin certainly wasn't wasting away. He wore his jail joggies as well as any of his designer tracksuits. Helping himself to some other poor sod's lunch, Lottie guessed. Trading on his notoriety, no doubt, though he was a big unit too, and handy, which probably made life behind bars easier. That and being a moron. Hard to lose your mind from being caged up when your idea of entertainment was seeing how high you could pish up a wall anyway. Still, Colin looked noticeably older, sitting across the table in the visitors' room. He'd always been a daft wee boy to his Auntie Charlotte, but there was a childishness missing from his face now.

"An are ye gettin oan wae everywan?" his maw, Ginny, asked. She sounded as if her son was at a summer camp. A pretence needed to keep the last of her sanity, Lottie thought. It was more painful to look at her sister than her nephew. Of the two, she looked like the one who'd been locked up this past year. Her skin hung loose on its frame, her hair a grey nest, eyes dry from not blinking enough. No tears left. She was the one being tortured.

"Aye, fine. Gettin a new room-mate soon.'

"How? Wit happened tae the other boay, wit wis his name again?"

"Graham."

"Aye, Graham, he sounded nice."

"He tried tae cut his ain ear aff wae a bit ae broken mirror so thuv moved him away, stuck him in wae the mongs an mentalists."

Ginny's mouth dropped and she covered it with her hand as if stifling a yawn. Her breathing came in trembling wheezes and she had to look away, her "So how was school today?" chat derailed.

"Said he wis hungry, wis gonnae cut it aff an eat it."

Ginny's shoulders shook and she folded in on herself. Lottie gave Colin a hard look that said, "Enough." She wanted to come back and have a word with the wee fanny alone—"See wit yer daein tae ma sister?!"—but getting angry wouldn't help anyone. And it was Lottie who convinced her husband to give Colin a job in the first place. At her sister's insistence, but still, without Lottie's wheedling, Paulo wouldn't have taken him on ("Away an shite, he's a useless, lazy eejit—an a mean that wae aw the love in the wurrold") and the boy wouldn't now be sitting in the jail, blamed for killing Paulo himself in a shoot-out over an arms deal gone sour. Fucksake, anybody who knew Colin well—scratch that, anybody who spent about five minutes in Colin's company—would know how ridiculous that sounded, how obviously he'd been scapegoated. If Forrest Gump was the butter knife in the block then Colin was a misplaced spoon.

"Needin any fags, son?" Lottie asked, an abrupt change of subject requiring no subtlety.

He shook his head. "Am vapin noo, Auntie Charlotte. They gee ye these kits an that. Could dae wae some better flavours though if yer offerin."

She wasn't but she said, "Aye, awright. Wit's yer favourite?"

"Bubblegum. A hink ye can get, like, Bucky flavour too…"
Big, glaikit smile which faded. "Wit's that *green* flavour?"

"Green? Ye mean lime?"

"Aye, lime is green, int it? A hink maybe some ae the lads in here would like that, if a could get them some *green* lime flavour." His eyes widened in a desperate attempt at telepathic communication.

He opened his mouth to speak again but Lottie twitched her head, sucked her lips in, miming silence. She'd be surprised if she and Ginny didn't get pulled up on the way out for Colin's bit of expert spy craft there. "Al try," she whispered.

Ginny was oblivious though, still tucked into herself. "This cannae go oan," she mumbled. "Cannae go oan."

By the time the car crunched up the driveway outside Castle McGuinn, Lottie had shaken off the oppressive blue-roll-and-bleach atmosphere of HMP Barlinnie and could feel the warmth of the sun again. The three storeys of centuries-old, renovated sandstone hidden among a shroud of guardian oaks off Nitshill Road never failed to lift her mood. Ten years she'd been there now and it hadn't worn off—not just the sense of pride the house gave her, but the feeling of having something solidly her own, bedrock to lie down on, a centre to the universe. She needed it now more than ever.

The place had been run down and they bought it in cash for less than it should have been worth. She'd had it stripped from the foundations to the attic and refurbed in her own personal style. "Yer like Kirstie Allsopp oan crack," Paulo complained during those first years when the house was constantly bustling with tradies. He loved it though, really, an endless parade of lads to force his patter on and wee apprentice boys to scare. Bartering to do, deals to make, hands to shake, the crumbs of stories to leave out which hinted at his reputation. His voice and accent had to be louder and rougher than any of the guys on the tools, his laugh heard in every corner of the house. Lottie had to work hard to make sure he didn't fill the place completely, take it over, as he seemed to do instinctively. This house was hers too. Now it was hers alone.

Her heels gave a rich clack on the herringbone parquet in the hall. The original panelling on the walls had been melted, scraped and sanded back to the wood, the warped and tool-marked spars mended and recoated in slate eggshell. A chandelier that would be ostentatious hanging in the Taj Mahal draped down from the double-height ceiling, the original ceiling rose and mouldings sharpened and thrown into relief by a pattern of similar-but-not-quite-the-same shades of white and grey. Clean, tasteful, and a total ball-ache for the decorators. To juxtapose, Paulo's contribution to the ambience of the main hall sat in the crook of the curling staircase: a white baby grand piano with a brushed-gold statue of a puma leaping from its lid. "Why no just get a sculpture ae yersel wae a foot-lang stawner made?" Lottie had said upon its installation.

She looked at it now and part of her thought of getting rid of it again. There was nothing to stop her, was there? "Stay," she said to the puma, and threw her coat over its head. Needed a cuppa.

"Where've you been?"

Lottie jumped. "Fuck!" Ari was in the kitchen, already ahead of her with a steaming mug in one hand. "A didnae know ye were stoappin by. Ye didnae text."

"Clothes to wash. Do I have to ask permission to come home?"

Lottie didn't answer that, it was a big arrow pointing to "Argument". "Mhari isnae in the day, huv ye goat enough clean stuff tae last ye till Thursday?"

"Can you not do it?"

"A could ask ye the same hing."

Big huff, eye roll. The classics. Infuriating when coupled with the west-end accent she'd grown.

"Try askin wae a 'please' oan the end."

"Could you do my washing, Mum? *Please?*"

"Could *you* make me a cup ae tea an aw, *please?*"

A smile broke and Ari got another cup down. "So where were you then?"

"Visitin yer cousin."

Ari froze with a teabag dangling over the cup. Her jaw tightened and her voice came out low and clenched: "Why would you be visiting him?"

"Am no gettin intae this again wae ye."

"You really think Aunt Ginny knows better than the police—"

"Ari, it's no just her. Av known that boay aw his life an, God bless him, he's dumb as dug shite. There's nae way in hell he widdae bin plottin against yer da."

"But—"

"An he loved him like he wis his ain faither. His Uncle Paul wis mare ae a da tae him than that useless sod who walked oot oan him an Ginny when he wis knee-high. No chance it wis him. Colin has his faults, plenty ae them, but he's loyal tae his faimly, and so ye should be an aw."

Ari huffed again and finally dropped the teabag in the mug. The chance of hot water being added now was nil, but.

The doorbell rang. "That'll be Ross. Why don't ye go an meet yer sister oot ae school." Lottie took some money from her purse. "Go fir a coffee or somethin. Al get the machine oan fir ye."

Ari left and the agent came in.

"Coffee, Ross?"

"Would a man lost in the desert drink a glass of pish? Please, Lottie, hen." He took off his glasses, mopped his brow and the top of his head with a handkerchief. Ross Brownlee was a man who had stressed himself bald and skinny. Both a lawyer and a money man, he did the books for the McGuinns, among lots of other things (work the whole spectrum of grey), including sorting out the buying of the house. It was hard to ascertain where he sat in the hierarchy of Paulo's firm or whether he was perched outside it altogether. Certainly, he hadn't fucked off as soon as it all went tits-up at that car wash last year and Paulo found himself with an air hole through his skull. Most of the other associates of her husband had stopped coming round, finding employment with other firms vying for the throne. Several sources of income had dried up and Ross had helpfully spent a lot of his time in Paulo's home office untangling all sorts of interesting forms of insurance. He was no stranger to the castle.

They took their mugs up to the second floor and into the office. Lottie slid up a sash window so Ross could smoke—the only person she made this allowance for. He almost went to sit down in the Big Man's chair, comfortable as he was in it, but stopped himself and motioned for Lottie to sit there instead. He pulled up a smaller seat a fitbaw pitch away at the other side of the massive desk which had been lifted in through the window by crane—another of Paulo's few furniture choices. Lottie had at least convinced him the tarnished silver gorilla to sit on it was unnecessary.

Ross lit up using a Zippo lighter the size of a deck of cards. Not just a hip affectation: arthritis in his hands had left his knuckles gnarled and limited his dexterity. (He also wore an elastic tie and slip-on shoes, although these accessories were admittedly less cool.) He chopped the lid open and turned the flint with the heel of his hand, sooked in a breath of life. "What can I do you for, hen?"

"Howsit goin wae the appeal?" Lottie had summoned him as soon as she'd dropped Ginny off at her gaff. Ginny had spent a lot of time trying to get Colin to move out to his own place but now that he had, in a manner of speaking, she was rattling about in there like a lost pea at the bottom of the freezer drawer.

Ross took a long drag. "All they can really do is rehash the arguments that were laid out before, hope a different judge takes a different view of things. Nothing new has come up."

"Wit aboot the car-wash goons?" Sean Prentice—the owner of the car wash where Paulo was killed—and his employee Davey Burnet had vanished into the ether following the hit. Colin swore blind they were both involved but the polis couldn't track them down. "Are they even still lookin fir them?"

"Nothing but dead ends. Still no sightings, no pings from phones or bank cards… Like I said, there's nothing new to add."

"Then *we* need tae find somethin new."

"We're pushing for further investigation but—"

"Fae the polis? Naw, they awready fuckt it. We need somedy who's oanside."

"Like who? You wanting Netflix to do a season about it?"

35

Lottie scrunched up a sheet of paper that was lying on the desk and launched it at Ross, who batted it away with a laugh. "Hinks he's a funny fucker so he does. A wis hinkin mare ae the likes ae Billy Jamieson."

The name paused Ross's mug on the way to his mouth—held in two hands like he was polishing off a bowl of soup. He managed a sip before he spoke. "Billy Jamieson? Lottie, hen..."

"That's wit he does noo. Investigations an that. Paulo knew him fairly well. He sent a cerd eftir, ye know."

"Paulo would have known him. Do you?"

"A know his reputation, if that's wit yer meanin. But he's a straight arrow noo."

Ross made a noise between a snort and a laugh. Smoke came out his nose. "Aye, and the Pope never misses confession. A man like that..."

"Goat tae dae somethin, Ross. Cannae just keep goin alang hopin it'll aw work oot. Will ye set somethin up?"

"He's a legitimate businessman, as you say, you can call the number on his website. I'm going on record as counselling you against this though." He stubbed out his cigarette in an ashtray shaped like an upturned hand. "Strongly."

"Feel free tae say ye telt me so later oan doon the road then."

"I wouldn't, hen... Well, I might, but I really do hope I won't have to."

"Me an aw."

4

DS Slater popped a mug down on her desk next to a framed photo of a gangly, glaikit-looking dog with brindle tiger stripes along its back. There was an old one of the twins somewhere behind the stacks of paperwork too—blonde, blue-eyed *Village of the Damned* weans who shared their mother's general turned-up expression of flat contempt for everything but hadn't yet earned the forehead creases and grey roots that complemented it.

"Dark-roasted arabica beans crushed under the bare feet of virgins, served with the froth of the milk of the sacred red doe of Ben Lomond." Slater dropped the James Earl Jones voiceover and smiled. "Only kidding. Tesco's Shitest, as requested."

McCoist lifted the mug in salute and took a mouthful, grimaced. Must have had at least three spoonfuls of instant coffee in it and as many sugars. "That could give a lesser mortal organ failure. Good work, Sergeant."

"I'll take that as a win. As good as we'll get today, I think."

Progress on the Super Rats victim had quickly ground to a halt after early success and now they were stuck waiting on an orthodontologist to take a look at the hideous smile—he had no wallet on him, no phone, no record on the PNC, no misper report that fit the description of what was left of him, so for now had no name.

The PM confirmed Caruso's theory that he'd been strangled elsewhere and then dropped, after death, from a height.

Then the CCTV trawl had spotted a van stopping on the hard shoulder of the slip road during the wee hours a day before the discovery. The driver—gloved, hooded—got out, went round the back and did something, likely dodgy, for a while, out of site of the camera, hidden by the open rear door and the side of the van. Then he closed up and drove off. They had their killer on tape. Exciting. Further along the road the cameras got a nice view of the van's reg plate. Very exciting. A quick check showed the van had been reported stolen the morning after Super Rats's estimated time of death. Shite. The owner was clean as a bean, the report appearing legit, so they were back to waiting again. Waiting for the van to show up, dumped somewhere, maybe torched or at least cleaned. The CCTV dredge continued.

"Gaz, get on the phone and find out how many stiffs are in the queue for the dentist, will you?" McCoist said. The lad didn't look up from his desk. "Gaz?" Still nothing. "Gaz!" Oblivious.

"I can do it, ma'am," DC Suffia Khan, the fourth member of their team offered.

"Ask if anyone can do something and it's always a woman who does it," McCoist said, skewering Slater with a look because Gaz was still absorbed in whatever was on his desk.

Slater conceded the point without complaint. He was a little older than McCoist—grey wings in his military haircut, burst blood vessels on the fat tip of his nose, handsome crow's feet giving his mud-coloured eyes some liveliness—but couldn't be described as "old-school" as far as detectives were concerned. While occasionally gruff with the underlings when he needed to be, he was far from the blowhard bullies McCoist had encountered throughout her career, and he certainly didn't mind taking orders from a woman who was a few years his junior. There was no awkwardness in going from informal banter to serious discussion to carrying out orders. It was rare. "DC TRAVIS!" he bellowed, and Gaz jumped, hitting his knees on the underside of his desk.

"Sorry?"

"Lost in space?"

"Huh?" He looked dazzled by the high beams Slater was blasting him with.

"Use your words, Gaz."

"Sorry, sir, it's just I've been looking at these again…"—he held up some partial prints that had been taken from Super Rats's suit jacket which hadn't been usable—"…the thumb-print that appears, it's all scuffed." This had been noted. There was a repeated thumbprint, right hand, which was cracked all over, the pad of the thumb damaged. "Look." He gave them a thumbs up, beckoned them closer.

The skin on Gaz's thumb was broken up with myriad cracks and nicks and islands of shiny hard, dry skin, most of the whorls of his thumbprint lost underneath the wreck. Just like the print. "Skater's thumb!" he grinned.

"Sorry?"

"Skateboarding. You get it from the griptape on the top of the board. It's like sandpaper, takes the top layers off the skin." He rubbed his index finger against the callus of his thumb proudly. "And look." He pulled out the crime-scene photos and flicked through them: "The classic diamond pattern. Our bloody footprint's a Converse All Star, out of favour but some older guys still like to skate em… the graffiti on the pillars… patches of fresh cement on the concrete to cover potholes…

ingress and egress through the hole in the fence... and look here, where it slopes up towards the underside of the motorway, that's a natural flat bank right there, ready to go. These usually have, like, Tetris bricks sticking out of them to stop homeless folk sleeping there, but not here. Dynamite."

The three of them were looking at him as if he were sitting there bollock naked.

"It's a skate spot! Some skater must have found the body—it was called in anonymously, right? But not before they bumped the wallet and phone. If I go back down there, check a few other spots, lean on the locals, maybe I could find something to ID our man." His excitement was not contagious.

"Skate spot?" Slater said, as if it were from another language. "How d'you know all this?"

"Well..." Gaz's puppy smile started to fade as he counted six raised eyebrows around him. "Well, I do a bit of skating myself, actually."

"Skateboarding?"

"We call it skating."

"You call it skating... Aren't you a grown man? With a house? Job? Hair on your testicles?"

Suffia stifled a giggle and McCoist had to cover her own smirk by taking a mouthful of coffee.

Gaz laughed it off. "'You don't stop skating because you get old, man, you get old because you stop skating!'—Jay Adams," he paraphrased, slapping a huge grin back onto his face and jumping to his feet.

"Who?"

"Legendary OG skater. *Dogtown and Z-Boys*."

"What?"

"Never mind. But it's a lead, right? And it's better than sitting around here waiting for the tooth fairy!"

"Fair-y enough," McCoist agreed. "See what you can do. Suffia, go along with DC Sk8er Boi, make sure he's not just sneaking off to play."

McCoist had clocked off—metaphorically, as there was no real break when working a case, she just moved her physical self away from the office—and was taking Bruce for a walk around the neighbourhood (lamp posts to be sniffed, territory to be reclaimed, cats to be bullied) when the call came from DC Travis. He was every bit as excited as Bruce, who had discovered a turd that was a vintage to his liking. McCoist wrestled the lead with one hand, phone in the other:

"Got the wallet!"

"Really?!"

"You sound shocked."

"Because I am."

"So little faith." He tutted but McCoist could hear his smile bouncing off the satellites and into her ear. She was going to have to let him have his moment. "Me and Suffy questioned a few skaters we found at the scene—got a nice wee chase off them too—and got passed around a few different crews. The story had got out. We were looking for someone who was probably older, still skated Cons, likely had some problems with addiction or money."

"How so?"

"You saw the body, gaffer. The face. Imagine seeing a zombie like that and going through its pockets? You d have to be at Desperation Station."

"Watch what you say, Gaz, or at least how you say it."

"Sorry, ma'am."

"He maybe came across it earlier, before the critters." A flush of excitement kicked her heart up a gear. She tried to step outside her body and scan for stupidity, something she might have missed, before speaking. "This druggy old skate dinosaur of yours didn't see it get dropped there, did he?"

Rustling hiss of a sigh. "Sorry, unfortunately not. We did ask, and we're bringing him in now for a proper interview, but I think he's telling the truth. He was pretty mellow when we caught up with him—the money went on something of decent quality by the looks of it."

"You were right about the addiction?"

"Aye." The smile was back. "When we asked around, he came up a few times. A guy they call Shags. Bit of an outcast from the scene but always hanging around. Drink, drugs, homeless on and off. Scares the younger ones, annoys the other old heads. He was trying to sell the driving licence to underagers at the skatepark but even the kids are too savvy to try and pass themselves off as a balding fifty-six-year-old... So?"

"So what?"

"How did I do?"

"If you want constant positive affirmation, Gaz, get a dog." (Bruce was still straining to get his chocolate lolly.) But truthfully, McCoist was impressed, and happy to be so. Her team were proving good. Slater, Khan and Travis. She'd wanted a DC who she'd worked with before called Findlay because his head seemed screwed on, or at least the threads were lined up straight, but he'd handed in his notice and fucked off around the time of the WhatsApp scandal. Jumped before getting pushed, probably. *Stupid boy*. The disappointment had worn off though and McCoist had landed with a half-competent squad. Wholly competent, she would admit, when feeling generous, which she was. "Kidding. Good work, Detective Constable Travis. Seriously. So how do you celebrate when you do one of your skateboard tricks?"

"You do it again, ma'am. 'Two to make it true' is the saying."

"You're going for the phone?"

"Shags says he lost it but we'll see if we can jog his memory when he comes down."

"Find it and I'll get you a wee sticker for your warrant card."

"Rad!"

"So who's our Jock Doe then?"

"Carter Lennox."

The name dropped into McCoist's belly like a shot of sour milk.

"Done a quick search online, he's a criminal defence lawyer, office in the Saltmarket, his own firm, 'Lennox & MacGillivary'. Sounds like it might be juicy."

It did indeed. And McCoist would have been excited about it if she hadn't recognised the name. If she didn't already know Carter Lennox was a criminal defence lawyer, one whom she'd met before when she investigated the death of a client of his. The client was an informer. He informed on Paulo McGuinn. He was dead—murdered. And now, so was his lawyer.

McCoist had let the lead go slack; Bruce had scoffed his prize. He licked his chops and wagged his tail, very pleased with himself.

5

McCoist took out her other phone. Her other other phone, actually. It was nothing fancy. Quite the opposite and deliberately so. She dialled the number, let it ring and waited for the callback.

She stuck a Thai curry in the microwave and poured a small glass of red while she waited. She tried to watch something on the telly but couldn't manage it. When the microwave pinged, she found she couldn't manage the meal either. Her gullet was tight, her stomach a fist.

The phone finally rang and she didn't know whether she was relieved or about to be sick.

"Bear?"

"Sir." Voice professional, eyes rolling in a perfect impression of the ever-icked Tess. Ally McCoist, codename: Broxi Bear, the blue-nosed Rangers mascot. Very clever, never got old.

"What's going on?" His voice was only a little more formal than chit-chat register. She could picture his glasses perched on his nose, his helpful librarian's smile and that thing that lurked behind it which she tried to imagine was not there.

"Interesting body showed up."

"The one without a face? Heard about that. Hope you can get something with the teeth or it'll be anthropological artists and Europol and all the paperwork that goes with it. Total ball-ache."

If the man didn't make her so worried, she would have laughed at that. Superintendent Devlin had the nervous habit of scratching his balls every few minutes. Mr Itchy Baws, she'd christened him in her mind. Maybe irritation caused by the all the paperwork he had to do.

"No need, we've got an ID."

"Which I'm not going to like?"

"Carter Lennox."

There was a whispering of air on the line as he considered this. "Might not be such a bad thing." McCoist, with Devlin's help, had buried the murder of Lennox's client, as it was one more thing that linked her to Paulo McGuinn and his untimely demise. Best kept hidden. Lennox being dead was potentially just more topsoil on the grave.

"Why now though? He hadn't caused any fuss, I assumed he'd just let it go."

"It's a good question, so find the answer. If somebody is doing us a favour, I'd like to know who and why."

"I don't think it's a favour."

"Those instincts of yours, Bear. You still trust them?"

"I'll keep in touch."

She put the phone and then her head down on the kitchen table. Her eyes stung. She smelt car soap and blood and burnt gunpowder, heard the echo of the shot around the stone walls of the car-wash unit. It was self-defence. Wasn't it? But she was armed and he wasn't. She saved someone's life though, right? McGuinn was going to kill Davey Burnet—a luckless and bone-thick employee of the car wash who'd been sucked into working for the gangster under duress. McGuinn was strangling Davey to death with a hose. She'd told McGuinn to stop, to let go. Hadn't she? Her memory of the whole thing was in bits, all of it a rush of overexposed, frazzled sensations.

The only really clear thing was the shot—the way the noise clapped over her ears and didn't release them for days, the outside world half submerged under the sound of her own blood pumping through her body. At night, in the quiet of being alone, there was still a distant whine inside which didn't seem to be improving.

Before that, she'd been an honest cop. Mostly.

6

There was no family, which was why there was no misper report. With no social media presence and no phone as yet to go off, Khan and Travis were knocking on doors up and down the west-end tenement building on Great Western Road which Lennox called home to see if they could scare up some spare keys or some friends. So far they'd managed to find a house cleaner. She did a few of the flats there—one single, common link between Lennox and his neighbours.

It seemed the only thing that would miss him was work.

"He was on annual leave..." MacGillivary said, face white as Casper but with none of the boy ghost's cherub-cheeked cheer.

"You don't keep in touch socially? You started this firm together, how long ago?" McCoist questioned. Slater took notes, perched with vulgar overfamiliarity, arse cheek and thigh, on the edge of the lawyer's desk.

"Twenty-three, no, twenty-four years." He had to sit down at that, as if the decades had suddenly landed on top of him all at once. "And no, not really. Not any more. Friendship can't survive business. Not for as long as all that... Twenty-four years... Lord."

"You weren't on good terms then?"

"I didn't say that. I just said we weren't pals any more, not buddy-buddies. We didn't fall out. Working together in this way just saps that part of your relationship, slowly, over time. You don't really think about it. And then..."

Sounds like my marriage, McCoist thought.

MacGillivary started to push things around his desk, rearranging them to no purpose, then fell slack against the back of his chair after the fit of activity, looking confused, as if he wasn't in control of his body. "What happened to him? I mean, how?..."

"Somebody strangled him then dumped his body off the side of the motorway."

His hand came up to his forehead, as if his fingertips were feeling for a headache, his eyes covered. "Leads?" The professional in him was trying to take over.

McCoist brushed past his question. "Is there anyone you can think of who'd want to harm Mr Lennox?"

This brought a glimpse of a smile, a hint of old fondness for his partner, maybe. "He was a criminal defence lawyer, DCI... sorry, what was it again?"

"McCoist."

"Sorry. DCI McCoist, yes."

"Easy one to forget," McCoist said, knowing full well he hadn't. Slater snuck her a cheeky grin.

"He was a criminal defence lawyer, you could fill the Hydro with people who'd want to harm him." He counted them on his fingers, movements expansive now, not aimless fiddling: "The clients from the cases he lost; the families of the victims from the cases he won. Journalists, campaigners, politicians, your brothers and sisters in arms—there's plenty of polis who've cursed him throughout their careers, no doubt. It's the nature of the job, but it needs to be done."

"Was there any recent case that was a source of trouble? Any threats made?"

He looked as if he was considering the question, but McCoist knew he wasn't. The expected answer came: "None I can think of. We didn't work on cases together in that way, so I wouldn't really know."

"You didn't ask each other for advice?"

"On occasion, but Carter is, sorry... was... quite a *singular* man. He had his own ways and kept his own counsel." The initial shock had clearly worn off that his partner of twenty-four years and friend for longer was dead. Murdered. MacGillivary was becoming the man who stood in court. Self-assured, voice smooth but with a broad, confident masculinity to it which would ring with sincerity across the polished wood benches. Juries probably liked him, trusted him. McCoist didn't. *Smarmy prick*. But then she had to admit to her own prejudices against defence lawyers. He was right about that, she was biased. All the "People have the right to a fair hearing" sales patter in the world couldn't make her buy it. It was like trying to punt hair gel to Vin Diesel—he wouldn't even take the shit for free.

MacGillivary took them across the busy waiting room to Lennox's office. The auld wifey with the Glesga patter behind the front desk gave herself a broken neck to get a look at them; the punters found their feet fascinating as the two detectives (Slater in particular just *looked* like polis, haircut to Clarks) passed by.

Having his "own ways" and keeping his "own counsel" were obviously euphemisms for being a mad bastard. The room was a tip. There were as many empty takeaway containers and stained mugs as there were stacks of paperwork and bursting box files. An old desktop PC with a genuine CRT monitor sat among the detritus, no leather left on the office chair in front of it. A spare suit in a dry-cleaning bag hung from the back of the door and a row of buckled filing cabinets took up the back wall opposite. "Paperwork filed by shade of white, I'll bet," Slater grumbled.

MacGillivary's nose wrinkled at the smell of greasy meals and BO. He looked irritated, then seemed to remember his partner was dead, and a slack confusion entered his face and body again, like he wasn't strung together properly and might flop down onto the floor. "They do say practising law makes you an eternal student—Carter expressed that in a very literal way."

He lifted a mug, green mould growing on the teabag left inside it, and dropped it back down. The mug had the firm's name on the side in the same style as the sign above the door: Lennox & MacGillivary. Shopfront in the Saltmarket, cheek to jowl with a whole host of law firms just down the street from Glasgow's High Court, broken up here and there by a random assortment of independent shops: a fishmonger's, a pet shop, a place on the corner which advertised "XXX DVDs" in large writing across the window and was remarkably still in business.

"You don't have a cleaner?" McCoist asked.

"We do, but she doesn't come in here. Carter doesn't want his things disturbed. Sorts it himself."

"So I see."

"A took a black bag in here masel wance an picked up aw the foil tubs an biscuit wrappers an that, an it's the only time a ever saw the man angry." The receptionist was at MacGillivary's shoulder.

"Oh, Sandra, it's getting a bit busy out there, could you let everyone know I'll be with them as soon as I can?"

"You can get back to work just now, Mr MacGillivary, we'll be in touch," McCoist said. "Can we borrow Sandra for five minutes?"

"Sure, um, thank you. I... Sorry, I just can't get my head around this." He looked to the full waiting room, at faces sullen, scared, defiant, gormless. For a moment he appeared lost, then his features clicked back into place. He strode out and his voice called to the next client in that sonorous, reliable baritone of his. Back straight, a sure pair of hands.

McCoist closed the office door and sat Sandra in the deep bum groove on the remains of Lennox's chair, did the introductions.

"McCoist, eh? Yer no relatet tae—"

"No."

"A pal ae mine used tae bide oan the same street as his maw, ye don't mind a—"

"We're not related."

"Aye. Course. It's just, there's no many McCoists aboot."

"Just me and one other, apparently."

"Och, sorry hen, dye get dug up aboot it aw the time?"

"Nope."

"Could we maybe ask you a few questions, Sandra, then come back to this?" Slater butted in, clearly enjoying it but seeing the veins standing out on McCoist's temples.

"Sorry, son. Aye, go ahead, hen."

McCoist took a calming breath before starting. "Sandra, I'm so sorry to have to break this to you, but we're here because your boss Carter Lennox was murdered."

"Wit?!"

"His body was discovered—"

"Wit?!" She barked out a laugh which turned into a cough. "Naw." She wheezed. "Wit's this? Yer wrang. Murdered? Cannae be true, cannae…"

"I'm sorry, Sandra, but I'm afraid it is. His body—"

She started hacking again.

"Do you need some water?"

Then the tears came. Her sobs were like twisted laughter, shaking her whole body, making her gasp for air. Slater whispered in McCoist's ear that they should maybe be ready to call an ambo.

It took a while for her to calm down. When she finally did, she answered their questions in a voice so meek it seemed to come from a different woman. Carter was a good man to work for. A lovely man. He really cared about the people he took on. He worked pro bono if need be. Mr MacGillivary didn't like it but the books all balanced out so it was fine. She didn't know him socially, she knew he wasn't married, had no kids, no parents left. A solitary life. If he had no friends it was only because he was at work all the time, didn't have the hours in the day for socialising or maintaining relationships. Because he was a lovely man, had a good heart. Metaphorically speaking, that was, all the coffee and crap he ate, it was surprising he'd had no problems with his ticker yet. Sandra had been there herself. This couldn't have happened, though. Mr Lennox murdered? Surely they were wrong.

They asked about whereabouts and itineraries on the last days Sandra had seen him, if there was anything out of the ordinary recently, etc., but nothing caught. It was all business as usual.

"Och, Wee Tim's gonnae be heartbroke. How am a gonnae tell him?"

"Tim?"

"He's oor student, bin doin work experience here fir a wee while noo. Mr Lennox hud him oan a stipend though, no workin fir free. Good man, nae exploitin the weans. Seemed tae huv taken a shine tae the boay. An vicey versa. Thick as thieves lately."

"Could we have a contact number for him? Tim?..."

"Tim Drummond. Aye, sure."

When they finished, the receptionist didn't get up to escort them out. "Are you OK, love?" Slater asked.

"Aye... aye... Could dae wae a coffee. Yous want wan an aw? A can make thum. Wid be nice tae sit an huv a coffee."

"I can get them." Slater sat and had a coffee with the old woman while McCoist left a voicemail for the uni boy.

7

Chuck was under the covers with his phone, the screen burning his eyes even with the backlight low. "Moan tae fuck. Come oan, come oan." Seven. Bust. "Fuck!" He tapped to put money in for another hand, then also stuck a bet on MovesLikeShagger69 who was on a winning streak. Five and three. Shite. *Hit us wae yer rhythm...* Ten. *Stick!* He hissed out a "Yass!" and gave a small, involuntary punch to the duvet over him. *Moan tae fuck. Come oan ye wee dancer ye...*

The dealer hit: blackjack.

Chuck lost his own hand and also the money he put on auld Mick. He groaned. His stomach clenched, his teeth clenched, his arse cheeks clenched. He dug his nails into his palms to stop himself from screaming. Two-fifty down in a baker's dozen of hands. His thumb hovered over the screen. Close the app or go again. He could at least scrape the balance back to zero if not make a profit. His heart raced and his breathing, stifled under the covers already, was shallow and sharp. He was about to click to bet again when his wife's voice made him drop a brick.

"Haw! Are you watchin porn under there?!"

He slapped his phone to his chest to hide the screen and whipped the covers off his head, cheeks flushed a dazzling dayglo pink. "Naw! Eh, a... a mean, can a man no huv a wank in peace?"

Bell's face wrinkled. "It's no even eight in the mornin." Bell was dressed in her scrubs and comfy trainers, her badge clipped to the pocket: Isabel Gardner, Advanced Nurse Practitioner, Greater Glasgow and Clyde. Flattering little passport picture.

"Didnae realise there wis an agreed upoan time fir it."

"Well, it's definitely no socially acceptable tae huv porn oan when the sun's up."

"Al keep tae the safter stuff then, eh?"

She picked up a pillow and smashed it over his head, half a grin on her face. Chuck laughed. His heart was still thundering but he could feel the relief spreading through his body. If Bell had seen what he'd actually been doing it wouldn't be a pillow she'd be hitting him with. Or it would be full of doorknobs rather than feathers.

"An av just cleant those sheets, so gee yersel a rest an get ready fir work."

"First joab's no oan till ten. How aboot ye climb in here wae me instead?"

"Am awready dressed, practically oot the door!" She gave him another bop with the pillow.

"Ye know a like tae try ma luck!"

Bell's face turned to stone.

"It's a turn ae phrase, Bell. Just a joke."

"No a funny wan. Am aff, see ye the night."

"Bell! Come oan!"

He waited until he heard the door shut to look at his phone again. Close call. He shut the app, fear still ringing inside.

The near miss kept him on the straight and narrow all through the morning. He stayed off the apps, didn't go into the shop for a couple of scratchers or a lottery ticket (EuroMillions was up to a hundred and ten mil though, fucksake!), and he

55

kept on driving past the Ladbrokes, Coral, Betfred, Willy Hill's, Paddy Power, Paddy Power, Betfred, Willy's, Ladbrokes, Paddy's, Bill's, Lad's, Pat's... their signs and posters bright and blaring, clawing their way into the mirrors of his van on the way to the Saltmarket. A plague of them. He was getting angry, irritable with other drivers. But by the time he pulled up outside Lennox & MacGillivary he had a text from Bell—nothing important, she was just having a quick cuppa, checking in, but it made his heart soar. Relief. She wasn't angry any more.

While he was on his phone, he deleted all the apps. *Fuck it aw. Done wae it.* (Except for the Great Accumulator, which was on anyway, no way to stop it, no point cashing out...)

Inside the solicitor's, there were a few guys moping on hard-looking chairs, but it was a tidy place, smelling of wood polish and coffee. The receptionist was a woman with a hard-lived face and voice to match who had a nice smile for him.

"Hiya, hen, am here fae Simply Shred."

"Ye must be Mick Hucknall then?"

Chuck ran a hand over what was left of his ginger hair. "Aye, the years huv no bin kind, music's a fickle industry!"

"Yer tellin me, son, a used tae be Marti Pellow."

She took him to an office off the waiting room—"Carter Lennox" peeling off the door's frosted-glass window—and apologised before she'd even let him inside.

"Jesus..." It was a tip. Like they kept the rest of the place looking tidy by stuffing all their shite into the spare room. There were mountains to move.

"A geed it a wee tidy-up, ye should ae seen it afore, yed ae bin takin Muhammad and Buddha's name in vain an aw. If ye bring yer van roon the block, ye can get in the back door fae

Steel Street, make hings a bit easier fir ye. Noo, a know am sposed tae watch ye but wur busy an, uh, short-staffed…" She turned her face away from him and made a rasping, gurgling noise into a crumpled tissue she'd pulled from her sleeve. "So al be comin back an to, awright?"

"Fine wae me if it's fine wae you. Don't want ye gettin in trouble wae the gaffer, but."

"Nothin else a can dae, is there? Tea or coffee, son?"

"Am a takin aw ae it?"

"Everyhin but the furniture."

"Better make it coffee, ta."

He was mostly left to feed the animal himself. Sandra, the receptionist, came through for a natter now and again but to call it supervision would be a ligament-snapping stretch. That suited Chuck fine. Not just because it was awkward having someone watch over your shoulder while you worked, but because a law firm was exactly the kind of place where he might find something interesting to bring to Mr Jamieson. Which would be good considering the money he'd lost not only that morning but the day before and the day before that.

He kept a secret account where he siphoned off some of the wages he paid himself, so he had money to play with that Bell had no idea about. She also had no idea about the loans. It filled him with shame, of course it did, but…

A positive thought punctured through the misery that had descended on him while clearing out the solicitor's office: if he was done with the gambling, then maybe he could be done with Jamieson too. If he kept the secret account going, kept paying into it but not using it for anything, then he could save enough money to pay back what he owed to the various lenders Jamieson was protecting him from. It would take some time but the idea of shaking hands and walking away from Jamieson, going back to being a straight citizen, would sustain him, wouldn't it?

If he'll let ye just waltz away, came a pessimistic thought to pish in his peanuts.

No, no, no. Sure, he'd heard some of the stories about Jamieson's past but that was a long time ago now. He'd been running his legit business for longer than he'd ever been in The Life. And fine, he still knew people in low places—which Chuck was thankful for because it had saved him from being nailed to a cross by his scrotum—but that didn't mean he wasn't, largely, on the level. (Despite the definitely illegal shit Chuck was doing for him currently.) No, when the books were balanced, the deal was at an end, and Jamieson, a businessman, would respect that. Right? *Right?*

"Eejit." Chuck kicked at the lower desk drawer he'd been emptying—ancient folders, textbooks as old as the Dead Sea Scrolls, loose, mummified Haribo—and it juddered in on its old runners, stopping short of closing. It was so unsatisfying that Chuck had to give it another hard kick with the steel toe of his work boot. This time, it gave a little then bounced back out. It wasn't the runners sticking: there was something wedged behind the drawer, stopping it from closing over. Probably just another folder that had slipped back there from the pile.

Chuck took the drawer out completely. Sure enough, an A4 Manilla envelope much like many others he'd already thrown to the steel maw of the shredder was loose in the back. He pulled it out, saw there was hairy gaffer tape on it, like maybe it had been stuck to the underside of the table, rather than sitting in the drawer. There was one word written on it in biro:

TIM

It had been torn open already. Chuck pulled out some crinkled sheets of paper covered in a messy scrawl, and a folded-up poly pocket which had something in it. A small trinket of some kind, looked like a metal fag dout...

Chuck dropped it, realisation hitting him like the nip of a static shock. He'd never seen one in real life before, but he'd seen plenty in films and computer games. It was a bullet casing. The empty cartridge shell that gets ejected from a gun when it's fired. He snatched it back up and stuffed it into the envelope. Quick look at the office door behind him before he turned his attention to the papers. They were loose and well thumbed. The handwriting was atrocious, even Chuck had a tidier script and he wasn't exactly a calligrapher himself. He scanned for words which popped out. Near the top was a name which made him want to stop reading immediately: Paulo McGuinn.

What the fuck was this? His heart started to drum like the Orange Walk on a quiet Saturday morning when every other cunt was in bed. Gold. He'd struck gold, he was sure of it.

He stuffed the papers back in the folder with the shell, tucked it into the middle of a stack of junk he was about to throw to the machine and scrambled through the back and outside to the van before Sandra could reappear asking if he wanted a fifth coffee.

He pulled the TIM folder out of the stack and secreted it under the driver's seat, then chucked the rest into the hopper, where the folders and papers, staples and all, slid down the shoot to the open throat of the robo-Sarlacc pit. As he hopped out the van, high on excitement and coffee, the apparition of a suited man at the back door popped his balloon, brought out a cold sweat on his back and the old beetroot beamer on his freckled face. *Shite, must be the other name above the door—did he see somethin?*

"Hiya. Chuck, is it?"

"Aye. Mr MacGillivary?"

They shook hands, Chuck's clammy and calloused, everything you want in a good shake.

"How are you getting on?"

"Fine, cheers. Reckon am aboot halfway done noo. Al need tae go an empty the van soon, she's nearly full, then al come back fir the rest."

MacGillivary nodded, half listening. He took a pack of fags from inside his suit jacket. "Smoke?"

"Naw thanks, a geed it up."

"Me too. Fifteen years, started again yesterday."

"Sorry tae hear that."

Again, he seemed not to listen, studying the picture of a throat tumour printed on the otherwise plain packet. "Marlboros, not that you can tell any more. It was always Marlboros for me. I wonder if you can taste the difference without the branding?"

"Aw pretty much the same, a used tae hink. It's like which shade ae shite dye like the best."

No smile or laugh or indication he'd even heard the joke.

Chuck watched the man smoke, not making any move to unblock the back door. "Right, eh, a better be gettin oan wae it, sorry…" Chuck had to squeeze past him.

8

There was one other person in the waiting room of Firestane Consultancy. She looked like a footballer's wife. Dressed up for a Tuesday morning, shiny rocks hanging from her, bag that cost half a year's graft, nails that could gralloch a monarch stag. Or a man for that matter—probably trying to find out who the husband's been shagging behind her back, Chuck decided, pity the poor bastart when he gets caught. Her face held more steel than his shredder, and she was looking right at him.

"Mr Jamieson chooses who tae hire as carefully as a do then," she said, her accent betraying working-class roots. A Scheme queen. "A hired a plumber tae refit ma whole hoose cause his company wis callt Plumbog Millionaire." She gave a slight smile, nodded towards the company logo printed on Chuck's shirt. He must have looked confused. Small talk was unexpected in a place like this. There was a telly on in the corner of the room with the sound off.

"Aw, right, aye, well, a cannae take credit, it wis the missus who came up wae it—she didnae hink ad actually go ahead an use it, but." He chuckled. Bell had called him a dafty: "Am no takin the blame if naebdy wants tae hire ye, ye big eejit."

"Clever wummin, yer missus."

"Aw aye. She's a nurse, an no just an ordinary nurse, she's an ANP. Advanced—"

"A can tell yer very proud."

He felt his cheeks redden but just laughed at himself. "Aye. Aye a am." True. Not that he always remembered that. The day's find had put him in a good mood right enough.

"That's nice." Chuck couldn't decide if the comment sounded sarcastic or sad. It bolstered his theory about her man playing away. She's wanting to have him followed, or maybe she's here to see the evidence. He wondered if she was hoping for him to be guilty or not guilty.

"Wit dye dae yersel?" Drink champagne at lunchtime, have the nanny pick up the weans from school, he thought, though not uncharitably, it sounded quite good. Nice, even.

Before she could answer, the door opened and Marble's beautifully crafted visage peeked through. He spoke to the woman in an accent Chuck had never heard from him before: "I'm so sorry to have to ask you to wait for another five minutes. Something urgent has come up." There were obviously two tiers of punter here, and Chuck definitely didn't get treated to that accent. In fact, Marble didn't even speak to him, just hooked a finger.

Chuck didn't have an appointment: he'd burst in and told the secretary/sentry he had something for Mr Jamieson, something good. "Ark ae the Covenant," he'd said.

"If it's anythin less than the word ae God, yel be leavin here in a fancy box yersel, son," Jamieson said, as close to a joke as Chuck had ever heard from the man. Was he as excited as Chuck? Whatever it was, it was unnerving, and Chuck handed over the envelope with a growing sense of dread.

The waiting room had stewed him: that invincible feeling that he'd clawed a diamond from the coal had become a state of panic. His heart galloped, he sweated. What did he know really except that the name Paulo McGuinn was on that sheet of paper? What if it was nothing? Just bullshit. Nonsense. But what about the bullet? What about the tape on the envelope that suggested it had been hidden? He ground his jaws as if he'd just spanked a line of top-flight flake, the kind the waiting woman's Premier League husband probably had for breakfast.

Jamieson shuffled through the papers, the sleeve with the shell inside pinched between two fingers. He would never do anything as obvious as smile but Chuck could sense something, the guttering of a candle within the man's tumshie-lantern heed.

"Where did ye say ye foont this, Chuck?"

"A telt ye yed want tae see it."

"Where?"

"Law firm callt Lennox an MacGillivary. The man Lennox is pan breed apparently, they hud me clearin oot his office. Stacks an stacks ae shite everywhere, ye shouldae seen it. Still goat tae go back an finish it aff but a thoat ad better get this right oer tae ye…" He was bubbling, excitement and nervousness unleashing a torrent of chatter.

"Huv ye read it aw?"

"Naw, just skimmed it. Saw, ye know, *that* name, an wae the bullet… Didnae want tae risk any cunt catchin me, an the writin's pish poor—"

"Ye sure yuv no read it?"

He felt Marble's presence close to his shoulder.

"Very sure."

"Good. Ye better get back tae the joab then."

Chuck's knee-jerk reaction was disappointment, but then he knew better than to expect open gratitude from Jamieson.

Stingy with emotion was an understatement. Pre-ghost Scrooge was a warmer chap, and freer with his money too. No, he could tell the auld boy was pleased, and his parting words made him sure of it: "A shouldnae huv tae say this cause ye know awready, but ye don't breathe a fuckin word ae this tae anycunt, right?"

"It's practically written oan the side ae the van."

On his way out he heard Marble address the woman in that posh voice he was able to dial in: "Sorry about that, Mrs McGuinn, as I said, something urgent came up..."

The name was like a fist snatching Chuck's heart, holding it still. McGuinn. That was McGuinn's wife. Reeking of money, working-class accent. It made sense. Paulo McGuinn's wife, fucking hell. Widow, actually. And here was Chuck just dropping off some kind of scribbled tirade about the man along with a used bullet. Totems and weird omens. He shivered and his heart restarted.

He'd parked on double yellows but it was fine—he drove a van. The Merchant City was a nice area so he was a bit further east before he finally saw a bookie's. An auld yin was smoking outside. Posters of magnificent racehorses covered the windows, obscuring the dim world within. Chuck strode past the wasters at the puggies (ads emblazoned in a black and yellow hazard warning on the unoccupied machines: HOW MUCH CAN YOU AFFORD TO LOSE?) and the anoraks with the *Racing Post* at the school tables which took up the centre of the room.

It wasn't like he'd actually quit, was it? He might have deleted the apps and kept the radio tuned to some country-and-western shite all morning but the Great Accumulator had always been on. That had never gone away. And with his luck running hot it would be silly not to have a flutter. He wasn't really into the ponies but he needed a quick hit so he stuck a wedge on a horse he liked the sound of: Spry Stallone.

He won a hundred quid. *Yasssyafuckindancer!*

Then he lost three hundred quid.

He mooched back to Lennox & MacGillivary. The lightning rage of losing had passed, leaving the dark clouds to linger. He hadn't stopped by the warehouse to empty the van but it didn't matter, that had been a lie anyway, an excuse to get away to see Jamieson.

He parked around the back again and let himself in. The back corridor ran behind MacGillivary's office and turned left into the reception area, Lennox's shit pit on the right. He could hear raised voices through the wall. As he approached the other office, Sandra almost threw herself over her desk to get to him.

She took him by the arm, tight bony talons threatening to bruise skin, and led him back the way he came. "Sorry, son, it's no a good time the noo, al gee ye a ring when ye can come back. Yel get paid no worries though, an the rest ae the joab is still yours…"

The door slammed shut behind him. The portentous noise signalled the rain to start.

Wit the fuck wis that aboot? How had it happened? He'd been winning this morning, but now it was turning to shite. King Midas had a wee brother, and his power was not so well appreciated.

As he rolled the van back onto the Saltmarket he saw a slate-coloured Beamer parked outside Lennox & MacGillivary. It was plain; it had polis written all over it.

9

A long time ago, William Jamieson had an argument with a man over a parking space. The man told Billy he couldn't park there but Billy didn't see the man's name written on the ground. Yet the man persisted in telling Billy that he couldn't park there. Billy said he could park anywhere he liked. In fact, Billy parked right outside this man's house in the dead of night, where this man's wife and children were inside sleeping, and Billy crept in, and with nothing but his car keys and a wheel brace, he turned them into confetti. The man stopped arguing and let Billy have his space on the street.

Paulo had told Lottie this story. The argument wasn't about a parking space, obviously, and she assumed the rest was gross exaggeration, the projection of her husband's own, gleefully vicious nature. It was meant as a campfire ghost story. Seeing the man himself now, a shrivelling face in a suit which sat too big at the shoulders, it seemed even further from the truth.

"A wis waitin fir ye tae come an see me, Charlotte. Did ye get the cerd?"

"A did Mr Jamieson, much appreciatet."

"How are yer wee yins hawdin up?"

"They're no so wee these days. Gemma's fifteen an Ari's nineteen. They're, um, doin as best they can. Considerin."

"It's a cryin shame. He wis a good man."

Lottie didn't agree to that and Jamieson didn't put any pressure on her to. They both knew what kind of man Paulo was.

"Yev come tae see if a can find oot who killt him." To the point.

"A huv, aye." No need to tiptoe around it.

He leant forward, inscrutable eyes boring into hers. For a second she thought he might reach for her hand. "Good. Cause a want tae help ye. A want tae know an aw." He sat back at rest, his neck lost to the collar of his shirt. "Thoat ye might be here sooner, a goat worried ye might ae bought that shite fae the polis aboot yer poor nephew."

"No at aw. No fuckin way wis it Colin. It wis they car-wash cunts—Prentice an Burnet—and the polis are daein fuck aw tae find them," Lottie seethed, words crashing from a burst dam. "How hard could it fuckin be? They're no likely a pair ae fuckin Einsteins, are they? They work in a fuckin car wash, thir no the Kray twins. Penn an fuckin Teller just disappearin aff the stage. Moan tae fuck."

"I can dae this properly fir ye, Charlotte. A mean it."

Something about his countenance, something treacherously soft which could draw out confidences, explanations, justifications, made her add, "Ma sister's goin aff her fuckin nut wae the stress. A need tae dae this as much fir her as me."

"Poor lassie, we'll sort this oot fir her then."

As if to wrest back control of the conversation, reassert herself, Lottie went straight to the chequebook. "Tell me yer rates."

He held up a hand. "Let's no talk aboot money the noo. Av been wantin tae get goin oan this wan, wis just waitin fir you tae geez yer blessin first."

She drove away cursing herself for not insisting on setting up a payment plan. But it felt like there was no room to argue the point. The man was intractable, but not in the boisterous, overbearing, bratty way of her husband. Jamieson was like quicksand. Soft, fluid, seemingly malleable, but when you tried to pull away it was hard as cement setting around you. She could hear Brownlee's "I told you so" already. But what was done was done, and if there was a chance to find out who killed her husband and set Colin free, then Jamieson was it. There was no better person—a man who commanded a team of experts in investigation and security, who knew The Life, who'd been there and back, who knew the Hampden Roar, the right trees to shake. Having him in her corner and eager to do the job could still be a good thing. Tallying up the balance of favours was something she could worry about later, when Colin was a free man and Ginny's hair started growing back. When things started resembling normality again. Normality for the woman who married Paulo McGuinn, anyway.

He was a right wee chancer as a lad. Spontaneous, wild. You might even call him vivacious, if you didn't mind getting a sore face. Could be funny too, sometimes, when he wasn't putting it on as a show for everybody. They met on Lottie's twenty-first birthday. He was at the same pub with his pals and sent two bottles over to their table: a bottle of Bollinger and a bottle of Lambrini. He was making money even then. Lottie carefully caught his eye and raised her glass as she poured the Lambo into it.

They liked to go out together. They liked to party and fuck and fight. It was exciting. She grew out of it. And by the time she did she had two kids and a nice car and a husband who was rarely home. She knew what he did for a living from early on.

She was looking forward to getting home, releasing the pressure that had been gripping her since the meeting, the maudlin dive into the glory days she could do without, but as she turned onto Nitshill Road she could see a polis van parked up on the kerb, and even at this distance she knew they were at her house. Her sanctuary.

"Wit's goin oan? This is ma hoose." She went into the gangling chappy in high-vis at the end of her driveway with studs up.

"Aw, eh, sorry, um—"

"Am Lottie McGuinn. This is ma gaff. Let me in."

He still had acne on his fizzog, poor boy. "Eh, Sarge—"

"Wit's happened?" Her own words tipped the ice bucket in her belly, unlocking the terrible "what if?" scenarios no parent wants to think about. Gemma was in school, she should have been in school. And Ari should be in uni. She might have come home though, what if, what if—

"Lottie!" Mhari, the maid, came running down the drive, crunching over the gravel in moon-boot Nikes, leopard-print leggings and a blue tabard with pockets. "Somebdy broke in! Door wis hingin open when a goat here, a goat such a fright, a, a—"

"Callt the polis?"

10

Noses were pressed against windows all down the street. Looked like half the polis in Glesga had heard about it and came to do the same. McCoist was one of them.

"What brings you to my humble housebreaking, Super Ally?" DS Jarvis said, a former colleague and terrible cop who couldn't catch the clap from a gas cooker. (When McCoist moved up, he moved down, another one who got the belt because of the WhatsApp scandal. Cost him his marriage too.)

"Could ask you the same, I thought CID had given up trying to solve crimes altogether."

"Maybe we should all just follow your lead and bang up whichever convenient sod is nearest."

"Works for your wife."

"Fuck you," he hissed, storming away.

"If you need help looking into the mystery of your missing pension, give me a call!" Childish, sure, but it felt good. The perks of rank—shitting on those beneath you like a pigeon on a lamp post.

Le Palais de McGuinn was a sight to behold. McCoist had been before when she was "investigating" Paulo's murder, but as she entered the hall, the brash radiance of the chandelier, like a spaceship about to land on a parquet runway, hit her afresh. There was a maximalist elegance to it until you spotted the big gold cat on the baby grand. Cannae buy class, McCoist thought—something her maw always said, usually whenever the neighbours bought something marginally nicer than the version they had.

On the wall where the stairs twisted up to the first floor was a family portrait. A decade old maybe, the daughters were young. Paulo looked young too, compared to the man McCoist had killed. She remembered the first time she saw this painting, the cringe of guilt it caused in her belly. In her mind, Paulo's big smiling face—one arm around his wife, the other hand resting on the eldest girl's shoulder—erupted in an explosion of burnt mince.

Bang. There goes a husband. There goes a father. There goes Alison McCoist's somewhat ordinary life as a somewhat ordinary polis.

Lottie hadn't aged at all. McCoist found her in the kitchen, elbows on the sparkling granite island, scrolling studiously on her phone with a manicured thumbnail. Her whole appearance had the sheen of varnish to it, skin included. Next to her, a cup of tea scooped up in his two arthritic hands, a Superking tucked behind the ear, was Ross Brownlee, the family lawyer or accountant or fixer, whatever he called himself. McCoist just called him a crook.

A harried-looking maid jumped up to get the kettle on again. At the movement, Lottie looked up and glared at McCoist as if she was something that had just crawled up out of the toilet. "Nae need, Mhari. DCI McCoist only likes the cheap stuff, an a don't huv any ae that."

"So nice you remembered, Mrs McGuinn." McCoist plastered a smile on her lips.

Lottie's nostrils just about flared like a bull's. "Come tae gawk?"

"I heard about the break-in and was concerned, came to see if there was anything I could do for you."

"Aye, ye could find oot who actually killt ma husband, if yev goat a spare minute."

McCoist forced some sincerity into her voice: she had to be careful here, and being snippy might cause her to say something she shouldn't. "I know you're not happy with the verdict, Mrs McGuinn, and I understand why it would be hard to accept but—"

"Naw, ye don't undertsawn. Cause if ye did, ye widnae be in ma kitchen right the noo offerin me a turd wrapped in foil an callin it a Kwality Street."

Brownlee inserted himself between them. "Detective Chief Inspector, why are you here? Not really your area, housebreaking, is it? Mrs McGuinn has already answered a whole barrage of questions from your colleagues at a most distressing time and I think she has a right to call it time."

"Trampin aw oer ma flairs in their bloody great boots an aw. Av never met a polis who knows how tae wipe their feet oan a doormat."

"I'll bring my slippers with me next time, shall I?" Lottie looked like she might go for her, and McCoist could imagine the damage those nails would do—easily lose an eye. She dropped the jokes, took a breath, dialled in a bit of humanity. "I'm sorry, I don't mean to intrude, I am genuinely concerned. Your... *situation* has changed a lot, hasn't it? Just you and the girls here now." She thought of her first nights alone in the house after she and Mark split up, the kids away with him during the week. It was quiet, she had to have the telly on in the background all the time. At night, the place was full of shadows and absences. A gap where Mark's turntable and records used to be, the missing trunk where Tess kept her Beanie Babies, the clutter of bikes and scooters and skates and helmets in the hall gone. They left the rooms bare and echoing. "Having someone invade your home like this, it can be so damaging. I've seen it before."

"It wis just some wee shitebag brekkin in tae nick stuff, that's aw. It's goat nothin tae dae wae... everythin else." Her anger was gone now. She didn't sound sure.

"Was something stolen then?"

"Some jewellery was taken," Brownlee answered. "DS Jarvis has a list."

"Just the jewellery, nothing else?"

"Speak to DS Jarvis and let my client have some peace."

"Can I take a look around? I'll check the windows and the locks for you."

"Somebody is already doing that."

"Another pair of eyes won't hurt."

"Do wit ye want." Lottie waved her away and rested her forehead in her hand, eyes closed, as if trying to pinch shut a splitting headache.

"Thank you, Mrs McGuinn. Mr Brownlee." She gave the lawyer a curt tip of the chin and he returned a look of mutual loathing. She'd see the cunt behind bars one day, and he probably knew it.

He stopped her at the kitchen door: "Just a reminder, detective, my client is the *victim* of a crime. She has allowed the police into her home to search for evidence which might solve that crime. Nothing more."

McCoist put her hands up and backed away with a smile.

Understood. This wasn't a raid: no prying beyond what related to the break-in. But there was prying and there was *prying*.

Back in the hall, she rounded on the puma leaping from the piano, gave it a tickle under the chin. "Bruce would like you. Good size for humping." The carpet on the stairs was thick and lush, absorbing all sound of her footsteps. The wall appeared to be covered in glittering sand. She had to go sideways to let a uniformed officer past. "Ma'am."

"Did you check all the windows, Constable?…"

"Ampor, ma'am. Aye, all locked up. Back door too. Looks like he went in and out the front."

"Is there a camera?"

"Nah, that would be too easy, wouldn't it?"

"Any other break-ins in the area?"

He tucked his hands into his stab-proof, shook his head. "None I know of. DS Jarvis might have a bigger picture though."

"Doubt it," McCoist mumbled.

"Sorry, ma'am?"

"How did he get in the door?"

"Shouldered the storm door, broke a bit of wood, easy, but the lock on the inner door is a serious bit of kit."

"Technical know-how?"

"I'd say so. More than the av-er-age bear."

"How about the av-er-age cat burglar looking to pinch a few shiny things to pawn?"

He sucked air in through his teeth, evaluating. "One that takes a lot of pride in his work, maybe. Most of them… eh."

People who have maids have tidy houses. Tidy houses are easier to rob. Lottie's bed was made as if it were in a hotel room, sheets tucked in tight, throw pillows on top of actual pillows. A total pain in the arse getting into bed at night after you've dragged yourself through another fucking day. Big vanity mirror on a walnut dresser, a stack of jewellery boxes presumably missing some ice. The chair back had absolutely nothing hanging over it. Very tidy, especially considering some sneak had just been through it. His attack must have been targeted indeed. McCoist's nose detected a waft of bullshit along with the perfume which scented the room with fresh floral notes.

The younger daughter's bedroom was more akin to something a person might actually live in. Couldn't see the floor for the clothes. Cups and bowls forming penicillin dotted around the place. Obviously made to do her own tidying up, some kind of attempt not to spoil her. McCoist wondered what kind of dad a man like Paul McGuinn would have been. Did he indulge his daughters with all his money? Was he kind to them? Did they miss him?

The office had been exempted from the maid's Marigolds and feather duster when McCoist had been here before—Brownlee a permanent fixture at that time, dwarfed by the massive desk and the stacks of printouts and box files. Busy, busy. It looked worse this time, but based on McCoist's own beleaguered workstation she couldn't be sure somebody had been rifling through it. The one thing which indicated it had been worked over were the action figures scattered on the floor, tossed from their open display case. Man-child nonsense—McGuinn had seemed altogether too scary to be the type, but maybe they were all the type.

Her eye caught the framed football jersey on the wall and she muttered a "fucksake": Rangers Football Club home strip from the mid nineties, name and number, signed by you-know-fucking-who.

Her phone rang. "Suffia, what's up?… Oh for *ffflippin*, moth-er*ffff*—" She took the phone away from her mouth and roared like the big cat downstairs. "On my way."

11

There was no amount of gin that could wash the taste of a meeting with that polis wummin out the mouth. Lottie continued to try though. *"Your situation,"* she quoted in a haughty, approaching-posh voice. "Situation. Tryin tae fuckin scare me, is she?"

If she was honest, Lottie was scared already. The violation of someone entering her home, touching her things… though the only room they seemed to have been interested in was the office. Drawers turned over, papers rifled, pictures hanging crooked. The glass-fronted cabinet with Paulo's collection had been jimmied open, the action figures, his precious wrasslers, shuffled around and knocked over—probably feeling for a false back panel or something. She'd righted Stone Cold Steve Austin, tapped his baldy head with a finger, panic falling to a simmer.

"Lottie, hen…" Brownlee put a stiff hand on hers, the curl of his fingers digging in more than he meant. "She's right about that. Things are different now without Paulo around. You aren't afforded the same protection, his crew are off finding new work with different people."

"Didnae take them lang. Turncoat bastarts."

"A good few are with Callaghan now—and that's probably a good thing for you, he's the up-and-comer and you have friendly voices in his ear."

"Wit would they fuckin want fae me anyway?" Brownlee gave her a steady, searching look but she was too busy draining her glass to notice. "He's goan. He's fuckin goan." The glass hit the granite hard. Her eyes stung and a sob threatened but turned into a chuckle instead.

"He is, hen. And this place… it's big. Ari isn't living here any more either. If it's just you and Gemma, maybe you should think about—"

"Sellin? Sell ma fuckin hoose?! Eftir aw the shite av bin through. Ma hame."

"I know, hen, I know. But it would be safer to go somewhere less… conspicuous. Where not so many people know. And to be frank, if you downsize, the money you'd get for the house would be good for you to put away for the future."

Lottie had been going to college, studying interior design, when she met Paulo. It all fell away the closer she fell in with him. Not just the ambition, but the friends she'd made too. The house had sparked something in her, she felt a need she'd thought was gone, satisfied by nice clothes and luxury package holidays and looking after the kids. No way would she leave it now. But she never finished college, never got a job, and now had no means of making money beyond what Paulo had left to her—and how long would that last?

"I'm only thinking of you and the girls."

"A know…" Lottie whispered.

Ross headed off. The polis were gone too.

"Want us tae go an get Gemma fae school?" Mhari asked, her usually chatty, stage-whisper-gossiping voice reduced to a mouse squeak.

"A can dae it."

"Yev hud a few drinks, Lottie."

"Mrs McGuinn."

"Sorry?"

"It's Mrs McGuinn tae you."

Mhari, who was older than Lottie by a decade, looked like a shiteing schoolgirl. "A, am sorry, a—"

"Yel get yer severance an a reference if ye need it, but yer finished here."

"M-Mrs M—"

"Pack up an go."

"But—"

"Ye *never* bring the polis tae this door."

"Am sorry, am so sorry, a just goat a fright an didnae know wit tae dae. Please, please don't—"

"Be goan when a get back."

Lottie tried to slam the front door behind her but it bounced ineffectually, broken where it had been forced in. Her legs felt rubbery as she crunched over the gravel, the fresh air going to her head, the house casting its shadow over her. She got in the Merc and waited a few minutes for things to stabilise. She took a roll of Polos from the glovebox and gubbed a few. As she crunched down on them, working the molars, the tempest of rage and anxiety and helplessness subsided. She flicked the radio on and some idle Radio 1 banter gibbered out, chipper and bland. The arguing in her mind cleared, a crystal purpose growing in its place.

Sell the house. Oer ma lifeless, boggin corpse.

12

McCoist decided she'd need some new, tougher shoes for booting bollocks and made a mental note to go shopping when she got a day off. Something with a pointed toe would be good. When Khan and Travis had shown up at the law firm to collect Lennox's computer and start dredging the office, the receptionist had happily told them they already had someone in to clear up the mess. The bloke had shredded his way through half the potential evidence. McCoist ripped MacGillivary top hole to bottom hole but the lawyer insisted he'd done nothing wrong. There was no warrant to seize evidence; he needed the place cleared out. She'd seen the state it was in, hadn't she? Like something on a daytime reality show: *Honkin Hoarders* with former-TV-contestant-turned-TV-personality Hugh Givesafuck. McCoist called bullshit, pointed out it was highly suspicious to be getting rid of his partner's work so soon.

"I didn't think—"

"Clearly. This is a murder inquiry, Mr MacGillivary. Somebody killed your partner, and you appear to be helping them cover it up."

He coughed and spluttered and laughed in a bumbling, posh disbelief, his mouth forming sentences and abandoning them, as if he just couldn't put into words how ridiculous the accusation was. Eventually he managed: "Preposterous! And defamatory, I might add."

"And I might add your name to my list of suspects," McCoist countered. "How big is my list of suspects, DS Slater?"

"Not big at all, DCI McCoist. Why, it only has one name on it. Now."

They let him stew while the work started on what was left of Lennox's office. McCoist made a note to speak to the shredding guy and see if anything could be done about the potential clues he'd torn up. She also made a note to get an address for the intern, Tim Drummond, who still hadn't returned any of her messages. The list now read:

Baw-booters—wingtips? Steel toes?
Shredding guy—mag glass & tape?
Student Tim—address?
Dug food/chews

It was getting on but she went to the station to pick up the keys they'd got for Lennox's flat and head over there. Scenes of Crime had started working on it during the day and the preliminary verdict was that it wasn't the murder site, unless their man was very careful indeed. Still, McCoist wanted to have a shufty, at least make sure MacGillivary hadn't been over to torch the place.

"Tag along with you?" Slater asked.

"You're all right, Si, cheers. Get on up the road, poor wee Maisie will be waiting for you."

"If you're sure. Here, we should take Maisie and Bruce out for a stroll together when we get the time. She's a mad thing, could do with some socialising."

"Same," McCoist laughed. "Aye, that would be good. Bruce isn't exactly Crufts material himself. Make sure Gaz and Suffia head off too, will you? Last thing I need is getting chinned for unauthorised overtime."

She called Mark as she drove to the west end. "How's everyone doing?"

"All fine here. Cam's away playing five-a-side and I'm dropping Tess off at Samantha's in half an hour."

"She staying over?"

"Yes."

She could tell Mark was waiting for it. The question. She tried to hold it in, but: "You confirmed that with Sam's mum?"

Long breath out, crackling in the mic. "No, I trust our daughter."

"Hmm." Mark was an open book in person, over the phone it was a little trickier. "Well, in the spirit of trusting our daughter, I was thinking we should let her go to the festival."

"Yeah?"

"Make her more amenable to having a proper chat about what's happening at school."

"So let her have her fun, get in the good books, soften her up then, *bam!* Cuffed to the chair, shadeless light bulb, two-way mirror, interrogation time. Right?"

"How were we together so long and you still know no more about detective work than what's in the fillums?"

"It's not like that?"

"You missed the towel and bucket of water."

"Of course," he chuckled.

"Speaking of which, I've got a new case and—"

"You'll be working this weekend." The bantering trace of who they used to be vanished, replaced with divorce papers tone.

"Sorry, is that all right?"

"I've got plans on Saturday night."

"Could you ask your mum?"

"She does enough—"

"Please, Mark. I can't get out of it. I'll sort it for the following weekend instead, I promise."

Heavy sigh. "I'll ask."

"Thank you, I really appreciate it. And I'm sorry. I'll speak to the kids."

"Yeah... Is this the real reason you're wanting to let Tess go to TRNSMT?"

"Did you really not confirm with Samantha's mum about the sleepover?" There was a moment of silence before Mark's laughter filled the car. Mark's laugh was lovely and easy, one of his most attractive features, which had always counted for a lot against the list of less attractive features in the other column.

"What are your Saturday-night plans then? Out to the dancin? Axe throwing? Top Golf with the boys?"

"Eh, no, dinner, actually." There was a hesitance in his reply.

"Dinner? Oh, dinner, like... with a, um—"

"Yeah..."

"Dinner with a woman. Gotcha." McCoist felt her cheeks redden. *Get a grip!* Blushing was not something she did often.

"Uh huh, it's, um—"

"You don't have to explain. Enjoy!" She screwed her face up, clenched her teeth. *Enjoy? What?! Stop talking!* "I mean, I hope you have a nice time. At the weekend."

"Yeah, um, thanks. I—"

"Speak to you later."

"B—"

She hung up.

She blew her fringe away from her face. Her forehead felt hot too. *Christ, what was that?* Realistically, Mark had probably been out with other women since they broke up—it had been years—but the topic had never been broached. Ignored rather than carefully avoided, McCoist had thought, but she was surprised by how much it had thrown her now it had finally arrived. She held no fantasises of them ever getting back together—McCoist had been a pragmatist too long for that, and a cynic for even longer—and it was inevitable, maybe, that he or she or both would meet someone else, and of course there were still some feelings, there always would be, they'd had a life together, had children together, but love—

Fuck! McCoist swerved to avoid clipping an Uber Eats delivery man on an e-bike she hadn't noticed pulling out onto Byres Road. He took a hand from its handlebar mitt to communicate his anger.

"Sorry, pal."

It was a relief to eventually find herself outside the row of tenements on Great Western Road where Lennox lived and turn off the engine. Fading purple light on clean sandstone, bay windows top to bottom like a turret, window frames painted in regulation black and white, fresh coat on the ironwork that sectioned little front gardens neatly sprouting plant life. Where the McGuinn mansion screamed pharaoh-like riches, these buildings humble-bragged affluence.

McCoist let herself into the close with the fob on Lennox's key ring. Colourful, highly decorative tiles covered the walls like a Moscow metro station, a chequerboard stripe at shoulder height, Mackintosh roses up above. The concrete floor was clean to a polished finish, no smell of pish. There were bikes leaning against the bars of the stairwell, none of them chained to the railings. Potted plants outside doorways were healthy-looking, watered, smelling of clean earth.

Lennox lived at the top. McCoist remembered the sagging, grey wee lawyer from the time they met, the shining, spotty dome of his scalp like a tarnished cloche over wild, shaggy hair (a monk's tonsure, if intentional, though probably not), fingers stained with ink, shirt creased, tie off-centre. A man who matched his work environment, as if a crumbling tower of dilapidated, coffee-stained law books had gained sentience and thrown on a suit. And with his evidential penchant for biscuits and takeaways, it must have been a killer getting back up the steps every night.

Though McCoist had sensed something steely hidden beneath the trodden-down, middle-aged veneer. He had worried her a little in his lack of showiness. His partner MacGillivary was more what she expected in a lawyer: arrogant, overbearing, righteous. The kind of person you could slap guilt-free. Lennox was something else, something harder to pin down. She suspected a Q-car—the shell of a rusty banger with an engine like a Ferrari rocket ship hidden under the bonnet. Maybe he had no problem getting up the stairs.

Midpoint of the climb, McCoist heard something that made her pause. Rattling from up above. A soft thump. More rattling. Hiss of exasperated breath which susurrated around the tiles like a ghost's sheet flapping through the air and passing through her. It lit up her nerves like a string of pulsing fairy lights. Muscles clenched, pores opened, heart danced.

She slipped her shoes off and continued up in her socks, cold floor on her big toe revealing a hole. As she approached the top floor, she lowered herself until she was using her hands as well, the way Tess and Cam used to when they went tearing up the stairs as wee ones, fast and animal-like.

Getting higher, she could smell warm pizza dough, and worried her stomach might gurgle and give her away. She'd missed dinner.

Peeking up, she could see a man on the top landing. He was fiddling at the storm door with a bank card, trying to slide it between the latch and the strike plate, and pushing against it with his shoulder, making sure not to disturb the police tape crossed over the doorway. He was tall but slight in a loose hoody and chinos, trendy New Balance trainers on his feet. McCoist's fight-or-flight gauge tipped towards "fight". Ever since the Car Wash Catastrophe she'd been taking an MMA class ran by an ex-SAS hard nut who called himself Sledge, and a wild part of her thought putting her training into practice could even be fun.

There was a Domino's box on the floor—neat method of getting into the close, McCoist thought, but he was pishing into the wind with that old credit-card move.

"Better to just give it a boot," McCoist offered, as she stepped up onto the landing. "Neighbours might hear it and call the polis though."

He spun around, eyes wide with panic. Young, bum-fluff beard from lack of shaving, needing a trim, mouth like a goldfish because he didn't know what to say.

He lunged.

Not at her; past her.

McCoist was ready, body-checked him with her elbow jutting out into his solar plexus. He gasped and staggered backwards, hands on his chest, a nice swinging distance for McCoist to bang his ear with the heel of her hand like the bottom of a sauce bottle. Off-kilter, his brain sloshed up the side of its tub, it only took a gentle shove to put him on the ground.

One hand was covering his abused ear, the other waved in the air. "Please! Please! Stop!"

McCoist pulled her warrant card. "DCI McCoist. I'm arresting you under the—"

"No, please, don't. Please. It's not like that."

"...Criminal Justice (Scotland) Act 2016 for—"

"McCoist. Ally McCoist! I know you!"

"Very funny. Really not the time for it, I promise you. I'm arresting you under the Criminal Justice (Scotland) Act 2016 for attempted housebreaking. The reason—"

"No, we've met before! Please, just listen a second. Please."

There was something to that... Gears coughed and turned and tried to bite together in McCoist's brain. He was familiar. He was. Where though?

It clicked. The eureka light bulb which had lit up in McCoist's brain at solving the puzzle fizzed and shattered with the implications that followed it. "The car wash..."

"Yes! Yes! Please, can we just talk? Don't-don't arrest me. Please. Honestly, I'm not trying to steal anything or..."

"Fuck." McCoist gripped the banister, adrenaline draining, anxiety filling up the empty space it left behind. The car wash again.

"I can explain."

"I think you'd better... What's on the pizza?"

13

"A cheeseburger pizza... You're a man of excessive tastes."

The lad gave a shy smile, the first since they'd sat down at the table in Lennox's small galley kitchen—the lawyer's gaff was the Jekyll to his office's Hyde, everything kept tidy by the cleaner. The boy's face had been a twitching, trembling thing since McCoist had pulled him up off the floor. Shiteing it. He wasn't someone used to being in trouble, but it was more than just the presence of the polis. Worrying. "At the counter I asked myself what Oscar Wilde would order," he said.

"I go for the spicy beef with extra chilli. De Sade." The pizza had gone a bit cold, the cheese thick and stringy, but to McCoist it was manna from heaven. A pure hit of salty, greasy, doughy comfort to settle the dread which had been chewing up her stomach since the doorstep revelation.

This was Tim Drummond, the student intern who had been working alongside Lennox, who she'd been trying to reach. He was also, it turned out, a former employee at the car wash where Davey Burnet had worked, where McCoist had shot Paulo McGuinn dead in order save Davey from being strangled. That was where the vague recognition had come from—they'd only met the once, briefly, and it had seemed entirely inconsequential, but now here he was, the dead lawyer's apprentice, and another link to the Car Wash Catastrophe that didn't want to stay buried. "I've been trying to get hold of you. Left a few messages."

"After Sandra told me Mr Lennox had been found…"—he rubbed the heel of his hand into his eye, sniffled—"…found dead, I switched my phone off."

"Why?"

He licked his greasy lips, adjusted himself on the wooden chair, eyes flicking to the doorway, to the window where everything had gone dark, summer rain spitting against the glass.

"You were scared, I know. But why were you scared? Come on, Tim, you said you wanted to talk to me. We can do it over dinner or we can do it at the station." She waved a crust dripping garlic mayo at him then chomped it.

"My boss was murdered. Of course I was scared. I'm still scared. Because it's fucking scary!" He realised he was shouting, dropped his voice low. "Maybe not to someone like you, but most people never know a person who gets murdered."

"Fair enough, but I think it's more than that." Dip, bite. "Uh, I fucking love this sauce, I could swim in it. You should have got more than one."

"Didn't know I'd be sharing."

"Look, I get it. It's not something most people come up against. It's awful, it's…"—she chewed and swallowed—"disturbing. A person is torn away, unnaturally, violently. You recoil from it, at the same time you're pulled to the void it leaves behind. Fear is the simplest aspect of the response. Understandable. But you said it yourself, you turned your phone off. You hid. Then you show up here trying to break in. Why?"

The lad didn't have much of a poker face. He was battling the arguments for and against lying so hard his eyes were watching tennis.

"Tim, I can help you. Protect you. I'm the police. Trust me."

He snorted. "I know I'm not exactly Top Cat when it comes to street smarts, but even I know not to blindly trust someone just because they're a cop. No offence."

"Well, too bad, I'm offended." McCoist laughed. He'd hit the bullseye, or 180 in her case. She did want to help though, that was true, it was just her motives that were getting all twisted up until she couldn't tell which strand of spaghetti was duty and which was self-preservation. "Look, on the day I retire I'll happily have ACAB tattooed on my knuckles, but right now I want to find out who killed Carter Lennox, and I want to make sure you don't come to harm as well."

Tim stared at a textured print of a cityscape. Nothing but a little colour to liven up the wall, inoffensive, like the rest of the flat. The whole place had been decorated as if Lennox had pointed to a picture from a catalogue: "I'll have that yin." It screamed terminal bachelor with a bit of cash and no interest in pop culture, made no dramatic use of the original mouldings or the incredible skylight above the living area. A paltry 9/10 on *Scotland's Home of the Year.*

"Sandra said you and Lennox were close."

"He was a good guy."

"Then he didn't deserve this?"

"No."

"So help me catch the person who did it."

He rubbed his face, looked tired and unwashed like a greasy teenager dragged from his scratcher before noon. "Off the record?"

McCoist turned her hands up to their surroundings, the empty pizza box between them. "Neither of us should really be in here. You're not under caution, you're not being recorded. This conversation is just between us. Call it 'intelligence gathering' if that makes you feel better."

A big yoga breath then he started: "Something was going on at the car wash involving Paulo McGuinn. You probably know that."

"I was the SIO in charge of investigating McGuinn's death."

Something in the reflex of his eyes made McCoist curse her blethering gub. Should have stayed quiet, let him get on with it. Schoolboy error. She needed to be more careful or she would lose him. Everything he said was being carefully balanced inside, she would only get a partial picture for now.

"I didn't know what it was—got the sack when things started getting weird—but my friend there, Davey, was caught up in it. He asked me for advice, which I couldn't give, cause I know fuck all, but I told him to speak to Mr Lennox."

"And did he?" *Shut the fuck up!* But she couldn't stop herself, her heart was keeping time with the rain drumming on the skylight.

"…He did."

Aw fuck, this was bad. Maybe very bad.

"But Mr Lennox couldn't help him in the end."

Not so bad?

"Then McGuinn was killed and Davey disappeared. Do you know anything about that?"

Yes, after he saw me put a bullet through McGuinn's thick skull I told him to run away and never come back. Devlin helped cover his escape, all leads going nowhere, requests bouncing. "No, do you?"

Bad move again. Tim slouched back in his chair, pulled the cuffs of his hoody over his hands as if they were cold then folded his arms. Shook his head. "We'd been trying to find him, but... Do you think he's dead too?" His voice squeaked out, making him sound younger than his years.

McCoist wanted to say no, to let him know his friend was probably OK wherever he was, to soothe the look of hurt on the lad's face. There was pain and fear there, spoilt innocence, and his sad wee mug brought out the urge to comfort in her, as if it were her own boy Cam sitting there and not a stranger. Instead she said, "I don't know." *Rotten bitch.* But she didn't want to hint she had any knowledge of what happened to Davey at the car wash and, truthfully, Tim was more likely to come round to trusting her if he felt he had no one else, if he thought he was alone. *Despicable cow.*

"He left a letter for me."

Now it was McCoist's turn to practise the straight face, try not to snap the arms off the chair.

"A kind of record of what had happened to him. Grim reading. I took it to Mr Lennox. I wanted him..."—he heaved a great sigh which turned into a chuckle—"...I wanted him to do something about all the shit that was in there. The dirt. The corruption. God, I was so fucking stupid." He covered his face with his hands, then slid them down his face, pulling the skin and his features into a contorted *Scream* mask. "Fucking idiot. And now Mr Lennox is dead."

"And you've lost the letter."

He nodded, then slumped forward onto the table. "Thought it could be here," his voice muffled by a mouthful of oak.

McCoist tried to subtly take some deep breaths of her own.

Davey Burnet, that stupid wee prick. What had he done? Had he named her? Her gaze searched over the leather armchair and the big-screen telly and the kitchen cupboards, the unused cooker. Three doors she could see off the living area—bedroom, bathroom and, just maybe, home office.

"No copies?"

"He said not to."

"Did he show it to anyone?"

"He wouldn't."

"You've read it though?"

Tim's head shot up, naked suspicion in his eyes.

Time to pull out the wrecking ball. "Tim, it's clear you think Lennox was killed for whatever was in that document, to silence him. If so, then as the only other person who knows its contents... I'm sure you can join the dots. That's why you turned off your phone, why you hid, why you risked coming here after dark."

The boy's eyes were starting to tear up. He covered his hands with his sleeves again, shivery. "Maybe just being paranoid."

"Maybe. Depends on what was in there. You mentioned corruption. What kind of corruption?"

"Political, judicial... police." His wet eyes lingered on hers. "McGuinn had people working for him everywhere."

"And did Davey name anyone specifically?" Her words came out low and breathy, dry mouth betraying her panic. The cheeseburger pizza was sitting uncomfortably high in her belly, threatening to climb back up her gullet. She could taste the gherkins again already.

They stared at each other, both attempting to read something in the bloody vessels of the eyes, the twitch of a muscle below pasty flesh, hook of a cracked lip. Nothing to see. McCoist knew there was a reason body-language experts were not allowed in court, and that reason was it's all bullshit.

"Tim, I want to help you. But to do that I need to know what you know."

He looked towards the door.

"I didn't want to bring this up again but I caught you trying to break through a police cordon into a potential crime scene." McCoist was getting desperate. "It's late, if I take you in now you'd be in the cells for the night before anything can get done."

Tears ran down his cheeks.

"Tim, look at me. Look at me." He did. "I don't want to do that. You're a good lad, trying to do the right thing, and you've got in over your head in something you've no business with in the first place."

His voice was quiet and broken with sniffles: "I just wanted to help Davey."

"You can, son. You can still help Davey and help Lennox too. Tell me about the letter. Were there any names?" She touched his arm.

"Davey had to help them with all sorts of awful shit. Cleaning up after, after murders and... There was a lorry. They were into people trafficking." He wiped his eyes with his sleeve, composed himself. "Bringing in girls to work in brothels. Not all of them made it alive. Davey wrote it all down, all the things they made him do. He didn't seem to know many names, but he wrote about a young policeman he met a couple of times, who turned out to be working with McGuinn, helping him cover things up. Thought his name was Finney."

McCoist's heart did a backflip, her stomach plunged, her blood a sea of sour pickle vinegar. Not Finney: *Findlay*. Fucking hell. It couldn't be, could it? DC Findlay, who had been her gofer for a short while before handing in his two weeks'. She thought he'd pre-empted a sacking over the WhatsApp scandal, but maybe he was actually on the run now his secret gangland boss was dead. DC Fucking Findlay. Dark horse. Bright boy in a bright suit, stylish tie. McCoist had been disappointed thinking he'd been part of the WhatsApp boys club because he'd seemed so, well, *nice*. A good sort. Was she less or more disappointed to now discover he was actually a bent polis rather than a gross twat?

"Thank you, Tim, that's great. That's something I can look into. This guy would certainly have motive."

"But how would he know about the letter? That his name's in there in the first place?"

"Good question. Anyone else?"

"...Not in the letter. But Sandra told me Mr MacGillivary was clearing out Mr Lennox's office already."

"Another reason to come looking here?"

"They'd been arguing a lot recently."

"What about?"

"Don't know."

"Do you think MacGillivary knows about the letter?"

"Mr Lennox said he didn't show it to anyone."

"MacGillivary has been his partner at the firm for a long time now."

"He said he didn't and I trust him."

"You're a very loyal friend," McCoist said. Tim gave her a sheepish smile, but it wasn't entirely a compliment. He was naive, and it was going to get him hurt. Even if he came through all of this business with the lawyer unscathed—and if McCoist could make any wish come true it would be that he did—there was heartbreak down the line for a boy like him.

Tim didn't want a police car to sit outside his flat. Who could blame him? McCoist thanked him for the slices and gave him a stern warning about breaking and entering. "Here, while we're on the subject, you wouldn't have done something even stupider than this and broken into Paulo McGuinn's house to search for your letter?"

"Fuck no!" He was rightly horrified. McCoist believed him—based on his attempts at Lennox's, he did not seem to have the technical skill necessary to get through that second lock on the door of the McGuinn fort. It did, however, raise the possibility that whoever did break into Lottie's was hunting for the letter too.

She sent Tim on his way: "Smile, son, you're on the winning team now." And God love him, he actually smiled. As if she didn't feel bad enough already.

As soon as he was out, she tore open the remaining doors in the flat. First one: bedroom. Bed made and turned down, small potted cacti on the windowsill, stacks of books and newspapers by the bedside lamp. Second: bathroom. As expected, Flash-ad clean, all-in-one soap/shampoos, grey slate. Third time lucky? Though if Lennox kept his office at work in that state, she could only imagine what his home set-up was like, maybe "lucky" wasn't the word.

She pulled open the door and her chin touched her toes. No home office.

The left half of the room was what could only be described as a glittery, feathery, carnival-coloured sex fungeon, whereas the right was entirely dedicated to the building, painting, and displaying of Warhammer figurines. A folding screen in the middle did a half-hearted job of separating the two. Which to be more ashamed of? McCoist wondered. Though she had the distinct impression Lennox was ashamed of neither. The room was, like the rest of his flat, neat as a pin and had surely been kept that way by the cleaner. If the space outside this room had suffered from a lack of personality, the space inside had an overabundance of it.

Once over the initial surprise, McCoist considered it through her business goggles. Tim was sure Lennox himself was clean. But whips and Warhammer were a serious source of kompromat. But then, if he was unmarried and unashamed...

She put the light out and closed the door over. Scenes of Crime should have at least given her a heads-up about that. It was a grim job though and they had to take their fun where they could find it. Couldn't begrudge them a wee laugh at her expense.

McCoist got her thoughts in order. If Davey's "record"—*fucking wee eejit, what the fuck did he think he was doing? Saved his fucking life and everything, should have let him get throttled by McGuinn, wouldn't be in this bloody mess at all then*—wasn't in Lennox's flat, then maybe his killer had it (unless the break-in at the McGuinns' was connected, in which case the killer likely did not have it) or it was in his office at the Saltmarket. His shithole of an office which was about to be probed by the long, gloved and lubricated arm of the law.

Not good.

...Unless it had been shredded already.

14

"He looks like shite. Magine bein that wealthy an still lookin like that." Bell was watching the morning news with a plate of Pop-Tarts and a fag rolled up ready for after—she liked to take her coffee in the garden with a smoke. She was more a do-as-I-say-not-as-I-do kind of healthcare provider. An MP was on the telly delivering more budget cuts to the nation. Time to tighten the ol' belt again, punch in some new notches, forgo our small luxuries. You can switch your heating off, I'll switch off my heated pool. Every penny...

"Auld money, isnit?" Chuck said. "His maw an da are probly cousins."

"Aye, but that's wit am sayin, ye could afford tae get yer pus sorted. Easy."

"Then people widnae know ye were auld money, but."

"Cunt's so posh he can barely speak."

"There's nae operation wit can fix that. It's a sad hing, man, a cryin shame."

"A cannae even tell if yer jokin, by the way."

"Am gonnae donate some money tae the wee fella."

Bell honked with laughter. "Tories in Need."

"A wis gonnae say Rid Nose Day based oan yer boyfriend there."

"He'd be fuckin lucky."

"A wouldnae mind if ye moved intae his second mansion as lang as ye take me wae ye."

"We don't need a mansion. Wuv goat this place, an that's enough fir me." The sweetness was put on, almost as much added sugar as the Pop-Tarts she loved, but beneath it Bell was being genuine. She loved the home they shared together, she was happy here. It wasn't much but it was a step up from the council terraces they'd each grown up in. And it was theirs—a dream they never thought would be realised. Chuck prayed she would never find out how much of it was leveraged against his debts. They could be doing with a room in that horsey old man's estate in the near future if Chuck didn't get his shit together.

The headlines changed to sports, multicoloured jerseys running about the screen with the logos of betting shops and gambling apps emblazoned across the fronts. Just the sight of them made the strings that worked Chuck tug hard. Bell went for the remote. Before it switched, he saw the score he was waiting on and his heart punched his chest in celebration. The Great Accumulator had made it another round. It was on, it was fucking on. He licked his lips, was aware of the stupid, involuntary smile spreading across his face and carefully rearranged it. It gave him a feeling like coming up on eccies.

"Here, are there any mare ae those?"

Bell took a big bite of her Pop-Tart and spoke through a mouthful of crumbs: "Aye, but ye cannae huv them. A bought them fir me."

"Fucksake. Al remind ye ae that when they're choppin yer feet aff wae the diabeatiss."

She smiled and took another big bite. The doorbell rang. "Away an get that."

"Guess al huv tae." Probably a parcel for Bell.

Chuck opened the door to find a couple on the step—blandly suited man and woman, too old to be Jehovah's Witnesses doing field service. Polis then. Everything in his body tightened up a little except his guts, which had received a different message from the stress chemicals in his brain and sagged treacherously loose and lazy instead. Their timely appearance at the lawyers' just after he'd handed that weird letter with the bullet over to Jamieson had been gnawing at him all night, now here they were at his door. The woman looked to be in her forties, the man a bit older, though he'd maybe just had a paper round in Castlemilk. Both gave off the aura of seniority, confident to the point of arrogance, unbothered by catching someone unawares in their jammies and dressing gown and the unfair advantage that allowed them.

"Mr Gardner?" the woman spoke.

"Aye."

"I'm DCI McCoist, this is DS Slater." They held out their cards but he didn't have his contacts in or his glasses on so the letters were too small and blurry to read. "Sorry for knocking on your door but we did try your business address first."

"Am no startin till ten the day."

"Is that why you didn't pick up our calls either?"

"A keep a strict work/life balance."

"That's very sensible," the man, Slater, chimed in, sarcasm assumed.

"Well, I'm sorry for the intrusion into the 'life' part of your day but since we're here now do you mind if we ask a few questions?" There was something severe about the woman, McCoist—he'd almost said something about the name but thought better of it.

"Eh, a guess." He wiped a sweaty palm against the scraggly fabric of his dressing gown. Bell was looking at him from the living room, fag in mouth, coffee in hand. "*Who is it?*" she mouthed, forehead creasing.

He waved her away to the garden for her morning ritual—"*Willnae be lang*"—and let the sodjers into the hall. "A need tae be gettin ready tae head oot soon, yel huv tae firgee us fir no puttin the kettle oan."

"That's all right, Mr Gardner."

"Call me Chuck."

"Isn't your name Stuart? Stuart Gardner?" The man, who looked so much like a polis he probably had a uniform on under his shirt and tie, looked at him with an accusing stare.

"Aye, it is, but evrybdy caws me Chuck. Cause ae the hair an glesses." They looked at his shorn dome and his face completely unadorned by spectacles. Their eyebrows huddled together, perplexed, and they snatched a glance between them. "Chuckie, fae the programme *Rugrats*, ye mind it? It's fae back in school. A used tae huv..."—he ran a hand over his baldy heed—"ginger curls an..."—he made circles with his thumbs and forefingers around his eyes—"big glesses. Chuckie. Chuck. Witever, just forget it." He licked dry lips, told himself to stop rambling.

The cops surveyed him in silence for a beat before the woman started up again. "Right... Chuck. What can you tell me about a job you were hired to do at a law firm called Lennox & MacGillivary yesterday?"

"Eh, no much really. Pretty standard. Hud a call fae a wummin there, the receptionist—"

"Do you remember her name?"

"Sandra."

"Go on."

"They were needin wan ae their offices cleared oot, an cause ae the nature ae the business they needed it done by someone like me. Confidential material an that."

"Have you ever done work for them before?"

"Naw."

"When did you get the call?"

"Day afore last it must ae bin."

"The day before yesterday? The day before you went there to do the job?"

"Aye."

"Bit short notice?"

"They wantet it done as soon as, an were offerin good money. A moved a couple ae hings aboot. Hings a should be settin aboot doin the day, actually."

"Hint taken," the man murmured.

"We'll be out of your hair soon."

"Good wan."

"Sorry?"

"Hair." He patted his head again and smiled but it was clear from the set of the woman's face the joke had been unintended and, even when pointed out, was not funny. He felt his cheeks redden, the sweat start to run in the small of his back. *Better chat if they were Jehovah's Witnesses.*

"What time did you arrive?"

"Ten."

"And who did you speak to on arrival?"

"Sandra again, at the desk."

"You didn't speak to Mr MacGillivary?"

He remembered their one-sided chat out the back of the building, MacGillivary sucking on his fag, adrift in his thoughts. "He said hello but no really."

"Who supervised you while you cleared out the office?"

They could probably see his Adam's apple bob up and down in his throat he swallowed that hard. He hid his dripping hands behind his back. He didn't want to get anyone into trouble, especially not a client. He wasn't a grass, and he lived in a greenhouse in that respect, the wee rickety kind that could be completely levelled by a wean's stray football. "Sandra wis watchin."

"The whole time?"

"Aye, well, a hink so. A mean, a wis in an oot the back carryin stacks ae paperwork an aw that, so a wisnae really payin attention tae her or anythin, but she mustae bin aroon, aye."

"You seem unsure."

"Sorry, a wis hard at it. That office wis a fuckin state. Scuse the language. It's the client's responsibility tae keep an eye, ask them, a wis busy gettin stuck in. Graftin.'

"Were you told the circumstances of the job?"

"How dye mean?"

"The reason they were clearing out the office."

"Naw, an a didnae ask. A just dae as am telt an get oan wae it." Chuck felt himself get off the back foot. This was solid ground for him. Get the word "confidential" into the conversation as many times as he could.

"What happens to the stuff you shred with your van?"

"It gets stuffed intae bales an then goes tae recyclin."

"And the materials you shredded at Lennox & MacGillivary, where are they now?"

"Why dye want tae know?"

"Are they still in the van or your warehouse?"

"Listen, evrythin that goes intae the shredder an comes oot ae it in bits is *confidential*. You check wae the law but am tellin ye yel need the right permissions if yer wantin tae get a swatch at any ae it."

"I think that can be managed." There was a deliberate menace to the woman's voice. She made Chuck feel like a child about to get a skelped arse. "We'll be in touch soon."

He closed the door on them, took a moment to calm down, then turned around to face the second inquisition:

"Wit wis that aboot?" Talk about a skelped arse, the face on Bell could've turned honey sour, never mind milk.

"Polis." Lying as little as possible was the best way forward. "Aboot a work hing. A client a shredded some paperwork fir yesterday is in trouble oer somethin."

"They hink they've hud ye get rid ae, wit, *evidence?*"

"A dunno really."

"Yer no in trouble, are ye? Stu, please fuckin tell me yer no in trouble."

The pent-up anxiety of the past couple of days had fermented into anger and exploded out of him. "Aw, course yed fuckin hink it wid be me in trouble! Always just waitin fir me tae fuck up again aren't ye?!"

"Stu! Wit the fuck?"

"Wid that make ye happy, aye? So ye can go aff an tell yer maw how she wis right aboot me!"

"Fuck. Aff." Bell stormed into the kitchen and slammed her empty mug down by the sink.

Chuck stood with his back to the door, a bright-red bellend.

15

"He was sweaty and weird, wasn't he?"

"Let's get Suffia or Sk8er Boi to see what they can dig up on him." Slater pulled away from the kerb outside Gardner's fairly pleasant suburban semi-detached with a grimy-but-competent-looking Renault Avérage in the driveway.

"Think there'll be something to find?"

"Aye, I can smell it on him. Nose like a bloodhound, me."

"Speaking of hounds, do you mind if we take a detour?"

They slotted into a dual carriageway through fields into a roundabout onto another dual carriageway through fields and past a furniture shop and a garden centre then more fields and a funeral director's, one suburb into another, housing estate against housing estate, an unbroken concrete frill ten miles thick which circled the city, one hooped New Town to the next, the whole pattern conceived and birthed most of a century ago by the factory-line automobile, the factory-line job, the factory-line family.

"Need to get myself a look at that room of Lennox's," Slater said. McCoist had shared her own findings along with the SOC report on Lennox's west-end penthouse—leaving out her meeting with Tim. She had to keep that to herself, maybe share it with Superintendent Devlin if she felt she really had to. Her gut told her to hold on to it as long as possible, though her gut had been wrong before.

"Are you interested in the sex room or the figurines?"

"The trajectory of a man's life tends to go from the figurines to the sex room then back to the figurines. I want to know how he had time for both."

"And therein lies the secret to a long and happy life?" McCoist smiled.

"If you don't get strangled to death. You think the kink theory holds water?"

The discovery at the flat had led to the idea of death by misadventure being floated: a sex game involving strangulation going too far, the partner panicking and dumping the body.

"Nah. The stolen van—that doesn't seem spur of the moment. That's planned. Plus there's no evidence of a body being moved through the flat, no sign he was even killed there. No way some random hook-up who'd accidentally choked his partner to death could manage that without leaving traces while completely freaking out. He'd have had four floors of tenement stairwell to contend with as well. The effort, the noise. No chance. It's bollocks, and make sure everybody knows it." McCoist was keen to stamp the idea out at its larval stage—a gay man being accidentally killed by his lover was a convenient solution which could easily cause Operation Troy to slip down the priority and funding ladders. (She'd let Travis name the op—he wasn't into Greek mythology; it was a reference to Nicholas Cage's character in *Face/Off*. McCoist hoped people would just assume it was the Greek thing.)

"Fair enough."

There was also Tim's information about Davey's secret, incriminating letter, which bolstered her confidence that the shagcident scenario was a no-go, not that she could let anyone know about that. While Slater drove, McCoist started drafting the application she would send to the fiscal, requesting a warrant to search and seize any evidence from Gardner's van and warehouse. She tried and failed to envisage how she could position herself to be the first to read the letter if it did indeed appear. (And, of course, get rid of it if it was incriminating.)

McCoist directed Slater to her front door. "Come in for a quick cuppa."

"And meet the man himself?"

"In all his disgusting glory."

Bruce had been ill since eating that turd the other night. McCoist wanted to check in on him, clean up any mess he might have made while she was out before the dog walker turned up.

The silly mutt's reaction was unusually subdued, skulking over to the door with his head low, looking for pets, feeling sorry for himself.

"Aw my poor boy." Slater knelt down and Bruce sniffed at him, licked him, let himself be clapped, his tail giving a half-hearted wag. "He's a handsome fella, isn't he?"

"He was a rescue." A half-truth. McCoist had pinched him, sorry, *liberated* him, from a puppy mill she'd been sent to shut down. So he was a rescue, technically, she just didn't go through Dogs Trust. "Looks like you've got a fan."

"He probably smells Maisie on me. No matter how many times you wash your clothes you can never get the dug hairs out."

She refilled his water bowl; food hadn't been touched. "We should get that walk sorted when he's feeling better." She almost didn't say it, and when it came out she felt her heart flutter. Her conversation with Mark popped back into her head. *Dinner with a woman.*

"Aye, that would be great! Maisie will love it."

16

Jamieson did her the courtesy of leaving his muscle man outside the office door, where he waited like the statue of a Greek god. Lottie wouldn't have minded chipping a piece off him. It had been a while. She hadn't shared a bed with Paulo for years and taking a lover would have meant giving someone a death sentence. Not any more though, and for just a moment the idea of whispering something filthy into the young man's ear rushed through her like a flash fire then petered out. Not a smart thing to do.

"A hadnae thoat ad hear fae ye so soon, Mr Jamieson."

"Billy, please." By contrast, the gaffer was an ugly man by almost any measure. He wore it well though, rotting away with dignity. "An am sorry tae say, this isnae directly aboot wit happened tae Paulo."

"Ye said oan the phone it wis urgent. A thoat yed maybe foont the car-wash lads." Her tone was irritable. She spent too much time chiding her teenage daughters, it had become her natural register.

Jamieson didn't notice, or was pretending not to. His craggy face gave nothing away—he'd turned what would have been considered a weakness into an advantage. "That's aw in hawnd, don't ye worry aboot that, but this… Ye might want tae prepare yersel fir this." He leant forward, elbows on his desk.

Lottie's heart quickened, she felt tingly, her legs crossed themselves, her hands gripped the rests and pushed her back into the chair.

"Ross Brownlee's bin stealin fae ye."

"Wit?!" If the chair had been pulled out from under her right then, she wouldn't have fallen over, she'd have floated there like a cartoon character, frozen in her seated position, defying gravity by the sheer muscle-tensing shock of what had been said.

"Bin goin oan fir years."

"Ross?"

"Aye. Bin lookin eftir the faimly fortune a long time noo, an helpin himsel tae a fair whack alang the way by the looks ae it."

"Cannae be. How? Ye must be wrang."

"Am sorry, Charlotte. Am no wrang." He hefted some documents from a drawer under his desk and slid them across the table. There were spreadsheets and numbers and Latin words and code, a Liquorice Allsorts of mumbo-jumbo data. Stuff beyond Lottie's comprehension. Stuff she would usually have Ross look at. "A hud wan ae ma guys check him oot an—"

"How? A thoat ye were tryin tae find oot who killt Paulo. Ross has bin wae us—"

"Since the beginnin. A know. But a huv tae look at evrywan. That's how this works. Am sorry fir the bad news."

Ross… How? He'd been a rock since Paulo died. And a good friend to the family for long before. She remembered him opening savings accounts for the kids for her when they were just little. "Never too early to start, hen." He was one of a small number of people Paulo would actually listen to, and even fewer who he respected. When Ross was diagnosed with early-onset arthritis, Paulo was so upset he made a generous donation to Arthritis Action. Paulo McGuinn, giving to fucking charity! It couldn't be.

Lottie sat there with her eyes fixed on the desk. The big side of beef came in with cups of tea and went back out. Lottie didn't even notice him.

"A hink the best way tae handle this is if a huv a quiet word wae him masel."

She found her head bobbing in agreement. If there was anyone she could trust since Paulo's death, it was Ross. He'd stuck around. He was loyal. Everyone else had fucked off to work for Ruaridh Callaghan or whoever else, but not him. He cared about her and her family. Didn't he? Or did he just care about the money all along? She remembered how against the idea of contacting Jamieson he was.

"We can see aboot gettin some money back, but maybe best tae just cut the losses and cut him oot fae noo oan, rather than cause a stink aboot it. Aye?"

"Aye," she croaked.

"A can recommend some money men fir ye, an some solicitors an aw. Good guys. Guys a can guarantee will be straight wae ye, cause if they're no they answer tae me."

"Uh huh."

"Am sorry aboot this again. But al be in touch wae some good news soon, am sure ae it. Pullin oot aw the stoaps fir ye."

"Aye... thanks."

The T-bone opened the door for her, but his sculpted body and film-star face held no allure for her now. Dead meat on the rack. When she stood, the tingling she'd felt turned to dizziness. The last time she saw Ross he was trying to talk her into selling the house. For her safety, for financial security, for the long future ahead. "*I'm only thinking of you and the girls.*" Or was he only thinking of the fat cut he could slice from the sale?

She stumbled in the waiting room and a man caught her arm.

"Ye awright?" Recognition in his eyes, then in hers.

"Simply Shred."

17

Touching a gangster's wife was something you'd usually want to think twice about, but she looked like she was about to collapse so Chuck grabbed her by the arm. "Ye awright?"

"Simply Shred."

"If You Don't Know Me by Now..." he grinned. "Ma name's Chuck. Well, it's no, it's actually Stuart but—"

"Cheers. Sorry aboot that. Am fine, thanks." She took her arm back, straightened out her skirt although it didn't need it.

"Sure?"

"Nothin a bit ae Night Nurse cannae sort oot." Her smile was weak and fleeting. Chuck wondered what she'd discussed in that room with Jamieson which had rattled her composure so. Or maybe it was just the effect the man had on everyone—Chuck certainly always felt a bit wobbly whenever he had to speak to him.

"Look eftir yersel," he called to her back as she left, then realised how odd it was to be attempting to comfort a woman like that. Obscenely wealthy, married—formerly married—to one of the most dangerous men in the city and probably beyond, an elite person for whom doors would open and heads would bow. A star of sorts. Michelle Obama of the Glesga underworld. *Look eftir yersel.* He snickered at his silly, redundant offer. What an eejit.

"Gardner." Marble called him to the door and closed it over behind them, then helped Chuck down into the chair with a hand on his shoulder, where he loomed.

"Back again awready. Busy boay." Chuck detected disappointment in the bluntly carved hollows of the man's eyes but it could have been his imagination. "Another loss? How much this time?"

What was left of Chuck's pride was offended by the insinuation—the part of him which still wanted to deny he had a problem. The rest of him took it on the chin because he'd earned it. "It's no that. The polis were at ma door this mornin."

Jamieson gave no visible reaction, but the temperature in the room dropped so low steam was pluming from his breath. Marble had turned into a yeti. "Wit did they want wae ye?"

"They were askin aboot that joab the other day. The wan a foont that, ye know, *hing* at. The envelope wae the..." He made a finger gun, gave the trigger a couple of squeezes.

"An wit did ye tell them?"

"Nothin. Just ad bin phoned tae clear oot the office. They were wantin tae know wit happens tae the stuff a stick in the back ae the van, a says they'd need a warrant if they want tae go near it."

"Anythin else?"

"Naw, but a reckon they'll be back. The polis wummin wis as hard as the fuckin Terminator. Fuckin laser eyebaws. McCoist, her name wis."

"McCoist?" Marble butted in. "Ye hink she's relatet tae—"

"Fuck up, baith ae yeez. Chuck, am gonnae gee ye some advice, son."

"Tired ae wankin, tired ae life?" Chuck blurted out and immediately regretted—he was trembling with nervous energy.

Something happened to Jamieson's usually impassive face. The light inside the tumshie lantern was there again, but this time it was flickering and spitting a dangerous red from his eyes and nose and his stubby, misaligned teeth, probing through the cracks and wrinkles of his crumbling skin. "In fact, it's less advice, mare ae an order. The kind ae order that needs tae be follied, cause if it isnae follied, the cunt who didnae folly it ends up as a fish-tank ornament at the bottom ae the Clyde. Are ye follyin me?"

Chuck felt Marble's hand on the back of his head, making him nod.

"If the polis ask ye a question ye say, 'Nae comment.' Even if they ask ye yer ain name ye reply, 'Nae comment.' If they say 'Agayboaysayswit', ye say…"

"Wit?"

Marble sniggered; Jamieson's face cooled—definitely disappointment in there this time. "Ye say, 'Nae comment.'"

"Nae comment, aye, goat it."

"If they drag ye doon the station, ye only open yer mooth tae ask fir a lawyer. Then ye call me. Right?"

"Right, Mr Jamieson."

"Good, sortet. Am glad yer here actually, Chuckie, it's geed me an idea. There's somethin a want ye tae help me wae the night."

"Aye, nae problem." Chuck's voice was sickeningly subservient, a bully victim asking to be hit again. *Av goat mare money in ma other poackit if ye want it.* But he was overwhelmed by the desperation to claw his way back into Jamieson's good books. The response was involuntary, a lizard-brain reaction. It was fear. "Wit dye need?"

"Meet me at yer warehouse later—al let ye know the time but it'll be dark oot. Bring yer van."

18

Slater warbled the chorus from "The Waiting", doing his best Tom Petty, which was fucking woeful. Karaoke bars have been emptied by better performances. McCoist smiled anyway. "A coffee might make it go easier."

"On it, gaffer!" Travis sprung from his seat.

"D'you remember how the boss takes it, Gaz?" Slater chirped.

"Toxic?"

"Attaboay. Downright offensive to the Platonic ideal of coffee. I'll have a normal one while you're at it."

"Suffy?"

"Normal please, Gaz."

Travis saluted her and skipped out the room.

They had reason to be a in a good mood: the van had been found. "Looks like someone took it off-roading," McCoist's new favourite SOCO Amy Caruso had told her over the phone. It had been left in woodland off a farm down in the borders. A dog walker stumbled across it. (Praise and hallelujah to the weather-hardened dog walkers of the world! Sniffer-outers of dead bodies and dumped evidence. They'd put more criminals behind bars than Taggart and Rebus combined.) Caruso would soon be going over every square inch of the van looking for any signs of spit, blood, semen, hair, urine, snot, greasy prints, skin cells and sweat—all the good stuff. If their guy already had a file on the PNC—and there was a good chance he did as people don't often go from zero to murder—they'd have him in the bag. A bag for life at that.

Plus the juicy info Khan had unearthed about their new paper-shredding chum, Stuart "Chuck" Gardner. Slater had been right: Gardner had a record. Five years back he was caught with his hand in the till at a DIY shop he managed. He'd skimmed a fairly serious amount of cash over the course of twelve months and cooked the books to try to hide it. The owner got wise and shopped him. He pleaded guilty—he'd been trying to cover gambling debts. A promise to go to addiction therapy and the fact it was a first offence had kept him from jail.

McCoist had gleefully pasted this info into her application for the warrant to search his business and home addresses and sent it off with all the joy of a wean throwing a paper aeroplane. She also applied to have MacGillivary's office given the Kim and Aggie treatment. He was a dodgy bastard too, and getting Gardner in to immediately shred his way through Lennox's office was a desperate move—3 a.m. Best Kebab desperate.

Now all she had to do was wait for the phone to ring.

"Boss." Gaz gave her a mug of steaming shite. She swallowed a mouthful of liquid death and felt it burn all the way to her toes. A moment of sheer bliss.

Then the phone rang.

"DCI McCoist?" A man's voice on the phone. Unfamiliar. West of Scotland accent but "proper" spoken—McCoist heard a wealthy suburban enclave, private school, fencing lessons, a love of horses and fine wine and killing small animals, Daddy's name on a university building and a first-class degree in law from Oxbridge.

"Speaking."

"This is Sheriff Cresswell."

The team's eyes were on her, and she returned their stares with raised brows and mouthed the word *sheriff* at them. They crowded closer, coffees forgotten, Khan grinning with a thumbnail stuck between her teeth, Gaz clenching his fists, ready to punch the air in celebration. A call from a sheriff was a sure sign the warrants were approved. They could push forward, another solid avenue for the investigation to go down.

"Good afternoon, sir."

"I'm calling about two search-warrant applications which were put in front of me with your signature on them."

"Yes?"

"I have to deny them, DCI McCoist. Both of them."

McCoist must have looked aghast because the rest of the team shared confused looks with each other, deflating, worried. "Sorry, sir?"

"I'm denying your applications because they do not meet the evidential threshold for me to grant them."

"But the procurator fiscal—"

"I'll be speaking to them too. Good day."

"But—" The line cut.

McCoist slumped in her chair, dazed. "Why would he call just to deny them?"

"Who was it?" Slater asked.

"Cresswell—you know him?"

"The name's maybe familiar. Must be a jobsworth tosser."

There was a post-Scotland-match mood in the room. Defeat snatched from the jaws of victory. "At least we've still got the van," Travis tried, a dedicated soldier of the Tartan Army.

"There's sure to be something there." Khan picked it up, adding a half-hearted smile.

They went back to their desks, working in silence. After a while, Slater tapped at the door of McCoist's office, slid his head in. "Sorry." He kept his voice down, tiptoeing on the thick atmosphere like Jesus Christ afraid of getting his sandals wet.

"Not your fault. I'll email the fiscal, see if they know what the fuck happened."

"Do that. But Suffy and Gaz are right. The van's a good win, we'll get something off the back of it for sure."

"Aye."

"Listen, would you like to grab a pint after this? Talk about it? Send the kids to bed early." He pointed his thumb at the DCs studiously adhered to their computer screens.

A tingle of nerves rippled through her abdomen. *Get a grip, wummin.* It was just shop talk at a pub with a colleague after hours. Commonplace even these days when the hard-drinking, lunchtime-pint detective had become all but extinct. "Aye, go on then."

19

If the man in the passenger seat was Marble then the man driving was Roughcast. They were parked off Victoria Road in a bland family sedan between rows of sandstone tenements on the corner of poverty and gentrification, eyes on the gastro pub down the street. A lick of paint, a refit and, most importantly, a rise in the cost of a pint had displaced most of the regulars. The man they were waiting for clung on though. Like the bar, he was a rags-to-riches story himself.

"They huv a decent wine list in there, actually. An they're doin these, like, Korean bao buns which are class," Marble was saying. "But there's a load ae nice wee places roon here noo, bigtime competition."

"That so?" Roughcast was looking at him with a *Weans these days* expression.

"Fuck aye. There's a wee Jamaican place just yards doon the road fae here that dae a goat curry wit has, like, thee *perfect* mooth-taste ever createt."

"Mooth-taste?"

"Aye. Hits every spoat oan yer tongue. It's salty, sour, sweet, bitter, rich an creamy an full ae oo-mammy."

"Oo-mammy?"

"An orgasm fir yer mooth, am tellin ye."

"A don't hink goats an orgasms should mix," the older man sneered.

"Very funny. Ye should try it. Widen yer horizons."

"Widen ma horizons? Dinnae talk pish."

"Suit yersel. You're the wan missin oot, but. Livin oan tatties an Bovril or witever."

They both laughed, easy in each other's company. Roughcast looked at his Padawan with an appraising eye. "Can a ask somethin, son?"

"Aye, shoot."

"Aboot the food an wine, yer nice nails an trimmed goatee an aw that?..."

"Wit aboot it?"

He tried to elaborate: "Ye know, aw that goin tae the gym an the sauna an clathes shoappin..."

"Am no follyin."

He huffed a deep breath. "Are ye... a *leaded roof*?"

"Wit?"

"Are ye a leaded roof? Ye know, a wonky toof."

"Sorry?"

"An alky-free beer, a word-in-yer-ear. A two-man tent..."

"Fuck ye oan aboot?"

"Ye know. A *two-man tent*. Aff wummin fir Lent. It's no a problem, am just askin."

"Am still no follyin ye. Yer zoomin right oer ma heed. Am no a Cathlic if that's—"

"Naw. A mean, are ye a *Joe Strummer*?"

"Never bin intae punk. Safety pins an Swasies isnae ma style."

"A Christopher Plummer. A Wemyss Bay, Theresa May."

"Are ye askin me if am a Tory? Cause av leathered cunts fir less."

"Fuck naw, ad never—"

"Just cause yev treatet yersel tae a nice fuckin suit disnae mean yer wan ae them dirty—"

"Fir fucksake, *are ye gay*?! A bummer! Bent! Queer! A poof!"

Marble sat back in his seat, mouth open. Roughcast realised he was shouting and scouted the windows and mirrors in case he'd drawn anyone's attention. Marble started to laugh. "How the fuck wis a sposed tae get that, ye rocket?"

"A didnae want tae say anythin offensive. Like a said, it's no a problem, a wis just askin."

"Well, it's no yer business but am bi, actually."

"So wit's that, yer no fussy?"

"It's no like, 'Well av no pullt a burd the night so al settle fir a guy,' it's… A find some lassies tidy, an a find some blokes tidy an aw. Understawn?"

"Aye… Sounds awright."

They sat in silence for a minute, Roughcast tempted to turn the radio up.

"Ye hink goin tae the gym's gay?" Marble had a smirk on his face.

"Well, no like a boxin gym or somethin, but the kind fir blokes in Lycra, ye know—hawd oan, here he is."

Their guy came out the door, alone. He took some time getting a packet of cigarettes and a Zippo the size of a hip flask from the inside pockets of his suit jacket, then had some trouble lighting up. A few too many, maybe.

They let him head round the corner, counted to twenty before starting the engine and creeping after him. The road was quiet, nobody else but their mark, and dark between the street lights. They passed him by and stopped at the kerb. Marble hopped out and opened the rear passenger-side door.

"Gee ye a lift hame, pal?"

The guy stopped. Read Marble's face, his suit, the hard body it struggled to contain. He took a deep draw on his fag, his hand hooked around it in a claw-like grip. He was middle-aged but there was something fragile in the way he held himself which gave the impression of being elderly. He had a wise face to go with it. "I'm not going far, thanks."

"It's nae problem. Dark oot noo. Eftir oors. Who knows wit folk are aboot." Marble stepped towards him.

"Who indeed. But if it's all the same to you, son, I'll walk."

"Well, it's no aw the same tae me. Get in the car."

"You one of Callaghan's boys? If he wants to talk to me he can just call, no need for the theatrics, you lads wasting your time sitting about with your thumbs up your arses while I have a pint."

"Get in the car."

"Can I finish my fag first, son?" He put it to his lips.

"Last time al ask. Get——"

Marble screamed—the cigarette tossed into his face, catching him square on the beak. "Fuck!" He batted at his burning face. His eyes streamed. By the time he cleared his eyes the mark had turned, making a run for it, but the drink was causing him to make only staggering, winding progress.

The engine of the sedan revved, then the car bounced backwards, released from the handbrake. The still-open door slammed into the mark's back and he hit the pavement with the sound of a chisel hitting brick.

Marble ran over. There was blood on the slabs. "Fucksake, man!"

"He's no fuckin deed is he?" Roughcast hissed, getting out the car to check his handiwork. The guy started to gurn and tried to roll over onto his back. "Ooft, thank fuck. Get him in."

He was skinny but non-cooperative, which made it hard even for Marble with all his sculpted muscle to lift him into the back seat without bruising both of them off the car's chassis.

Marble jumped into the motor and Roughcast tore away. The man in the back started to cry.

20

The Fishery was, of course, known to its regulars as the Pishery. And, fair play, the place was bogging. It was down the Broomielaw in the perpetual gloom cast by the shadow of the King George V Bridge over the Clyde. Sawdust on the floor would have improved its style, smell and ambience. The choice on tap was McEwan's 60/-, 70/-, or 80/-. Bottles were for whisky. There was no telly and no music. Entertainment was a dartboard on the wall and a line taped to bare wooden deck, for serious players only. The drinking done here was serious too. Not a place for a cheeky pint before heading out or heading home. Even the gamblers stumbling through from the Riverboat Casino next door after a heavy loss found it too depressing and turned around before sitting down. Not a place for a celebration or a quiet catch up. Not a place for two off-duty polis.

"I once went into a house where the old boy who lived there had been dead for two weeks and it smelt better than here," McCoist murmured. "He looked in better nick than half the punters and all."

Slater smiled. "Get a table and I'll get the drinks in."

McCoist was the only woman there and was drawing some looks—angry rather than sleazy. The denizens of the Fishery, who bloomed like mushrooms out of the mouldy woodwork, could sense an interloper. A tourist invading their misery. McCoist felt her pulse quicken, but stared back until they looked away. They were all fucked, no fight in them, and she relaxed a little. Trouble was unlikely at the moment, but she wouldn't want to stay too late.

The modern problem of who could use what toilet had been solved here already: a stick figure wearing a skirt had been crudely drawn in marker pen under the much more official gents' sign. "They refused to let women in until the mid-nineties when they were forced to," Slater explained, putting a couple of greasy-looking pints of heavy down on the scarred table. "Made the toilets unisex to avoid doing any work to the place."

"How... progressive?"

"Could be. Honestly though, I'd pop next door to the casino if you need."

"Is this your regular, Si?" She smiled outwardly but wondered why Slater had brought her to such a hole. She was old enough that she didn't need to pretend to be cool any more and would have asked, but then wouldn't that make it seem like it was a date? Like she was expecting to be wined and dined or something? And it wasn't a date. It was a pint after work. Discuss the case, kick some ideas around outside the constrictions of the office, the distracting buzz of the station. She took a mouthful of dark beer. At least the lines were clean if nothing else was.

"Thought it be best to give the pigpen a miss—drug squad are in celebrating their big bust, having a lively one according to the report from Sk8er Boi. Fair play to them but if they can actually tie it to Ruaridh Callaghan, I'll eat my bunnet." He supped his own pint and wiped a foam moustache off his upper lip. "I come here now and again though."

"Why?"

"You'll see in a few minutes."

"That sounds ominous."

Slater chuckled. "It's a converted warehouse, used to be a fish market. The fish came from the firth of the Clyde. You can still see some of the guttering in the floor for the, eh, run-off."

"Probably still useful," McCoist replied, looking around at the grey, sickly specimens nursing half-and-halfs. Easy to imagine pish running down their trouser legs unnoticed, or a casual whitey onto the floor between mouthfuls.

"Did you get a reply from the fiscal?" Slater asked, getting to business.

"They're as stumped as I am, but what the sheriff says goes, so we need to find something more implicating, I guess." She sighed and sipped, as ground down as the other patrons of the Fishery. "I thought the idea behind this was to cheer us up a bit?"

"Oh no, cheering up isn't what I do, it's wallowing I go in for."

"My mistake, it should have been obvious as soon as I stepped into this time warp."

"Joking aside, Alison, I think we'll get something on the van. That's the big one, that should be our focus. While we wait for the DNA match, we can check the CCTV, ANPR, see if we can get a better look at our man in the van."

"You're pretty confident about the DNA?"

"My confidence about the DNA is at Muhammad Ali levels." He made his hand into a gauge and held it above his head, as high as his arm could stretch.

McCoist smiled, a genuine one. He had cheered her up after all. Also, she reminded herself, she didn't have to put all her eggs in the DNA basket. There was another lead: ex-DC Findlay, who Tim had said was named as a bent polis in Davey Burnet's love letter. Her smile shrank—she would have to follow that path alone. She couldn't tell the team, couldn't tell Slater. In fact, investigating in that direction would probably necessitate lying to them. If she needed support, the only person she could turn to was Devlin and the thought of relying on him further was as unappealing as his ball-scratching habit.

"Here we go." The bartender put two pies down in front of them. Golden brown, hot-water-crust pastry, crimped edges slightly caught by the heat of the oven, steam that smelt of succulent, roasted meat curling from the holes cut in the tops.

McCoist's stomach rumbled. "I hope it's not Clyde fish in there."

"Shredded ham hock and leek with apples," Slater said. "Give it a go."

McCoist took a bite of the best pie she'd ever tasted. "How?" she said through a mouthful, pastry spraying, her fork pointing to the dinge and damp and despair all around. (Christ, she didn't want to even begin to picture what the kitchen must look like. The pie was too good not to eat.)

"A miracle, I think. This is what we came here for."

They got halfway through the pies before they spoke again. Slater told her a bit of his background. From Airdrie originally but worked all over the country. A stint in Fife, then up in the north-east, then back home to North Lanarkshire for a long time before coming to London Road after being promoted to DS a few years back. "I've been shimmying up the bamboo scaffold rather than climbing the career ladder, I guess."

McCoist searched the comment for some kind of barb, all too used to the whispers and snipes about her own career progression, but it sounded innocent. "How come?"

"I went part-time for a while, which didn't help. My maw was unwell." Slater gave a painful, pastry-flaked half-smile that said she didn't get better. "It was just me and her growing up, so I needed to help look after her. It was, eh, a slow deterioration and…"

"I'm sorry, Si."

"After she died, it took a while to get back into gear, you know? I was…" He wiped his mouth with a napkin instead of finishing the sentence. "Still, I'm here now. Detective Sergeant, finally."

"'What's for you won't go by you,' in the words of my own mother." Like the bullet in McGuinn's noggin that gave McCoist her own promotion. "And I'm glad you're on the team."

They cheersed.

Chat was firmly in the personal end now. Slater was divorced, lived with his dog. McCoist had her dog and her ex too, plus her twin teenage kids, Cam and Tess, who she saw on the weekends. She grumbled to him about Tess and TRNSMT festival coming up. And how they were off to their gran's caravan in Tyndrum soon after that.

"How many times will I actually see them in a year?" she said, the words spilling out her mouth before she could stop them.

Slater gave his awkward sympathies; McCoist decided not to have any more alcohol. They both gushed about how good the pie was, the delicious, soft, tender, torn meat.

21

"They're ootside," Jamieson said.

Chuck pressed the button to raise the shutter, headlights blinding like a fast-forward sunrise as it clattered upwards. The car crawled in, parked in what little space was left in the warehouse between Chuck's shredding van and the waste baler. Jamieson had been dropped off by a driver half an hour before and spent most of the time checking his watch while Chuck twitched uncomfortably, offering cups of tea or coffee while Jamieson offered no reason for what he needed doing here in the middle of the night in his warehouse.

The headlights switched off; Marble and Roughcast got out of the car, bickering.

"So punchin bags an weights are fine but treadmills are gay?"

"Aye. Treadmills, rowin machines, fuckin wit-dye-caw-them—moonwalkers?"

"Elliptical machines."

"Aye. They're gay."

"Al agree wae ye oan that wan, actually. But are ye really tryin tae tell me the blokes doon yer boxin gym arenae pumpin in the changein rooms eftir gettin aw sweaty thegether?"

"Coarse they are! But it's prison rules in the boxin gym, isnit? Disnae coont."

"So two men shaggin's no gay as lang as they punch fuck oot each other first."

"Eh… Aye."

"Baith ae yeez shut it," Jamieson said, and they obeyed. "Chuck, get the shutter back doon. The Krankies, quit bletherin an get the fucker oot the motor an let me see him."

Chuck felt the fine hairs on his skin go rigid. *Get the fucker oot the motor.* What was happening here? What was he to be part of? The shutter hit the ground with an ominous echo. He felt sweat on his body and shivered.

More Chuckle Brothers than Krankies, the two goons pushed and pulled from one side and the other to manoeuvre something out of the car.

"Wit the fuck huv yeez done tae him?"

It was a man. Skinny and baldy and curled up in the foetal position on the concrete floor of Chuck's warehouse. His head was pishing blood—vivid and bright like red paint under the harsh fluorescent tube lights. He trembled, breathing hard.

"Ye goat a chair fir the man, Chuckie?" Jamieson said.

The victim—surely a victim, the man's been fucking kidnapped, Chuck's mind reeled in a blabber as if four pints in—smelt of smoke and pub grub and urine. His suit was too big; he had Velcro shoes on.

"Chuckie!"

"Sorry." Chuck ran to the table at the back where he kept some of his own paperwork and his kettle and rolled the desk chair over.

Marble and Roughcast lifted the man upright, sat him on the chair as if playing with a mannequin. That seemed to calm him a little. The tears had stopped though his breath still hitched in his throat.

"Hawd oan." Marble took a pair of cracked glasses from his pocket and stuck them on the man's face, crooked because one of the legs had been bent. He then felt around inside the man's suit jacket, pulling out a crumpled pack of Superkings and a large lighter. "Open." He stuffed a fag in the man's lips and lit it with a venomous smile before slipping the oversized Zippo into his own pocket.

"How ye feelin, Mr Brownlee?" Jamieson asked.

A glow at the end of the cigarette indicated a draw. Smoke flowed out his nose.

"The boays gee ye a wee bump oan the heed?"

"Aye, only eftir he chucked his fuckin lit dout in ma pus."

"Quiet."

"Probly goat a fuckin burn scar, fuckin disfigurement—"

"QUIET!" Jamieson roared and the warehouse roared with him. Every other man clamped shut, testes shrivelling. "Mr Brownlee..."—his voice was now a whisper by comparison and despite the fear, they all pulled in closer to listen—"a huv some questions fir ye, an if ye answer them tae ma satisfaction ye can go oan yer way."

Brownlee took his fag from his mouth with a stiff hand, curled up on itself like a dead insect. He'd stopped visibly shaking and now sat with as much dignity as a man with pish-soaked trousers could muster. "That's not how you used to do it, Jamieson. Nobody was ever left to 'go on their way' in the good auld days."

"Hings huv changed."

"So I see. Delegating the dirty work now." He risked a glance at Marble and Roughcast. "Aff the tools?"

"The privilege an curse ae gettin auld."

"So if the new you won't kill me, and the old you certainly would no matter what, maybe the best thing to do is just keep my mouth shut." He was calm to almost cool now, no stranger to scary people even though violence wasn't really his bag.

"That's a very black-an-white view ae hings. There are increments in between." He gave the signal and Marble slammed a punch into Brownlee's gut, launching the fag from his mouth and making him dry heave.

Chuck jumped at the speed of the movement, the ferocity, the thick, slapping sound of the contact like a meat hammer pounding a side of beef.

"Ye drapped somethin." Marble picked the cigarette up and stubbed it out on Brownlee's cheek, who squealed and scratched at his attacker with his gnarled fingers. Marble caught Brownlee's wrist, took his frozen pinkie—"Let me straighten that oot fir ye"—and yanked it back the wrong way.

You could hear it break. *Snap.* Like a pencil. Acid burbled up Chuck's gullet. His heart pumped sheer panic through his system, making his muscles and tendons wobbly and his guts unreliable. There are actually three possibilities, rather than the famous two, when adrenaline kicks in: fight, flight or shite (yourself).

Roughcast rolled his eyes at his pal's one-liner, but a smile played on his lips as the man screamed and fell off his seat.

It took some time for Brownlee to stop crying and gurning again. Jamieson waited with the patience of a stained-glass saint. Eventually, he nodded to the boys to lift the crooked suit back onto his chair.

Brownlee sniffed and hawked up a rattling, phlegmy grog which he spat on the ground, like a knackered football player. "Break them all," he wheezed. "They aren't doing me much good these days anyway."

Roughcast seemed genuinely impressed: "Hard cunt, eh?"

"We'll see." Marble approached again but his boss stopped him with a look.

"Yed huv tae be tae rip aff Paulo McGuinn."

Brownlee's head snapped up, like smelling salts had been stuck under his nose. His eyes were focused, intense, desperate.

"Tae get close tae him, tae become his pal, an then, oer the coarse ae *years*, fill yer ain poakits wae his money. Two big cannonbaws ae iron, hangin in a chain mail sack."

"You didn't, you didn't tell…"

"She knows."

"Fuck." His chin dropped to his chest again. his face screwed up as if he were indeed having his fingers broken one by one. "Is that what this is about?"

"Well, a did say tae the wummin ad huv a quiet word aboot it—"

"I never meant to hurt Lottie or the girls," he croaked. "It was stupid and selfish and greedy, I… I—"

"So consider yer quiet word tae huv bin had. But naw, yer here cause a huv questions fir ye, like a said. Really it's just the wan question, so it shouldnae take lang." Jamieson lowered himself on stiff legs. Brownlee came eye to eye with the carved, glowing hollows in the depths of Jamieson's sunken fizzog.

"McGuinn's Shit List: Where is it?"

Their eyes were locked for nearly a full minute when the lawyer blinked. "What?"

Jamieson straightened up, relaxed. "Ye know, Ross, ma boay, maybe yer right. Maybe a huvnae changed that much at aw. Increments? Wit a load ae pish." He gave a thumbs up to Marble and Roughcast, who swarmed Brownlee, took an arm each and lifted him up off the seat, the toes of his Velcro shoes dragging on the ground. "Get the door, Chuck."

"Wit?"

"Open the van door." Those eyes were on him and he couldn't say no. He unlocked the van, slid the side door back. Brownlee was hoisted inside, whimpering.

Naw, naw, they widnae, Chuck's brain rambled. *They're just gonnae scare him, right? Right?* "Yer just gonnae gee him a wee fright, that's aw?" he whispered to Jamieson. The eyes found him again, then Jamieson winked. It was so incongruous, Chuck felt like he'd seen something he shouldn't have. It was against nature, like seeing a chicken flap its wings and take off one day. Maybe he'd imagined it.

"Switch the machine oan," Jamieson commanded, and Chuck did as he was told with fumbling, sweaty paws. *Just a wee fright, just a scare tae get him talkin.*

The engine rumbled, the steel cylinders rolled, the thick blades coming together like interlocking fingers and passing through as they spun with oily efficiency.

They had the back of the lawyer's head against the lip of the hopper, as if about to give his hair a wash at the salon. He was sucking big panic breaths in through his nose, his mouth clamped, his eyes wild.

"Where is it?" Jamieson asked.

They pushed his head further down the chute towards the gnashing, churning teeth, the dual shafts turning with the steady, inevitable power of train wheels. More torque than a politician caught in a lie.

"I-I don't know!" he screeched.

"Where is it?"

"I don't even know what the fuck you're talking about!"

Marble had him by the scruff of his neck and Roughcast lifted his legs, tipping him back, deeper into the hopper, closer, and closer. If he had any hair on top he'd have been getting a trim.

"Where did he keep it?!"

A number three with the clippers.

"I don't know!"

Two.

"Where?!"

"I don't know!"

One—scalped by the razor if it went another degree closer.

"Where?!"

"I DON'T FUCKING KNOW!" The scream came out hoarse, painful, words barely sounding like words, clawed from burnt, raw vocal cords.

Jamieson gave the signal and they lifted him back up, still perched on the edge of the hopper. "Maybe al just ask Lottie then," Jamieson said.

"No!" Brownlee lunged forwards but Roughcast caught him with an elbow.

He tipped back.

Marble snatched out, grabbed him by the tie—"Goat ye"— smirked, for a fraction of a second, at the look on the man's horrified face.

But then he kept falling.

It wasn't a real tie.

It was elastic. A thread-thin string of it around his neck to hold his tie in place.

And it was stretching.

Stretching.

Snapped.

22

Viscera, blood and bone shard sprayed from the shredder like a blender with the lid left off. Warm, wet, chunky liquid like minestrone soup hit their faces and they recoiled, covering their eyes. A sharp pain stung Chuck's forehead. He screamed and tasted grimy pennies. He dove for the big red button and slammed it.

The machine stopped.

There was silence, except for the pitter patter of something dripping from the roof of the van to its floor. Chuck, Marble and Roughcast had all been hit hard by the splashback and were spitting bits of Ross Brownlee's cranium from their mouths.

The shredder had eaten the top of the lawyer's head and face down to his jaw. His tongue was still attached.

Chuck reached for the sore point in his forehead, felt something hard lodged there. He pulled it out: a tooth. Like shrapnel from an explosion, its long root had embedded itself in Chuck's head. It was a molar with a silver filling. The contents of his stomach ejected onto his boots in a hot surge of bile and half-digested biscuits which he'd scranned before he'd headed out for the night's show.

"Better oot than in," Jamieson said, his voice flat. Not joking.

"Wit the fuck wis that?!" Marble screamed. He picked at his tongue as if there was a hair stuck on it.

"Me?! A thoat ye fuckin hud him!" Roughcast yelled back.

"Wit the fuck dae we dae?!"

Beyond throwing up, Chuck had no idea. He'd just seen a man killed. Chomped by his own machine. Which he'd switched on himself. *Just sposed tae scare him, just a wee fright,* his mind gibbered.

Roughcast took a breath and peered closer into the mess in the hopper. The body hanging out of it twitched and he squealed like a child. "Fuck! Fuck! Fuckin hing!" He flapped his arms as if trying to shake a spider off himself, then held a hand over his mouth as if he were on the verge of whiteying too. After a few seconds, he swallowed it down, spat the taste of vomit out his mouth. "Can we reverse the turnin ae the blades? Haw, you! Paperboay! Wake up."

Chuck looked at him, dazed.

"Can ye reverse the blades? The back ae his heed an neck an aw that are chewed up an stuck in there. We need tae reverse the way they shafts turn tae pull him oot."

"Or get an axe or somethin?" Marble suggested. "Chop through the, ye know, stuff." He mimed chopping his own neck with the blade of his palm.

"Am in blood, stepped in so far that should a wade nae mare, returnin were as tedious as go oer." The flame behind Jamieson's tumshie-lantern visage was a cool blue pilot light.

"Wit?"

"*Macbeth,* ye numpties. The Scoattish Play. Shakespeare. It means: wur gonnae huv tae get rid ae him somehow noo— choap him up, get rid ae the teeth an fingers, aw that—but wuv awready made a big mess ae the van wit'll need cleant up anyway, so..."

They looked back and forth between each other as they all slowly made the connection. Marble and Roughcast looked

137

worried. Chuck was about to hit the boak again. He wanted to cry. What the fuck? What the fuck was going on? He shouldn't be here. This wasn't him, wasn't his life.

"Great hing aboot Shakespeare, he's fuckin timeless. Chuckie, hit the switch."

"Naw, naw a cannae. A cannae, Mr Jamieson." The tears came. "A cannae dae this. It's no, it's no ma hing, it's… a-a…"

"Chuck. Look at me. Calm doon." Jamieson put his hands on Chuck's shoulders, and in a strange way it did calm him. He recalled the wink. It was an accident. A terrible accident. Brownlee had made a move, surprised them, got knocked back. "Yer in this, son. Ye huv bin since ye startet hawndin oer trinkets tae me, since a startet protectin ye from yer creditors. Wit did ye hink this aw wis? Wit a do?"

Chuck closed his stinging eyes, felt tears roll down his cheeks, opened them again to Jamieson's deep, flickering stare.

"We get this done, we caw it a bad night, an we move oan. Sooner it's oer wae, sooner we can aw go hame."

Marble and Roughcast took a leg each.

Chuck switched on the machine.

Jamieson and Shakespeare had made it all sound so neat.

It was not.

A human body is around sixty per cent water, and a lot of Brownlee's water had sluiced through the small gaps in the body of the shredding van and onto the floor. Blood water, brain water, kidney water, liver water, bladder water, gut water, fucking eyeball water. Then there was the pulp. And the chunks. And the splintered bone. Some recognisable things—a fingertip with nail, a short hose of human tripe—but mostly an oozing, congealing black pudding stew sloshing about in the back of the van.

Jamieson's driver had returned in a Ford Transit, bringing with him buckets, mops, sponges, bleach, a pressure washer, and a change of clothes for each of them. The sun was up by the time Chuck, Marble and Roughcast had finished, eyes and hands stinging and stinking of chemicals, backs breaking. For the final act they stripped off their soiled clothes—Jamieson included this time, as he probably had fine particles of Ross Brownlee on him too—and threw them into bags, then the driver turned the hose on them. He handed towels out to the four trembling men and their freezing, shrivelled wee dicks. Marble was shining wet and still looking good, the others like they'd been dredged up from the bottom of the Clyde.

The buckets they filled with Brownlee sludge were sealed and put in the back of the Transit.

"Which colour bin does that go in?" Roughcast asked, back to smiling now the job was done.

"Waeoot the EU it disnae matter. Ye can pour it intae the sea at Largs," Jamieson said. "Fuckin Brexit. It'll go somewhere safe. Don't worry aboot that."

Marble and Roughcast headed off to dispose of their car.

"Chuck…" Jamieson rounded on him. "Am sorry aboot the mess. Forget this night ever happened. A mean that. Best hing fir ye."

Chuck nodded, still shaking from the DIY decontamination shower. Maybe he'd never stop.

"Consider aw yer debts wiped. Al square up wae the boays ye owe, as a thank you, awright?"

"Th-thanks, Mr Jamieson."

"Don't fuckin waste it, noo."

"A-a willnae."

"Nae mare wee flutters, aye?"

"N-naw. Cheers." Chuck's voice was quiet and froggy. He felt a pinprick of hope, of relief. He was free. Free of one thing, at least. How he'd ever forget what had happened in his warehouse last night he didn't know.

"It never happened," Jamieson said, as if reading his mind. "There's nothin tae remember. Ye went oot, ye goat blootered, ye loast track ae time, dragged yersel hame in the mornin, nae memory ae the glorious night afore, a wee scratch oan yer heed as a memento. Aw this…"—he waved his hand to the warehouse, the scene of the horror—"…wis just some fillum ye must ae seen, geein ye nightmares."

"A-aye, Mr Jamieson."

"It'll protect yer heed, a promise." He leant in closer. "And yer body. Right?" The eyes smouldered like glowing coals. His breath was rank. "Like a says, yer wae us noo."

"Right."

"An we don't breathe a word tae anywan or else we don't breathe again."

23

The main street was the same as all town main streets: five different hairdressers, the chippy, the Indian takeaway, off-licence, betting shop, a greasy spoon clinging on, a petrol station breaking up the flow and ambience of the charming scene, and the boozer. It was a Spoons.

There was also a dry-cleaner's: IRN MAN. The sign was done in blue and orange. Copyrights had been jigged upon. The woman outside the door—fortyish but fucked with the stress—finished her snout and went inside, bringing the smell of smoke with her into the shop where dresses, suits and kilts hung in plastic on a rail behind the desk, representing weddings, funerals, graduations and court dates.

Lottie followed her in. "Luce?"

The woman's eyes widened. She took in Lottie then snuck a look behind her, to see if anybody was waiting outside. "Eh, it's nice tae see ye…" Didn't sound like it.

"A word?"

"Hows aboot a word an a cuppa?" Luce quick-marched her through to the back, where she kept her office among the clutter of the lost and found. There was no window and the press of the soft, dampening garments made it oddly cosy. Nice in winter but currently suffocating.

Luce put the kettle on and they watched each other across a desk. They were a similar age purely by number of years, but Luce had a lifetime on Lottie in terms of living. It was etched into her face, and no amount of Lottie's hundred-quid-a-pop facial rejuvenation cream—*created using deep organatural mineral-infused jizz-embalment oilology*™—could have fixed those lines.

"How ye bin keepin?"

"Sane, just aboot. How's tricks?"

"Ye know…" Luce shrugged slightly.

"Loads ae work comin through?" Lottie accused.

Luce gave a guilty, hands-in-the-air smile but wasn't cowed. "Am sorry, Lottie, but dye know wit it's like fir a wummin in this game? Hud tae dae wit a hud tae dae, a need tae work, hen. There wis naebdy steppin up tae take oer fae Paulo, maistly cause he didnae keep anywan capable enough aroon tae dae the joab. Thoat he'd be oan tap firever. Am sorry if that's harsh, but ye know it's true."

Lottie swallowed the medicine. She was right. Paulo's mind was blindly compartmentalised. He thought himself immortal despite the facts of the life he lived, the way he behaved, the people he hurt and humiliated along the way. "Wit aboot yersel, Luce? Ad say yer a capable wan."

She smirked. "Oh, a am indeed. Ye know how much organisation goes intae movin anythin in or oot ae this country aff the books? But as a says, am also a wummin. Ye know how difficult it'd be tae get even a few ae these fuckin knuckle-draggers tae folly me?"

"Times change."

"Times don't change. They swing. Backwards an forewards, an right noo wur goin back faster than Marty McFly in a DeLorean." She poured two mugs of tea, left the bags in, no milk on hand, just sugar. "Ye wur marriet tae Paulo. A dunno if that means yel undertsawn or if ye really fuckin don't get it at aw."

142

It was disbelief that hit first, then anger afterwards. No way Luce would have spoken to her like that if Paulo was still around. But he wasn't. The utter bastard. Lottie fumed, sipped the tea. It was scalding, bitter, sticky sweet on her teeth.

"Am sorry, Lottie. Am no meanin tae make ye feel bad, am just… tired."

"Don't be sorry. Am here tae ask a favour."

Luce went rigid, her eyes sharpening to needle-points.

"No a favour, really, al pay fir the service."

"Lottie… ye know who a work fir noo?"

She brushed it off. "This has nothin tae dae wae Callaghan or Rogers or whoever yer shacked up wae. This is just between you an me."

Luce smirked again. "Ye know, a always thoat ye deserved mare credit than ye goat. Ahint evry great man an aw that pish. But maybe a wis wrang. Maybe ye really know fuck aw." She leant across the table. "There's a battle comin, hen. A big wan. Evry cunt's tryin tae pick the right fleet tae be part ae, hopin it's the winnin side. Naebdy wants tae be left sittin in a fuckin dinghy oan their tod when it aw kicks aff. Evry decision is crucial. Evryhin affects evryhin else. Nothin can be 'Just between you an me.'"

Lottie swallowed her anger again. "Ye shouldae backed yersel."

Luce sighed. "Am surprised yer here in person an no goin through Ross Brownlee. It wid be safer."

"Ross has goan his separate way fae the faimly." The betrayal was still fresh. It reminded her of the first time she'd caught Paulo cheating, before it became the accepted norm. Fury and self-pity and a terrible drouth which saw her drinking every night by herself for months. She could murder a Pinot or ten right now. "Am oan ma ain. In a dinghy, as ye put it."

Luce appraised her again, sighed again, took a fag from her pack and stuck it behind an ear. "Fuck… Look wit is it ye want? Nae promises but tell me."

"A need tae get some grass through tae Colin in the jail. Am worried he's in trouble, needs some kind ae asset he could trade or witever."

"That big, buff lump?" She cocked a brow. "His ain chiselled *ass*-et no enough currency?"

"Fuck aff."

"Sorry. Speakin ae Colin, there's murmurs Billy Jamieson is askin aroon aboot yer man's death."

"Aye, a asked him tae."

"Be careful wae him; he's somethin else."

"Aye, aye, so folk say. Av heard the stories."

"Believe them."

"Ma husband wisnae exactly Gandhi himsel. Look, a need tae get ma nephew oot ae prison. Ma sister's losin her fuckin Pogs oer it. An findin oot who actually did it is surely worth knowin, don't ye hink? Fir yer battle an yer armada or witever?"

Luce played with the flint of her Clipper, her own wheels turning in her brain. "A can get a delivery tae Colin. Cost ye, but."

"Am good fir the money."

"*And…* ye keep me in the loop wae the investigation."

"Fine." Lottie stood to leave. "A mean it, Luce. Wan ae these days, back yersel. Be the captain."

24

She swung by Mark's house in the morning.

"Time for a cuppa?"

"Better not, I'm on my way in, just wanted a quick word with Tess before she goes out today." Despite Mark's scoffing at McCoist's narc-attitude towards music festivals, he didn't try to discourage her from having a Very Serious and Frank Talk with their daughter the morning of.

Tess was in her room, already in her short-short denims and Scotland top, applying glitter to her face. A giant, floppy sunhat and a pair of pristine wellies waited by the door.

"Excited?"

She got the pout in the mirror first, but a smile broke as she turned around.

"Who's all playing?"

Tess listed off a string of musicians' names that sounded like automated high-strength passwords. McCoist was more the Radio-2-in-the-car kind of aficionado. Her music taste had stopped evolving sometime around her mid-twenties, when her career was getting serious and her relationship with Mark was getting serious, and having more than a couple of drinks caused a hangover that lasted a couple of days—also very serious.

"Where are you meeting the girls?"

"Bus stop at the town centre, then we'll walk to Glasgow Green."

"Emma's mum still picking you all up after?"

"Yup." She turned back to the mirror, her face contorting as she applied the sparkles. She'd sprayed on a lot of perfume, not unpleasant, but certainly overpowering. Gucci and Hugo Boss—the official smell of teen hormones.

"Listen, and don't *Muuum* me till I'm finished, OK?"

Tess said it with her eyes rather than her mouth but McCoist took that as the go-ahead.

"People will be drinking there. And taking drugs. People might offer you a drink, or drugs. You don't know what is in the drink, or in the pills or powders. You don't know the reason they want you, an underage girl, to have them. But you can probably hazard a guess. So just don't accept anything, stay with your friends, look out for each other, don't let anyone wander off with someone you don't know. Call me if you need me. OK?"

Tess had cringed herself into origami.

"OK?"

"OK."

"Have fun." She kissed her daughter on the top of her head, tasted enough hairspray to keep a building in place during an earthquake. "And stay away from open flames."

"Muuum."

A quiet office meant it was time to follow up young Tim's other lead: ex-detective constable Matt Findlay, formerly bent copper under the employ of ex-gang lord, formerly breathing Paulo McGuinn, and maybe also the killer she was looking for.

Unfortunately, McCoist had to do this one solo to avoid telling anyone about Tim and risk bringing her own shady deeds into the light. (At her desk, she shouldered away the sensations of hot, fresh blood on skin and acrid gun smoke singeing nostril hairs. Tamped it all down into her toes—a built-in reflex of powerful Scottish emotional repression that she would need to get through the day.) This meant forgoing most of her police powers, all of which would leave a digital breadcrumb trail leading right back to her for detectives Hansel and Gretel, Anti-Corruption Unit, to follow. Avoiding leaving her signature or key-tapping fingerprints on anything meant no Data Protection Requests, no way to access bank accounts or other protected info, no access to CCTV or ANPR, no phone data… Pretty much all the easiest ways to track a person down in the twenty-first century. She could hire a private company to see if they could get hold of some of this stuff but their reach was limited, legally, and easily evaded by someone with a few wrinkles in their grey matter. The alternative to all this was burning shoe rubber.

She put in a call to HR to scrounge Findlay's last known address. ("It's been nearly a year now and his stuff is still clogging up my office space, I'm happy to pay for the delivery, I just want it out of here.")

The flat was by Queen's Park, bottom floor in a red tenement on the corner across from the Ivory Hotel. Not his name on the label by the buzzer, but McCoist pressed it anyway. These were nice gaffs. Findlay was working-class stock, his accent east of High Street, he must have been renting on a DC's salary. Unless he had income from other sources—which, if what was in Davey Burnet's account was true, he very likely had.

"Hello?" A woman's voice (her accent east of the Danube).

"DCI Alison McCoist. Can you let me in for a word?"

"Sorry?"

"Police." She held her warrant card up to the button camera, though it probably wouldn't be clear enough to read. The door buzzed and as she stepped into the close, the smell of hot, lemon-scented degreaser steaming up from the floor tiles, the door of the flat to the immediate left opened up, the woman coming to meet her.

"Hello," she said again, her body an awkward barrier in front of her door. Defensive, but not because she was hiding something, just standard mistrust of the polis.

"Sorry to bother you, but does Matt Findlay live here?"

"Findlay." Recognition. McCoist's heart gave a few rabbit thumps. "Ah." She held up a finger—*one second*—and stepped back into the house, returning with a stack of letters. "Lived here before us. We're still getting his post." She thrust them towards McCoist, glad to have someone to pass them off on. "This isn't all, we've been getting them all year, we usually just score out the address and stick them back into the postbox though. Sorry."

"That's OK. Did you know him at all?"

Shake of the head. "Only that he likes climbing. Magazine kept arriving for him for a couple months after we moved in." _

"Thank you for this." She turned to go.

"Wait—is there anything you can do about stopping the letters?"

"Eh, try speaking to the post office."

"We have but they still keep coming."

"Sorry."

The woman tutted and closed her door. McCoist had a quick flip through the envelopes, smiled at the sight of bold, black lettering threatening "DO NOT IGNORE" across a few of them. A collection agency—could be a good lead. She knocked on the other doors in the tenement first, asking for anyone who might have known him while he was there. Most were "Hello/ goodbye" familiar but had little more to say—he was in and out a lot for work, often during unsociable hours but they knew he was a police officer so it was expected. "Kept to himself," was the refrain. City living, nobody knows who's just through the wall. The only notable blip was his sudden disappearance. Nobody knew he was planning to move out, just Houdini'd it one day. A moving van showed up and he went with it. The landlord must have been left in the lurch because it was months after he'd gone before people started turning up for viewings.

So Findlay had moved in a hurry and without warning, left his name on everything, been still paying subscriptions to a magazine at that address. McCoist wondered if his Netflix was still logged in—wouldn't be the first time a streaming subscription or an Uber Eats account had led the polis straight to some master criminal's secret lair.

Back in the car she called HR up again, told them the address was out of date and asked for his next of kin.

His mother was in a terraced council house in Cumbernauld. She'd done her best with a small front garden and the house matched inside—well kept if not fashionable. The same could be said for Mrs Findlay herself, who in her sixties had a healthy, well-exercised look about her undermined by a pensioner's hairdo and trousers. When McCoist held up her warrant card, the poor mother's face aged to match. "Is everything OK?"

"Fine"—McCoist tried on a reassuring smile—"as far as I know?..." She waited for Mrs Findlay to speak, fill the silence.

"Sorry, it's just, well, considering Matty's job, and your job, I just had a wee fright. Thought it might be... bad news."

She didn't sound at all like her son. Her accent was that of a generation who'd had the need to "Speak Properly" drummed into them at school. His hinted that he'd spent more time with friends than at home growing up.

"Matty's not here then?"

Her face creased in confusion. "Oh no, he's up in Inverness. Transferred there a while back. Don't you know that?"

He hadn't told her he'd resigned. "Oh... oh yeah, right, of course." She tried not to slap her forehead with a "Duh", keep the am-dram to a minimum, the woman was already suspicious now. "Sorry, I knew he'd moved but didn't realise he'd gone so far—"

"Why are you looking for him?" Very suspicious.

"Nothing important, just he'd left some things in the office—a magazine subscription keeps arriving there, you know, and, uh, I thought he might want them or he might not know, so..." Floundering.

"Is he all right?"

"Fine. Honestly."

"It's the middle of the day."

"I'm on my break." Big smile.

Mrs Findlay glowered, nose wrinkled. Wrong tactic. Should have come better prepared. McCoist's explanation was a spaghetti strainer. Full of holes. "Nobody calls him Matty but me; he hates it. Please just tell me if something's wrong."

"Really, there's not, Mrs Findlay. I'm so sorry if I've upset you coming here, I should have phoned, but it really is nothing. I just wanted to return his things."

"He heads up north without a moment's notice, barely calls, and now you're here at the door looking for him. I'm not stupid." Her eyes were starting to shine with a film of tears but she kept them back with her anger. "You might think so and he might think so too but I'm not. What's going on?"

Now McCoist was the pouting teenager getting the parental inquisition, and she felt a pang of sympathy for Tess. *Nothing, Muuum.* She was on the back foot, had to change gear, regain control: "What do you suspect?" Aloof, haughty, let her know she's speaking to a senior police detective, that the shoe is only ever on one foot: DCI McCoist's. Crime-solver, gangster-killer, maw-terroriser. "If you think Matty's in some kind of trouble, tell me and I can help."

The righteous indignation was cracking the tears were winning. Her voice fell to a deflated monotone. "I don't know. I don't. It's just, he's so far away now. He's never been good at staying in touch, and now that he's all the way up there... He never told me he was even applying for the job or thinking about moving or anything. I'm his mother. What does that say about me?"

McCoist backed down too, shrivelled with guilt and a hint of fear. Would this be her in ten or twenty years? Kids moving hundreds of miles away without a moment's notice, no calls. At least in Mrs Findlay's case, the reason her son had fucked off without explanation was that he was on the run and couldn't leave a trail or involve her in any way. In McCoist's, it would probably be because they'd got so used to being without her anyway.

"I'm sure he's just busy. Don't worry about any of this. Please."

She waited till she'd driven well out of the street before punching the steering wheel. "Fuck!" Poor. Poor work.

. . .

The notices from the collection agency took her to a big, grey, corrugated-metal box of storage units in Rutherglen. "Sorry, hen, the unit wis auctioned aff and cleant oot a wee while back. Only made a couple ae payments."

"Detective Chief Inspector, thanks."

The guy behind the reception desk gave a hard, phlegmy sniff in response to the correction.

"Do you have a record of what was in it?"

He made a face like he'd been asked to repaint the Forth Road Rail Bridge using an artist's brush held in his nostril. "Naw, but there's a photie oan the file here taken fir the oanline auction." He turned his monitor around so McCoist could see it.

A snapshot from outside the unit with its shutter open:

Couches standing on end, wrapped in plastic, boxes with marker scribbled on them ("LIV RM" and "BED 1" but no detail about the contents), a couple of stereo speakers which looked expensive and more things in the back which couldn't be seen, tantalising for treasure hunters. The contents of the flat at Queen's Park. She'd spoken to the landlord, who'd received no notice of Findlay moving out, was only alerted when a payment was missed. When they went round, the gaff was empty—except for the landslide of post blocking the door—and damp. Similar tale to the storage unit.

He'd fled and given himself a few months' grace on paper before cutting the direct debits. Or maybe he'd left an account to drain, while keeping his ill-gotten gains somewhere separate. If she put in a Data Protection Request to the bank with another officer's name on it, say Khan or Travis, and signed it off with her own authorisation, she could—

No. That was a bad idea. Could easily come back and bite her on the arse, and if the thread was pulled, well... Forging a DPR was a petty misdemeanour compared to shooting a man (*a dangerous, evil man, mind*) in the head and covering it up by framing somebody else. Forging a DPR meant a disciplinary, maybe even getting sacked, but the other thing/s would win her a long prison sentence. And a polis in jail was like Christopher Lee in any film: soon to die. It wouldn't be quick or dignified either. Boiling water, blades made from screws and tooth-brushes, a bludgeon from a pillowcase filled with pool balls, a bar of soap shaved to a cone and stuffed down the throat.

McCoist jammed the thought back into the bulging DO NOT OPEN file in her brain before it caused her to crumble into a moaning puddle of tears and pish, unable to move or think.

She had to be able to think:

Findlay was secretly working for Paulo. Paulo dies and Findlay fucks off. Maybe he's worried about retribution from rival gangs, maybe he just wants a fresh start. He could be in Inverness as he told his maw, or maybe/probably, he's somewhere else. However, he's named as a bent polis in a letter handed to Carter Lennox. If he knows this—another maybe, big missing piece right there—it gives him motive to murder Lennox. Bonus problem: if he *is* aware of this school report of Burnet's and has seen its contents, does he know about her killing Paulo?

Fuck.

She needed to speak to Tim again, see if he would let her know more about the contents of the letter, see if she could better gauge if she was in the shit with this thing or not. And she needed to make the phone call she was avoiding.

25

"Bear, what's the weather report?"

"We're in Glasgow, assume it's pish."

"I've got a big umbrella." She imagined Devlin's librarian smile at the other end of the line, the glasses perched on the end of his nose, held by a chain—the world's least cool bling, even Mr T. wouldn't go that far—him having a little scratch at his nads, just a little tickle of the scrote, a comforting twitch. All of it surface, hiding something cold and unknowable below. A human costume, worn lightly.

"I need help finding someone."

"You're a senior detective."

"He's involved with the car-wash *thing*, I'm hobbled."

"Hmm."

"Matt Findlay, ex-job, bent, worked for McGuinn. He disappeared after the Big Man… died. And he might be the one who killed Carter Lennox."

"What have you got linking him?"

"Davey Burnet made a written record of everything that happened to him at the car wash with McGuinn and passed it off to Lennox. Findlay's name is in it."

"Davey Burnet, the SpongeBob?" There was a sound that might have been a chuckle. "It's always the ones you least expect who fuck you, isn't it?" His almost cheerful calmness gave McCoist stomach pains, caused the veins in her forehead to throb. "Do you have this record?"

"Do you know where Burnet is now?"

"Attention needed deflecting at first, but he and Prentice have done a decent job of fucking off and staying fucked off. Don't answer a question with a question, you're not a politician. *Do you have this record?*"

"No. It's missing." To the top of the shit pie she added the problem with the paper-shredding and the warrants.

"Goodness gracious. So how do you know his name is in it? Is your name in it?"

McCoist gave herself a beat to work up some steel. "Answer one: a protected source, I'm not willing to say for now. Answer two: I don't know."

"Protected source... Bear, do you know what an asset is?" Thick condescension in his voice but still no trace of anger. "An asset is someone who brings me intelligence and solves problems. You, however, are causing problems and withholding intelligence. Do you know what the opposite of an asset is?"

"I guess you're going to tell me." Her irritation was hitting dangerous p.s.i.

"A liability."

Wanker.

26

Chuck had got in the door early morning, the summer sun already obscenely bright, and crashed out on the mattress in the spare room. He thought he'd never sleep again but it swallowed him whole. The dreams made him wish he'd been right.

He woke with a sinkhole of dread in his stomach. For a fleeting moment he thought, wished, it might all have been one long, horrible nightmare. But no, he'd seen that man get killed, chewed up by the turning blades of his pet shredder, and he'd helped clean it up. The sudden, murky, pungent smell of shite—when most of the top half had been fed in, five shirt buttons down, and the teeth reached the abdomen—was still in his nostrils, overloading the already rich, whitey-inducing, butcher's-shop aromas of blood and fresh meat.

Bell was downstairs, knocking the hoover off the skirting boards. He'd told her he was going out in town with pals last night, so she was expecting him to rise late and be hungover. The exhaustion in his bones, the ache in his muscles, the queasy, greasy sloshing in his belly were not unlike a hangover. If only he had the blackout to go with it. *It never happened. There's nothin tae remember*—Jamieson's advice/threat. He tried to push aside the sight of the body being eviscerated, the sound of churning meat and breaking bone popping over the industrial rumble of the machine; he spewed in the shower.

"You look like shite," Bell said. "Must ae bin a good ni—wit the fuck happened tae yer face?" She rushed him to get a close-up of the cut the tooth had left in his forehead. "Tell me yev no bin fuckin fightin."

"Wit?! Who's bin fuckin fightin? Why wid ye hink that? Fuckin fell oer didn't a."

"Aye?"

"Aye! Av no bin in a fight since a wis at school, fucksake."

"A know wit yer pals are like, but, an when yer aw excitet aboot a night oot thegether like wee boays."

"A wisnae fightin, Bell. Geez peace. An a bit ae fuckin credit an aw."

He could feel her eyes scanning him like an airport X-ray machine, and he passed. "Sorry. Geez a look." He bowed his head towards her and she held his head between her hands. Her cold palms felt good against his temples. "Al get a Steri-Strip oan it. Ye cleant it?"

"Hud a shower."

"There's bacon if yer needin it," she said, going to the cupboard for the first aid kit.

How to tell her he was thinking of going vegan? "Am no ready fir solids yet."

He spent the day in a haze, a dead numbness, stranded on still water in a thick fog, with occasional blasting winds of clarity causing trembling panics, lashing sweat, threatening to capsize him, pull him under, swallow him down to the deep. Bell kept getting on at him for not listening to whatever the fuck it was she was on about. "Wit did a say then? Go oan. Tell the class."

"Stoap nippin ma heed, man!"

That went down well.

About as well as a man in an industrial paper shredder. Head first. He felt again the blood splatter on his face, the tooth sink into his head, diving for the red button, the unbelievable sight of Brownlee with the top half of his head gone and his bottom jaw sticking out like a broken Pez dispenser.

Jamieson, the rotten ghoul, whispering: "Like a says, yer wae us noo… An we don't breathe a word tae anywan or else we don't breathe again."

His heart was bumping up hard against his insides. He was giddy with sickly adrenaline. He couldn't eat dinner—Bell chastised him for getting so mad-wae-it. "Ye arnae eighteen any mare, a hangover'll dae ye in fir days."

"Might never recover," he mumbled. He looked at his pie, chips and beans—a favourite—and saw greasy bone shards and viscera. He forced a small mouthful of pie in but the texture of the mutton was like the little bits of Brownlee gristle that had been minced through the shredder. He forced it down, clenched his jaw against the threatening boak.

"State ae ye." Bell shook her head.

"Dye ever hink…" He couldn't get the words up, the chunder trying to come with them.

"Somebdy aroon here has tae," she laughed.

He faked a smile, swallowed the whitey and the visions of meat and murder, gathered his courage. "Dye ever hink aboot us just leavin? Gettin the fuck oot ae this place an goin somewhere else?"

Bell chuckled. "Wit? *A Place in the Sun*? *Wantet Doon Under*?"

"Am serious. Sell the gaff, pack the bags, get tae fuck. Somewhere new. Somewhere better."

"Wit?" The smile was still there but the laughter behind it was gone. "Where's this come fae?"

"Nowhere, a dunno, it's just. Dye ever hink ae gettin away, gettin oot there, daein somethin else, somewhere else." He was warming up to his pitch but Bell wasn't. Her face was contorting, edges hardening, eyes lighting up like Cyclops from *X-Men* about to melt some cunt.

"Yev bin bettin."

"Wit?!"

"Tell me yev no. Fuckin tell me yev no bin bettin. That ye don't owe money. That yer no askin me tae run away fae ma hame an ma faimly an everywan a know cause folk are eftir ye fir money." She looked at the cut on his forehead again.

"Bell, no—"

"Stuart." Proper name in full; here it came. "TELL ME YEV NO BIN FUCKIN GAMBLIN!" she exploded.

Chuck covered his face with his hands, rubbed at his temples as if they were sore. Playing cards had given him a good poker face. Addiction had made him a good liar. He gathered himself to respond, hated himself already for what he was about to do.

"A huvnae. Bin. Gamblin." His voice a rasp. "A huvnae bin fuckin gamblin fir five fuckin year. An ye still willnae trust me. Ye still throw it in ma fuckin face evry time we disagree or fall oot oer somethin. Wit mare can a dae? Will it ever be good enough?" He dredged together every petty little resentment he'd ever felt towards his wife—and truthfully there weren't many—and used it to make himself believe the lie, make his face a mask of hurt.

And she bought it. The DEFCON number rose faster than Popeye's dick after a can of spinach. "Sorry, a... a didnae—"

"Naw, don't. Am sorry. A dunno wit's up wae me. Maybe it's the hangover blues, eh? Feelin shite. Maybe a just need a holiday."

She put a hand on his arm, coaxed him up out his chair and into a cuddle. "A holiday wid be nice if we hud the money."

That was the rub. A new life costs a fair wedge. There was the Great Accumulator in his back pocket, but there were still a good number of matches left. Plus it was a long shot. Long, long shot. The thermostat in hell would lower a couple of degrees before it paid out in full. (Didn't stop Chuck having a good feeling about it, but.)

He needed more money, and quick. And he couldn't borrow from anyone who Jamieson knew—he didn't want him to suspect Chuck was trying to do the Richard Gough. Also, the man had just cleared his debts with those "lenders", another reason he couldn't go back to them.

Trepidation crept into his panicked, pacing-the-floor thoughts. *Nae mare wee flutters, aye?* His ledger was clear for the first time in years. He was no longer in danger of losing his house or his legs. *Don't waste it.* Maybe he could just embrace that. Freedom, of a kind. Enjoy it. Bin the gambling for good, for real this time. Stop lying to Bell. Because she would find out eventually, of course she would. And it would break her heart. She was as much in the balance as the house and his legs.

He'd been living with the constant fear of losing everything for so long now, it would be nice to let that go, wouldn't it?

Yer wae us noo.

It would also be nice to never feed another human being to his paper shredder ever again though.

27

Another day in the can. McCoist flopped back on her bed. Bruce hopped up and scrambled around, digging himself a cosy spot in the sheets. The great lump was too warm to be sleeping next to in the summer but there was more chance of him learning to tap-dance than sleep in his own bed. As a pup he would cry with his paws up on the side of McCoist's queen-size until she broke and lifted him up. Once he was fully grown there was no stopping him. She put a hand on his fur, could smell his musty dog-scent, and she started to calm, let the thoughts of the day slip from her mind...

The phone rang.

"The fuck is it now... Hello. DCI McCoist."

"Sorry, Alison, did I wake you?" Slater. Her heart did a wee stumble at his voice in the dark. Then reality clicked in and she knew it would probably be bad news. He was on the night shift this weekend, and he'd only call her if it was serious. A time-sensitive break in the case at best, another dead body at worst.

"No"—though her voice was gummy with sleep-drool—"what's happened?"

His next words were a mule kick to her already overwrought gut: "I have Tess here."

"What?!"

"It's OK, it's OK, she's fine. She got pulled into London Road because she'd had a bit too much to drink—"

"For fucksake!" A burning cocktail of fury and fear lit McCoist head to toe, chased off any hint of sleepiness.

"She dropped your name when they were clerking her in and the desk sergeant put in a call to the department—got me."

"Is she OK?"

"She's OK, I promise."

"Thanks, Si. I'm on my way in."

"No need, I'll bring her to you."

"You've done enough, really, I'm so sorry you've been involved—"

"It's no problem, honestly, we'll see you soon."

She threw her work clothes—rumpled on the bedroom floor—back on and headed to the kitchen for a quick, seething coffee, her hands tight around the mug as if trying to crumble the ceramic into dust.

She phoned Mark but it went to voicemail—he was on his date, wasn't he? Still? It was after eleven... Fuck. She'd have to call her mother-in-law and let her know what had happened. Fuck, fuck. She made the call and, as expected, Granny Cath deemed the whole mess to be McCoist's fault, despite her golden boy being the one keen to let Tess go to the festival in the first place. Fuck, fuck, fuck. And she'd have to call Emma's mum too...

A knock at the door sent Bruce bounding down the stairs and barking his gormless head off. "Quiet! Stop! Stop! *Shhhh!* Come on, you bloody animal, *shut up!*"

Slater wore tired eyes and a sympathetic, *happens-to-the-best-of-us* smile. Tess skulked in his shadow, her body weaving, eyeliner and glitter in clumpy runnels all down her cheeks. "Get in and go to bed," McCoist snapped at her. She didn't need to threaten her about The Talk they'd have in the morning, it was implicit in the steam coming off McCoist's raging face. She was livid. Now the girl was home safe, the worry had left her and what remained was an anger that could tear buildings down.

Tess stumbled past her, head down, staggered up the stairs using the wall for balance.

"Go easy on her, we've all done it at her age," Slater said.

It was a testament to McCoist's temper in the moment that she very nearly told him to shut his stupid fucking man-gob— what did he know about looking after weans? The instinct passed quickly, a spike, and she was glad she hadn't. He'd done her a big favour, potentially saving her daughter a night in the cells and further professional embarrassment for her senior-polis mother. And he meant well.

"Thanks again, I'm so sorry about this."

"It's nothing."

He hovered on the doorstep. McCoist almost asked him in for a cuppa but in the circumstances, her daughter upstairs, him on the clock, it felt wrong. "Sorry. Again. I'll let you get back."

As he got back into his car, McCoist noticed the light on next door—that auld biddy Edith had got the full show then. *Wonderful. Nosy cow.*

The night was filled with retching and remorse. McCoist held Tess's hair back and cleaned up the spillover. Lessons were learnt, for now.

In the morning, McCoist had the bearing of an egg-timer stuffed with plastic explosive. Tess tiptoed around her, putting the kettle on, getting the mugs. Things she wouldn't do under normal circumstances. Youthful resilience meant that despite spending hours chucking up her digestive juices during the night, she was already on the mend. She'd been for a shower and brushed her teeth, with only a slight grey pallor to her face as evidence of her adventures at TRNSMT. McCoist looked like the one who'd been on a bender. Felt like it too—eyes gritty, head thumping, bowels fluctuating. She waited until coffee and toast were on the table before starting: "Are you gonna tell me what happened then?"

Tess filled her mouth with toast as a way of saying "No comment". She chewed slowly, maybe not as fresh as she looked.

"Whose idea was it then? Sounds like you all had a wee tipple."

"Sorry," she mumbled. Again, not an answer.

"Emma's mum was just about having a heart attack at you not showing up with the rest of the girls. You owe her a sincere apology."

"Sorry."

"You're all going to chip in to get her car cleaned too."

"I wasn't even in it." Pouty, teenage, *life's-not-fair* voice.

McCoist crucified her with a look and she went back to meekly grinding up mouthfuls of toast into paste. "How do you think it makes me look? My own daughter getting booked."

"It's all about you, isn't it?" Under her breath, not bold enough to say it clearer, angry enough she couldn't keep it to herself.

"Don't you dare. You don't get to be angry at me!" McCoist shouted. Her finger was pointing. "Anything could have happened to you in that state! It's maybe even lucky the polis *did* pick you up!"

Tess kicked her chair back and thundered up the stairs to her room.

Good work again, Alison.

McCoist was already late for work and would have to drop Tess off at Mark's on the way, making her even later. The atmosphere in the car was better than in the kitchen, both of them having cooled off and McCoist turning her worries to the day ahead.

"Dad says he's making us do a 'digital detox' when we go to the caravan," Tess said. "He's even bought a box to lock our phones in. Can you talk to him?"

McCoist couldn't hide her smirk. "No. A detox of every kind would be good for you right now."

Humph.

"And you know what he's like with these things. Ask your gran, if anyone can talk him down, it's her."

"Did you know Dad was going on a date last night?" Tess sounded genuinely curious, no intent to hurt.

"I did, yeah. You're not feeling…"—McCoist searched for the right word—"…upset about it, are you?" Best she could come up with.

"Are you?"

Jesus, what a question. "Tess, I'm here to look after you, to make sure you're OK, you don't need to worry about me. I'm your mum. Maybe one day, when I'm in the retirement home you've put me in—a nice one, of course, very expensive, with handsome nurses—"

"*Muum.*" She was smiling though.

"—we can swap places, but for now, let me worry about you. You're feeling all right about it?"

"I am, it's just, he's being all sneaky about it? Like, he thinks me and Cam are idiots and have no clue what he's up to."

"He's just trying to protect you both. Meeting new people is different when you have kids. You don't want to—"

"Let them know you have any?"

McCoist burst out laughing. Tess joined in but it was half-hearted, there was real concern beneath.

"No, no, of course not. It's more like... you can't just let *anybody* into your life, your family, d'you know what I mean? You need time to see if they're right first."

They drove in silence for a while, Tess chewing on the information, before she piped up with: "Have you been out with anybody since Dad?"

"Christ! I'm driving here, Tess, are you trying to get us killed?"

She laughed, and McCoist did too, and it felt like a long time since the two of them had enjoyed each other's company like this, despite the subject matter and the circumstances.

"That detective who drove me home last night... he was telling me all about how great you are." She had a cheeky red-devil smile on her face. "How you're so clever and wonderful to work for." McCoist had the cheeks to match.

"You really were plastered."

28

The client was late so Lennox sent him to the cafeteria to get a scran and some coffee. "Could be a long day, son," he'd said. "Fill up."

Tim was more dressed up than most of the people on trial at the High Court. He was getting glances from hard-looking guys in tracksuits and it made him quiver like his bones and organs were gummy sweets. The lawyers, with their document cases and cloaks and wigs, moved with a vicious purpose—Tim didn't want to accidentally step in front of one of them any more than he would a bus.

The cafeteria was mercifully quiet—too late for breakfast, too early for lunch. Tim bought a coffee and a muffin, not really hungry but heeding Lennox's words. He was a clever man, Carter Lennox—Tim had known that the first time he heard him speak, as a guest lecturer at uni—but he also had a quiet, deep compassion that Tim had come to respect since he started interning with him. He took his duty as a defence lawyer seriously, but also his duty to his fellow man. No matter who their daddy was or what he did. No matter whether they had a nice suit and shiny shoes like Tim or showed up in old gutties and a Diadora two-piece jogging suit from when it had been cool the first time around. A lot of his clients fell into this second category. He did a lot of pro bono work.

As Tim nursed his coffee and picked pigeon crumbs from his muffin, just such a character stoated into the caf. He looked like a scabby, waterlogged football and moved with a gait just as heavy and unpredictable. He stumbled table to table, asking for some cash to buy a bowl of soup. He nodded off a few "sorry, pal"s, bounced off the indifference of those who refused to acknowledge him at all and kept their eyes on their phones. He landed across from Tim, the musk of drink and fags coming off him in waves.

"Any chance ae a few quid fir some soup, pal?" His voice was ragged and nasal. "Just need a wee bowl ae soup, that's aw. A bowl ae soup. Get some ae ma five a day." He smiled, his teeth black at the gums, though he was probably not much older than Tim. Hard life.

The look, sound, and smell of him had turned Tim's brain into a ringing alarm bell, but he'd been trying to examine his own prejudices lately, inspired by his boss. "Yeah OK, come up with me."

Tim went to the counter, the man ambling ahead. "Soup, soup, soup fir the soul, doll!" he sang to the woman behind the counter, who smiled at him the way you smile at your senile old granny. "Tae go, please, am in a hurry." When she ducked down to a low cupboard to get the takeaway cup, he pinched a Kit Kat from the rack of sweets at the till and stuffed it into the kangaroo pouch of his hoody. He turned to Tim: "Can a huv a roll an aw?"

"Eh, I guess. Whatever you like," he said, trying to give him a look which conveyed: *I saw that, you cheeky git!*

"A roll an aw, hen! Ta!" When she turned to get the roll, he snatched another Kit Kat. "Cheers, cook!" He tore a chunk from the roll with his teeth—"Cheers, pal" to Tim, mouth full—and stumbled out.

"A soup and a roll… And two Kit Kats. Is that all?" the woman asked, ringing it up, hint of a smile on her face.

"That's it, thanks," Tim said with a sigh. His dad's voice in his head lectured: "Give them an inch and they take a mile." He tried to ignore it.

Five minutes later, he got a text from Lennox telling him to come back. The client had arrived.

Tim followed an orange snail trail of spilt soup out the door, up the stairs, down the corridor and all the way to the main hall where Lennox had been waiting, now standing with a swaying, cream-of-tomato-covered drunk.

"You're late," the soupy drunk said.

Tim's face was an angry goldfish.

"Better to arrive late than be *unfed* on time," Lennox quipped, and gave him a wink.

Memories of the early days kept coming back to him, and afterwards he had to remind himself that Carter Lennox was dead and it was his fault.

He had begged Lennox to take him on as an intern; he had ulterior motives. His friend and former colleague at the car wash Davey Burnet had got himself caught up in organised crime, and Tim had believed Lennox could help him out. Then Davey vanished and the letter appeared in his place. A record of all sorts of wrongdoing involving "alleged" OCG kingpin Paulo McGuinn with potential ties to Glasgow's rich and powerful. And with the letter, an empty bullet casing. McGuinn had been killed with a bullet to the head, and the chances were high this might be the very one.

He begged again. He guilted him. They needed to do

something about this. They couldn't just leave it to continue festering. Or else what was the point? They'd already let Davey down once before, and now he was God-knows-where. Time to fix it.

And Carter agreed. Not such a clever man after all. They were both exhilarated at first. To be doing something important, something dangerous. It was like being in a film. *GLA Confidential. Chinatoon. The (Auld) Firm.* Then Lennox started to get scared, really scared. Said the depth and breadth of it all was "Staggering. It's like we're trying to scoop the ocean up in a bucket. And the bucket's got holes." He stopped letting Tim in on what he was doing. And then one day he stopped answering his phone. And soon after...

Tim was miserable and afraid and alone.

Maybe.

DCI Alison McCoist. To trust her or not? The question had chased its own tail around Tim's head since she'd caught him trying to jimmy the door of Lennox's flat like an eejit. He wanted to believe she was on his side. *You're on the winning team now,* she'd said. He also wanted to turn back time to when his main concern had been where to go out and get smashed that night with his pals, but that wasn't possible either. His life had been reduced to hiding and hoping and skulking in the shadows, looking over his shoulder. And by his own meddling too. A fight for justice he might have called it if he was feeling charitable or grandiose, but he'd felt neither since Lennox was murdered.

Which brought him back to the door of Lennox & MacGillivary for the first time since his boss went AWOL, soon to turn up as a corpse. Sandra had been the one to tell him, over the phone, and grief was a convenient cover to go to ground and not show up for a while.

Today he turned up in his smartest civvies—not there to work but not wanting to look like he'd spent his last few days locked up in his flat, shiteing it, snatching sleep whenever it came, subsisting on dry cereal and black tea because he didn't want to go out to the shops for a few messages in case he was being hunted. Jumping whenever his phone rang—just his mum, always, the only person who called him now. How was the studying going? How was the internship? Was he eating and sleeping? He couldn't truthfully answer a single question.

"Aw, son." As soon as he was through the door, Sandra got up from the desk and pulled him into a bear hug. "Ye awright? Yer lookin affy skinny, even fir you."

"I'm all right. What about you?"

"Och, a just… still cannae believe it, ye know? Still expectin him tae come through the door each mornin. A go tae stick the coffee machine oan an am halfway tae his office tae ask if he wants wan afore a mind he's no there." If Tim was looking skinny, Sandra was also wearing her grief on the outside. She seemed old to Tim, elderly, like his gran, in a way she never had before, always some kind of bright burning energy at her core, keeping her young, that was now fizzling.

"You not taking some time off yourself?"

"A widnae feel any better sittin in the hoose. An anyway, this place wid faw apart waeoot me."

"True. How about Mr MacGillivary?"

She pretended to spit on the floor. "He'll get oer it, am sure. Were ye lookin tae speak tae him? Cause he's no in the noo, aff tae court."

Tim knew that. He still had access to the firm's schedule. "No, that's OK. I just came to pick up some things I left here now that, well..."

"Ye leavin us?"

"I guess so. I never did anything for Mr MacGillivary and I haven't heard from him since Mr Lennox..." He finished the sentence with a tight smile and dropped his eyes to the floor.

"Sorry tae hear that, son. If it wis up tae me..."

"Thanks, Sandra. I'll just go and grab my things from the office."

"Aw, son, the polis huv bin through it aw, taken a load ae stuff away, ye might huv tae get in touch wae them."

"Shit." He didn't have to act hard to seem despairing. "I'll take a peek anyway, if that's OK?"

"Course. Fancy a coffee an aw? Fir auld lang syne?"

Sandra set about the machine and Tim headed out of the waiting room and over to Lennox's office. He did indeed have a peek through the door—the place had never been so tidy. The floor was visible. Without its occupant, the room felt dead too. An empty office—the Lennox family tomb. Then he swerved across to MacGillivary's, letting himself in to the sound of the coffee machine crunching pods and spitting boiling water. "Syrup?"

"Caramel, please!" His voice cracked a little with nerves and he hoped she hadn't noticed. His heart picked up to a steady runner's pace, sweat prickled on his skin.

He'd never been into MacGillivary's office before. It was the yin to Lennox's yang. Orderly, efficient, rubbish exclusively in the wastepaper basket, a computer manufactured in the past couple of years without a crumb on the keyboard. The only point of similarity was the lack of any personal effects—no family photos, no knick-knacks, nothing that hinted at a life beyond the walls of the court. Which was curious because MacGillivary seemed exactly the type of guy to stick a picture of his yacht or something on the wall of his office. But the only thing hanging there were his framed credentials. Some kind of lawyer thing, maybe, Tim thought. The kind of clients that came through a defence lawyer's door might not be the sort of people you want knowing you have a wife and kids at home, and bills to pay for a boat.

Tim had no idea what he was looking for. A pair of leather strangler's gloves in the drawer? A confession written in verse? An invoice from a hired hitman? "Item: man asphyxiated ×1, corpse removed ×1, cost before VAT, registered charity number..."

He started by trying various drawers in the desk and filing cabinets to see what was unlocked. Nothing. He shook the mouse and the screen woke, asking for a password. A hacker Tim was not. Waste of time.

A shelf of leather-bound law books stood well dusted on a high shelf. He scanned the gold-foiled titles, each one as lengthy, dry, archaic and impenetrable as a Renaissance poem. Not stuff Tim had been assigned to read at uni. This was some kind of set MacGillivary had assembled and had bound. Maybe Tim had been wrong before about the lack of vanity shots—this was MacGillivary's yacht, his selfie with massive dead fish, his secondary-school badminton-league trophy. And there was his name on one of the spines: *Analysis of the Historic Convention of the "Bastard Verdict" and the Advance of Criminal Rights in Scotland following the Restoration and Their Continuing Impact on Twentieth-century Jurisprudence* by D. A. E. Cresswell PhD, LLB (Hons) & A. R. MacGillivary LLB (Hons).

Tim pulled the tome off the shelf, creaked it open. As the pages fluttered, something slipped out and drifted to the floor. A folded piece of paper, "PLU" written on the external side. A note from another many-named upper-class collaborator? Tim picked it up and unfolded it. The words inside were written with a heavily slanted, curly, looping, ostentatious hand. If it was a font it would be called "Boarding-school Communal Wank Sock". It read something like:

Bit of a fix, ole mucker. Services might be needed if all else fails. Owe you a sherry.

Tim put the note back in the book, though he wasn't sure exactly whereabouts it had fallen from. He flipped further through the text, its pages thin like a Bible or dictionary, until he found another note, again from PLU:

Not just about me any more. Drawing a target on the lot of us. It has to stop. Make him play ball or we go the other way—Yours *in extremis*

Did they mean Lennox's investigation? Tim thought. No way to tell when the note was written. Whoever this PLU was, it sounded like he was in the cross hairs—was he mentioned in Davey's letter? Tim strained to recall if there were any names to match the initials but nothing jumped out. Was he putting pressure on—

"Mr MacGillivary!" Sandra's voice from the reception. "Didnae expect ye back awready, geed us a wee fright there."

Fuck! Tim's heart cannonballed to the floor. Adrenaline picked it back up, electrifying his body like a triple-threat rail of coke, gunpowder and Viagra.

"Postponed—I'll stick the new date in the diary."

Tim stuffed the note back in the book, shoved it onto the shelf and scurried to the office door, whipping it open, diving through and pulling it closed before doing an arse-wiggling speed walk towards the reception, where he almost crashed straight into MacGillivary.

"Mr MacGillivary!" It was almost a yelp. He attempted a meek smile but with his heart moshing with his other internal organs it came out a manic, crazy-eyed grin.

"Mr Drummond." He measured Tim's circus-freak look and sweaty forehead, his red cheeks. "What are you doing here?"

"I, uh, had some things I'd left..."—he gestured with his thumb towards Lennox's office, too big, too wavy, too much hand and arm flapping going on—"...and wanted to collect them since, eh, I guess that's me, um, finished here. Is it? I don't, eh, nobody has said..." He ran out of puff, and his out-of-control hands rested on his hips like Paul Hollywood appraising a shoddy Bakewell tart and the useless specimen who made it—a pose he'd never previously adopted in his life. It looked as natural as you'd expect.

"The police have taken everything from Mr Lennox's office for their investigation. I'm afraid if you left anything in there, you'll have to speak to them."

"I know—I mean, Sandra told me that but I wanted to check myself just in case." He stood there under MacGillivary's searchlights. He felt like one of those cardboard-cut-out security guards you get in pound shops, about to get folded by a light breeze.

"Anything else?"

"No."

"Well, goodbye then, Mr Drummond."

"Bye, Mr MacGillivary."

Sandra gave him a funny look as he buzzed back into reception—"Sorry, I can't stay for that coffee, it was wonderful working with you and I'm so sorry it ended in these circumstances"—and out the door.

He managed to control himself until he was through the gates of Glasgow Green, then he started running. Not even in the direction of home.

29

MacGillivary had decades behind him as a defence lawyer. He could smell guilt a mile off, and that boy was wearing the scent like it was CK One and he was off to the dancing.

He went into his office, to the computer first: screen saver. He tapped the keyboard and the login screen showed. He tried his desk drawers, but they were all still locked, as he'd left them, as he always did.

He slumped into his office chair. Maybe he was just being paranoid. Drummond was just a lad, after all. Barely more than a schoolboy, really, here for something to stick on his CV. "Spent the summer fetching coffee for so-and-so..." He may have taken a liking to Carter—a lot of people did, including himself, once upon a time—but surely he couldn't have been involved in—

His eyes caught on the bookshelf... something not quite right... His own contribution to it was sitting ever so slightly proud of the rest.

30

"I did something a little stupid." He looked a little proud.

"A great start to any conversation. How stupid?" McCoist could feel that special tingling in her gut she got when things were going bad—or maybe it was the beginning of an ulcer.

"Remember you warned me not to break into any more places?"

"Aw, what the fuck, Tim?" He would only agree to meet in a public place, so she couldn't choke him. There were kids everywhere in the park, cycling on the path, kicking a ball about in the shadow of the Hope Sculpture, the blank figure atop the towering plinth reaching out to embrace the city. She'd brought Bruce to give herself a plausible reason to be there, and the dog was bounding around, chasing smells and bees, tail thrashing, fully recovered, the happiest being on the cratered face of the fucking planet. ("He's friendly," Tim had commented upon meeting the dug, who immediately jumped up, licked his face, then attempted to make sweet, sweet love to his leg.)

"Well, there wasn't really much breaking this time—"

"Or last time."

"Fair enough. The door was open."

"What door?"

"The one to MacGillivary's office." He smiled. He actually smiled.

"Bruce," McCoist commanded, "sick im!" Bruce ignored her, continued to snoover around for some decent fox crap to wear. "Christ, do you know how much trouble you'd be in if you got caught?"

"What about you? Would you be in trouble?" He was trying very hard to be tough, but McCoist had met plenty of tough guys and Tim Drummond wasn't one of them. There was something gentle at the core of him that couldn't be hidden. McCoist felt sorry for what was happening to him. She remembered seeing Bruce for the first time, a little pup in a cage of too many others, all of them keening and hungry and filthy. Hapless victims of bad human business. She couldn't bring herself to be too harsh with him.

"Don't you worry about me. Well, tell me what you found then. That letter from Davey Burnet with a nice bow on it would be good."

"Sorry, not quite." He hesitated, and she could see again the battle playing out inside his mind. If he really was going to be a lawyer then anything court-facing was probably not for him.

"Come on. You were the one who called me. Meet face to face, not over the phone. What have you got?"

He watched Bruce playing on the grass, carefree and silly. "There were a couple of notes tucked away in a textbook—one MacGillivary co-authored. Not his handwriting, the initials PLU were on it. I think they were about Mr Lennox, like, they were angry with him about something. Whatever he was doing."

"Whatever he was doing with you?"

"Um, yeah, maybe."

"Did you take pictures of them?"

"No time."

"Christ, you didn't remove them from the office, did you?"

"No, no. I put them back when I heard him come in."

"He caught you?! Fucking h—"

"No. It was close, but no."

"You're sure?"

"Yeah, sure." He wasn't sure, she could tell. *Fuck.*

"What did the notes say, try to remember as best you can." McCoist was all nervous prickles, synapses crackling, looking for something to pounce on.

"One was… like, asking for help. Legal help, I think. The writer said he was 'in a fix' and might need MacGillivary's services."

"Was it addressed to MacGillivary? Did it have his name on it anywhere?"

"No, it was just a note. Like something passed in class."

"The other one?"

"Said it was more than just him in trouble: 'a target on the lot of us'. Wanted MacGillivary to do something about it. Signed off with some Latin."

"Fucking posh boys. What did it say?"

"'Yours *in extremis.*' It means—"

"I think I get it, thanks… They were plotting to kill Lennox if they couldn't get him to stop his investigation?" McCoist mused out loud. "And there were definitely no names on it?"

"No, just the initials PLU on the other side again."

"Right…"

"What do you think?"

"I think it has potential but plenty of deniability. I think if we can get a warrant to get his office searched properly—by the polis and not Tintin here—we might be in business."

"You won't tell anyone what I did though?" Panic made him look even younger. First she saw Bruce the pup in him, now she felt she was looking at Cam, in a flap because he'd forgotten about some piece of homework he had to hand in that day.

"No. I won't. I'll work something out. Go home and keep the heed down."

He took a deep, shuddering breath of the braw summer morning, gathering himself. He shouldn't be here, shouldn't be involved at all, McCoist thought, with a mixture of pity and shame. "Tintin?" he smiled.

"Timtim, if you prefer. And listen, I'm only going to say this one more time: for the love of the Almighty's Great Tits, *Please. Stop. Breaking. Into. Places.*"

The smile widened. It was infuriating. Bruce came over to him again for a clap and a lick. "You religious?"

"No, but I grew up going to Sunday school. Once you learn to blaspheme it's hard to stop."

31

It was just the obnoxious, exploding pop of a boy racer's fire-spitting engine as his choad-mobile ripped past her on the road, but it made her soul jump right out of her body. Her fingers choked the steering wheel, rigid and white. She slammed the clutch and brake. Horns blared behind her. She couldn't see—blood in her eyes. Whistling in her ears, the reverberation of the gunshot bouncing off stone walls, smell of soap and dead fireworks. Blood and dead bodies. The black hole in the head—the one facing her—was almost neat. Especially compared to the one on the far side of the skull, which yawned open and let all the yolk out.

Horns again.

The walls of the car wash receded, opened, disappeared, revealing the road in front of her. Cars, pedestrians, traffic lights, the bright sun making her squint. Her car smelt of Bruce, the spent gunpowder wafted away.

Still shaking, she apologised with a raised hand to the car behind and pulled away.

By the time she reached London Road she'd crushed the experience under the hydraulic press of denial. Everything was fine.

"Interesting news from the water cooler, gaffer," Khan said, already at work and two coffees deep judging by the chirpiness in her voice and fizzy edge to her bearing.

"Aye?"

"Pal of mine got a misper report through on a lawyer called Ross Brownlee. Known to have been a longtime associate of—"

"The McGuinns." She'd spoken to him only recently, in Lottie McGuinn's kitchen, waving his dick about—as was his occupation and pleasure. "He's missing? Since when?"

"A few days. Wife said he went to the pub Friday night and never came home."

"SOP?"

"Uh... Standard Operating Procedure?"

"Still Oot Pished."

Khan laughed. "That's what my pal told her, but he knows I'm working for you and thought we might want to know before they step it up. There's still no sign of him. And considering who he rubs shoulders with..."

"Hmm. Let's go speak to the wife."

"Are we allowed?"

"Well, we've got one dead lawyer who defends criminals, now we maybe have another. The link's good enough for me." Not to mention all the stuff she knew about Lennox tying him to McGuinn and the Car Wash Catastrophe which she couldn't share. "Coffee to go."

"I'll nip to the loo first."

The house was on Orchard Drive in Giffnock, one among a row of century-old sandstone villas with up-to-the minute SUVs parked outside, protected from the street by black iron railings and neat box hedges. Clean, green and affluent. Enough to make you sick. A lot of them were no longer homes, repurposed for business use as private healthcare clinics, dentists' surgeries, nurseries, solicitors' offices... Brownlee's was both.

"Mrs Brownlee? I'm DCI Alison McCoist, this is DC Khan." They held their cards out for the woman to squint at—she adjusted the distance between her specs and her eyes to try to get them in focus, but to no avail. Late fifties, she kept herself looking young—she had the money—but the work of the spa and stylist was slowly being undone by the amount of time she must spend in the sun, her skin turning to pork crackling.

"Is there any news?" Not urgent, not desperate to hear anything. There was a lack of tone or feeling to her words that hinted at tranquillisers. Who could blame her? She might have been up all weekend, sick with worry.

"I'm afraid there's nothing yet, Mrs Brownlee. I just wanted to go over the report you made, make sure we have as much information as possible. Can we come in?"

She looked between them again, slow, searching. (A wee glass of something as well, to wash the Vallies down?) It gave McCoist the feeling of being see-through, not quite solid. Creepy. "I thought... the man on the phone said he was probably just out. Drinking or something."

"Is that the kind of thing your husband does often? Goes out for a few nights at a time? Doesn't call?" McCoist found herself speaking loudly, over-enunciating, the voice she used when talking to her demented aunt.

"Hmm. I don't... That's what they said."

"Who? You mean the police?"

"Yeah. The policeman I spoke to. He said not to worry." She didn't seem worried, but she was not at all *right*.

"But you've still not heard from him?... And it's been how many days now?"

"Uh, three?"

"Can we come in, Mrs Brownlee?"

"You said you had no news." She was already turning away, closing the door.

"Yes, but we'd like to go over everything so far—"

"I already told him!" she snapped, a sudden burst of lucidity in her eyes, a rage cutting through whatever was keeping her Chill Bill. Then it was gone and she went soft and mushy again, personality like a plate of mince 'n' tatties. "I told him everything on the phone. It's not changed. Nothing to worry about, he says to me."

"Mrs Brownlee—"

She shut the door.

McCoist and Khan shared a look. "That was a bit sus, right?" Khan said.

"Wrong. It was very sus."

An alarm started beeping from behind them, a crunch of tyres on gravel—a van backing into the driveway.

"What the actual fuck?" McCoist whispered to herself when she saw the decal on the side of the van:

SIMPLY SHRED

"Wrong again," Khan muttered. "Extremely sus."

Stuart "Chuck" Gardner hopped down from the driver's seat, clocked the detectives and made a face like he was about to drop an ostrich egg out his hole.

"What are you doing here, Mr Gardner?" McCoist asked. Back straight, chin up, face chiselled from stone, the entirety of her a living, breathing expression of *don't-fuck-with-me.*

Gardner's forehead was shiny, his cheeks red, and it had nothing to do with the summer sun or the fucked-climate temperature. "Goat a joab tae dae."

"In Ross Brownlee's office?"

"Eh, aye."

"To do what exactly?"

He tapped the side of the van, where the sign said: SECURE DOCUMENT DESTRUCTION. "The usual."

"When were you hired?"

He made out as if he was recalling something, poor performance. "Bin in the diary fir a few weeks." Lying bastard.

"That so. Is Mr Brownlee a regular customer?"

"Here, a don't hink a can be tellin ye stuff like that waeoot seein some paperwork, right?"

"Why so defensive, Chuck?"

His boots crunched the gravel as he shifted around for steadier footing. "Wit? Naw, am no, it's no like that. No at aw, yer bein unfair, that's wit." He'd mustered some anger, got over being caught off guard. "This is ma joab. Ma business. *Ma livelihood.* Wit happens if a fuck up an gee oot information am no legally sposed tae?" He stuck his tongue out and sprayed a wet farting noise at them. "Am done, finished, finito, fuckt. There's proper ways tae dae hings, an yous know it, so don't act like am the wan bein unreasonable."

McCoist gave him a slight, begrudging nod that said, "Fair enough." He was, indeed, right.

"So, are ye arrestin me or can a get oan wae it?"

"Big job is it? Gonna be grafting all day?"

He snorted. "Yer a chancer, Ally McCoist. No unlike yer namesake. Ye need tae learn tae play fair."

"DCI Ally McCoist, if you must."

He huffed away to knock the door.

"Wait. What happened to your head?"

Gardner had a butterfly stitch over a small wound on his forehead, a hint of puckered bruising around it. He put his fingers to it, as if he didn't know it was there. "Paper jam," he said. "A wis usin a broom handle tae try an dislodge it an the machine snatched the broom aff me. Big splinters came firin oot an wan goat me."

"Lucky it missed your eye."

"Wis wearin ma goggles, if yer hopin tae catch me oan some PPE violation or witever."

McCoist and Khan got back in the car, did not turn the engine on. She called Slater at London Road and explained the situation. "Get me a fucking warrant before he shreds everything in that dodgy cunt's office."

32

They watched Chuck carry bundles of papers and folders out the front door and into the van.

"Like holding a winning lottery ticket over a candle," Khan grumbled.

He hadn't been out with any computer equipment yet, which was something to hold on to, hope he was leaving it till last.

McCoist checked her phone by the minute for any messages. "Reminds me of when I first got my dog, Bruce. It was early days and he'd howl every time I left the house. It was horrible for both of us, so I decided to put a nanny cam in so I could check on him while I was at work. Throughout the day I kept going on the app to peek, watching as he shat all over the kitchen, tipped his food and water bowls onto the floor, nibbled all the skirting boards, pished on the doormat, broke into the cupboard and tore into the tatties and carrots, ripped up packets of pasta and rice… And I couldn't do anything cause I was stuck at the office. Sat there like a plum watching him wreak utter destruction on my home."

"What did you do?"

"When I got back I cleaned up the mess, and the same the day after and the day after. But I never used the nanny cam again."

The phone rang.

"DCI McCoist speaking."

"Hello detective…" A familiar voice. Shite. "This is Sheriff Cresswell." Didn't mean it was bad news though, just that the request had been put in front of him again: there were only so many powdered wigs in Glasgow, it wasn't an unlikely event. And if he was calling, it was probably to give the go-ahead—"I think you know what I'm going to say about this request."

"Sorry?"

"I thought we'd covered this last time."

She sank back into the chair, pressed into the headrest and closed her eyes, bracing.

Denied. Again. And once more accompanied by a preening, condescending, bollock-clacking rebuke. "I've a mind to take this to your superintendent if any more half-baked warrant requests cross my desk, do you understand?"

"Fuck!" She tossed her phone into the pocket in front of the gearstick (having made doubly sure to hang up first).

Khan sat stiff in the driver's seat, trying not to notice her boss having a mini meltdown. Her eyes were left to dwell on Chuck, still cheerfully tossing away mountains of potential evidence, feeding it to his van.

"Let's go, I can't watch any more of this," McCoist said, kneading her temples, headache brewing.

She picked up her phone and called Slater again. "Spiked."

"I know, I got an email from the fiscal. Sounds like it caught them off guard too."

"Did he give them an earful or was it just me who got the lecture?"

"Our favourite sheriff again?"

"Yours maybe. Mine is Alan Rickman in *Robin Hood: Prince of Thieves.*"

"Never seen it. Can't stand Robin Hood. Who the fuck does he think he is? Robbing the rich to give to the poor?

Aye, that'll be right, his whole charitable organisation stinks of tax write-off."

McCoist laughed in spite of the gloomy sickness she was feeling. "If you've not seen the Costner film I'm assuming you're talking about the cartoon fox?"

"Going around pretending to be blind? He's a sick bastard."

"I think you're jealous of his good looks and charisma."

"Good looks and charisma? Listen to yourself. He has fleas and eats out of bins!"

McCoist snorted, then became painfully aware of Khan stealing glances at her. Prayed her cheeks weren't literally turning red. "We're on our way back."

"OK, well, if you fancy stopping by the Greggs for a box of doughnuts on the way, there has been some good news at least: Caruso is finished with the van and she's got some fibres and DNA she reckons belongs to our killer."

"YES!" McCoist slapped the dashboard, hung up on Slater chuckling.

Khan looked over again, expectantly.

She put on a DJ voice: "Fibres & DNA—'In the Back of the Van'," then turned the radio on.

There was something of Tess's cringe in the smile of the junior officer.

33

Thank fuck they'd gone. But Chuck's relief at seeing the polis drive away was short-lived. A chance to put it all right and get back to something like a normal life slipping further away and out of sight as they turned at the corner. He was a criminal now. Well, a serious one. Stealing money was one thing, and dealing in protected information was another, but aiding a kidnap and murder and then covering it up were a whole new league. With bigger stakes to match. There would be no taking into consideration of his wee gambling problem for this. If he was caught it meant jail, if he confessed it meant jail and, likely, a painful death.

He humped another armful of ancient, mothy folders into the van and dumped them down the shredder. The van was haunted. Chuck could still smell what had happened—finely grated human matter, blood and shite and all manner of effluvium, the eye-stinging chemical reek of bleach doing its best to cover the sins and failing. Every time he had to look at the rolling steel cylinders and their relentless blades he could see Brownlee's head wedged in there, the rest of the body hanging out, muscles in spasm.

Chased out, he took a breath of fresh, untainted air and tramped back inside to the office which took up a couple of large sitting rooms in one side of the house. He could hear Mrs Brownlee's uneven steps creaking around upstairs, which didn't help his feeling of being stalked by spirits. Even in her drugged state, he couldn't bring himself to look Brownlee's widow in the eye. She was only unofficially a widow though. If all went to plan and the buckets containing him (what was left of him—a sloppy goo fit only for being made into Big Macs) were never found, it would be seven years before she could get her husband declared dead and claim her title.

Chuck took the next drawer and emptied it out onto the floor. He sifted through, scanning for anything potentially useful for Jamieson. *Yer wae us noo.* He had no need to be clandestine—the missus knew the score and was well warned, and well cooked on a combo of over-the-counters and white wine—and Brownlee was a potential gold mine of information, so he took his time. He would be taking the PC on the desk and any other laptops, memory sticks and electronics whole to the Firestane office.

The debts were gone but the work continued. Jamieson had better leverage now.

More precisely, those particular debts were gone. Chuck had since created whole new ones. Because escape was the only viable option, and for that he'd need money. He'd worry about trying to convince Bell again when he had enough—it would certainly help his case.

He'd gone to two lenders, one in Bellshill, one in Possil. "Lender" was euphemistic, they were loan sharks. "Loan shark" was euphemistic, they were hardened criminals who'd smash their own grannies' false teeth in for forgetting to put a score into their birthday cards. Sharks were nowhere near as dangerous. But nobody legitimate would be willing to lend Chuck a wee bawbee, never mind enough cash to execute a getaway. He'd already made some plans on where to place his bets.

He'd already lost some money playing online poker. It was fine though, he'd get it back. Just had to move fast. The interest was steep, steep like a sheer cliff wall, and every day he hadn't paid the money back he owed even more. Didn't matter. He knew what he was doing. Even if he had to give them half his winnings, the remainder would be enough for a fresh start.

And, tipping another sheaf of paperwork into the hopper and down the churning steel maw of the shredder which had only days ago ground a man into slurry, he really fucking needed a fresh start.

34

"We're still payin fir that west-end flat, are we no?"

Ari made a face. It was slappable, Lottie thought. She'd never smacked her kids, not even a quick skelp on the arse the way her own maw and da used to when she was a wean. Now Ari was legally an adult, was it more acceptable or less?

"It's got damp."

"So clean it."

"Mhari could've done it if you hadn't fired her," she pouted.

"Geez peace. And no, she widnae huv. It's *your* gaff, it's *your* responsibility."

"Oh, it's *my* gaff, so *my* name's going on the title deed then, is it?"

"Eee-nough, ye greedy little witch!" The words tore out of Lottie's throat, bounced on the parquet floor of the hall, rattled the wood panelling and carried up to the high, high ceiling. Ari looked like she really had been slapped. "Wit would yer faither hink if he could hear ye noo?! He—"

The doorbell rang.

Lottie swallowed the rest of the tirade, breathing hard, digging her nails into her palms. Ari looked like she was about to greet, bottom lip so petted she could trip over it; the years fell off her. Gemma appeared at the top of the stairs. "The door," she squeaked.

Lottie turned to the screen by the front door, hooked up to the new camera and lock which had been installed after the break-in. The flattering fisheye-warped image of DCI McCoist filled it. "Fuck," she breathed. She whispered "polis" to Ari, who begrudgingly headed for the stairs and her sister.

"Good evening, Mrs McGuinn," the detective said, close to neutral but grinding the gears a little.

"Wit ye here fir noo? It's no a good time."

"Can I come in?" A polis never answers questions, only asks. "Better inside than having me here on your porch. The neighbours got enough of a spectacle last time, no?"

Lottie opened the door but didn't step completely out of the way, so the detective had to squeeze past just a little, feel her presence, her stature. The detective pretended to admire the hall as if she had never been there before, taking in the moulded ceiling, the chandelier, even the bloody ridiculous golden-knob puma statue. Her eyes rested on the staircase, as if she could still see the trail of steam piping off Ari as she went up them. "Teenage girls," she said, an obvious attempt at both letting Lottie know she'd been overheard losing her shit and creating a rapport, but there was a streak of genuine understanding there too. More communal commiseration than sympathy. "You know, some animals just eat their young before they reach maturity. Sometimes I think they've got the whole parenting thing figured out."

"Fuckin tell us aboot it." Whether it was being wrong-footed, doorstepped, or because she was not quite herself, still on the comedown from the not-quite-peak of her rage, the summit snatched away, she almost smiled. *Fuck ye daein makin nice wae this useless coo who locked Colin up?* she berated herself, stoking the fire again. "Wit ye daein here, then? Is it aboot the brek-in? Cause av heard fuck aw fae DS Fannybaws since he wis roon here drinkin ma coffee and stuffin his gub wae ma bickies."

"It's not, sorry. DS Jarvis probably has a lot on his plate—"

"Aye he does, four fuckin Jammie Dodgers he helped himsel tae." Lottie noticed a smile play on the detective's lips.

"I'll give him a nudge."

"A nudge willnae dae it, stick the elbow right in."

Another tiny flicker of a smile.

"This is about Ross Brownlee."

Icy tingles tickled her inside and out, springing the fine hairs on her skin, which rippled like waves across her body. Fuck, had the polis found out about his embezzlement? The last thing she wanted was them using it as an excuse to get a look at her accounts. "Wit aboot him?"

"He's missing." She could feel McCoist's eyes on her as she said the words, trying to read her like some hen-party psychic.

"Wit?" A cold fist squeezed her heart, pumping it too hard, making her giddy.

"Went out on Friday night and never came home."

"Yer kiddin…" *Wit in the actual fuck?! Missin?! No, no, no.* Her mind raced. Jamieson said he would just have a quiet word. There was no reason to go further. She didn't want that, hadn't asked for that—maybe it was unrelated. Did he do himself in? Was he that upset about what happened? She didn't think so. Who else though? Callaghan? Maybe he approached him after Lottie binned him and something happened between them… Aye, that was a possibility. Like Luce said, these were volatile times, nobody knew who to trust, misunderstandings would escalate easily. She gave herself a mental shake, like a dog after a swim.

"You've not heard from him over the weekend?"

"Naw. Huvnae spoken tae him since durin the week."

"And how did he seem?"

"Fine. Look, wit is this? Ye shouldnae be comin roon askin me questions waeoot a lawyer here."

"You're not being interviewed under caution, Lottie."

"It's 'Lottie' noo, is it?"

Tight smile. "He's worked with your family a long time, I just thought you'd want to know. And you might be able to help find him, give us a steer."

"Well a cannae. Av nae idea wit he does wae his weekends. Ask his missus."

"We did. And, you know, it's the funniest thing. When she filed the report, she was very anxious and insistent. Understandably worried. She made a few calls to press the issue over the weekend. But when I dropped by today it was like she was suddenly reluctant to speak. It was like she was trying to avoid me."

"So?…" A response straight from the mouths of her daughters.

"What d'you think of that? Why has she suddenly lost interest in finding her husband?"

"Ask her. A never met Molly, evryhin a know aboot her's came fae Ross."

"And what do you know?"

"A dunno, she likes fuckin *Game ae Thrones*. Wit, ye want me tae gee ye her star sign an ye can divine whether she's affed her man fae that?"

"You think she might have killed him?"

Lottie forced a laugh, which howked some burning bile up her throat. "Fucksake, course no. Is humour ootside yer jurisdiction?"

Another little smile—not placatory, smug. Ari's wasn't the only face she wanted to slap tonight. Giving DCI McCoist a face-five would definitely make her happy though.

"Look, a know wit this is. Don't mistake me fir some fuckin bimbo. Yer fishin, come tae check oot ma reaction. Well here it is: am shocked. A dunno wit's happened tae Ross. He's bin a good friend tae me an mine an a want him tae turn up awright. So why don't ye get the fuck oot ma hoose an dae yer fuckin joab fir wance."

She held her hands up. "I've never thought you were stupid, Lottie. It's funny you mentioned offing husbands... There were a few wild theories flying around that you might have done something similar."

"AW PISS OFF!" There was the peak, the top blown right off, enough burning rage to bury Glesga like it was Pompeii. Her hand flew through the air, open palm, rings flashing silver, completely out of her control.

McCoist slipped back, a boxer's dodge, lithe little fucker. Lottie's hand sailed past, tips of her nails just missing the detective's nose.

The fuck huv ye just done?! Fuck! Fuckin hell! Lottie was breathing hard, simmering down, trying to pull all the exploded parts of herself back together, get a handle on it. *Just tried tae slap a fuckin polis, wit the fuck ye daein?!* It hadn't made her happy after all—maybe if she'd actually made contact...

McCoist stared, stupid disbelief on her face which slowly, slowly twisted into something like a sardonic smile. "I'll get out of your hair, then," she said and went to the door. Her hand on the handle, she turned back. "I always find a takeaway and a hot chocolate helps mend the bridge." She motioned to the staircase.

"Good idea," Lottie rasped, starting to shiver.

There was a night out at a new club—about a year into her relationship with Paulo. The owner had invited Paulo and his friends, and they were treated to a private booth with bottles of Grey Goose in ice buckets and a velvet rope separating them from the proles on the dance floor. Lottie and Ginny were on their way back from powdering their noses (literally) when they saw Paulo arguing with the owner in their booth. Paulo was stabbing his finger against the guy's chest. The guy tried to look away, but Paulo slapped him, made him turn back to face him. The guy left the table in tears.

Lottie forgot about it until a few days later when the night-club burned down.

She understood. And she told herself it didn't matter. Because she was young and life was wild and exciting. The present was everything, the future held no fear and the past was dead and buried. She didn't think, what if Paulo ends up in jail? Or, what if he gets killed? Will he ever hurt me the way he hurts other people?

She could choke those worries out with holidays and good times, drink and drugs, sun and sex, nice clothes, a fancy flat above George Square. Her mum worried, of course she did, but she was also partial to the spa and a shopping spree. There was money and there was love. And when eventually there wasn't love, there was still money. And the kids came along and grew up and Lottie had this life she never expected and wasn't sure she'd ever wanted.

Not that she didn't love the girls—hard as it was sometimes—but constantly staying in the present, on to the next thing and the next without looking forwards or backwards, meant that when she finally did take stock, she had no idea where she was or how she'd got there. It was like she was living somebody else's life. Wife to a dangerous criminal, mother to his children. Complicit in unspeakable things, there was no hiding from that. Every time she tapped her bank card she aided, abetted, approved. Every time she came back to her house and felt that soothing rush of home, like stepping into a warm bath, revelling in the pleasure of the space she'd created for herself, she signed off on everything Paulo had done to make it possible. People had suffered for her parquet floor and her Christian Lacroix wallpaper, the claw-foot tubs and the home gym, the cinema room and sauna. The choice of Farrow & Ball over Dulux could have cost someone their life, and Lottie had picked the expensive, lush, opulent, rich option. Knowing.

Lottie sat in the office. Its tasteful and muted, calming tones, chosen to free up brain space and promote industriousness, were undermined by the embarrassing man-cave shite Paulo had accented it with: a framed football strip; an acrylic poster of Al Pacino as Serpico; a mannequin sporting a bascinet supposedly worn by Robert the Bruce (like fuck was it real—and here's Abe Lincoln's hat with the bullet hole in it); and, of course, the display cabinet of wrestling figures—his childhood favourites, heroes from what he called the "Golden Era" of the WWF. ("It's aw goan saft these days. Nae blood. Cannae even tell some cunt tae sook yer dick any mare. Shite.") She stared at the knots and imperfections in the expansive, lacquered-hardwood desk.

What if Jamieson killed Ross because of her?

She had an urge to get online and book a holiday. Pull Gemma out of school. Get Ari back onside with a luxury all-inclusive trip to Barbados, a new poolside wardrobe to go with it. Same for herself.

It passed. She had to be more careful with money now. Ross had cautioned her many times since Paulo died and the business crumbled, the seedy, secretive world of illegal trade rumbling on without him. A bigger help would have been to not steal a fortune from her. A bolt of anger for the stupid, two-faced prick passed through her like a railway spike being driven into the ground. It too passed, and she hoped, with a frothy sickness in her belly, that he'd just done a runner, taken his money and fucked off somewhere sunny. Barbados. She smiled. But she knew he was dead.

35

The Hope Sculpture was a blank child-mannequin standing atop a twenty-metre-high, six-legged plinth in the middle of the Cuningar Loop, casting a sundial shadow across the dew-wet grass. It had been built to commemorate a climate conference held in the city, the decisions of which were currently being reneged upon by those in power. Around its base, poems by the great and good of Scottish literature had been carved into the stone. Bruce and Maisie sniffed around at them, tails wagging.

"Big Jackie Kay fan is she?" McCoist said.

"Peter Kay, more like," Slater replied. "Poetry's not really our thing."

Bruce cheerfully cocked his leg and pished up one of the monument's legs. "Bruce! For God's sake, there's a whole field of grass right here, trees and benches and bins everywhere, and you've got to desecrate a bloody art installation." His tongue stuck out, panting, made him look like he was smiling.

"Look how proud of himself he is."

"He has to be proud of himself, nobody else is. I'm worried he'll lead Maisie astray."

"Nah, she can misbehave with the best of them."

The dogs bounded off across the grass, chasing each other and tumbling, the occasional excited bark. McCoist and Slater had finally made it out to the park with the dogs. McCoist had suggested the Loop after going there with Tim. It was a nice place, and it would be a good idea for McCoist to make it a regular haunt in case anybody had seen her there before. *I'm there all the time with the dug, Your Honour.*

They were the only ones about, meeting early doors before work. The open sky gave a slight chill but promised a hot day ahead. Slater had brought a couple of coffees with him. "From the twenty-four-hour Starbucks, so probably not as bad as you like it, but it's the best I could do at this time of the morning."

"Thanks anyway."

They began with a bit of work chat, discussing the missing Ross Brownlee and how it might fit in with the dead and feasted-upon Carter Lennox. She mentioned she'd been over to the McGuinn estate and scoped out how the black widow took the news. Her surprise seemed genuine but McCoist couldn't afford to trust her. She almost mentioned the attempted slap but didn't. That was something private between them, something she wanted to hold on to. The fury on the woman's face followed by a shared disbelief at what had happened, what had almost happened.

They meandered into the personal. Slater asked how Tess was doing now ("Regretting her life choices but showing it by being a mardy arse") and if they had any plans or holidays ahead. "The kids are off to their gran's caravan with their dad soon—I think I mentioned it at the shitehole amazing-pie pub?"

"Oh yeah, Tyndrum, wasn't it?"

"Aye, but I've not got anything sorted myself. Maybe see about booking something last-minute when this case is over. You?"

"Same, when I can get the leave, you know?" He winked.

"You'll be lucky, I've got you rota'd in until Ragnarök."

They laughed and their eyes met, and for a second there was—

McCoist's phone rang. One of them. It was perfectly legitimate for a polis to have two phones—work and personal. Three was for dodgy cunts. She slipped phone no. 3 from her jacket pocket, hoping Slater wouldn't notice it was different from the ones he'd seen her use already (not like he'd got a close look at the make and model and they all had the same sleek minimal design these days).

Tim's number was on the screen. Foreboding coincidence. McCoist felt a lurch in her belly and tapped to hang up, slipping the phone away again.

They carried on walking in silence, following the path up and around the play park, into some trees, past some metal sculptures of deer with motorcycle wing mirrors for antlers. Her phone rang again. Tim again. Hung up.

"Do you need to take that?" Slater asked. "I can go on ahead a bit with the dogs?"

"No, it's fine—" It rang again and she thumbed the red phone icon, feeling the heat in her cheeks. "—Not important. I…"

As they rounded the corner, out of the trees and back to the main path, a sight stopped them in their tracks:

DC Khan wearing a helmet and pads, standing on a skateboard, holding on to DC Travis as he walked crabwise, rolling her along the path.

"What is going on here?" Slater asked.

They looked up and sprang apart, Khan nearly falling over as she dismounted the skateboard. Each of them took a beamer, as if they'd been caught shagging in a cupboard at the office Christmas party.

"Sir. Ma'am," Gaz nodded to each of them with a silly grin.

"Gaz is teaching me to skate," Khan said with a girlish laugh which was so unlike her usual demeanour it could have come from a completely different person.

"So I see."

"When we were out looking for that wallet, it seemed really fun and…" She motioned to her helmet and pads.

"How about you?" Gaz asked, and it was their turn to take a riddy.

"Walking the dogs," McCoist said. On time, Bruce and Maisie came to the rescue, distracting their juniors with playful demands for affection. "We should probably all get a move on."

Back in the car, McCoist listened to the voicemail Tim had left:

"I think I've maybe got something else. Not sure, just maybe. Can you look up anything you can find about a murder that happened last summer? A sex worker at one of McGuinn's places. Stabbed to death. Involved a couple of our mutual friends on the clean-up end. Call me back."

Oh she'd call him back all right. Call him back, reach through the phone and rip his lug right off for speaking about this shit over the phone. He hadn't used names at least, and apart from his request, he'd only alluded to what they were up to. Still.

She called but it was his turn to ignore it.

36

When Lottie dressed to the nines, she dressed to the tens.

She descended upon the Merchant City with the swagger and self-assurance of the tobacco lords who built the place with the suffering and misery of others—bricks of flesh, blood mortar. Lottie, their spiritual descendant, kindred destined for the circles of hell, rose up the building to the offices of Firestane Consultancy, made her entrance like the lash of a whip.

"Wit happened tae Ross?"

Marble, the chiselled slab of holy, horny vision, looked to his boss with guilty panic on his face. Jamieson's crumpled visage remained implacable. He blinked slowly, pointed to the chair opposite. "Huv a seat, Charlotte. Please."

"Wit happened?"

"There wis an accident."

"Wis there, aye? A 'quiet word' ye says tae me. How did that cause an accident?"

"A mean it. There wis an accident, he wisnae meant tae get hurt, like a says. Well, no hurt badly."

"Ye telt me ye wur just gonnae put him aff? Wit the fuck were ye daein?"

"Seat. Please." He didn't raise his voice but the words came out harder, imperious. Lottie found herself sitting down. "Get us a couple ae coffees will ye?" he said to the assistant/bodyguard/*Baywatch* hunk. They watched him leave. "The burds' knickers drap like thuv bin weighted aroon that cunt. Lads' an aw."

"Must be distractin."

Jamieson didn't laugh but he didn't look offended either. A lot of guys in his world were fragile about that kind of stuff. Even a suggestion could send them into an over-compensating fit of rage. Paulo was like that. Made sure everybody knew about all the wee lassies he was shagging. Fucking pitiful. Even more than making her angry and embarrassed, it had made Lottie ashamed to be with him. She missed him.

"Look, am sorry, awright? A really am. It wisnae meant tae happen, but it did, an noo we just huv tae get oan wae it." He spoke as if he were talking about a clerical error.

"So he *is* deed?" The vehemence Lottie had been channelling deserted her. Her voice came out small, the reality of it hitting her, diminishing her.

"Aye, am afraid so." The coffees arrived. "Some tissues, please, son." He turned back to Lottie, who was sniffling. "A know ye were pals. Even eftir wit he did, a understawn yer upset."

"Dae ye? Wit happened?"

"An accident, like a says. We wur askin him some questions."

"How hard were ye askin?"

"Ye know wit he wis like better than me. A tough auld cunt. A respect that. Don't make many like us any mare." Despite the words, Jamieson didn't sound world-weary or as if he were being nostalgic for pish-pots and asbestos like so many others his age. It was a flat statement of fact. Self-aggrandising but not self-satisfied. *We just huv tae get oan wae it.* A terrifying, surgical pragmatism was at his core. Cut, stitch, survive, adapt.

"Were ye askin him aboot Paulo? Ye didnae hink—he didnae huv anythin tae dae wae it? Surely tae fuck he didnae."

"Naw, naw. He wis a thief but other than that ad say he wis loyal tae yer man. We hud tae ask, but."

There was some solace in knowing Ross hadn't been involved in killing Paulo. "If he wis honest, why did ye huv tae be rough wae him?" She remembered the first time she saw Ross after she'd been told the news about Paulo. Without even a "hello" he'd pulled her in close, his gnarled, crumbling, pain-riddled hand squeezing her shoulder, his stubbled cheek resting on her head. He smelt of cigarettes and aftershave. He spoke to her with a gentle whisper. *Yer gonnae be awright, hen.*

"There wis somethin else an aw. It's no the main part ae the investigation but it is relatet."

"Aye?"

"The Shit List."

"Wit?"

Lottie could feel the shine of his eyes, buried in the fleshy, wrinkled divots of their sockets, focused laser-like on her face. Sweat prickled the small of her back. Botox stopped it visibly beading on her forehead, at least.

"Come oan, Charlotte."

"Am no follyin."

"Paulo's List. The Shit List." He did that thing with his voice again. Low, compressed, hard, pushing slow but unrelentingly firm like a car crusher.

"Repeatin it willnae help, tell me wit yer oan aboot." Her heart quickened, her toe tapped.

"Ye awready know. Paulo's Shit List. Where is it?"

"The fuck is this?" she spat out. "A came here askin ye tae find oot who did Paulo in, an so far yuv done fuck aw except kill an innocent man. Now yer geein me the fuckin inquisition?"

"Keep yer fuckin voice doon," he growled, and for the first time Lottie saw something like emotion flare in him. "Am offerin ma considerable services tae ye pro bono in respect ae Paulo's memory."

"A never asked ye tae work fir free."

"Don't be ungrateful. Where's the List?"

Lottie had to break away from his eyes, shook her head and took a shuddering breath. "A don't know wit yer meanin, a never hud anythin tae daw wae aw that."

"Naw?"

"Naw."

"Just a WAG, then, eh? A hoosewife."

He was trying to wind her up, goad her, and after the incident last night with that bitch McCoist, Lottie knew better than to let herself be riled. She clamped down hard on the part of her that wanted to reach out and choke him with his tie. Instead, she smiled: "Hoosewife isnae fair tae hoosewives, a dae fuck aw hoosework. An am no 'just' a WAG, am THEE WAG. Paulo McGuinn's WAG. An a would like some fuckin answers soon."

Jamieson sat back in his chair. Something shifted in his beady-eyed appraisal of her. "Yel get them, don't worry. Ye sure ye don't know wit am talkin aboot?"

"Sure."

"OK. If ye say so."

She stood to leave.

"Again, am sorry aboot Ross." He didn't look sorry.

37

Ginny was hyperventilating in the passenger seat. "Thuv killt him. Thuv fuckin killt him."

Lottie, driving, reached across and grabbed her hand, squeezed hard, leaning towards her but keeping her eyes on the road. "Naw. He's gonnae be OK. Listen tae me, he's gonnae be fine, yel see." Ginny was going to be the one who died if she didn't get her breath back, Lottie thought.

She put her foot down, yanked into the overtaking lane without indicating, Audi rings in her rear-view flashing their high beams at her.

The hospital loomed ahead—tall, boxy, its wings sticking out from each corner making it look like a landed Space Invader, pixels of light from its many windows, rooftop aglow. Staff called it "the Death Star". It disappeared from view as she veered left again, down the slip road.

She beeped a few cunts getting into the car park. Relatives of the sick and dying—*feel bad aboot it later*. Parked it like it was stolen. (The motor was a gift from Paulo, so there was a good chance it was.)

It wasn't that the woman behind the reception desk was unfeeling, just that she was used to people's panic, used to emergencies, used to distraught relatives and mangled bodies. She was too calm and it made Lottie want to lash out. They had to wait for a doctor to come down and take them by the hand to the ICU. It wrong-footed Lottie, made her unsure of how worried she should be. Were they not supposed to be hurrying? Were they not supposed to be in a flap? Howling? Looking ready to collapse on the floor like Ginny was? Her face so white it almost glowed under the strip lights, her scalp visible through her thinning hair. Somebody would be offering her a wheelchair next, she looked terminal.

Eventually they were escorted through the vast, bustling building, badged through sealed doors, then into a private side room off the main ICU ward, where a uniformed polis jumped up out of his seat as they entered, stuffing his phone into a pocket.

On the bed was a slab of raw meat leaking its juices into the bandages and bed sheets.

"It's no him," Ginny said at first. It was indeed difficult to make out Colin's face among the bruised flesh, the strip of tape hiding the broken nose, more across the brow which had been sliced open.

"He's alive," Lottie said. "See? A telt ye." She gave her sister a hug that could crush her into dust.

Stable for now. He'd been jumped by a group of his pals, stabbed a few times by a sharpened toothbrush handle, slashed with the lid from a tin of beans. The DIY weapons had not been sharp enough to do serious damage but the kicking he'd got was severe. He'd be bed-bound for a while, monitored and tested, watched over by Constable Clit-sack until he could be returned to the cage, the dogfights.

Ginny pulled the seat up to the bedside and laid her head on the mattress in a space next to his shoulder. The uniform looked a bit miffed he'd have to stand from now on and pretend to be watchful, as if the unconscious prisoner might leap from his bed any minute.

"Al be back soon," Lottie said, and slipped away.

She picked Luce up on a street corner in Govan and went to the nearest McDonald's drive-thru. "Want anythin?"

"Ad huv a choaclit milkshake if the machine's runnin."

Lottie got a burger for herself and a Happy Meal to take back to Ginny. Her sister didn't have the biggest appetite anyway and since Colin went to prison she only seemed to manage a handful of birdseed a day.

They parked and Lottie dug in—a good place to have a clandestine conversation in a car without seeming suspicious. The downside being her car was already now honking of fast food and the perma-fog of cigarette smoke that hung around Luce.

"Colin's in the hoaspital. Did somethin go wrang wae the green?"

"No oan ma end. If he's stepped oan some cunt's toes tryin tae deal it, that's oan him... Sorry, hen."

That was entirely possible, Lottie thought, chewing and not tasting, stuffing it in. It was Colin after all. He had less business nous than Del Boy and was more irritating. Easy to imagine him flashing it around and getting right up some cunt's nose. "A group ae them attacked him thegether. Couldae killt him easily."

"Ye hink they held back?"

"Maybe."

"A message then?"

"Maybe." Lottie finished her burger in silence. Luce slurped her milkshake down to the dregs and kept going, making a sound like a stone sucked up the hoover.

"How is Colin then?"

"Battered half tae fuck. They jumped oan his heed. Lad's no goat enough brain cells in the first place tae be daein wae that. He needs aw he's goat."

"Well, maybe that's a blessin, like, if he's goat brain damage, naebdy'll even notice."

A guilty smile. "It's ma sister though. Aw this is gonnae end her, a need him oot."

"Aye, so how is Jamieson's investigation goin?"

"Fine," Lottie said, and the pit of her stomach felt heavy with the cud of her eaten-too-quickly meal.

38

Yesterday had been a washout, may as well have just stayed in the park. The DNA found in the dumped van had no hits on the PNC. A killer with no record. The fibres were from clothing and so common even Sherlock Hames wouldn't be able to tell you which Glasgow haberdasher's they came from. She'd tried to get hold of Tim a few times while taking breaks but he hadn't picked up. Hadn't left her any more messages either. She attempted to follow up on what he'd given her without context—a young woman killed by stabbing the previous summer—but no open case file seemed to match. No body then. Plenty of misper reports that could potentially be the victim though, didn't help much. A day of deep sighs.

Today had been more of the same. CCTV trawls continued. A sighting of the van post-stolen, pre-dumped sent Khan trudging off to do some door-to-doors. *Excuse me, do you remember seeing this completely unremarkable white van out your window a week ago?* "Clutching at straws" was too optimistic a description. Pinching at pubes, more like. The priority would be slipping down soon, it was coming, and with it, McCoist's hopes of getting in front of whatever shit was out there about her. Not for the first time she cursed Davey Burnet. *Should've killed him too.* A bad joke, even for her, and the well of shame she'd filled in with cement over the past year threatened to crack open.

As she was making her millionth coffee of the day, her phone rang. The dodgy one. *Yass, fucking finally, wee man.* But it wasn't Tim.

"Bear?" Devlin, the baw-tweezing bastard.

"Speaking."

"Colin Kennedy was hospitalised last night."

"I'm surprised it took this long—cellmate must have the patience of a saint."

"Be serious."

"Yes, sir." You put him there, she reminded herself. If he does die inside it's your fault, another to add to the list.

"A group of inmates attacked him for reasons currently unknown. He'll live but he'll be taking the sea air for a while. Something to have on your radar."

"Thank you, sir."

"And the other thing, our former friend Findlay: the net's closing in. Your opportunity to speak to him will be limited, a small window, so be ready."

The call cut. "Goodbye to you too."

McCoist sat at her desk, sipping her dreadful coffee and feeling none of its usually bracing effects. Devlin's words echoed like rumbles of thunder inside the ominous grey clouds which had rolled into her head. It was too much. What she was doing. With Tim, with Devlin. She was adrift in a storm, soon to be swallowed by something. What if she'd waited at the car wash after she shot Paulo? Told Devlin to shove his offer of protection up his arse and taken her chances. Told the truth about what had happened. Faced the sack or maybe the jail. Neither a good option but honest at least. Free from the sinking pool of

Devlin's corruption, the tainted idea of justice he represented, the greater good he supposedly served by any means necessary.

Was it too late? What would happen if she exposed it all? Would the consequences be worth freeing her conscience? She thought of Tess and Cam and decided the answer was no.

Too agitated to stay put any longer, she stepped out of the office and tried Tim again. No answer. Fuck it. She made the relevant calls and got hold of his address, jumped in her motor and sped off towards the north end of town.

Tim's gaff was in a warren of low flats in Townhead, not far from Strathclyde Uni, one block of grey roughcast among many, a black eye of damp under every window, a view out to more of the same, the whole place a dreary hall of mirrors. Cars and vans were parked right up against the ground-floor windows.

No answer with Tim's buzzer. Probably out. Could be anywhere, it didn't mean anything. But her agitation, fuelled by all the coffees and the conversation with Mr Itchy Baws, crept up again. Why wouldn't he just answer the bloody phone? Now she was skulking about a seventies utopian afterbirth of modern living, The Scheme, looking for him. She tried some other buttons, got a couple of answers but as soon as they heard "polis" they stopped talking. She took a page from Tim's book with the next one: "Domino's." That did it.

Stepping into the stairwell, she was reminded of where she first met Tim, in the close at Lennox's place in the west end, all patterned tiles and wrought-iron balusters, a carved mahogany handrail polished to a shine. In comparison, this place was utilitarian, and that was the nicest thing that could be said about it.

Second floor, the door by the window overlooking the car park. She gave it a knock and waited. She could hear music coming from inside. She knocked harder, and her heart knocked harder too. Just listening to music a bit too loudly, he's a kid, that's what they do. A student. Maybe he'd decided to get back to studying and getting plastered. Being normal. She banged her fist against the door. Her palm stung. Flapped open the letter box, view clouded by its heavy lashes, and sniffed—because she couldn't help sniffing, as much as she desperately told herself she was overreacting.

And a hint of something off wafted to her nose. *Aw fuck. No. No, no, no.* She staggered back, the floor listing like a sinking ship. *Please not that.* She called Slater, shaking, gave him the address. "I need you to bring tools, need to get a door open. Right now, get here now… Please."

CRUNCH. Crumpling metal, outside.

Dashed to the window—bloke in a hat, hooded jacket too hot for summer, rolling down off the roof of a van, over its windscreen and bonnet, bad landing in a heap on the ground.

McCoist took the stairs two, three at a time, jumping the last ones to the next landing and the next until she was wrenching the front door open, sprinting out into the car park, past the van.

There he was straight ahead: limping with his left, right doing the work, like he was in a three-legged race with the invisible man. Even hobbled he was moving at a decent speed.

McCoist pumped her arms and legs, her throat and chest burned like she was sooking on an exhaust pipe.

He took a turn, into the warren, another car park, out of sight.

Not for long though. McCoist kept pushing. She rounded the corner, saw him bolting across a small, overgrown park, where she lost him again among trees and hedges.

She crashed through the bushes and onto a path.

No sign.

She followed the path at a jog to a small playground, where a group of young mums were pushing their wee ones on swings, lifting them onto the slides. Primary-school-aged kids had the roundabout going like a NASA centrifuge for G-force training, seeing who could hold on the longest. When they saw McCoist appear, red-faced and panting, they pointed over the fence and into more hedges, the high-rises beyond.

She was off again. Lunged over the fence, through the bushes and trees, out to the green on the other side. There he was: glimpse of hat and jacket in the car park by the nearest high-rise, which was shrouded in scaffold, skips and Heras fencing and warning signs at its foot. Flashing neon invitations for bored, poor kids in the summer.

He was fast but dragging now. Injured and overheating in his unsuitable clobber. McCoist would outlast him, all she had to do was keep going.

Into the car park.

Where was he?

Motherfucker, he was right... where? He—

A flash in the eyes before the pain registered. The sense of falling was slow, like she was removed from her body, and she could feel the pavement against her shoulder before it had fully stopped, like there was a delay in certain senses. Pain bloomed at the top of her skull, a headache pouring down like falling rain inside her head. She closed her eyes. Screamed. Curled up and put her hands to her head. Sharp jolt as her fingertips brushed the tender egg of swollen, bruised flesh, ragged cut at its epicentre, the pain leaching out from it in nauseous waves.

She dragged herself upright, brushing brick dust and tears from her face.

He was gone.

39

By the time she got back to the flat, Slater and Travis were waiting for her outside, tooled up, and the paramedics were en route. Every car, bicycle and foot soldier in the vicinity was scrambling to form a cordon around the area with more bodies inbound, blue lights all the way.

"What's happened?" Slater touched her shoulder.

She'd been hit over the head with a brick, she thought. They could see the dust on her too-pale face, a spaced look in her eyes, but the blood was hidden by her hair. "Come on." She took them up to the second floor. "This one."

"Who—"

"After. Just get it open."

Slater wedged the crowbar into the jamb by the lock. Travis took a great swing at it with the sledge.

Bang.

Bang.

Bang.

A couple of neighbours had opened their doors. McCoist held up her warrant card but it didn't shoo them away.

Bang.

Bang.

The door was jumping in its frame but not giving. Not yet.

"The cavalry'll be here with a proper ram soon enough, why—"

"He might be hurt, we can't wait," McCoist answered, voice cutting.

Bang.

Neighbours were coming up from downstairs and down from up now.

Bang.

"Put yer back intae it, lad!" Slater yelled.

Travis swung the sledge right back, like he was holding a rounders bat, then hurled it forwards.

"*AAAaaargghhyefuckinbastaaart!*" Slater dropped the crowbar, cupped his right hand in his left. Blood was dripping through his fingers and weeping down his wrist.

"Oh shite, sorry gaffer. I'm so, so sorry, I didn't mean to."

The assembled audience finished gasping, began snickering and gossiping, phones started to record. Somebody brought a tea towel and gave it to McCoist. "Fucksake. Wrap this round it. Paramedics will be here soon at least."

Slater had taken on a Kermit hue. McCoist worried it was even worse than she'd thought and regretted being flippant, but her head was killing her, her stress levels were higher than the Burj Khalifa, and now she was dragged into a Three Stooges skit when she needed, desperately, to be on the other side of that door.

"It's fine, it's fine. Just, not so good with blood, that's all. Makes me feel…" He was swallowing hard, fighting the whitey.

"Sit down." He slumped to the floor.

McCoist picked up the crowbar, now slick with Slater's blood. She jammed it into the frame. "DC Travis, I'm going to count to three and you are going to pan this fucking door right in. If you don't, you'll be getting a shiny new company car with bells and whistles on top, do you understand?"

"Ma'am."

"One. Two. THREE!"

Smash.

The lock tore through the wood of the frame, sending the door crashing inwards, the inside handle driving into the wall and eating a chunk of plaster. DCI McCoist had a lucrative post-retirement career as a motivational speaker ahead of her. If she ever made it that far.

"TIM!" The smell was stronger. Bad ham. "TIM!" Bad drainage.

Music pulsed, a thumping dance beat, vocals a mid-orgasm groaning over the top.

The flat was poky: living room with a telly sat on the sloping shoulders of a third-hand Ikea unit; your gran's couch, buckled in the middle; a music stand folded back on itself like a broken wrist serving as a tea tray; stereo and speakers, the most expensive things there; kitchen along the back wall with a rusted electric hob; bedroom a swamp of clothes, curtains pulled shut, bed somewhere under the gloom and air-thick damp...

A length of extension cord ran from the living room into...

The bathroom, avocado suite...

He was in the tub. Water was running from the shower head somewhere under him. Work had already begun on taking him apart. Legs gone to the knees. Presumably, the shins, ankles, feet and toes were in the heavy-duty rubble sacks on the floor. The rest of the roll was waiting to be filled. A power saw was plugged into the extension reel. The blade was in need of a toothpick.

Tim's face was turned away from her.

40

McCoist couldn't remember much after that, except for Slater's hands on her shoulders, bleeding on her, lifting her off her knees, dragging her out the door as she wailed.

Next thing she was in his car, the Soviet blocks of Townhead replaced by ancient stone, the Bridge of Sighs overhead, leading into the necropolis, the back garden of the black-and-verdigris medieval cathedral, where Slater had parked. Old, old Glesga. He reached out and she pushed her face into his shoulder, closed her eyes, tried to let the smell of his aftershave and cheap washing powder clear out the butcher's-shop stink of the bathroom and what was in it.

She wasn't sure how long they sat like that for but the tears had stopped and the mania had gone, gutting her out, leaving her hollow, numb.

"There's a nasty cut on top of your head," Slater said. "We should get it seen to."

"What about your hand?"

"Can't be fucked with the paperwork, I'll go to minor injuries tomorrow morning if it looks bad, tell them I was doing some DIY or something. Off the job."

"I'll keep your secret if you keep mine."

"Speaking of which, what were you doing there? On your own too. Did you think our man would be there?"

She pulled away from him, studied her shoes, scared if she looked him in the eye right at that moment she would tell him

223

everything. *I killed Paulo McGuinn. I covered it up. The evidence is out there and the person most likely to lead me to it is now in pieces.* "I don't know, I guess, in the back of my mind, I..." The headache was coming back for round two. "No, that's not right. I was scared something had happened to him. I was scared, so I went round there, but I didn't expect..."

"'Him', you mean the lad in the bath? Who was he?" His voice was soft. Interrogation-of-vulnerable-witnesses soft. No. That was unfair. He was concerned. Worried for her. Genuine human reaction, not textbook tactics.

"Tim Drummond. He was working with Lennox."

"Oh, the intern. What? Why would anyone... I thought we hadn't heard from him?"

The headache, the shock, maybe the brick to the head, whatever it was, something was keeping McCoist from feeling the guilt and grief and she was thankful. Thankful and sore. "He contacted me. Wouldn't go on record so I kept it to myself, thought if I played it well then maybe, down the line..."

"What did he have to say?"

Tim was facing away from her, his head lolling against the tub. She couldn't bring herself to look. The memory of his boyish face, marred by worry and bad sleep, his too-naive smile urging her to feel something. Not more than a boy. Nineteen, twenty. Alone.

"Come on, Alison. They killed his boss and now they've killed him. What was it he knew that was worth that? You can't keep him off the record any more. There are SOCOs up there in the flat right now, there's a dragnet out for this bloke who jumped out the window and brained you, we've got a platoon of uniforms doing door-to-door—you know how many fucking doors there are in just a couple of streets in that neighbour-hood?—and DC Singing Kettle is at the park questioning a bunch of seven-year-olds to find out if they saw anything."

McCoist cracked a smile. "I don't think the Singing Kettle are a thing any more."

"Showing my age," he smiled. "Please, tell me. I can help. I want to help you. Trust me."

"Have you got cold hands?"

"Sorry?"

"Cold hands." She took his left hand—uninjured but stained with dry blood—and placed the palm against her forehead, closed her eyes to the slight, cool relief it brought her. "Lennox was in possession of a file, a written record which contained dirt on someone, several someones actually, and one of them took the initiative and silenced him. That was Tim's theory."

"A written record? Would someone really kill over that? Evidentially, it's—"

"Two people are dead, so."

"Yeah, sorry, right. And Tim had this file?"

"His killer certainly thought so. But no. Or so he said."

"You believed him?"

"Like you said, Scenes of Crime are up there now, so we'll find out."

"Killer might have taken it. You saw what it was like in the bathroom, the uh, *gear*... He'd been there some time, time enough to search the place."

"I believed Tim."

"OK. That's not too bad... You'll have to answer some questions but I think if you tell them all that it won't—"

"It gets worse."

"Shite. It does?"

"Tim broke into MacGillivary's office, he found something there, or thought he had. He called me—"

"At the park?"

"Uh huh, and I hung up. He left a message, and I tried to get hold of him but..." Tears burned again. "No answer. Two days, no answer. Two days, I waited and he was..."

"It's not your fault, Alison, it's not your fault."

"It is. If I'd—" Her breath shook, eyes and nose started to dribble.

"You can't think like that."

"He'd still be here if I'd done my job properly. My. Fucking. Fault."

Slater put an arm around her, pulled her in as close as he could with the handbrake and gearstick between them. She heard his voice rumble in his chest with her ear pressed against it:

"After my maw died, I was... not doing great. I should have taken more time off, but I didn't know what else to do with myself, so I came back, but I was in a state most of the time, mind only half on where I was, what I was doing. A report was given to me—DA, not the first time the victim had complained against her boyfriend. I kicked the can down the road, but it must have slipped between the cracks.

"Her name was Melanie. Just a few days later she ended up in hospital. Broken jaw, broken ribs, needed surgery on her eye. She was twenty-three weeks pregnant—it was in the report.

"When I found the boyfriend, I... I can't remember if he said something, or if it was just the bastard look on his face, but... I hit him. Over and over, couldn't stop myself, like I'd gone feral

226

or something. I gave him a doing, trying to make myself feel better, but all I did was make sure he was free to go. Because I couldn't nick him then, could I? Couldn't drag him to the cells with my knuckles bleeding and his face looking like he'd stuck his head in a wasp's nest... Told myself I was justified. That he'd deserved it, and that what I'd done would scare him enough to never hurt anyone else again, but..."

McCoist could feel Slater's breath jerking now, starting to sob. "She lost the baby."

She looked up, saw his tears, felt the heat of his face on hers.

"We're human, Alison. We fuck up."

She kissed his cheek, stubble spikes pricking her lips. He kissed her forehead, her mouth. She held tight to him.

They parted, McCoist's brain a sea of clashing emotions and chemicals. "We need to get back."

41

"A heard the bad news aboot yer nephew."

"Ye did?"

"No much gets past me, if yel pardon the professional pride. How's he daein?"

"Stable. Fir noo."

"Good, that's good. They keepin him in a while?"

"Aye."

"Well, it's no much consolation but it's good that he's oot the jail fir a bit, good fir yer sister tae be wae him, see him regularly, in a different settin."

"Eh… aye. Um, hopefully, it willnae be lang till he's oot fir real."

"Right, right. Hings are comin alang, don't worry yersel, wull get there."

"Anythin ye can tell me?"

"No oer the phone."

"Aye, course."

"A wis just wantin ye tae let yer sister know a wis askin fir young Colin, that's aw."

"Thanks, Mr Jamieson. She'll appreciate that."

"A hope he'll be awright this time." *This time.*

"Doacter says he'll make a recovery, just needs rest."

"Ach, that's good. That's good. Actually, while av goat ye, a also wantet tae ask if yev thoat any mair oan that hing a asked ye aboot last time. Noo yev hud a bit ae time tae hink oan it."

"…Like a says tae ye afore, a don't really—"

"Nothin joggin the auld memory?"

"…Eh, naw, but al put ma mind tae it, aye?"

"Cheers, doll. That wid be helpful. A sound idea."

Lottie put her phone down, her hand shaking. No doubt now. A dot-to-dot with only two points. He didn't believe her about the Shit List and the squeeze was on.

I told you so, hen.

42

It's never the thing you worry about that fucks you. While McCoist had been stressing about the priority of the Lennox case slipping down the rungs and forcing her onto something else, with a second murder chained on, the opposite had happened. Now there was a roomful of detectives leaving coffee rings all over her office space and prying with grubby digits and beady eyes into everything they had so far, going over it again, adding their own ideas and looking for leads to chase down. DI Griffiths, who had stepped in to take charge of the Townhead scene when McCoist went AWOL, was leading the briefing and handing out jobs. McCoist had her own line to follow.

"Anybody spoken to you about yesterday?" Slater asked, closing her door to the now-bustling office.

"Not yet but it's in the post."

"I reckon if you tell them what you told me it'll be fine. Say you were 'cultivating a sensitive information source' or some bollocks like that."

"Chief constable material, you are." They smiled at each other, and McCoist felt heat rising in her face. Too cutesy, it was gross. Get a fucking lid on it. "What about the part where Tim broke into the office?"

"Maybe keep that bit quiet."

"But I can trust you with it. Right?"

Slater looked in her eyes, a frisson of yesterday's moment in the car prickling like static between them. "Of course."

"Good... Good. Because we need to talk about it. He found some notes hidden in a textbook which sounded suspicious, maybe pertaining to Lennox, wanting MacGillivary to talk to him or do something about him. He was causing trouble."

"Any idea who the notes were from?"

"Tim said they were signed with the initials PLU, didn't mean anything to him. Ring any bells for you?"

"PLU... Nah."

"Anyway, the message Tim left me the day he, uh—he sounded excitable, he thought he maybe had something. Wanted to see if I could find anything out about the murder of a young woman, a sex worker, last year."

"A sex worker... one of McGuinn's girls?"

"One of his slaves, yeah. Tim didn't say any more on the phone. If I could have spoken to him..." She saw the back of his head, in the tub, the livid bruising on the neck... "I couldn't find anything anyway, not enough to go on, really. But anyway, MacGillivary saw him leaving and—"

"Then he turns up dead."

Half dismembered in his own home. "I've bagsied us interviewing MacGillivary. On our turf this time."

Lawyers were used to polis interview rooms. Cooncil-brand Abu Ghraib did nothing to unsettle them. Even in the hot seat, MacGillivary looked calm and self-assured, the kind of lawyer you'd want sitting beside you if you were het for something.

McCoist gave him a coffee she'd made herself, to her own taste, see if that put the shits up him.

"I've come here out of respect for the boy," he said. "But it'll be the last time unless you want to arrest me and do this thing for real."

"Before beginning this interview, under Section 31 of the Criminal Justice (Scotland) Act—"

"Skip it, will you? I know my rights. Like I said, this is a tragedy, I'll do anything I can to help, I just don't appreciate you demanding I come down here when I've currently got the work of two solicitors to do."

"You taken his name off the sign yet?" Slater asked.

"I beg your pardon? If this is how it's going to be—"

"Apologies, Mr MacGillivary," McCoist butted in. "Let's all take a breath, start again. Please, sit back down. *Out of respect for the boy.*"

MacGillivary snorted and took a mouthful of coffee. Choked, spluttered. "Are the budgets really that bad?"

"Worse. You should see the biscuit selection."

McCoist shot Slater a warning look which he acknowledged with an innocent *who, me?* smile. "Mr MacGillivary, can you tell us how Tim Drummond came to work for you?"

"He didn't work for me. He was Carter's intern. Begged him for a bit of work experience, ended up staying with us quite a while, getting a wage too."

"Begged? Why did he want to work for Lennox & MacGillivary so badly?"

"Oh he didn't, he'll have been up and down the Saltmarket going into every firm with the same spiel. It's a highly competitive industry, any experience you can add to your CV is going to help."

"But Carter Lennox had quite a reputation, no? Spent a good

part of his career in trials involving organised crime, then all that 'helping the helpless', pro bono stuff..."

"There was a certain glamour to him, if that's what you mean. On paper, of course, you saw what his office was like. His appearance was an extension of it." His appearance, when McCoist had last seen it, had looked like something whipped up by Tom Savini for an eighties video nasty.

"Is it possible Tim wanted to work with him because of his history then?"

"Could be. Carter did guest lectures at the uni sometimes, maybe he just felt he had a foot in the door with him because of that. Who knows, I don't. I didn't interview him, and aside from the odd coffee or pastry run, he didn't do anything for me."

"Did you think it unusual that Carter took him on?"

"No, he was always looking for strays to help, and God knows he needed some help himself when it came to his filing."

"But keeping Tim on so long..."

"He was eager to work, didn't mind the hours."

"There was nothing personal to their relationship?"

"Do you mean were they friends or are you insinuating something inappropriate? If so, it's a gross stain on Carter's character, not to mention wildly defamatory."

"His flat was full of whips and chains and, you know, kinky sex stuff," Slater said.

"I didn't realise we were sitting in the TARDIS," MacGillivary replied without missing a beat, not even a hint of surprise on show. "What year have we gone back to? Being into BDSM does not make you a predator. Carter abhorred the abuse of power. He dedicated his life to fighting against it. He and Tim worked

well together, they got on well together, that's the whole of it."
He took another mouthful of coffee and didn't choke this time,
even looked like he was savouring the taste.

"So what do you think about not one but two of your colleagues being murdered?" McCoist asked.

"I honestly don't know what to think. It's…"—and for the
first time words seemed to slip away from the lawyer, and his
ramrod-erection bearing shrivelled a little—"…incomprehen-
sible. It's awful. I don't understand it."

"No?"

"No."

"When we spoke to you after Mr Lennox's death, you said
he wasn't short of potential enemies, is there any reason why
anger at him would also be deflected onto Tim?"

"I can't think of any."

"When was the last time you saw Tim?"

McCoist could feel Slater tighten up in the seat beside her
and she willed him to be cool, not to hint that the suspicious
arrangement of leaves on the floor hid a hastily dug hole with
pointy sticks at the bottom.

"It was a few days ago."

"Three days ago?"

"No, it was… four. He came to collect some things he'd left."

"And you spoke?"

"Briefly, just to say goodbye."

"You didn't want to keep him on? Considering all the extra
work you were just talking about."

"I need a highly trained and experienced criminal defence
solicitor, not a tea boy."

"He wasn't cross about that?"

"Didn't seem so."

"And that was all? Just 'goodbye'?"

"Sandra, our secretary, was there too, he probably spoke more with her. They got on well."

"Everyone got on well with him except you," McCoist said.

"The implication being... what?" He finished the coffee to the dregs. "No, there's no implication because there's no evidence, and there's no evidence because I didn't have anything to do with either death. This *exercise* here, or whatever you want to call it, is nothing more than a baffled and criminally useless police detective trying to look like they're actually doing something when in reality they're sitting with their thumb up their arsehole, absolutely clueless."

Slater bristled. McCoist took it on the chin, parcelled it up to detonate it later at a safe distance. "You're quite worked up about it."

"I am. For reasons I've made clear. You know, most of all, I feel angry for the boy's parents. It's bad enough I've got to deal with you bungling the investigation into my friend and colleague's death, but to have you fumble all over their son's murder. It's a damn disgrace."

That one hooked in low, to the soft belly, took the wind right out of her. McCoist had been round to see the Drummonds the evening before to break the news. Semi-detached suburbia, a scene so ordinary McCoist's presence seemed a violation, like she'd arrived wearing a black cloak and holding a scythe. She had to quell a nervous laugh on the doorstep. Pictures of Tim at various ages broke up the painted-over woodchip in the hall. His mum screamed until she made herself sick. His dad tried to hold on to her, as if tending to a wounded, wild animal, almost confused as to what had happened to her, as if he himself hadn't heard McCoist's words at all.

"Mr MacGillivary"—McCoist addressed her final question in a quiet, chastened voice—"do you know anything about the murder of a young woman last year which Mr Lennox may have been looking into? She was a sex worker, maybe attached to one of Paul McGuinn's operations."

There: a flicker, a hesitation, dragging the beat by a millisecond. Twitch of panic spasming the muscles of the eye. "No. And I think you have enough murders to be working on."

"Thank you for your time." You lying, patronising pig-fucker.

43

Glasgow Sheriff Court was three storeys of colour-desaturated Tetris blocks assembled on the south bank of the Clyde. Judge Dredd would have approved of its design: in spite of its intended purpose it screamed "summary execution". Inside was warmer by dint of the number of people there, the main hall made for milling, waiting, the hard floor perfect for a lawyer to make a good sound while striding across it, purposeful and predatory.

McCoist went up to the first floor, to courtroom nine at its heart. She planted herself outside the side door used by the lawyers and waited. It was five to four, she wouldn't have long. He'd be out on the dot, they always were. Clockwork was jealous of the metronomic punctuality of the court. A hearing could be stopped mid-sentence, put off till the next day, if the words weren't concluded by the time the second hand clicked into place at 4 p.m. Tee-off would not wait for justice.

Her insides were a rattling, spinning tombola. Instead of numbered lottery balls, it contained hand grenades. She'd tried to push search warrants for MacGillivary and Simply Shred again but the fiscal was nervous after two rebuffs on the bounce. Time for drastic action. Tim had died because of all this, what did her job even mean compared to that? Though, to cramp Sister McCoist's pious reasoning, Devlin would be wanting to keep her as protected as possible. Her trouble was his trouble, as he'd sort of put it, and he'd gone to some lengths for her already. Even if his neck wasn't on the block next to hers, his itchy nads would be in a vice if she got rumbled. It gave her the bit of nerve she needed, some political armour, an umbrella for the inevitable turd-tossing.

She rehearsed what she was going to say, how she was going to say it. Be calm. Be deferential. Be apologetic at the intrusion but adamant of its necessity. Be sincere. Be polite. Speak nice. No glottal stops, cross those *ts*. Plead your case. Beg if you have to.

At the first sight of him, bewigged and cloaked with glasses perched at the end of his haughty nose and the underbite of royalty giving him a constant look of amused disdain, she knew she'd have to bite her tongue right off to stay civil.

"Sheriff Cresswell."

He looked at her like she was a fly who'd landed on his lunch.

"I'm DCI Alison McCoist." She held out her warrant card. "We've spoken over the phone."

"And what are you doing here?" He talked through his nose, accent Scottish but geographically unplaceable. Posh had its own higher region.

"I've come to ask about warrants pertaining to my case."

"This is highly inappropriate. Go through the proper channels."

He started walking away. McCoist skipped to catch him. "Sir, sir. I have to know what's needed for approval."

"You are a detective chief inspector, an experienced, senior police officer, you should know." He spoke without looking at her. The lackeys who followed behind did it for him—staring, sneering, looking for a chance to jump in and have a go.

"There's been another death. Lad who worked for Carter Lennox."

"I'm sorry to hear that but it doesn't change how the system operates."

"An intern, nineteen years old, strangled in his own home, chopped up in his bathtub—"

"Chief Inspector McCoist." He stopped on his heel and rounded on her, like a soldier turning in a parade. People hanging around the hall were looking at them. "Please leave before I am forced to make a formal complaint. You know the proper procedures. Follow them."

"I have. I have, and you turned me down time and again. Why? Those requests were fine, even the—"

"They were *not* fine, they did *not* meet the required threshold to be granted, and this is *not* the place to discuss it. I will give you one more chance to get out of here without serious consequences for your career." He towered above her, eyes pressing down, vehement, unblinking.

Part of McCoist, a sensible part, told her to walk away. Maybe throw in a bow or curtsy or something like a grovelling peasant. Instead she looked right back up at him. "They were silenced. Both of them. And I will find out why. Your help would be appreciated."

"More likely, you will find yourself out of a job."

Without looking away and without consulting her pride or ego, she added: "...Please."

With an almost imperceptible shake of the head he walked away.

One of the lackeys gave her a smile. "Can you detect your way to the exit?"

"Can you detect the sheriff's prostate with the tip of your tongue?"

Slater was waiting in the car. He'd wanted to come with but McCoist argued it would be better if only one of them ended up on gardening leave. "I'll order you to stay if I have to," she'd said. It came out flirty and he smiled and she smiled and she wanted to be sick in her mouth. Tess was in her head, "*Gross*," laughing at her/with her.

Returning, she got back in, shut the door, and stared at the glovebox as if all the world's ills were stored inside it, rather than just the car manual and alloy key.

"That bad?"

"Something else to add to any upcoming inquiry into my competency, probably, keep the conversation lively."

"You wouldn't want them to run out of ammo. That could be awkward."

"True. Giving them a little more wouldn't hurt then, would it?"

"What d'you mean?" He dropped the bantering tone.

McCoist put her hand on his. "It's a big ask and I completely understand if it's a no and I won't hold it against you. If you don't want to, just, please, pretend this conversation never happened."

"What?"

"I need to know how MacGillivary and the shredder are involved in all this. Warrants or no warrants. Whatever we find out, we can come up with some official mode of discovery retroactively, but the important thing is that we know."

"You want to run surveillance on them?"

"Yup. Take one each. Cover them best we can, see what turns up."

"Shame," he laughed, "for a second I thought you were about to ask me to do something inappropriate."

"Fuck off." She punched him on the shoulder. Then she kissed him.

44

This was the third lot of cash he'd borrowed now—from some-body else again, of course. He had to use some of it to pay back a chunk of the first loan, at least a bit. Then the rest of the wedge could go on the next bet, get himself back in the black, pay off the credit and the interest on everything, sail away with Bell and the winnings. Drink rum from a hairy coconut. (How he'd convince Bell to go was a problem he still hadn't made much progress in tackling, but he was sure money would help. He just needed lots of it. Easy.)

The third geezer was the worst so far, his whole look, demeanour and dingy office space at the back of an imported American sweety shop screamed Dodgy Dan. His face perma-nently gurned with the key bumps he spent all day taking. He gave out cash in brown paper bags. His contract didn't explicitly list body parts under collateral but it may as well have. Chuck came away from the place feeling as slimy as the inside of the Variety Bar fish tank. Or maybe it was just the permanent panic-ooze which had been leaking from his skin since Brownlee had been grated through his machine, made worse by every dicey decision he'd made since, every bet that hadn't come off. No such thing as a losing streak, he told himself. Again. No such thing as luck. Just crunch through it and eventually you win. Las Vegas lurkers came to mind. Auld biddies who waited until some poor sap gave up on their slot machine after hours of playing then swooped in for the jackpot after only a handful of goes. You only lose if you give up. Grind through. Keep putting the coins in, keep pulling the lever. It was like bursting a dam. You just had to keep the flow of cash going in and eventually...

He switched the machine on. Despite the thorough cleaning he, Roughcast and Marble had given it, he was sure he could smell lawyer tartare as it powered up.

Today he had a couple of Joe Public jobs to start with, then he was off to the west end for a couple of commercial ones. Last stop was out of town—a new customer, some kind of ancestry DNA service, he gathered. They'd only called this morning but he'd said he'd fit them in today, hoping to get a bit of repeat business out of them. One of his west-end stops was an accountant's in Hyndland—maybe something in that for Mr Jamieson. He hadn't been asked to do anything specific for him since emptying out Brownlee's office, but it wouldn't be long until he came calling again, Chuck was sure. While the horror of Brownlee's body cracking, tearing, compressing into the chomping rollers of the shredder had become a regular day/nightmare for Chuck, the image of Jamieson's face—the calm, collected cool beneath the sagging, caved-in surface—as he suggested simply feeding the rest of the body into the machine was one that visited him with more terror than any of the schlocky, unreal gore. A vision that made him feel as if he'd been plunged into a hole in ice.

"Are you OK?"

"Sorry?"

"Are you OK?" It was the woman he was doing the job for. He realised he didn't know how long he'd been standing there holding a stack of old papers above the rumbling machine. "I just came to see if you wanted a cuppa? You looked frozen."

"Oh, eh, aye, sorry." His cheeks flushed with the riddest of riddies, a high, glowing puce only achievable by those of the fair, ginger complexion. "Stuck in neutral there." He gave a weak laugh. "Aye, a tea wid be lovely, ta."

"Milk? Sugar?"

"Baith, please. Two sugars."

"Might as well. Life's short, eh? I'll bring you a biscuit too."

He thought of Bell's snout-and-Pop-Tart ritual. She was off for a couple of days. He could go home to her. She would be there. Spend the time together. Life's short, getting shorter.

45

Another fucking cup of tea. "Guy has more breaks than that lassie whose husband pushed her out the plane," McCoist mumbled to her phone on hands-free, sitting low in her car seat a block from where Gardner was having a cuppa and a bickie beside his van.

"I watched that one," Slater replied. "Decent."

"Too extravagant a method to get away with. Tampering with a parachute? It's almost baroque. Fucking Poirot sent in to investigate."

"Oh aye? What would you do?"

"Frozen ham hock to the head then eat the weapon, obviously."

"Not a blade made out of ice?"

"Paint a picture of a tunnel entrance on a wall, let them drive into it."

"You trying to kill a wife or catch a roadrunner?"

"Pretend to be a ghost haunting an old amusement park, and then—"

"Doomed to fail. Best detectives in the world and their dug on your case."

"I'm not afraid of meddling kids. I eat Glesga hard men for my brecky."

Slater laughed, went quiet for a moment. "Speaking of which, did you ever meet the Big Man?"

"Sorry?"

"McGuinn. Did you ever meet him before he got his ticket punched?"

Punched right through his fucking heed. McCoist the ticket collector, fingers numb around the grip of the pistol, eyes burnt by muzzle flash, face warm and soiled with splashback. Couldn't really call that "meeting". They had once before though. Again in the car wash, unexpectedly, McGuinn's sudden presence taking her by surprise, the bulk of him, his aura, his aftershave, the wild thing he kept on a frayed thin rope leash just below the surface causing a paralysing, play-dead animal response in McCoist's nervous system, bowels ready to evacuate if he made any kind of move.

"Yeah, one time… and it was enough." She wanted to say more, tell Slater how McGuinn had sent his thugs after her, how they'd ambushed her with knives and she'd barely escaped alive. She wanted to tell him it was her who killed him, to feel the relief it would bring, even if it was only temporary.

"I know it's not right to say it, but that lad whatsisname— your man the nephew who nailed him—did everyone a favour. He was a bad bastart all right. Evil. The stories you heard."

"Colin Kennedy. He's in hospital just now actually. Got attacked inside." *And who put him there?* She'd met Colin too, before it all went down. Thick, arrogant, young. This business, it pulled young boys in and told them there was only one way to be a man, with inevitable results. Even Tim had been a victim of it in some way. Although there was plenty of responsibility to share around for that. McCoist, Burnet, Lennox all included. The motherfucker who did it too, of course, but she couldn't overlook her own part. That would be a self-deception too far, and she was already lost enough.

"Ach well, it's all cleaning itself up then." He sounded like Devlin. The underworld was its own self-sustaining ecosystem, and the polis just played their part, making sure it didn't impact civilians too hard where it overlapped with the overworld. Or the right kind of civilians, at least.

Guilt crashed in on her, dragged her spirits down to the footwell. "It's my fault," she said.

"You can't blame yourself, Alison. It's the life these guys choose."

That was an easy way to look at it, but Slater's figurative understanding of what she said stopped her from going further: *It's my fault because I put him in jail for an execution I carried out.*

"Anything happening at your end?" she said instead.

"Nah, my gran has more going on, and she's about to get her royal birthday card. He's either in his office or out smoking. Spent half his evening on the porch last night puffing away."

"Stress?"

"Guilt, more like. Any day now he's gonna take me straight to PLU, whoever the bastard is. I can feel it."

She tried to let Slater's energy buoy her but worry niggled at her instead. She'd involved him now, and the implications were finally hitting her. Somebody was out there killing people who they thought might know too much about this letter. If anything happened to him too... She tamped it down. Si was a polis. A professional. "Stay on it."

Gardner had been a little more interesting. Yesterday, McCoist had followed him to one of those American "candy" shops on Rutherglen Main Street, a ten-minute drive south of the city, where he'd disappeared into the back room for a while. He came out half an hour later with a bag full of imported

Pop-Tarts, looking sweaty. She'd ask Devlin about the place, either he'd know what was going on there and could tell her, or he'd be interested in finding out, maybe buy her a little grace with him. Considering Gardner's history, she thought maybe an illicit bookie's. Whatever it was, she guessed he wouldn't want his wife to know.

"He's finishing up here. Speak soon."

She followed him around as he shredded his way through the day, going to this office and that, the odd gaff. Up the west end, riding tandem, Chuck on the front, McCoist on the back, they went to a private health clinic near Vicky Park then looped back to an accountant's on Hyndland Road.

Keeping a few cars between them, she followed him back down Great Western Road to the heart of the west end, past the Òran Mór with its blue-neon hoop sitting jauntily around its spire, continuing on through the shops and pubs and restaurants, across the M8— which bisected the city like the Judgement of Solomon—and into the centre, down Sauchiehall Street, the Gothic buildings broken by art deco anomalies and modern monstrosities, crawling east through the gridded streets and one-way traffic system until they entered the Merchant City.

He mounted a kerb, not in a space, and got out. White van's privilege. McCoist had to keep going past, craning her neck to try and see where he was going, snatching glances back out the windscreen to make sure she didn't plough into someone. He'd turned onto Garth Street—one-way traffic coming from the other direction.

McCoist kept on going, bundled into the first space she saw, jumped out and sprint-walked back the way she came.

There was a busy cafe on the corner, al fresco lunching set up outside for the summer, and she used its parasols and punters as cover to sneak round.

He was waiting at the door of an office block a few doors down, looking at the buzzer panel—a camera? Then the door was open and he went in.

A couple left their table and McCoist sat down to stained cups and sticky cutlery, crumby plates with napkins crumpled onto them, fags in the ashtray. Sun cream and cigarettes, the sweet smell of a youthful summer. First, she opened her parking app. She did not need to get ticketed while on an illegal stake-out. Second, she googled the building's address to see what was inside.

Definition-defying lists of surnames and consultancies abounded. All sorts of boring desk work going on. Insurers, accountants, techy wizardry. One called Firestane piqued her interest—security and investigations. Private eyes. But any one of these places could legitimately need the help of someone like Gardner. Just another job. But then why had he left the van back on Hutcheson Street? If he was about to haul a load of paperwork out of that building, wouldn't he have just gone around the block so he could come into the street the other way and park right outside it? Stick the hazards on?

A waiter came over to clear the table and she ordered a coffee, knowing full well it was going to be the good shit and not what she really wanted. She asked for it in a takeaway cup—maybe to help the flavour, but also because if Gardner came out in a minute, she knew there was no way she could just walk away from a coffee she'd just paid the best part of a fiver for. (Ruin an investigation over a few quid, really? Yes, it was the Scotch curse.) While she waited, one eye on the door, she began checking out the businesses' websites, starting with Firestane as it sounded the least yawn-inducing.

The website was slick in a boring, corporate kind of way. McCoist couldn't help the yawn after all. It was very far removed from the image of Philip Marlowe with his feet up on his desk, bourbon in hand, a dangerous dame on the other end of the rotary phone. Firestane's services covered a gamut of problems, including corporate theft, missing persons and various relationship issues, including scoping out your next Tinder date. *Fucking fair enough*, McCoist thought, *maniacs out there everywhere*. The heading "Infidelity" was accompanied by a stock image of a woman lying in bed, staring at her phone, illuminated by the glow of the screen, the edge of a man's face just visible over her shoulder, looming in the shadow. They boasted "Male and Female Investigators". Their security options ran through installing CCTV to posting guards. It seemed a fair-sized operation. Companies House listed a few names attached as investigators and secretaries and so on, and the director as "William Jamieson" with an address in Newton Mearns.

She was another couple of websites and half a coffee down when Gardner emerged from the door again, pacing towards her at the cafe. She turned a little, so she was facing towards the walls of the buildings rather than out into the street, and kept her eyes glued to the screen, her head down, hair falling over her face. He passed by. She resisted the urge to turn to watch him, instead listened for the sound of the van door opening and closing at the end of the street, the engine starting up.

Only then, she chanced a look round, saw Simply Shred pull out into the road. She sprang out her seat, coffee in hand, and ran round the corner to her car.

Fun and games.

46

The EK address he'd been given by the ancestry guy took him out to a weedy, half-forgotten corner of a sprawling industrial estate off a dual carriageway. Rusty shutters and weathered signs told of businesses opened and shut down. There was a unit that used to be a music studio, another that had something to do with customising motors. An odd place for a genealogy company. Though Chuck guessed their business was probably all online, all they needed was office space to work in, not a shopfront. There certainly wasn't any signage he could see.

There was a VW Caddy, wrapped in golden-yellow vinyl, parked at the dead end of the street, outside another closed shutter, this one advertising "SOLUTIONS FOR ALL YOUR HARDWOOD NEEDS", the slogan being spouted by a cartoon hammer with a pervy, knowing grin. Chuck rolled down towards it and stopped. He jumped out and saw the decal on the side of the flash van which read: "Who's Yer Da? Scottish Family History Uncovered". A man was sitting in the driver's seat. He spotted Chuck looking in his wing mirror and got out, strode over with his hand outstretched.

"Mr Hucknall?" he laughed. "Sorry, ye must get that aw the time." They shook. "Trav, we spoke oan the phone." Trav looked like a garden gnome in a suit. Short, round, beardy, and surely bald under his flat cap, which might have been trendy on a man ten years younger. He had a nice smile.

"Hiya. Chuck."

"Step intae ma oaffice." He went around the back of the wee van and opened the rear doors.

"Is it just aw in here?" Wouldn't be much then, maybe not a great source of new business after all, not unless they expanded—

The back of the van was empty.

It was less of a push, more of a tackle. It slammed Chuck's back, sent him crashing face first into the wood panelling in the back of the van, no time to get his hands up to break his fall. His shins caught the bumper as he went in, like a tree hacked down with an axe. "Wit the fuck?!" He tried to get up and turn. There was another man with Trav, a much bigger man—must have been in the passenger seat. The big man climbed into the back of the van, stooping. Chuck's heart vibrated like the bass drum in a metal song, he could feel the blood whooshing around inside him at a crazy speed, making him dizzy.

"Stay still," the big man said. But before giving Chuck the chance to obey, his huge fist slammed into Chuck's cheek, bouncing his head against the deck again. He cried out, pain driving in from both sides, spreading through his head, roots breaking through tarmac.

Rough hands rolled Chuck onto his belly. A knee pressed into his back, pushing the air out of his lungs. He tried to cry. It was breaking him. Going to break him. Snap his spine, crumble the vertebrae, mangle the cord. His wrists were cabled together. Then the pressure on his back was released and he gulped in air. "Stoap," he croaked. "Stoap." He couldn't shout.

They covered his mouth with tape anyway.

A plastic tie held his ankles together.

The big man got out, the van springing on its suspension as he did so. Trav climbed in. His smile still looked nice. He held up a black sleep mask with the words "Fuck Off" embroidered on it. "Willnae take too lang, just try an chill oot, awright?"

Then he was in total darkness.

47

Time and space had been robbed from him. He rolled about in the dark as if in the hold of a ship, carried off to fuck-knows-where. Voices murmured from the front, their words obscured by Bruce Springsteen coming from the speakers. A pal of Chuck's had once said there was a Bruce Springsteen song for every possible event in a person's life. Maybe the one playing was about being kidnapped and tied up in the back of a panel van.

The initial shock had worn off and become an all-consuming panic. Was this about the money he'd borrowed? The money he'd lost? Had Jamieson found out? Was it about Brownlee? He knew fuck all about the guy or who he'd been involved with before he'd backstroked into the shredder. Was this retribution?

Finally, the van stopped rumbling, the engine off. He heard doors open and close. This was worse, he was ready to puke, and it wasn't just motion sickness.

The back doors opened. Large hands closed around his ankles. In one great yank, like a magician pulling the table-cloth out from under the plates and glasses, he was pulled straight out of the van and onto the ground, slamming onto his face, shoulder, ribs, hip. He screamed into the tape over his mouth.

"Careful," a voice said. Trav's. Chuck could picture his friendly gnome-smile.

He chundered. Some of it came out through his nose, burning his nostrils, the bulk of it filled his sealed mouth with hot, chunky soup and he began to choke.

"Get that aff."

"Am no touchin it."

"Fucksake. Pure fanny baws, you are."

The tape ripped from his lips, taking some bristles with it, and the vomit flooded out like gunge at Noel Edmonds's gaff.

The voices cheered as if a glass had been dropped in a pub.

"Am no cleanin that up." Trav speaking.

"Aw, am gonnae whitey an aw, a cannae be aroon—" The big guy.

"Ye better fuckin no."

"A need tae get away or am gonnae boak."

"Fucksake, Jake."

"Calm it, Janet."

"Don't be moody, Judy."

"Lick ma rim, Jim."

"Up yer hole, Joel."

"…Eh… Flick ma bean, Jean."

"Fuck wis that? Way too late. Yev goat three seconds max fir a comeback, no hawf an oor."

Somebody was down at his ankles, cutting the ties. "We're headin upstair," Trav said. "Watch yer fittin, try no tae trip."

They took an arm each and levered him onto his jelly legs, then half marched, half dragged him along. "First step," Travis called. "That's it." They jostled him up a flight of stairs—"Last step… Next yin, here's the first… Last…"—then through a door, his elbow (hands still tied behind his back) catching on the frame. There was a chill, the sun not reaching wherever he was, a large space around him, their footsteps echoing.

"Stoap. Here, take a seat." He felt himself pushed down into something surprisingly plush and comfortable, but having his hands still behind his back caused a horrible wrenching sensation in his shoulders.

The sleep mask was whipped off and his eyes stung, although as his skin had sensed, it wasn't exactly bright in here. No sunlight, the rooftop windows all boarded up. Greasy yellow tube lighting, the silhouettes of dead insects visible in the coverings, cast their sickly pall over him.

He was sitting in a massage chair—the kind you put a quid in and it vibrates and squeezes and gently pummels your backside—in an indoor shopping centre. Abandoned for some time. A few signs clung on outside gutted units, and as well as Chuck's massage chair and its partner, there were a few children's rides—Postman Pat's van, and there was Bob the Builder on his anthropomorphic digger—and a golden retriever with a slot in its head collecting money for Guide Dogs outside what used to be a Safeway.

"The shoappin village ae the future, *the day*." The man in front of him spoke with faux grandiosity and spread his arms wide to take it all in. He wore a navy suit, no tie, classic cherry-red Doc Martens that matched a pocket square. Handsomely greying hair shaved at the sides and swept back with gel to go with his well-tended beard. Ear and nostril hair burnt off at the Turkish barber's, monobrow vanquished. "A mind comin here as a wee boay wae ma gran." His voice was deep and rich with a small, pleasant amount of gravel to it. "We'd go get the messages an then sit in at the baker's fir a scone an a cuppa. She'd sometimes gee me a fifty-pee fir the sweetie machine."

He sat down in the chair next to Chuck. Trav the gnome and his big pal smirked.

"Smoked hersel tae death, so she did. Emphysema, then the cancer."

"Eh, am sorry tae hear that." Chuck's voice squeaked out, his mouth too dry, his heart in his vocal cords.

"Aw thanks, Chuckie." The man patted his arm. "But don't worry aboot it, it was a lang time ago. An ma plans fir this place will dae her proud, yel see." He nodded to himself, stiff-jawed, resolute. "The notion ae addiction is pertinent tae oor situation here, but, don't ye hink?"

"Sorry?"

"Sick compulsions wit we know will only lead tae oor ain demise." He nodded to the big guy—"Ben Nevis, if you please"—then sat back, deep in his massage chair. Comfortable.

Chuck was grabbed by his collar and tossed onto the deck, his nose bouncing off the cold, dusty tiles. Snap, crackle, pop—blood streaming bright and thick and rich. Kicks pelted into his stomach, his back. He closed his eyes and tried to curl up but the way his arms were tied kept him from being able to shield his head. He squealed and screamed. Sole of a boot hit his mouth, burst his lips against his teeth.

Then he was back in the chair.

Breathing hard, feeling giddy, sore all over, too many different points of pain for any particular one to stand out, nerves overloaded. Tasted warm blood, everything fleshy in his mouth—lips, tongue, cheeks, gums—felt ragged.

"Yev taken oot a good few loans recently. Quite a bit ae cash when ye add it aw thegether. An a like tae meet ma big-money clients in person."

Who the fuck? Chuck's brain was fogged, it was the best he could do through the rancid fear which had made his whole body ill.

"Aw these lenders yev bin visitin, Chuck. They aw kick up tae me." He held out his hand for Chuck to shake—"Ruaridh Donald Callaghan. Oh, right"—then gave a sheepish smile as if just realising Chuck's hands were tied. "An some ae these bookies yev bin visitin, they're part ae the whole Callaghan Group an aw, ye see? So yer sort ae…"—he pedalled his hand in a theatrical gesture—"…robbin Peter tae also rob Paul. It's no good money management. Martin Lewis widnae approve, wid he?" The smile didn't fade, it simply stopped being a smile though the muscles remained frozen in the same position. "Would he?" Their eyes locked and Callaghan leant over the armrests until his nose was nearly touching Chuck's. "Answer me: *would Mister Martin Lewis, money-savin expert, Commander ae the British Bastart Empire, approve?*"

"N-naw?"

The fist smashed Chuck's head deep into the leather and lush cushioning of the chair's headrest—it probably saved him from bruising his brain—bursting a cut open high on his cheekbone around the eye. Ben Nevis pummelled him then rag-dolled him onto the floor again.

Chuck managed to manoeuvre himself up onto his knees. He spat blood. He felt his belly spasm and thought he was going to spew again. Already his eye was swelling up so much he couldn't see out of it. Everything felt raw. Tears stung. He saw Travis's smiling gnome face, the big unit marching towards him. He was going to die. He was going to fucking die. His life wasn't flashing before his eyes. All he could see was the impending, painful end that was Nevis's Timbies.

"Police! Get back or get a pus full of Sergeant Pepper!"

48

What the fuck to do next?

There were three of them (one of whom looked like he spent his weekends flipping tractor tyres and dragging boat anchors around for fun) and one of her, plus a small can of PAVA which she held out in front of her, praying her arm wouldn't tremble. Gardner had his hands tied and was in no fighting state anyway. Far from it, he looked like a protester who'd chained himself to the Heavenly Gates, begging to be let in. They'd kicked the fuck out of him.

McCoist's plan hadn't been overly organised. Improvised, in fact. Stupidly so. Tracking Chuck through the industrial estate had been tricky—it was a maze and there was no traffic to hide her, nightmare for tailing someone. She saw the gold van leaving a cul-de-sac, Gardner's own one sitting there empty, and with seemingly nowhere else for him to go (shutters all down), she took a reasonable guess he might have caught a lift and changed her target. The boarded-up shopping centre they stopped at gave her a thrill—he was up to something, definitely, right now, with her to witness it—then what she'd glimpsed through the door into the derelict mall told her he hadn't got into that van voluntarily. Adrenaline flushing madly through her, shorting out brain cells and filling her muscles with blood and wild confidence, she stormed through the door: "Police! Get back or get a pus full of Sergeant Pepper!"

World's Strongest Man and Lollipop Guild looked to the one who was dressed like he was off to a northern soul night. Must be the man in charge. His expression was hard to read. Intensity about the eyes, but not panicky. "What now?" he said, reading McCoist's mind.

She licked dry lips. Tried to clear her brain enough to think while keeping primed and ready to run. "I'm going to take your friend there to hospital. You're going to let me or you're going to the cells for the night. Maybe a few nights. Maybe a few years."

He put on a show of polite, mock surprise. "A hink ye might huv the wrang end ae the shitty stick here, officer..."—he clicked his fingers. "McCoist!" He grinned. "That's it, wis tryin tae place ye, yer face wis familiar. Ally McCoist, isnit? Av seen ye in *The Digger* a few times, in relation tae oor dearly departet Mr McGuinn."

"Detective Chief Inspector McCoist." Her irritation helped her summon some authority into her voice.

"Course, ma apologies. Detective Chief Witever McCoist, there's bin a misunderstawndin. Wur just huvin a wee chat. A business meetin, really."

"What business is that?"

He looked sheepish, or acted out "sheepish"—bad pantomime. "Well, that's client privilege, a cannae just tell anywan that."

"Grievous bodily harm," McCoist chanted.

"He slipped oan the tile. It's skitey." He squeaked his boot on it.

"Abduction."

"There's only two seats in the front ae the van. A know ye shouldnae huv anybdy ridin tailgun, but folk dae it aw the time, come oan."

"Conspiracy."

"Yev goat us, wur filmin the moon landin in here. Don't tell anycunt."

She moved slowly towards where Gardner was kneeling.

Northern Soul put his hands up—no harm meant. "Wur done anyway, right, Chuck? Hammered oot aw the necessary bullet points."

"R-right," he said, blood and spit spraying from his mouth. McCoist took him under the arm and helped him to his feet.

"Trav, Ben, gee the lassie a hawn will ye? Motor parked doon the stair?"

"Stay back," she warned, brandishing the spray again.

"Awright, awright. Just tryin tae help."

McCoist and Gardner stumbled down the empty plaza back to the door, waiting for the sound of footsteps behind them, but they didn't come.

"A cannae just leave ma van there," Chuck burbled through burst lips and flattened nose, slumped against the window. The smell of sick and blood coming off him mingled pleasantly with the ever-present hum of dug in McCoist's motor. "How will a get it back?"

"Take a taxi. You need to go to hospital."

"A just need ma bed."

"You look like Quasimodo; I'm taking you to A & E."

"A need hame tae see Bell."

"Wife or pet?"

"Wife," he grunted.

"I can phone her, have her meet us there."

"A just want tae see her noo."

"Is she in danger? From them?"

A racking cough caused him to fold up on himself, jittering. "Naw," he wheezed. "A don't hink so, but a want tae get hame tae her. Moan, stoap the car. Stoap the fuckin car!"

"Calm down. Fine, whatever. I'll take you home, but I bet your wife's going to be raging you've not gone to hospital. She'll have to take you herself."

"She's a nurse. Al be fine."

"You look like Sloth from *The Goonies.*"

"Yer a bit fuckin wide fir a polis, ye know that?"

"Lucky for you."

"It *wis* you a saw in toon then, sittin ootside that cafe. Ye bin follyin me aw day?"

"As I said, lucky for you. Am I gonna get a 'Thank you for saving my life' at any point?"

"Ye allowed tae dae that?"

"I don't know. Are you allowed to get into debt with a bunch of gangsters or will your Scots Blue Bell be upset about it?"

"Blackmail. Class."

"You're being melodramatic," McCoist tutted. "I'll put the attitude down to the head injury. What is it you've got yourself into then?"

Chuck huffed and curled in on himself as best he could with the seatbelt on.

"Come on. I know about what happened five years ago. I'm pretty sure you've been gambling with borrowed money again, and by the looks of it these people aren't going to just hand you over to the polis for it. I can help you, Chuck."

"Naebdy can help me."

"That's not true. There's no point at which you can't turn

back, can't put things right." Who was she talking to now? She recalled a similar conversation with Davey Burnet, pleading with him to trust her, despite the little protection she could really offer. She'd saved his life and failed him simultaneously. She could try again. Maybe.

Chuck turned to face her, swelling occluding one eye, a vicious cut spreading open on the cheekbone, nose out of joint and the accompanying double-shiner already visible, lips like squashed slugs. "She'll leave me, if she finds oot."

"Do you love her?"

"Aye."

"Then you need to do right by her. Don't you? Come on, talk to me. Who's the hip dad with the red boots and pocket square?"

Deep breath. "Ruaridh Callaghan. Ye know him?"

"That was Callaghan? I know his work. Seen a mugshot too but it's a good bit out of date. Christ, he's aged well."

"Fucksake. Are ye wantin tae arrest him or shag him?"

"I'm duty-bound to put criminals behind bars... You wouldn't swipe left though, would you? I mean, you should see what's out there in that age range, a bunch of guys who look like they've been on an 18–30 holiday twenty years too long—" Slater popped into her head and she stopped talking. The adrenaline comedown was making her gobby and weird. "You owe him money?"

"Aye."

"Can you afford to pay it back?"

"Depends."

"Depends on certain results?"

"Aye."

"And the interest?"

"Steep."

"Hmm." She recalled her "date" at the Fishery with Slater, what he'd said about the drug squad taking over the coppers' local for their party. "There was a big drug bust recently, a boat called the *Shippendale*—"

Chuck groaned.

"You're one to talk, Simply Shred—was searched when it came into Oban. More coke on board than David Bowie in his Thin White Duke era. A significant loss for whoever was involved, and the rumours point to Callaghan. Makes sense he's wanting to keep a close personal eye on his books, pinch the pennies. I take it the repayment deadline is tight?"

"As a nun's—"

"Behave."

"A wis gonnae say 'charity boax'."

"I can offer you protection, Chuck." *Could she?* "But only if you help me. I need to know what you were doing at Lennox and Brownlee's offices. Did Callaghan send you there? Did he do something to those men?"

He looked out the window at the lights whizzing by.

"You can be an accomplice or you can be a hero."

"This is me here."

Deflated but rattling from the excess excitement/knicker-ruining fear of the day, McCoist let herself into her house. Usually Bruce would come bursting out from the living room, a rammy of legs and tail and tongue, to meet her, jumping and slurping and whining with desperate happiness. Instead there was just the dark hallway. "Bruce? Bruce?" She put on the hall light. "Where's my boy?" The door to the living room, where Bruce liked to luxuriate on the couch with the radio on while McCoist was out, was open. "Oh, you little shit."

She marched upstairs, flung her bedroom door open. "Bruce!" The duvet rose abruptly and the dog looked out from under, ET in his ghost costume, expression just as gormless. "How many times do I have to tell you not to go in my bed when I'm not here?! Down!"

Now came the expected welcome. She couldn't stay angry with him. She rubbed his head and ears, clapped his back, smelt his fur, scrunched her face up, eyes and mouth closed, and endured him lapping his tongue over her.

"Come on then." They went downstairs and into the kitchen. McCoist grabbed a wine glass from the cupboard. Christ, she needed it. She got the corkscrew from the drawer along with the back-door key to let Bruce out into the garden.

She touched the handle and, before the key had even gone in, the door gently swung open. Not locked. There was something wrong with the snib, it—

49

Hands wrapped around her neck from behind. Gloved fingers pressed into her throat, digging in between the muscles and tendons and tubes, pressure hard enough to crush them all. She'd had no time to gulp in her last breath. The air was all gone already, lungs parched and screaming, throat doing nothing but choke and gurgle.

She stabbed at her own neck with the corkscrew, flailing, hitting something, the panting noises behind her turning to grunting. The hands shifted, one let go to bat away the corkscrew, knocking it from her hand.

Before it could return, McCoist jumped, braced both feet against the frame of the back door.

Pushed. Hard. With everything left in her oxygen-starved body.

And they fell.

Hit the kitchen island.

McCoist threw her legs up, into a backwards roll off the other side of it.

She breathed fire in. Giddy, blood rushing to her head. Sound of barking. "Bruce," she wheezed, "sick im!"

Bruce charged over, getting between McCoist and the man in the balaclava scraping himself up off the floor. McCoist prayed Edith was doing her usual nosy, was hearing the commotion and dialling 999.

Bruce jumped up on him, growling and barking in his face.

He backhanded the dog and was rewarded with a bite to his leg, making him scream.

"Good boy, rip his baws off!" McCoist's voice was a rasping shriek. She grabbed the kettle—nearest thing to hand—and stormed over as he managed to send Bruce away whining with a hard kick. "Cunt!" She swung the kettle at his face but he got an arm up to absorb the hit.

Jab to the gut doubled her over. He slapped the top of her head—right on the tender egg where the brick had landed only days before. She hit the deck, gasping with the pain, tears burning, blinding.

He lifted her by her hair. Her already raw throat blistered as she howled.

A hand went back around her neck again. He pushed her against the wall and she was silenced. Spitting, choking. His eyes the last thing she would see. They were ordinary.

Bruce leapt from the island like a WWE wrestler off the top rope, landed on the strangler like a sack of potatoes, took him to the ground, got his teeth into an ear and tore a chunk right out, the man screaming like a possessed banshee.

Kitchen warfare round two: the George Foreman grill. "Bruce! Move!" The dog jumped back. McCoist brought the grill down onto the man's skull like a hammer blow dealt by its namesake.

His lights were out for a minute and he was groggy and confused for a good while afterwards. There was blood oozing from a deep gouge in his head—corner of the grill must have got him there. McCoist had cuffed him to a radiator and bound his ankles with duct tape. She watched over him with a knife in one hand and her defence spray in the other.

Underneath the balaclava he was dirty blonde, round-faced and flushed. Reminded McCoist of a children's TV presenter. Nearly killed by Mr Tumble, she thought. That was the thing with killers—they didn't look like monsters. Their inner evil was not represented by outer ugliness or deformity. That was Hollywood stuff. Bullshit. Unfair bullshit at that. No, they looked just like anyone. *Blue Peter* here had strangled two people in the last couple of weeks. He'd calmly begun the process of sawing poor Tim into pieces with your da's power tools and some bin bags. He'd walk past you in the street and you'd never know. The sweat had turned icy on McCoist's body.

"Polis are on their way," she croaked. It hurt to talk. The back of her neck felt like she had whiplash. Edith had indeed called the emergency services—when McCoist put in her own call the cavalry was already on its way—her snooping good for something at last. "You can either wait on the floor comfortably, or you can wait on the floor uncomfortably." She brandished the can of salsa propellant at him. "Your choice."

He rattled his cuff experimentally.

McCoist gave him 50,000 Scovilles straight to the face. He screamed like she'd set him on fire and thrashed around as much as his bonds would allow.

"I can get you some milk for that, if you promise to stay still. No?"

Sirens outside.

"Sorry, I have to get that."

50

Getting herself dressed with the brace around her neck was tricky and without dignity but she managed it. She wondered what Bruce would think of her being coned like this, if he'd be sympathetic or if he'd feel some kind of justice had been served for his lost testes.

She sat on the hospital bed, rigid and uncomfortable, and waited for someone to come and discharge her. She'd been messaging Slater, Travis, Khan, Griffiths, everyone and anyone who might keep her in the loop.

Then Slater was at the door of her room in person. "Not quite the Balmoral but it's clean," he said, forcing a smile.

"And free." McCoist's voice was a chain-smoker's husk.

The smile dropped and he tried to hug her, gently as possible, still making her neck twinge. "Sorry, sorry. I'm just so relieved you're OK. Or OK-ish."

"Not dead."

"Not dead, yeah, it's good."

"It's OK." She smiled and tried to shrug but it hurt. She leant in, whole upper body stiff, for him to gingerly hold her again.

"You just been here by yourself?"

"Mark was here. He's still my emergency contact, apparently. He went to go get Bruce, take him to the vet today. Said he'd swing by with the kids later but I put him off, hoping I'll get out soon."

"I can take you to them after, if you need a lift?"

"Thanks for the offer, but I need you at the office keeping your ear in. What's happening with our guy? Any idea who he is yet?"

"Nothing doing yet, he's still being treated—in here somewhere."

"Shite." She felt unease scuttle across her skin. The bastard could be bloody well right next door. A double killer who'd just about made McCoist his third, the only thing between him and freedom a pair of handcuffs and a Hi-vis Harry.

"Aye, they've had to scan his head and all that bollocks cause he lost consciousness for a bit. Have to rule out brain trauma. The nurse was saying he couldn't remember how he got here or what happened before you stoved his head in with a bloody Breville."

"Convenient. And it was a George Foreman."

Slater chuckled. "That makes sense, no wonder he can't remember anything. Hooked by Big George. Oh, and he's missing a bit of an ear. Paramedics couldn't find it at your place so no hope of reattachment."

"If they can wait a couple of days Bruce will return it."

"He's a good boy."

"A hero."

There was a chap at the door and a thin grey man in jumper and chinos, wire-rimmed specs hanging on a chain round his neck making him look like a cartoon depiction of a librarian, came in with a bouquet of flowers. White lilies. Funereal. "Excuse me, Sergeant, could I have a word in private with DCI McCoist?"

Slater gave her a look and she nodded at him to say it was fine. When the door closed behind him, the librarian laid the flowers on their side on the overbed table and sat down in the visitor's chair, his legs wide enough to allow him to give his bawbag a wee scratch when needed. Which was frequently.

"How are you feeling?" Superintendent Devlin asked.

"Fit for duty, sir."

A benign smile played on his lips—benign if you didn't know every bit of his dorky patrician schtick was all front. "Not for you to decide I'm afraid. A couple of days off at least will do you good."

"Sir—"

"A short holiday, perhaps? Get out into the countryside, smell the flowers."

"But, sir—"

"What were you doing outside Firestane Consultancy yesterday?" Changing tack like flicking a little switch on a model railway—he looked exactly the kind of sad sack who enjoyed model railways.

"Firestane? Oh, eh, I was following a lead."

"A lead?"

"A person, I mean. The shredding guy who showed up at Lennox & MacGillivary and then at Ross Brownlee's house. He's involved with Ruaridh Callaghan, owes him money."

"Callaghan... That so? Interesting."

"I followed him to that building—assumed he had a customer there, but he came out empty-handed. What's the deal with Firestane?"

Devlin gave his bollocks a thoughtful itch before folding his legs, leaning forwards. "Do you know who owns Firestane Consultancy?"

"I looked it up but I can't remember—"

"William Jamieson."

"Right."

"Billy Jamieson. *The* Billy Jamieson."

McCoist cast her mind back to old war stories the ancient ones spoke of at the odd office do, usually around Christmas after a few pints. "There's that story, about the bloke's family and the tyre..."—she moved her hands in the air, taking an invisible tyre off an invisible car—"...thing. He was a big-time gang lord and then..."

"He went straight. More than thirty years ago. Had it all and walked away. Legend, almost myth."

"Do you believe that, sir?"

"Would I be telling you right now to stay the fuck away from Firestane Consultancy if I did?"

"No, sir. How did you—"

"Eyes and ears, McCoist. You know I can't say any more."

"You've been on him a long time?"

That smile again, fathomless, unknowable things lurking beneath which had never seen light. "He put me where you are once. In a hospitable bed. The end of my short-lived career as an undercover detective. Long time ago now, but I learnt my lesson."

"You're telling me you don't want me screwing with your personal vendetta?"

"I'm telling you a man like that never just walks away: he waits. And with McGuinn gone, his time is coming soon. He doesn't want the competition to know yet but he's lining up his ducks."

"What about Callaghan?"

"I'm not placing bets yet, but that time will come too. Taking my personal vendetta, as you say, out of it, Jamieson is the safer pair of hands. And there are already links between some of his 'legitimate' private investigators and some of ours."

McCoist bristled, everything was sore and sorry and awful. "You're talking about criminal enterprises, black markets, violence, human suffering," she rasped, every word a razor blade slicing her throat.

"I'm talking about stability. It's the best we can do, and it will save lives. Cheer up, Inspector, you've just dragged a murderer off the streets." He stood. "To reiterate my orders so there's no mistake: stay away from Firestane Consultancy, and take a couple of days off. Stop and smell the flowers." His eyebrows rose a hair and he left.

She turned to the lilies on the table. Twice he'd said it. She reached in for the card. Instead of "Get well soon", there were two long, decimal numbers. Coordinates. Then beneath: "BAR".

What? BAR—Burn After Reading.

Slater came back in. "Who was that? Polis, is he?"

"It's not initials."

"Hmm?"

"PLU. It's not somebody's initials, it's an acronym." She grabbed her phone and opened Google Translate. "Fucking posh boys. It's in Latin." She held her phone up for Slater to see: "*Post legendum ure.*" She did her best with the pronunciation.

"Burn after reading... Shite."

"MacGillivary was supposed to burn the notes, that's all." If she could have moved her head it would have slumped.

"Ach well, we've got the guy now, right? It doesn't matter. He'll be down the London Road interview room in a day or two giving us the goodies."

"Maybe…" She went to rub her throat but her hand hit the brace instead. "Nothing feels right."

"Alison, you've been through a hell of a lot. Maybe it's best if you don't rush straight back to work."

"Maybe not." She picked up the card from Devlin's flowers again. "Fancy a wee trip?"

51

She hit the Greggs for some yum-yums before heading to the hospital, even though Ginny probably wouldn't touch them and Colin had little appetite, although he was awake now and again, which was good. The doctors were happy with his progress. Ginny was briefly happy too, but then every day he got better he got closer to going back to Bar-L and the bad bastards waiting for him there. Whatever, the nurses could have them. If they promised not to share with whatever plod had been assigned to babysit. PC Shitfinger or Constable Fannychops or whoever.

Speaking of which, a familiar sodjer was coming towards her through the lobby, flanked by another plain-clothes. Lottie's jaw jutted, the greasy paper bag of yum-yums crinkled as her grip became an iron claw, thinking they'd been up to hassle Ginny and Colin. Then she noticed the brace around DCI McCoist's neck, the bags under her spaced eyes—red inkblot of a burst blood vessel in the white—and general aura of someone who'd just been chewed to cud, digested and shat out.

"Wit happened tae you?" Lottie asked. The partner gave her a look as if she were a fly that had splattered onto his windscreen, ready to flick the wipers on.

"Bit of rough and tumble," McCoist answered. Her voice made a sound like buffing a car with a curling stone. Reminded Lottie of her Auntie Ella—forty a day, started when she was eleven, a trachy and home oxygen hadn't stopped her yet. Lucky she didn't blow herself up.

"Hope ye gave as good as ye goat." Lottie felt unsure if she meant this or not. She remembered swinging at the woman herself, and her spry wee dodge out the way. Hadn't been fast enough this time. For all Lottie's anger towards the woman, seeing her in this state didn't give her the expected dirty high of schadenfreude.

"Thank you, Mrs McGuinn," she replied, seeming too tired for any more sparring. "Let me know how Colin is." She kept on going, the partner giving a double take after hearing the name.

"He'd be fine if it wisnae fir you!" she called after, but it was half-hearted, not feeling up for a barney herself. Another argument over the phone with Ari that morning—money, the flat, Aunt Ginny and Colin ("I'm glad he's in hospital!") and the usual bollocks—had drained her. Not to mention the mangey dog of Jamieson's threat shadowing her every waking moment. Ross would have known what to do. Paulo too—but then if he hadn't got himself killed then she wouldn't be in this mess in the first place. If he'd been more careful, if he hadn't been so fucking... *Paulo* about everything. She cursed the cunt and the mother who'd shat him out. She missed him. She was tired. She wanted to cry, no energy to rage. She took a deep breath, loosed her grip on the yum-yums and headed for the lift.

The minute she was in the door to Colin's room, Ginny pushed her back out. "Goin fir a cup ae tea," she called out, presumably to the guard. Despite wasting away from worry over the past year, her bony grip on Lottie's arm then was powerful and sharp as she marched her out of the ward.

"Wit—" Lottie started and stopped—Ginny's eyes were manic, days-without-sleep crazy. "Are ye OK?"

"Stupit fuckin question," she hissed under her breath.

"Fair doos. But a mean, like, has somethin else happened?"

"Aye. Aye it fuckin has." They didn't seem to be heading towards the cafeteria, just moving aimlessly with a purposeful stride. "Some *men* came last night."

"Wit? Here? Men? Wit men?"

"A don't fuckin know who they wur. But they said they wantet tae see how Colin wis daein. Hud a tub ae fuckin Celebrations an a balloon wae them. A big fuckin Spider-Man balloon, like ye get in the shoap doon the stair fir the weans."

"Wit the fuck?"

"Wit the fuck's right, Lottie. Wit the actual fuck?!"

"Did they say anythin else?"

Ginny stopped, Lottie skidding round to face her with the momentum. Her sister looked like she'd escaped from a secure unit. Her breath was rancid, smell of BO coming off her in thick, musky waves. "They asked if his aunty had bin by tae see him."

Fuck. "An wit did ye say?"

"A says naw! A telt them ye still werenae talkin tae me since, ye know."

"OK. Wit did they look like?"

"Wan wis young an big, in a suit. The other wis aulder, kind ae shrivelt up, looked like somethin scraped aff the flair ae the Savoy twenty year ago."

Double fuck. The first one could be Jamieson's secretary, the dreamy beefcake. Second one, who knew, he had plenty of unsavoury people working for him. Another warning? A follow-up to the phone call? They would know Ginny was lying, if it was Jamieson's outfit. They'd hurt Colin, she was pretty sure about that. Would they hurt Ginny too? Was that the message?

"Where wis the useless pillock who wis sposed tae be keepin watch?"

"Goan fir a slash or somethin."

"Convenient timin."

"The fuck huv ye got us intae noo, Lottie?" Ginny was crying.

"Wit dye mean, 'noo'?"

"If Colin hudnae gone tae work fir that crooket fuckin husband ae yours—"

"Wit?! *You* were the wan who asked us tae get Paulo tae take him oan!" Lottie screamed. People were looking, thinking about getting their phones out to film. "Like he wis desperate tae take oan some lazy fuckin eejit like yer son?! *You* wantet him oot the hoose, *you* begged me tae dae somethin aboot it. Then when it aw went tits-up, ye came tae me again askin me tae sort it oot! An if ye huvnae fuckin noticed that, oan toap ae grievin fir ma ain loss, that's exactly wit av been fuckin daein! Fir you! Ye ungrateful wee *BITCH!*" The shrill word filled the hallway and then died into sheer silence, like an explosive flame torching all the oxygen out of a space and leaving a vacuum behind.

Ginny sank down onto the floor, arms over her head, curling in on herself, shaking and sobbing.

Lottie got down next to her, tried to wrap her up in her arms. "Am sorry, am so sorry."

52

He hadn't gone to Inverness, as he'd told his mother, but had rather tried to lose himself in the West Highlands.

McCoist and Slater enjoyed a scenic drive into the mountains, McCoist trying to keep on top of her painkiller regimen and the lies she'd told so far.

"Matt Findlay."

"You know him? Put in a good shift in North Lanarkshire before moving to Glasgow, might have crossed paths."

"Maybe…" Slater was non-committal. "I'm better with faces than names. We'll see. But he's in this file Tim and Lennox had?"

"I think he's the one Tim meant; it would explain why he disappeared in a hurry after McGuinn…"

"Got himself *trepanned*." Slater's voice sounded smiley, a vulgar, childish wonder in his tone. "It's this ancient ritual where a hole is drilled into the cranium so—"

"Got it, thanks. You sound like Gaz."

"He was the one who recommended the podcast—"

"Fucksake. What's he doing to everyone? You'll be skateboarding as well next."

"If I still had the knees for it!"

"Anyway, so, yes, Findlay disappeared after McGuinn's death. Didn't even tell his maw where he was going. It seems likely he's the one Tim spoke of, though he didn't get the name quite right." She filled him in on the preliminary work she'd done trying to find the vanished Findlay which had come up against a dead end.

"Then you get a mysterious visitor who knows where he is." He couldn't keep the huffiness from his voice.

"Si, I'm sorry, it's not that I don't trust you—"

"Well, it is."

"Hey, I've brought you with me, haven't I?"

"Because you need a driver."

"Don't be like that." The neck brace stopped her from being able to turn towards him while belted into her seat. She reached out and pawed his thigh clumsily. "I'll let you know when I can. But honestly, it's better not to."

"For you?"

"And you. Deniability is power these days."

"Now who sounds like a chief constable?" The warmth had returned to his voice somewhat. "I'm just worried, that's all. Look what's happened already. You can't keep going in all this alone."

"I'm not. I've got my driver."

"Shut up."

"My valet, then, how's that?"

His hand found hers and squeezed. "Makes me sound like Parker from *Thunderbirds*. I'm not that much fucking older than you."

"If you're Parker, does that make me Lady Penelope, then?"

"We'll get you a pink neck brace, m'lady."

McCoist laughed and it hurt her throat. "I need to find this letter, Si. It's important."

"We have the guy though, don't we? The one who killed Lennox and Tim? Bloody nearly got you too."

"I think so. He's certainly the bloke I chased from Tim's flat. Hit me right on top of the head when he attacked me—knew it would be painful already."

"Fucking animal."

"And he tried to strangle me—fits the MO. It's him. He either thought I had the file or that I knew what was in it. Neither is true and I need to fix that. The case can't be solved until I do."

"If we get a solid DNA match from him to the van and the bathroom, maybe he'll tell us in exchange for a year or two off his hefty sentence."

"Maybe, but I can't afford to wait. It's important. To me."

"Sure. OK... guess I'll help then." He sighed. "A missing document, dodgy notes hidden in books..."

"Paper is privacy these days—oh, shit, I forgot to say..." She remembered to tell him about Chuck and Callaghan and the showdown at the shopping centre.

"FUCKSAKE!"

The GPS finally took them to the southern bank of Loch Leven, shrouded by trees, their backs to the verdant hills, facing the jewel-like water, resplendent and blinding in the late-afternoon sunshine.

"What a shitehole."

The caravan looked like it had seen better days—the moon landing, maybe, judging from the amount of rust on the brown paint job of the little one-bed two-wheeler attached to a car made on the other side of the century. Slater banged the door.

The curtain on the window drew aside and a young man with a thick beard looked out, immediately pulling it over again.

"DC Findlay!" McCoist shouted. "Nice to see you again!"

"Don't make me run round the back, son!" Slater chuckled, chapping the door of the tiny caravan again.

It creaked and rattled—pacing around inside. Eventually, the lock on the door snicked back. The beard added on a good few years to the boyish face McCoist had known, but the stress had done its work too, hollowing out the spaces between the bones, eyes loose and swivelling in their sockets, always on the lookout. "Ma'am," Findlay said, giving McCoist a slight nod. He looked Slater over, gave him nothing.

"I'm not here to bring you in, Findlay," McCoist said. "I just have some questions."

"Although, to clarify, if you don't answer them, then we will bring you in," Slater chipped in with a flash of a smile.

"That right, aye?" Findlay glared at Slater. "Ye eftir a new scarf tae match the gaffer's?"

Slater pretended to laugh. "You can go in the back seat or go in the boot, it doesn't bother me."

McCoist groaned. "Put the wee willy winkies away please, boys, I've not got my tape measure with me."

They kept eye contact for a good few seconds longer before Findlay finally broke away. "You can come in, boss. Yer dug stays ootside."

"Fu—"

"Fine."

"What? Alison—"

"It's fine, Sergeant."

"But—"

"Please. Si."

His face had turned blotchy and wounded. "OK. But open the curtain so I can see. If he tries anything—"

"Yel wit?" Findlay squared up again.

Slater's smile was ugly, sneering. "You know what it's like for a polis inside? They'll use knitting needles to turn you into a human KerPlunk. Then they'll fuck the holes they've made."

"Enough," McCoist warned. "Both of you."

Inside, the caravan was as lovely as the outside indicated. Only a little cosier than a worksite bothy, it smelt of tinned beans and the music they caused the human body to make. What it did have going for it, however, was an incredible view of the loch.

"Yer a coffee, right? Shovel ae grounds, shovel ae sugar—"

"To help you shovel the shite. Well remembered." McCoist felt an absurd and genuine flush of warmth towards the young former copper. Had to remind herself he was supposedly working for McGuinn all along.

"Yev gone up in the world since a last saw ye." The cups he slopped down must have come with the caravan, faded brown and green diamond pattern on beige ceramic with the odd chip. Matched the worn-flat corduroy of the bench seat by the window they sat on.

"Wish I could say the same about you, Findlay. You were a decent polis, so I thought."

"Hud enough ae it."

"Not long become a detective constable. Quite a milestone. Odd time to call it quits."

"Pressure goat tae me," he shrugged.

"So you decided to head up north and live the Good Life instead?" Her eyes took in the poky cabin, the unmade bed, the stack of climbing mags and pish bottle beside it.

"Laugh aw ye want, but it's simple, honest. A get up an a can go wherever a want."

"Honest. Right. So why did you tell your maw you'd taken a post up in Inverness?"

"She widnae understawn."

"Why you'd throw away a good job to live in a rolling outhouse?"

"Stoap fuckin aboot an just tell me why yer here," he snapped, his first show of aggression towards her, all others having been directed at Slater. He wasn't the man she'd known before. She'd never really known him though. She took a mouthful of coffee and made a show of savouring it's terrible, ashy, cultured-milk taste.

"You were working for Paul McGuinn, right? Bolted after he was killed. I thought maybe you were embroiled in the WhatsApp leak, but it just made for convenient timing, didn't it?"

He mirrored the move, sinking a decent draught from his own mug like it was a pint of lager. "Nae idea wit yer oan aboot."

"You were using your position as a police officer to aid his illegal operations."

"A wis usin ma position as a polis officer tae aid in ma chattin up ae the lassies doon the dancin. It wisnae a good enough reason tae keep it up."

"When McGuinn was killed you fled the city telling as few people as possible and leaving your direct debits in place to hide the fact you'd gone."

"Didnae want ma maw tae know fir a bit. Needed some breathin space. A take it yev spoken tae her?"

"Aye. She seems OK. Just worried about her son, that's all."

So far, he'd been batting answers back like in a friendly game of badminton; this time he shot back with a tennis smash. "Witdye say tae her?"

"Nothing much," McCoist answered sweetly. "Do you know Davey Burnet?"

"Who?" Agitated now.

"Worked at a car wash being used as a front for McGuinn's operations."

"Naw."

"That's funny, because one of the first things me and you ever did together was interview Davey Burnet after he ended up in hospital with a knife wound. And you told me how you'd met him previously—taken him to hospital when he was drunk one night."

"Am a sposed tae mind every drunk av ever booked?"

"You did then. You need to get straight which things you need to lie about, Findlay. The next people asking these questions might not ask so gently."

At that he sprang up to the window, looking out to the forest line, Slater's wee face giving him a stinking look. "Thoat ye said it wis just yous two."

"It is. For now."

He went to the other window, looking out at the water, the monumental hills on the other side, so clear and stark and colourful in the bright summer sun they looked as if they'd been painted on a backdrop.

"Talk to me, Findlay, come on. Davey Burnet. Last April, a girl was murdered. The two of you helped clean it up."

"Naw."

"You had no choice. It was McGuinn's orders. Clean it up or be the next victim."

"Load ae fuckin bollocks."

"It's not."

"Wit's yer evidence then?" He tried to make it sound like a challenge, but McCoist could tell he was actually eager to know, to know how bad his situation was.

She watched him carefully now. "A written record was made. It describes in detail this particular *event*." She laid it on a little, she didn't know how much Burnet's dear diary really got into the nitty-gritty, just the scant version Tim had suggested at.

"Written by who?"

McCoist held her silence.

"Burnet? Why the fuck wid he dae somethin fuckin silly like that? An wit wid it matter anyway? He said, she said, it's bullshit."

"It's enough to start a case on."

He snorted.

"Is that why you wanted to get rid of it?"

"Wit?"

"The record. You needed it and anyone who'd read it gone."

"*Wit?!*" He leant back, needing space from her, the accusation, face ferreted with incredulity "The fuck? Av only just bin telt aboot this hing an suddenly av sposed tae huv done wit exactly?"

"Ordered the deaths of two people."

He started to laugh, a full-bodied, drunken thing—a cosy fireside sound in other circumstances. "Ordered fae a take-oot menu? Aye. Aye that'll be right. Bin plannin elaborate crimes fae ma mobile HQ oot here in the fuckin jungle. Av no even goat a mobile phone. Who's the lucky punters then? Burnet wan ae them?"

"Not that I know of but, like you, he's hard to pin down. Lawyer called Carter Lennox and a lad who worked for him, a student intern called Tim Drummond. He used to work with Burnet at the car wash."

"Never even heard ae them."

"You sure?"

"Is Jesus a Cathlic?"

"...No. Jewish."

"Wit?"

"D'you mean the Pope?"

"Aye a mean the fuckin Pope. Noo, are ye done here? Cause am done."

"Thank you for the coffee, Findlay."

"Ma'am," he grunted.

McCoist stood. "Listen, son, you can't outrun this. Not forever. Help me and I can do the best I can for you."

He didn't look at her, picked at the peeling wood-effect vinyl of the table. "Here's some help fir ye—watch that cunt oot there."

"Who? DS Slater?"

"Aye."

McCoist's guts felt like a cold tangle of chains, jingling. "What? You know him?"

"No personally but he wis aboot when a wis in Motherwell an that, as a uniform. A mind him well."

"And?" Her heart was twitching faster. It was hot inside the cramped wee caravan, sun blazing into the window, bouncing off the water.

"It's funny ye mentioned the WhatsApp hing. Bunch ae lads gettin the sack oer durty jokes, an he's still here."

"He wasn't involved in any of that. The inquiry was thorough, relevant heads rolled."

"Guess he wisnae then."

"What are you getting at? Come on, just say it, I've had enough pissing about." Getting angry. Why though? He was just stirring the shite, that's all. Fucking bent polis, cleaning up after McGuinn's victims, helping him get away with all that and more. Scum of the scum.

"Am no grass, boss."

Now McCoist laughed. "Not a grass, no. You're compost—full of shite."

"If ye say so. But a geed ye fair warnin. If ye want tae look further, try tae get in touch wae a wummin cawed Cindy Ampleford. Used tae be a social worker, until yer pal goat her sacked. Lived in Jerviston but she may huv moved since."

Findlay's composure had completely returned, McCoist obviously looking like the one wrong-footed now, eyes dazed, mouth like a punctured sex doll. She had to fix that before heading out the door. "Thanks for the heads-up, I'll return the favour: skip the morning swim and get on the road now, you might still be a free man by lunchtime."

"What did he have to say?" Slater had recalled his face after all. ("A useless, swaggering wee shitehawk as far as I remember. Not surprised he was on the take.")

McCoist filled Slater in on Findlay's denials as they headed back south—he'd suggested a nice lunch or a coffee while they were "on holiday" in such a scenic part of the world ("You forget this stuff's right on your doorstep, it's mad!") but McCoist complained of needing a lie-down, feeling sore again, wanting to head straight home. She didn't tell him the real reason was that her body and brain were in turmoil, jostling between worry and disbelief, defiant, protective cries of "The boy's just a toalie-whisking bent polis" warring with insidious, niggling doubts which would not be ignored or bulldozed over. Doubts are like cockroaches, they survive and persist.

"Feeling all right?"

"Bit sick." She leant her head against the window, the scenery whipping past at the corner of her vision. Still swallowing razor blades, head keeping up in the pain contest, she could feel herself becoming unmoored from her place in the world. She thought of Tess and Cam and Bruce—they seemed far from her. A pang of loneliness and self-pity added to the overall feeling of full-body fucked-ness. Tears prickled.

"These windy roads won't be helping. Or maybe we should go back to the hospital—"

"No, it's OK. I just need my own bed."

He patted her thigh and she crossed her leg away from his hand. "Close your eyes for a bit if you need."

Her phone rang—DC Khan. "Gaffer?"

"Hi, Suffia."

"I'm sorry, I know I shouldn't be calling you but I thought you'd want to know."

"It's fine. What's up?"

"Your man's ready to leave the hospital. DI Griffiths is questioning him tomorrow."

53

He refreshed the results. Again. Again. *Moan tae fuck.*

The front door opened and he nearly threw his phone across the room. She didn't come into the living room though. Feet treading the stairs. Heavy, shoes still on. His heart was stuck in his throat, it felt like he'd swallowed a Jolly Rancher whole by accident. He stood up on treacherous stilts.

In the hall he heard thumping and bumping. He went upstairs as softly as he could. The bedroom door was shut all the way, his hand clammy on the handle.

Bell didn't acknowledge him in the doorway. She carried on moving her clothes from the drawers into suitcases which lolled open on their bed.

"Please. Don't, doll. Can ye speak tae me?" But he may as well have been Bruce Willis in *The Sixth Sense.* She carried on, though the set of her jaw and hyper-focus of her eyes straight in front of her at least gave away some awareness of his presence. "A know av fuckt it. Yer right. Ye gave me a second chance an a fuckt it. A wis lyin. A cannae help masel. A need ye tae help me." His voice a quiet, pleading whine. Making her cry again.

It had been bad. When he got home battered to fuck after his meeting with Callaghan. He couldn't deny it this time. She called him a gaslighting bastard. Like he was some kind of abuser. She wanted to know how long he'd been back gambling. "Months? Years? Is it fuckin *years*? A don't want tae know. A don't even want tae fuckin know—wis it years? Years yev bin takin me fir a fuckin mug?!" Had he ever stopped? Five years ago, when he lost his job and nearly went to jail, Bell had stood by him because he promised to get help for his addiction. Because she loved him. He'd done the meetings, he'd done the therapy. He'd managed for a while, chastened by his downfall, feeling lucky to be alive and free and to still have Bell by his side. He couldn't remember when he'd first slipped back. Was it a lottery ticket? A scratch card? Couple of quid, just a silly wee flutter, on match day? And when had it got serious again? The apps, the poker games, the loans? How could he even begin to explain how deep in it he was this time? How could he tell her what had happened with Jamieson and the dead lawyer? *It wis just an accident!* No, she didn't deserve that. Didn't deserve to be tied down by the weight of something so awful.

Still, he begged her not to go. Literally. On his hands and knees.

She left.

Gone to her maw's, though Chuck knew she wouldn't be able to stand that for long. Nat wouldn't be able to keep the gloating out of her voice as she delivered her sympathy with copious amounts of tea and tobacco.

Chuck slumped down on the sofa, breath still shuddering though he wasn't bawling any more. The house looked the same—she wasn't off with the furniture yet—but it wasn't. He'd been lonely a long time. The secret had put so much distance between him and Bell anyway. And every escalation had made it worse. Still, only now was he truly and utterly by himself in this mess.

His phone buzzed. Full time. A win. His stomach did a happy flip, his sick brain sucked at the dregs of hope it provided.

Fuckin eejit. Yer a fuckin eejit, a waste ae space. He should just delete the app right now. And the others. All of them. But he owed so much money again. His whole body was louping, top to bottom, bruises fresh and still growing into their full bloom. He had to keep going, didn't he? Even if Bell was no longer part of his getaway plan. The thought was a lump of shapeless, wet clay in his belly. She would come back, wouldn't she?

His phone buzzed again. Ringing, number withheld. He ignored it. Until it called for the fourth time and he couldn't. "Need tae be a bit quicker, Chuckie." A familiar voice. Theatrical, slick, for-the-telly Glaswegian.

"M-Mr Callaghan…"

"Thoat ye might as well make yersel useful, goat a joab fir ye doon at the shoap. Al gee ye a decent rate but it's set aff against the outstandin, right? Right."

Fuck.

Had to keep going. No choice.

54

There was something upper class about the way he looked. Healthy in a full, rich, red-faced way. Wholesome. (Apart from the bit of his ear that was missing.) Again, McCoist was put in mind of a children's TV presenter. They still didn't have a name for him so she'd taken to calling him "Mr Tumble".

Mr Tumble sat resolute and silent throughout the interviews. He hadn't requested a lawyer and sat alone at his side of the table while DI Griffiths and her sidekick sermonised and cajoled and pleaded and outright hassled him. They stuck pictures of his victims in front of his face. From the window, the pictures were too small for McCoist to see clearly, but Griffiths described them in detail for the recorder, and McCoist found herself seething and seasick at the details of Tim's strangling and partial dismemberment. Fresh guilt stung her.

They talked through both murders and the forensic evidence linking Mr Tumble to them. Mr Tumble did not react at all. He did not speak or shuffle in his chair or scratch himself. His big, ruddy moon face did not smile or frown or twitch. There was little doubt he'd killed Carter Lennox and Tim Drummond but no motive could be deciphered. Further DNA hits linked him to more deaths and polis from other parts of the UK were interested. There were rumours that Europol had been in touch with the big high heed yins.

"A contract killer," Slater said. "Bloody hell. You were right about it not being over, Alison. We need to find who hired the bastard." The office was pure buzzing with activity and excitement. It was like being in a packed pub on Christmas Eve, and McCoist just wanted to go home.

"I'm off, said I'd go see the kids at Mark's." She wasn't officially back to work yet anyway. "Let me know if anything else comes up."

Slater seemed a bit disappointed but his words were all sympathy. Findlay's hinted accusations had begun to colour his every action in McCoist's already overwhelmed mind.

She took a taxi out to Mark's. Bruce bounded from the front door and jumped her, his big slebbery tongue lapping at her face. "Calm down, baby!" she laughed. The vet had given him a clean bill of health and Mark had let him stretch out on the chaise longue due to his status as a hero.

Mark made her coffee, got some biscuits out for Tess and Cam, and they sat together with the telly on, watching some shite, all crammed in together on the same sofa, Bruce lording over his own throne. The twins were too old for this, but they didn't complain, and their quiet affection towards her was like a balm to her tattered, scabby soul. She let it soothe her. Tears began to drip and it hurt her throat even more.

But her brain wouldn't stop.

She made her excuses and tore herself away when her Uber pulled up outside. "I'll be back later to pick up Bruce."

Cam had doubts written on his face. Tess voiced them: "You can't go, not after what happened. What if something…" She was crying now.

"I thought you were off for a bit," Mark said. "Can you not just—"

"I can't."

"But—"

"Don't. You know I can't. Don't be silly, guys. I'll see you all later."

Tess stormed off to her room. Cam pulled Bruce into his lap and flicked through the channels. Mark's face was resigned.

Cindy Ampleford did still live in Jerviston, in a flaky, lemon-painted semi-detached in a row of the same. Visitors were greeted with the shoulder of the house as they pulled up—the arrowhead gable end faced the street while the front doors were tucked down each side. The building seemed to be guarding itself from something. The front garden was weeds-through-gravel and empty planters. A satellite dish perched on the roof livened the whole thing up.

Cindy positively sparkled among the drab surrounds. "Av bin waitin fir wan ae yous tae show up sometime. Yer a good few year late, mind. Guess wae aw that WhatsApp stuff in the daily rags yeez need tae look as if yer daein somethin, eh? A honestly cannae decide whether tae drag ye in or tell ye tae fuck aff." She immediately turned and said, "Moan."

"Getting ready for a night out?" McCoist asked.

"Wit makes ye say that?"

"Oh, you just, I dunno, you look all dressed up."

"Fashion polis, wis it? Can a see yer cerd again?... Alison McCoist." She gave her the look, McCoist returned a warning one. "Major Investigation Team. So they're pullin oot aw the stoaps then?"

"When you said you were expecting me, Miss Ampleford—"

"Cindy, please, hen."

"Cindy. Sure. What did you mean?"

"Well, yer lookin fir dodgy polis aren't ye? Eftir aw the recent scandals. Men who've bin abusin their powers. Historical abuse an that."

The words made McCoist's stomach do a bungee jump. "Can you tell me your story?"

"Al put the kettle oan—naw, actually, fuck it man, a need a proper drink fir this."

A proper drink was a Prosecco-and-gin cocktail in a champagne saucer with a raspberry floating in it. McCoist declined, although it was tempting. Dress glittering and glass in hand, Cindy looked like an extra from *The Great Gatsby*—apart from the thick slipper socks on her feet.

"A used tae work at Coleridge."

"What's that?"

"It's a wummin's shelter, an if ye don't know where it is am no gonnae tell ye. Less cunts who know these hings the better. Even polis."

"Fair."

"Almost ten year a worked there, seein the worst ae it. Wummin beaten black an blue, wummin carryin their rapist's babbies inside them, some ae them little mare than weans themsels."

"Must have been tough."

"Aye. It wis. But a loved ma joab. Ye genuinely goat tae help folk. Get them back oan their feet, start a new life. Ye see them come in, fuckt sideways an loast like rubbish oan the street, an oer the time, they become like new people. Or maybe the person they were afore they goat tore apart by some fuckin animal."

She allowed herself a long sook at the champagne saucer. "Anyway, as yel know, we huv tae deal wae oor fair share ae polis.

Some ae the wummin who came tae live wae us were marriet tae them, ye may well know."

"I do."

"Fuckin filth, if yel excuse me. Others were investigatin cases involvin oor girruls, came tae take statements and deliver updates an that. There wis this wan... *man*... but, who wis tryin tae use the place like a fuckin singles night."

"How d'you mean?"

"Och, he went aboot like he wis a fuckin knight in flabby armour, bringin lassies tae safety an punishin their wicked abusers, but he wis just as bad. Preyin oan them, no leavin them alane, wantin somethin in return fir his good deeds. An these lassies are just oot ae years ae bein battert an belittled, their strength an dignity stripped aff them. He used their need ae comfort an safety, ae somewan tae be gentle wae them, tae get them intae bed. It wis fuckin rank rotten."

McCoist had to make an effort to control her breathing, slow her heart. "And did you report him?"

"A brought it up wae ma boss an then next hing a knew, a wis gettin the sack."

"What for?"

She allowed herself another long scoop, dabbed carefully at her wax-red lips. "Some ae they lassies are strung oot till they're thinner than a minge hair—frightened, anxious, huvin night terrors an flashbacks, ye know? Some ae them are comin aff hings, the hard stuff, an aw. So, sometimes, ad gee them a wee bit ae grass."

"You were dealing weed to domestic-abuse victims?"

"*Dealin!*" she scoffed. "A wisnae fuckin dealin! Wur talkin aboot a joint here an there tae unwind them a bit. It wis fuckin therapy."

"Still, Christ, you were giving illegal drugs to women in your care. Some of whom, as you said yourself, had addiction issues."

Cindy gave a derisive laugh and finished her cocktail. "Such a fuckin polis. Am sat here tellin ye aboot wan ae yer ain bein a fuckin sex pest, usin vulnerable lassies fir their ain gratification, an aw you're worried aboot is a bit ae green bein puffed. Useless. An cunts are surprised when it turns oot the whole polis is fuckin riddelt wae wrang yins. Aye right. A lose ma joab an noo, years later, yer here tae add insult an cover arses."

"That's not how it is, Cindy."

"Ye know wit, hen? Go back tae Miss Ampleford. An get the fuck oot ma hoose."

McCoist retreated towards the door, Cindy close enough she could smell the gin and fruity perfume.

"Come back when yer actually plannin oan daein somethin."

"I am. Look, I'm sorry this got a bit heated, but I need to know—"

"Wit? A telt ye it aw. Did ye no listen?"

"His name, you didn't tell me his name."

"Ye must know it awready. Why else wid ye be here?"

"I need to hear it from you." McCoist's blood thundered through her body, made her tremble with the force of it.

Cindy huffed. "Simon Slater."

55

McCoist had to beg Cindy for a victim who could corroborate, was ready to drop to her knees on the doorstep for it. Cindy finally made a call—"only cause the lassie's daein awright fir hersel noo"—and gave her a name and address.

Melanie Coburn was indeed doing all right for herself. A four-bedroom new-build in Mearns with a double garage and a back garden you could play rounders in. Melanie herself was slight in baggy clothes, her hair was greasy and tied back, the red cracks in the whites of her eyes screamed for a good sleep. From the doorway, McCoist could smell why.

"He's six months. That's him just sittin up noo, aren't ye wee man?"

A chubby babe in a bursting-at-the-seams onesie, planted like a bag of sand on the play mat, gurgled and dribbled at McCoist, one fat hand grasping in her direction.

"Eatin food too, an aw that work's ruint his sleep. That's right, isnit?" Melanie addressed him in a cutesy, high-pitched voice and little Herby smiled at her.

McCoist felt an involuntary flutter in her belly. She'd never been gooey about babies until she had her own, and even then it wasn't like every drooler she spotted made her start feathering her nest—however, he was very cute. 'I know all about that. I've got two myself. Twins. They're teenagers now, but..."

"Twins! Fucksake, how did ye manage? A feel like am barely sleepin wae just the wan!"

"I honestly don't know. You have to, so you just do." She had a flashback of a fridge door covered in timetables—who's been fed when, who's napped, who's filled their nappy… "You'll be sick of hearing it, but this stage passes before you know it. Eventually you'll get to sleep, but they'll never be babies again."

Melanie grimaced at the platitude.

"What did Cindy tell you on the phone?"

Melanie turned to fuss at Herby, but McCoist could tell her eyes were not really looking at the baby, not taking him in. "She said ye wantet tae speak tae me aboot Simon Slater."

"That's right. I want to hear what happened, if you'll tell me."

A smile played on Melanie's lips. "If Damo wis here, just the soond ae the cunt's name wid set him aff oan wan."

"Herby's dad?"

"Aye. Ma husband. Damien."

"What's Damien like?"

"Don't." Melanie's eyes snapped to McCoist's, suddenly awake. "Damo's a great guy. A great dad. He just, he cannae stand wit happened, that Si goat away wae it aw. Ye know, Damo even hired a private investigator tae try tae get somethin oan him. Waste ae money, a telt him, an a wis right. Guys like Si don't get done. Hink Damo wis expectin Benedict Cumberbatch tae come waltzin through the door an fuckin crack the case wae his mind palace or somethin." She laughed. It wasn't bitter. McCoist could hear in it the fondness Melanie had for her husband.

"And what did DS Slater do?" McCoist had heard Slater's version of how they had met. The unease in her gut told her

Melanie's would be quite different. Their first kiss in the car assaulted her and she had to shoulder it aside.

Melanie took a shuddering breath. She lifted Herby onto her lap and let her hair down so he could play with it. "A wis nineteen an goat pregnant wae ma boayfriend, who wis a sick cunt. Used tae hit me. An worse. Aw that shite. We'd bin thegether since school. Years. A left him an went back tae him, left him again. Oer an oer. A couldnae… a dunno." There was a hardness in her face. "Wan night, he geed me a doin so bad a ended up in hoaspital. Loast the babby. A wis aboot… five, six month. Aye." She rubbed the heel of her hand hard against the corner of an eye.

"Si hud bin assignt tae the case. Only, instead ae bangin ma ex up, he beat him up. Said he did it fir me. Fir justice or witever. Said if he'd took him in, charged him, he'd be lucky tae get as much as six month inside. This way, apparently, he goat wit he deserved an he wis warned. But…

"A hud tae go tae a shelter, no matter wit Si says, a knew wit ma man wis like. He wis oot there, an he'd come back fir me. So, a says tae Si a need tae go somewhere safe, an he sets me up at Coleridge. An that's awright an that, but he keeps comin back. Nothin's happenin wae ma case but he keeps comin back. An bringin me wee gifts an that, choaclits an fags, witever. An he started like…"

"D'you need a break? Something to drink?"

Melanie shook her head.

"It wis confusin, fir me. Ad just bin, ye know… an Si's tellin me how he saved us an aw that. How he wis protectin me. That as lang as a wis wae him…" A tear broke free.

"Did he pressure you into having sex?" The words were ash in McCoist's mouth.

"Aye." Melanie batted the tear from her face. "Aye, he did. A wis nineteen. A didnae know how tae handle… evryhin that hud happened tae me awready, and then here he is—he didnae say a owed him but that's wit it felt like. Like it wis the only hing a could dae."

"How long did this go on for?"

"Months, an then just wan day it wis like, a dunno, he goat bored ae me. Foont some other poor broken burd he needed tae look eftir. Didnae know how tae feel. Relieved. Scared. Loast waeoot him. Wit wis a tae dae? Ma ex wis still oot oan the street, an Si who'd promised tae protect me hud fucked aff." Her laugh now was bitter. "Cunt."

"What did you do?"

"There were some good folk workin at Coleridge."

"Like Cindy?"

"Aye. An some good wummin stayin there too. They helped me. Si bein oot the picture made that easier. Sounds pure cheesy sayin it, but a could start tae heal."

Herby latched on to his mother's forearm and tried to suckle. "Looks like somebody's hungry," McCoist said.

"Again."

"Thank you for sharing this with me, I appreciate how hard that must have been."

"Aye well, Cindy says yer gonnae actually dae somethin aboot it. Is that right?"

"That's right."

56

"Close the door." Almost never a good sentence to hear in the workplace. Slater thought McCoist was about to share another piece of top secret, don't-tell-anyone-or-we're-getting-canned-and-maybe-arrested information, so he did it excited as a schoolboy playing spies, casting a quick, suspicious eyeball over the office first. He should have trained his beady eyes on McCoist instead. If he had, he would have noticed the set of her jaw over the top of the neck brace, the stare set to MRI—brain-cooking levels of radiation coming from it.

"Got something else from your man with the flowers?"

"Sit down, Simon."

"Everything OK?" He was picking up on it now, a crease of worry on his forehead.

"Coleridge."

"Sorry?"

"It's a shelter for abused women on your old beat."

"I know. Worked a few cases involving women there, not many usually want to pursue charges though. They don't trust us—"

"With good reason."

He sighed, put on something like contrition, more like *what-can-you-do?* "Fair enough, the stats are, um, yeah pretty bad—"

"I'm not talking about the stats. I'm talking about *you*."

"Me? What?" Confusion—a bravura performance.

"What happened at Coleridge?"

"Wha... oh this is, this, right. That Ampleford woman. I didn't think she'd even put it in writing in the end. It was so obviously just a vindictive... attack. On me."

"It wasn't in a report."

"You spoke to her? Wait, has this got something to do with Findlay, that corrupt little weasel—Alison, tell me you don't think I'd..."

"What?"

"That I'd, uh... *harm* anyone. Look, I caught that woman peddling drugs to the clients, I informed her boss, and she cooked up some story of, of... *impropriety* to get back at me. Spiteful cow."

"She wasn't charged with anything. Not even cautioned."

"Her boss dealt with it and that was enough, as far as I saw it. Maybe not strictly by the book but you're hardly one to talk on that front." He chuckled.

"Meaning?"

"What? Nothing. Alison, it was a joke, I wasn't—I wouldn't. What's going on here?"

"DS Slater, I'm referring you to the Anti-Corruption Unit based on—"

"Based on what?! The testimony of a bent ex-job and an ex-social worker who got the sack for selling drugs to abuse survivors? Alison, you can't—"

"Boss."

"Sorry?"

"It's 'boss', or 'gaffer'. I can. And I'm going to. It's not just Findlay and Cindy Ampleford either. I spoke to Melanie Coburn. Remember Melanie? Melanie whose boyfriend put her in hospital who you then let skip off free? Melanie, a victim of abuse who you then harassed into—"

He stood up, chair scraping backwards, looming over her.

McCoist held eye contact. She'd battered gangsters and hitmen, no chance she'd be intimidated by a shabby, middle-aged polis. This had made it easier. The betrayal, the hurt. Turned to anger in an instant.

"Bullshit. Nothing happened between me and Melanie."

"That's not what she says."

"You spoke to her off the record, I suppose? Your usual technique. How are you going to explain how you even came by this information? Findlay is a big thread to pull, is he not? His accusation led you to Ampleford. Who led you to him? Go on. Explain that."

McCoist played stone. Her mind thrashed around for a clever answer.

"You can't. You're absolutely fucking *mired* in secrets, Alison. All the stuff with Tim and assassins and this file, or letter or whatever, you're looking for. It's rotten. All of it. And you're up to the eyebrows."

"Who the fuck do you think you are?" she hissed.

His chuckle was ugly now, boorish. "A question just as easily levelled at you. Who d'you think has more to lose?"

"Get out. You're on sick leave."

"How?"

"Injury. Your hand. I put through the paperwork."

"This is fucking stupid. So fucking stupid." He slammed the chair back under the desk and stormed from the office.

McCoist wanted to press her forehead against her desk but the neck brace stopped her from being able to. She swallowed tears down her ruined throat. Angry, scared, alone.

As if to back up Slater's threat, her email pinged. She was required for a debrief. They had questions for her.

57

Marble and Roughcast came to pick him up personally. This was not a good sign. But the back of their motor was a lot nicer than the back of the Gnome's van. And he wasn't bound and gagged. A case of "better the devil you know", maybe. Though the job Callaghan had for him at the old shops was fine. He had him clear out the crap left in some of the back rooms, let him cherry-pick the boxes of CDs he found in the supermarket stockroom, chart hits from when it was last open. Took *Human After All, You Could Have It So Much Better, The Massacre* and a few others for the van. A wee freebie and the beating was forgotten about, apparently. *Fuckin Eejit*. That would be the name of Chuck's album. His self-disgust was working overtime since Bell left, and it was a muscular emotion to begin with, buffed up over the years with every lie, every bet, money won, money lost, all the same. He'd deleted the apps again. Except one—the Great Accumulator, against all odds, was still on. He'd almost forgotten too, almost written it off. Didn't dare to hope. *Fuckin eejit.*

"So say there's this tidy wee burd, right? But there's also this fuckin, eh, sort ae George Clooney-lookin guy, ye know, a handsome wan, right? How dye know who tae go fir?"

Marble seemed relieved to pull up at the office. The office was another good sign for Chuck. They weren't taking him somewhere remote or quiet. You couldn't come to harm in an office.

·   ·   ·

Chuck screamed as the blades of the electric pencil sharpener turned on his pinkie.

Marble was behind him, pushing his chest and head onto the desk with all his sculpted weight while Roughcast had an iron grip on his wrist. The pencil sharpener was automatic. Roughcast let his hand go and it sprang from the machine, Chuck squealing, panting, stars in his vision, acid in his belly. The nail had been torn off, a chunk of flesh was gone from the tip, and what was left had been flayed down several layers closer to the bone.

"Yer gonnae tell me wit yev bin up tae, Chuck, or wur gonnae dae each finger in turn. When wuv run oot ae fingers, it'll be yer foreskin goin in there." Jamieson's tumshie visage had that cool blue glow behind the eyes again. He tapped the sharpener. "Ye like it? Goat the idea fae yersel an Brownlee. Scaled it doon." He wasn't teasing. Jamieson never teased, never ribbed, never jested. The question was genuine.

Chuck struggled to catch his breath. The sharpness of the pain was gone, replaced by a throbbing, steady ache causing waves of giddiness. The compartment of the sharpener which caught the shavings was see-through. It did indeed look like a mini diorama of the Brownlee-shredding incident. Chuck did a mini sick in his mouth.

"Moan then, wit's the story?"

"A-a, eh, um—"

Jamieson huffed. "Next finger."

"Naw! Naw!" The breath was squeezed out of him again as Marble pushed down. Roughcast had to use both hands, was sweating and panting trying to manoeuvre Chuck's ring finger into place. Chuck had balled his hand into a fist but

Roughcast prised the finger out, bending it back close to breaking point.

"Callaghan!" He screeched the name, the vowels raking his voice box on the way out.

Jamieson held up a hand and they let go, letting him sit back in the chair.

"Callaghan's men j-jumped me." He pointed to his bruised face. "Made me dae some work fir them. Nothin like, like wit a dae fir you. Just clearin oot some shoaps he wants tae dae up."

"Why?"

"A borrowed money." Tears and snot were threatening to creep down.

"An yev loast it?"

"Some ae it," he sniffled.

"Maist ae it?"

"Aye." He couldn't look at Jamieson. Made himself look at the pencil sharpener instead, the compartment full of skin shavings and blood.

Big sigh. "Ach, Chuck. A says tae ye afore that a hate seein ye in here. An al say it again. It makes me sad. Look at ye. Look at wit's happened tae ye. Cause ye cannae get this fuckin demon ae yours unner control. A thoat eftir wit happened wae Brownlee that maybe, wae a clean slate, yed, a dunno—fuck it. Am no yer fuckin counsellor."

Chuck tried to smile.

"An am no yer financial advisor either, but if a hear aboot ye takin any mare money fae that shady cunt, or any other shady cunt, al put ye through yer ain machine." He leant over the table. Chuck could see the gleam of fire in the pits of his eyes, smell the rot from within. "An ye know a don't make empty threats. Yev seen it fir yersel." He sat back again, looked to his goons. "Dae the next finger."

Chuck screamed but he didn't have the fight in him to struggle away this time. His ring finger went into the pencil sharpener and its electric motor whirred to life and the rotating blades—the small, spiral-toothed maw of the shredder's bastard, suckling baby—chewed into him. Slivers of bloody skin fell into the compartment.

They gave Chuck a minute to pull himself together, stop howling and hyperventilating. Roughcast mopped his brow and flexed his hands. All this was a bit of a workout for him. Marble gave him a withering look.

"Wit's important tae remember, Chuck, is that yer wae us. Ye mind a says yer wae us noo?"

"A-aye."

"Good. Ye didnae forget. An yer no gonnae forget, are ye?"

"Naw."

"Yer no gonnae get confused an hink yer wae Callaghan, noo that ye owe him money instead, are ye?"

"Naw."

"Cause wit we actually huv here is a nice opportunity. Ye see where am goin?"

Chuck did see where he was going, and it was a path which ended with a tombstone with "STUART 'CHUCK' GARDNER" carved on it. No, *Fuckin Eejit* wouldn't be his album name, it would be his epitaph.

"Ruaridh Callaghan hinks he's gonnae be the main man noo, since the demise ae wan Paulo McGuinn. But Ruaridh Callaghan is wrang. Course, av hud the feelers oot fae him awready, but this geez us a chance tae get closer. So, whenever

Callaghan has ye dae any mare wee joabs fir him, ye come tae me straight eftir an tell me wit it wis. Ye keep yer eyes an ears *peeled* an report back anyhin an evryhin."

"Aye."

"Great. It's aw worked oot quite well." Something like a smile crinkled his old face and he leant back, at ease. "Sweet as a nut. An as it happens—another happy bit ae providence—av goat an errand fir ye tae run. Oh, an a joab loat ae shite tae take wae ye an aw."

Chuck received his instructions while Marble bandaged his fingers up.

Jamieson left him with a parting thought: "Here, if ye double-cross me, son, al gee ye the final send-aff masel. Ma ain personal touch. Naebdy's bin sae lucky in a lang time. Hopefully yer losin streak continues."

58

The puma hit the floor with a sound like her life coming apart. "Fuck you!" she screamed and laughed and started to cry. "Fuck you."

She wasn't exactly blameless though, couldn't put it all on her dead husband. She knew what he was, what he did. She could have walked away at any time. Couldn't she? What would he have done if she had tried to leave? "A relationship is fir life," he'd once said, "nae matter the ups an doons or wit it says or disnae say oan a bit ae paper." He meant that in business as well as marriage, another kind of business. He'd never been violent with her, though their arguments sometimes reached a level of scary that made her tremble for an hour afterwards. She could tell he was showing restraint and that made the fear worse. The things she heard about him too... And the latest trouble—Ross's death, Colin being attacked, her sister threatened, that had all started when she went to Jamieson. Another man of power and wealth and violence. And she was definitely trapped by him, that decaying auld cunt.

"Mum? What the fuck?!"

She sniffed hard and wiped her eyes with her sleeve. "It's OK, doll, it's—"

"That was Dad's!" Voice of an injured child—hear the trembling lip. For a second Lottie almost tried to claim it was an accident. That she hadn't taken the ugly bastard thing by its front legs and slung it onto the hard, varnished wood. The sound of it breaking echoed to the high ceiling, both heavy and brittle.

"You've been wanting to do that since the moment he died."

"Naw, Gemma, naw that's no true, it wis, a wis—"

"Ari's right. You don't care. You're glad he's gone."

"The fuck ye sayin?!" The pressure had been constant; the valves finally burst. "Ye huv nae fuckin idea wit yer even oan aboot! Neither ae yeez dae! So just shut yer wee fuckin mooth an try tae be grateful fir fuckin wance!"

Gemma snatched up a chunk of puma rubble and launched it towards her mother, missing and skelping the piano with a crash and a deep, atonal rumble from the strings inside. She turned and marched up the stairs, bawling.

Lottie turned her back also, sought a different refuge in the kitchen: a good pour of gin with a bit of fizzy water to top it up. Not long after, she heard the front door slam.

The text from Ari was predictably scathing and burning with a righteous anger that made Lottie simultaneously want to laugh at her and smack her and beg for forgiveness. Gemma would be staying at her flat for a bit. Probably why she was so angry—the inconvenience. Cloaked in something noble. The gin had not calmed Lottie or made her feel charitable. At least she decided not to reply just yet.

The doorbell went and she had business to attend to anyway.

"Simply Shred."

"Mrs McGuinn."

"Wit happened tae you? Ye look like yev bin put through yer ain machine."

The smile he returned was painful, maybe because of all the damage to his pus, but maybe something more behind it. "Sports injury."

"Aye. Right. Moan in. Get ye a drink afore we start?"

"If yer meanin coffee…"

Shite, had she really had that much? Could he smell the booze off her? Or was she acting drunk? Fuck it. "If ye want. Or the good stuff if it's no too early fir ye. An we can stoap pretendin this is a normal visit tae dae a normal joab."

"Fair doos. A could huv a small wan an still drive."

59

She was dishevelled compared to the stylish woman he'd met in the waiting room at Firestane. He couldn't exactly speak though, his face textured like Artex, coloured like rotting red cabbage, and his fingers bandaged up. He held his glass of Balvenie like he was having a cup of tea with royalty.

The gaff was like a film set, dramatic and vast and Insta-aspirational to a sickly extent. Looking closer, it was untidy, starting to look lived-in around the edges. A statuette was in pieces on the floor. A broken big cat.

She took him to the office. Big boss desk, a knight's helmet on a pedestal, framed poster of Pacino, signed Gers top, a display of wrestlers—the Rock, Stone Cold, the Undertaker, Mankind, all the troops were there. *Fuckin class*, Chuck thought, unable to keep a boyish smile from his cratered face.

"A see yer a man ae good taste like ma husband wis." Sarcasm as obvious as the drink on her breath.

"Used tae watch the wrasslin at ma gran's hoose cause she hud cable. She wis a big Rowdy Roddy Piper fan. Said he wis daein us aw proud. A mean, a telt her he wisnae actually fae Glesga but she didnae care."

"How are we daein this?" Not even a smile for his wee granny. "Straight tae it or are ye gonnae go through the shite first?"

"Well, it's goat tae look like a proper joab so—"

"So av tae pay fir the fuckin privilege?"

"A guess ye could talk tae Mr Jamieson aboot it—"

"*Mr* Jamieson," she snorted with a school-bully sneer about her.

Chuck felt himself flush, hardened his tone. "An he wants tae be sure yer no hawdin anythin back. So aye, a better go through it aw."

She leant back in the mammoth Bond-villain swivel chair. "But he knows there's nothin in there. He awready sent wan ae his wee stooges tae huv a look aroon while a wis oot. Right?" She seemed genuinely curious now. Her moods were slipping about all over. Another sip of gin wouldn't help but she took it.

"Nae idea, am no the man who knows. Look at me." And she did, flayed him with her eyes.

"Naw, a guess no. But then, who are ye?"

She got him started with "some auld shite" to sort and cart out to the van and he told her his sorry tale. Partly because he was expecting one in return, mostly because he needed someone to tell. The person he most wanted to speak to would not answer his calls. But Lottie asked and she would maybe understand—she was already entangled herself.

"So yer gettin spit-roastet by Callaghan oan wan end an Jamieson oan the other."

"That's the length an girth ae it, aye." That brought a smile to Lottie's face. "Hows aboot yersel? How dis the wife ae the city's biggest gangster end up bein extorted by the likes ae Billy Jamieson?"

"Some cunt kills her husband, then she's no langer the wife ae the city's biggest gangster. Hings slope doon fae there." She sighed, looked through the bottom of her empty tumbler.

Chuck let her have the space. "Jamieson wis sposed tae help me find oot who really did it. Who really killt Paulo. The polis huv ma nephew banged up fir it an ma sister's goin mental. A went tae him tae help her. Noo he's usin her against me tae get wit he wantet all alang. He fuckin killt Ross an aw."

"Ross? Brownlee?" Chuck's guts coiled up around his stomach like a snake choking a rat. He had omitted that part of his story. The look on Lottie's face made him regret asking.

"Aye. Ye knew him?"

"Eh—"

"Ye fuckin know wit happened, don't ye?" She was out of the chair, bearing down on him. Chuck noticed how lethal her nails looked.

"How... eh, how dye know him?"

"He wis ma pal," she hissed, seething, standing to pace the office floor. "An that bastart hud him killt. Accident he says, the lyin—"

"It wis an accident." The whisky was sitting in his gut like a puddle of bin-bag leakage. "Honest, it wis a fuckin accident, a fuckin awful wan, horrible, a, a huvnae bin able tae stoap fuckin hinkin, fuckin seein it when a sleep, it wis—"

"Wit happened?"

"Ye don't want tae know."

"Tell me."

And he did. He regurgitated it like off meat. He could see it right there in front of him—half the head gone, the bottom teeth, the bits and blood and buckets. Lottie sank back into the big chair, put her hands on the desk, spread her fingers as if feeling the surface for something. "Am so sorry," Chuck said, his voice a husk. He felt wrung out too, slumping into the chair opposite. "But a couldnae—by the time a goat tae the button it wis too late, an…"

They sat for a time. Eventually, Lottie stood and went to the display case full of wrestlers. She unlocked it and took one from the shelf. "Ye said yer granny's favourite wis?…"

"Rowdy Roddy Piper."

"Aye, well, this wis Paulo's."

"Stone Cauld." She put the action figure down in front of him. Steve Austin moulded in plastic, shining bald head and angry-man goatee, "Austin 3:16" on the back of his vest. "A liked him an aw." It sounded moronic, but Chuck couldn't think of anything else to say. Why was she showing him this?

Then she pulled him in half—split at the waist. Protruding from the bottom of his torso was the blade of a key. "The door this opens isnae noted in any ae this paperwork yev bin humfin aboot. It's no oan the computer either, if ye were plannin oan takin that an aw." She tapped her head.

"That's wit he's eftir?"

She nodded.

"So ye gee him that an it's aw oer?"

"Maybe, maybe no. Doubt it'll help ma sister or ma nephew. Hows aboot you?"

Chuck's problem was threefold:

1—He owed Callaghan a bathtub of money and was having to work it off.

2—He was under Jamieson's thumb because he helped clean up Brownlee's murder and was therefore being forced into spying on Callaghan.

3—He might be killed by either one of these psychos at any time.

So no, it would not be over for him. Not any time soon. Unless…

"Maybe we need tae dae somethin, Chuck, instead ae just goin alang wae it an hopin fir the best. Wid be takin a chance, but. A big chance. Freedom or fuckt… Wit dye say?"

Oh, and also:

4—He could not stop fucking gambling.

60

The summer sun was dragging the day out forever. The view across the city was still clear from the flagpole: Glasgow uni tower; the Finnieston Crane; the old Metropolitan College building, completely pink down its southward face with "PEOPLE MAKE GLASGOW" emblazoned on it, sticking up from the city centre like a fat middle finger. In the distance beyond the sprawl, the Campsie Fells were gentle waves of green meeting the sky.

"It's good tae see it like this sometimes," Chuck said.

"From a great distance?" McCoist replied.

"Ever the cynic, Inspector."

"Chief Inspector, Mrs McGuinn."

"Ye actually need that hing fir yer neck? Made ae brass is it no?"

"Makes it impossible to reel in," McCoist smiled. She eyed both of them—Chuck looking like the barely surviving bait from a dogfight, Lottie sleep-deprived and shifty. What a good-looking group the three of them made, standing in the cobbles and broken glass of the Queen's Park observation deck. "So how did this union come about then?"

"Assurances first, then we talk." Lottie took charge. Chuck backed her up with folded arms and a forced pout—though maybe with his pus in that state every expression looked like a painful grimace. Fizzog like a haemorrhoid.

"What kind of assurances? I can't offer anything without any idea of what you've got for me." All bluff. McCoist wanted to hear them out. She'd been almost salivating since she'd got the call. Was it Burnet's letter? Did they know about it? Did they have it? (She needed good news, really fucking needed it, especially now with Slater's shit-stained shank in her back and his threat pressing on her brain.) Walking into blackmail? Maybe, she'd thought. She weighed up what she knew about Gardner and his debts—she had too much leverage against him for him to try that on her, but Lottie McGuinn? Wouldn't put it past her.

"A want two hings," Lottie bulldozed on. "Wan: reopen the investigation into ma man's murder, get Colin oot the jail."

"Lottie—"

"We baith know it wisnae him. Stoap fuckin aboot. Get him oot an get it sortet properly this time. Two: ye take Billy Jamieson doon."

McCoist almost laughed. "Just a small favour then, is it? Billy Jamieson's a legitimate businessman, so I hear." Devlin's warning about staying away from Jamieson echoed in her head.

"Aye, an middle-aged men go tae Thailand cause they really like elephants," she snorted. "Yer a *chief inspector*, as ye pointed oot. Surely it's no ootside yer realm ae influence, big shoat."

"No." Although she really wasn't sure, she couldn't afford to give the impression she had nothing to offer. "But it's still a big ask. The information you promised would have to be pretty spectacular—"

"It is. But a make nae promises if you don't."

"A want protection," Chuck butted in. Lottie gave him a look that said this wasn't part of their script. He probably wasn't supposed to have any lines at all. "Ye says afore ye can help me. So help me. Get them aw aff ma back. Get me in the clear."

322

McCoist could hear the pleading behind the gruff, forth-right order. Her heart picked up the pace, she felt tingly, dry-mouthed. She had offered protection to Burnet too. And that had worked out peachy. If she agreed, would it be a lie? Half-truth? She picked her words carefully: "If you're straight with me, Chuck, then I can do my very best."

"Straight?" Lottie said. "Hows aboot yersel, McCoist. Are ye straight?"

McCoist swallowed a ball of steel wool. "You called me, Lottie."

"An you showed up."

"Look, it's time to shite or get off the throne. If what you've got is worth it, as you claim it is, I'll reopen the investigation into Paulo, and I'll get you somewhere safe, Chuck. As for Jamieson, I'll see what I can push for."

Lottie and Chuck shared a look but didn't speak. She could tell Chuck wanted to trust her; Lottie was harder to read. After too much silence and frowning and teeth-grinding, Lottie took a key from her pocket. "This is a copy. The original is goin tae Jamieson." She gave her an address on Borron Street in Port Dundas, a four-digit PIN code and a password.

"What's it for?"

"He cawed it the 'Shit List'. Yel need tae hurry if ye want a keek afore Jamieson gets his paws oan it."

61

Chuck was being played. Lottie was going against Jamieson and Chuck was there to take the fall if it went shiteways. His role was to delay handing over the keys to Jamieson so McCoist could get a look at this "Shit List" first, but beyond that he had no place in the scheme except as a human shield. McCoist wondered if Lottie had known she would figure that out, force her into taking on Jamieson for Chuck's sake. She was a devious cow, McGuinn's missus. McCoist had claimed to have never underestimated her, but maybe she had after all.

She headed straight from the park, over the Clyde and north through the city to the canal, which was going through massive redevelopment. People in colourful helmets and life vests kayaked in the cleaned-up water by the newly mani-cured walk along the bank. Factories and warehouses now played host to gyms and skateparks and cafes. Old distillery barns had become trendy apartments. She arrived at a former iron foundry that was now a business park—shops and office spaces. Around the back of it was a run of unmanned self-storage units.

The PIN code got her into the building. The key fit a lock on the second-to-last unit on the left. The shutter rolled up. A smell wafted out—chemicals and something more organic, rotten, underneath.

Shelving units stood against the left and right walls, piled with boxes. At the back was a desk with a computer. This couldn't be to do with Burnet's file, could it? It wasn't hiding in one of the boxes or copied onto the computer, was it?

McCoist stretched on a pair of nitrile gloves and pulled the shutter down to ankle level behind her. She couldn't bear to seal it fully. She started with a nosy through the boxes. Some were empty. Others had initials scrawled on them in black marker and were not. A peek in these initialled boxes revealed weapons of various sorts, pieces of clothing, smartphones and burner phones. Rags which smelt of petrol. One had some kind of costume—a curly judge's wig or the like—stained with patches of rust red. Another held a kit used to recover evidence from a woman who's been raped. McCoist's stomach lurched. *What the fuck?* The hairs on her arms stood up and she had the urge to run, snatch at the gap by the floor and haul the door up, get the fuck out of there.

Instead, she woke up the computer. Typed in "P4ul0i5theD0n". (Lottie had to repeat it several times, making sure the numbers and capitals were correct, even looked embarrassed, which sat awkwardly on her, and which McCoist had enjoyed.) The desktop was covered in folders, obscuring a picture of McGuinn resting against the bonnet of a black sports car like a *Knight Rider* poster. Each folder had a name. The Shit List, presumably. She scanned them. Mostly common names, nothing to go off without—then one poked her right in the eyeballs:

Cresswell

"Fuck. Me."

In the folder were a series of photographs of Sheriff Cresswell coming and going through the main entrance of a certain high-rise block of flats. A notorious one, where the top-floor windows were blacked out, and the girls in the beds were almost as young as McCoist's own daughter. The angle suggested they'd been taken from the tower of the nearby church. There were many visits, dates going back years. Another couple were dim and fuzzy, stills from a video maybe, button camera in a darkened room, Cresswell—presumably—on top in his sheriff's clobber, robe and wig. White slice of a bare chest and leg below the robe. *Rank.*

Cogs ground in McCoist's brain. This was Paulo's stash of kompromat. This was what he used to control the powerful men he needed to look the other way, to do him favours, and there were so many of them. She had a feeling of vertigo, like she'd missed the bottom step and was wobbling over a fall—the drop much, much bigger than she could ever have anticipated. The sudden clarity was stinging raw like a hot wax strip ripping the hair off your skull:

The break-in at Lottie's. The note in MacGillivary's office: *a target on the lot of us.* All this time she'd been chasing Burnet's letter and it wasn't about that at all. It was about this—the blackmail evidence held by Paulo McGuinn and what would happen to it now he was dead. Cresswell stymied her investigation deliberately. Maybe he'd even paid to have Lennox and Tim killed because he thought they knew about it. But would he really do all that over a shagging scandal? The girls were on the young side but he could probably claim he didn't know and—

McCoist jumped from the chair. The box she'd flapped open before—initials "DC" on the side. The stained wig on top. She lifted it carefully in her gloved hands. Not a costume, this was genuine court dress. Her heart wanted to tip the whole bastard thing out on the floor but she forced herself to slow down. If she was right, the evidence had been stuffed in this box for over a year, she didn't want to damage its value further. The wig and robe, stiff with blood; a bedsheet folded in a rough, rigid square even worse, saturated. Used swabs in specimen containers. And a knife, a palette of congealed reds and blacks and mouldy tertiary colours all the way to the hilt.

Tim's voicemail: *Can you look up anything you can find about a murder that happened last summer? A sex worker at one of McGuinn's places. Stabbed to death. Involved a couple of our mutual friends on the clean-up end.*

Cresswell wasn't just banging sex slaves. He'd killed one of them. Burnet had cleaned it up and Findlay had collected the evidence for Paulo to use against him. Burnet's little "memoir" had put Lennox and Tim on the trail. Cresswell must have found out. (*Passing notes in class with MacGillivary?*)

A shagging scandal might not be worth killing for, but this?

McCoist carefully replaced the sullied items back into the box. What was she going to do? Put it in the boot of her car and ride on over to London Road? How would she explain how she came to be in possession of it?

There were a lot more boxes too. And many more names on that computer. Shit List indeed.

Fuck. There was only one person she could talk to.

62

"I knew you'd be good to have around," Superintendent Devlin said, and smiled like he was about to bestow a sticker upon her for being a good girl.

"You called me a liability, sir."

"For motivational purposes only." He snapped on a pair of gloves and perched his librarian glasses on his nose. McCoist gave him a tour of McGuinn's evidence locker and showed him the exhibits that put Sheriff Cresswell in the frame for hiring Mr Tumble to kill Lennox and Tim and doing in the unknown girl himself. Devlin couldn't help showing a hint of being impressed, almost a whistle as he looked at all those names on the folders.

"So how did you come to intercept this?"

She opened up about Chuck and Lottie, her "confidential sources"—and their terms.

"Jamieson?!"

"This place is his now. Gardner will be handing over the keys at any time. A quickly closing window of opportunity, like I said." She shifted a glance towards the shutter, as if it was about to be ripped open. She hoped Chuck would give her a good lead time as promised—and a text before he made the delivery.

"*Fuck.* I told you to stay away from Jamieson."

"I did. He came to me—not that he knows it."

"Lucky for you."

"What happened with you and this guy?"

Devlin took his glasses off and let them hang on their chain, rested his arse against the computer desk. He pursed his lips; his eyes measured and weighed her. "My first and last case as an undercover detective. I was embedded with his crew. And I was found out. Inevitably. As punishment, they held me down, sliced open my scrotum, and removed one of my testicles."

There was a moment of silence for Devlin's lost ball before McCoist realised she was staring, mouth catching midges. "Sorry, uh—they didn't happen to use anaesthetic, I take it?"

"They did not." His expression and voice remained flat, bordering on conversational, while his eyes seemed to focus somewhere beyond her. "Lucky for me they decided to stop there and didn't kill me. They even posted the testicle back to me a few days later. At my home address. It was floating in a jar of pickled onions."

He gave an itch at his crotch.

"Is that why you…" she nodded south.

"What?"

"Nothing."

"Anyway, story of woe aside—"

"That would get you pretty far on *Britain's Got Talent*, sir."

"I'm more of a *Strictly* man."

"Could've guessed really."

"*Anyway*, as much as I dislike it, Billy Jamieson might actually be an experienced and safe pair of hands to take the reins, fill the void *you* created."

"But why does it need to be filled at all?!" McCoist had an urge to sweep the boxes off the shelf, kick something, pull at her hair. "Fuck the lot of them, bang them all up!"

"If it were so simple." He smiled his fucking smile, and McCoist wanted to staple his lips together. "Your mindset is too binary. Us and them. Overworld and underworld. Cops and robbers. It's all connected, different parts of the same ecosystem. Information, money, goods and services. Do you know how much money the black market contributes to the economy of a country?"

"But it's blood money."

"The UK is one of the biggest arms dealers in the world. Bombs are manufactured right here in Glasgow and dropped on poor people half a world away. Is that blood money?"

"Aye, it is."

"And who are you going to 'bang up' over that? Nobody, because it's not against the law. Black markets are black because we say they are. There's no morality to it, it's just politics. Inherited rules that slowly change over time depending on the mood of the day and who is in office."

"So what, we just let the McGuinns and Jamiesons do whatever they want?"

"No. We control them as best we can. We keep the system as stable as possible, and in doing so we limit the amount of collateral damage. He's tried to hide his hand, but Jamieson is the hot contender for us. Could mean peace on the streets for a good few years to come."

"He's a psycho who chopped your bollock out," she said, incredulous.

"That too. And one day, I'm sure, he'll be repaid in kind for his hospitality by somebody else—that is The Life—but we need to play the long game."

"And does playing the long game involve charging Cresswell with three murders?" McCoist spat. She could feel the heat on her face, too wound up to rein in her anger in front of a superior—one who knew her every dirty secret at that.

"These are big allegations."

"With big evidence to back them up!"

"It'll shake the ground the entire establishment is built upon." There was a hint of something approving in his voice, playful in the set of his lips. Infuriating for McCoist, who couldn't get a handle on which way was up with him.

"Good. Knock the whole rotten thing down."

"Patience. He'll pay for what he's done, I promise you, but we need to make our decisions carefully. We must be cool and calm. And detached."

"Like your baw." The words came out before they'd been filter-assessed.

He laughed. "Your mouth's quick, McCoist, your brain just needs to catch up." He squeezed her shoulder—the touch a shock but not menacing, the kindly-librarian mask firmly in place. "Good work, Chief Inspector. I'm on this, you must trust me. Meantime, keep the investigation spinning its wheels. Europol's input could be a good source of red tape. Oh, and there's something else you might want to sort."

"Sir?"

"Your DS Slater has been nosing around the Car Wash Fiasco—checking out files we don't really want people checking out."

"Shite."

"Do you know why?"

Anger became shame and embarrassment, McCoist going from towering inferno to damp bungalow. "When I spoke with Findlay he, uh, put me on the trail of... historical abuse allegations... against the sergeant."

"Which you believe?"

"...Yes. Sir." She had to look at the ground, fight back the sting in her eyes. She felt the knife twist afresh. Part of her still said, *It can't be true, he was so...* His heat against her, mouth on her mouth. *Bastard. Fucking bastard.* "I do. I corroborated the claims. And when I brought it up with him, that I was going to report it—"

"Damn it. Just when I think you're finally proving useful. How much does he know? Is he blackmailing you?"

"No. Well, not yet. He... he knows about Burnet's letter." Her voice came from somewhere down at her toes.

"Shite indeed."

"But not what's in it. Your visit to the hospital and the tip-off about Findlay also raised a red flag."

"You need to stop him before he goes any further."

"How?"

"Two ways. Diplomatic: make a deal. Your silence for his."

"No! He's a—a predator! He can't stay a polis—"

"Then there's the second way."

"Which is?"

"Family man, is he?"

"No. I mean, he lives alone with his dog, I don't know about other relatives." *Dead mother, ex-wife.*

"That's a good start, but you'll need to look for anyone who might miss him first."

McCoist wanted to shake her head, try to make it make sense, work out if she'd just misheard him or misunderstood or...

"If you have a third way, be my guest, but *take care of it.*"

"...Sir."

63

Meeting McCoist had all the suspense and terse communication of a military op. They snuck out the back door where an Uber was waiting down the street, not wanting to use their own motors. Chuck was fairly confident (fairly) his new role spying on Callaghan meant it was unlikely he was being tailed—Jamieson wouldn't want to blow his cover by hovering around him like a fly on a turd—but they couldn't be too careful. Lottie had taken apart Stone Cold Steve Austin with a flat-head screwdriver and a hammer to get the key out, so they didn't have to take the whole action figure to Timpson to get it copied. Telling Lottie what had happened to Brownlee had unburdened him a little, made him feel a smidge lighter, and it also bolstered his confidence in Lottie's plan that she understood exactly what Jamieson was capable of, the stakes of tattling to the polis. *Al put ye through yer ain machine.* And he would. He'd already begun with Chuck's fingertips.

The actual meeting with McCoist had robbed him of this feeling. As he later drove away from the McGuinn sanctum, he was circling panic like a coin hurtling round and round the throat of a charity money spinner—faster, faster, tighter, closer, inevitably down, down towards the black hole at the centre.

On his way to Callaghan's tumbleweed shopping arcade— the job continued—he stopped by a nearby Betfred. Used the cash he had in his wallet and no more. That's what he'd sworn to himself, and he felt a twisted pride at having stuck to that as he left the dim din of the horses on the tellies and the puggies chirping, clunk of buttons being slapped—warnings decaled on the sides of the units, repeated in the windows and on the door which he held open for a G4S bloke with visored helmet and armoured briefcase. Should be afforded the same get up, he thought, for what he himself was carrying in his van: the key to a secret vault and a USB stick on which the only information saved was a PIN code, password and location. The Shit List—the keys to the kingdom. Worth a lot more than a suitcase full of cash.

And then there was the other thing:

Roughcast had been het to watch him shred the stacks of paperwork Jamieson had given him, but Roughcast was not arsed for this, and believed Chuck to be well warned to stay in line, his fingers freshly trimmed and bandaged. And though Chuck was indeed well warned, emphatically so, he couldn't help himself. He'd spent so long training to snoop as he shredded that he did it on autopilot now. And what he'd seen and subsequently squirrelled away...

His van was a rolling bomb.

If ye double-cross me, son, al gee ye the final send-aff masel. He was already double-crossing Jamieson, putting off delivering the Shit List long enough for McCoist to do her work first. What if he triple-crossed?

Chuck's face was still a Picasso from the savage beating Callaghan's thugs had delivered, the Timberland tree symbol stamped onto his forehead. Weighed against the finger sharpening, who was more friend or more enemy? He wished the guy behind the counter at Betfred could give him the odds. The Gangster Form. Who was less likely to have him killed?

Chuck started to cry. He wanted to speak to Bell one more time before he died but she still wasn't picking up the phone.

64

Two ways: stay silent about a serial sexual abuser working in her ranks or... *get rid of him*, to use the accepted euphemism. No, McCoist didn't accept that, there must be another. She couldn't keep on letting him get away with it. Nor could she, you know, *remove* him. From the earth. She'd killed a man already, true, but that was different. Self-defence, of a sort. Kind of. To save Davey Burnet's life—that's what it was. To save his life. Culpable homicide at worst, legally, and something she could apparently live with morally. (She didn't dwell too much on it any more, with a bit of practice it was an easy line of thought to shut down, bar the odd uncontrollable flashback, itself a problem she did not want to deal with for now.) It wasn't calculated and it certainly wasn't premeditated, which this would be. She was premeditating it right now. As soon as those words were out of Devlin's mouth they "evinced malice and ill will". No, not a chance. There had to be another way.

She battered the dilemma about the walls of her mind like a squash ball for the rest of the day. She did a good impression of paying attention as DI Griffiths briefed her on the latest with the investigation. CCTV, ANPR, door-to-door, trawling the mispers and the stolen-motor records was all being done again in an attempt to corroborate the forensics, strengthen the case as much as possible—similar tasks being carried out in other parts of the country now where Mr Tumble was also linked to unsolved murders via DNA. "We're looking good but the home straight's going to be a slog, gaffer," she said.

Just wait till she finds out about Cresswell, McCoist thought, with a giddiness that made her want to blurt it out then and there. She then decided the best way to avoid thinking about Slater was to put her mind to organising the next steps once Devlin gave her the go-ahead to pull Cresswell in. Christ, she hoped he'd be in his wig and gown when she went to lift him. She checked her phone and checked her other phones and made her own coffee and kept her own company and checked her phones again.

She clocked off without receiving the call she wanted.

She hadn't seen Cam and Tess since the day she got out the hospital, their faces as she left them an etching titled "Guilt" carved on her frontal lobe, but they were off to the caravan with Mark and his mother that evening so she couldn't attempt to make up for it yet. With nothing on the auld dance card and unable to sit still, she took Bruce for a walk.

She'd put her exercise gear on but it was difficult to run and keep track of Bruce simultaneously. He zigzagged all over the place, nose to the ground, then would bound in and out of bushes, occasional fits of barking when a bird or squirrel caught his attention. It was a warm, bright evening and the park was busy. (She'd come back to Queen's Park, the scene of the crime, views of the city at a distance.) She had to chase Bruce away from a family having a late picnic, apologising profusely for the cocktail sausage he'd managed to snaffle before she caught up with him.

The best was yet to come though:

A dead seagull down by the pond. Bruce was on it in a flash, snatching the dirty feathered carcass into his jaws. "Bruce! Stop! Put it Down! I said PUT IT DOWN!" McCoist lunged for the rotten treat but Bruce was too quick. Tail thrashing with joy, he bounded into the pond, head and shoulders just above the water, launching ducks and swans in a fury of splashing, churning away from the bank where McCoist screamed and pleaded for him to come back while everyone watched on with amusement and horror as Bruce swallowed the dead bird down in three choking mouthfuls, barely chewing at all. "Aw for fucksake," McCoist wailed. "Bruce! Come back!"

Meal finished, he paddled over, jumped out the water and soaked McCoist with a great big shake, pleased with, and proud of, himself.

"Need to keep him on a leash."

McCoist whirled around. "What are you doing here?! Are you following me?"

"Don't flatter yourself," Slater snorted, a face on him like your Brexit-voting uncle complaining about the line at passport control.

McCoist felt disgust at having been attracted to him at all. The memory of him bringing Tess home that night twisted her insides, how Tess had told her all about the nice things he'd been saying about her… Who was that man? Was he real at all? *Bastard*. Becoming a nun seemed like a fine idea.

"Just a nice night for walking the dug," he said. Maisie padded over and sniffed at Bruce, who wagged his tail and stuffed his nose into her arsehole in turn. Unlike her owner, she seemed impressed by the gull-swallowing incident. "Though I was hoping to run into you."

McCoist felt a shiver on her bare arms. There were a lot of people about. No way he could try anything. Still, she couldn't shake the undercurrent of unease his sudden appearance had caused, like her thoughts had manifested him—did his ears burn when his superior suggested killing him?

Her running leggings had no pockets, which meant no PAVA spray. Have to be hand-to-hand if it came to it. Not that McCoist was an adherent to Queensberry Rules. Hand-to-bawbag, more like.

"How?"

"Well, it'll only be a couple of days till I'm back at the office— then what are we gonna do?"

McCoist had no answer, gave him a brick wall instead, tried to pull Bruce towards her in an attempt to stop him fraternising with the enemy.

"We need to talk this out properly."

"I don't want to hear about how you used your authority to screw vulnerable women, Simon. You can tell it to the ACU."

His face tightened in momentary anger. "That's bullshit. Adults can make their own decisions. You're twisting it—just like you twist everything."

"Is that right?"

"Aye, it is," he hissed. "You're a liar, Alison. A serial liar. What you've done…"—he forced a smile into his face—"…is so, so much worse than anything you could remotely accuse me of. I've been doing a little digging."

"A dog's prerogative."

"Oh, I wouldn't be acting snidey if I were you. I mean, from a distance maybe it looks like incompetence, but a little closer, from a different angle…"

McCoist felt the heat close on her skin, sweat on her palms, heart thrumming and belly knotting. She licked dry lips, gummed together.

"I found out a couple of interesting things. Tim Drummond, for instance, he used to work at that car wash, didn't he? The one Davey Burnet worked at, the one Paulo McGuinn was using as a front, the very spot where he was killed in a shoot-out with his nephew, supposedly. Funny coincidence. You didn't think that was worth sharing with the team?"

"News to me," she fibbed.

Slater chuckled. It was like a ratchet clicking in his throat. "Aye, right. Something else happened too—there were two cars crashed outside the car wash. One was McGuinn's, the other was hard to trace. Stolen, maybe, fake plates. Serial numbers filed off."

"Belonged to the other bodies."

"So the investigators—and you were part of this team, no?— surmised. But your car had been stolen that night, hadn't it?"

"So?" Her blood was pumping too hard to think.

"The same make, model and colour as the one which, supposedly, belonged to the shooters. A Škoda Octavia—very sought-after by car thieves, is it?"

"It has good boot space," she croaked.

"And as for the shooters themselves—all deed, of course— two small-time crooks down from Aberdeen and one John Doe."

"A professional."

"A guess—only supported by the lack of a solid ID or any information attached to him. Colin Kennedy claimed in his statement that he didn't know any of them."

"He would—"

"And nothing is found to link them at all. Yet Colin still takes the fall."

"Because he did it."

"No, Alison, he didn't. Somebody else did it, and it was covered up." Slater moved in close, she felt his heat, remembered his lips on hers. "Where did the owner of the car wash go? And his employee, Burnet? Who did it? Who shot McGuinn?"

McCoist flailed for an explanation, blinded by desperation and adrenaline. "You need to stop, Si. You don't know what you're getting into."

"Oh, I think I do," he smiled. After too long, too close, he stepped away. "Maisie, come on. See you on Monday, Alison."

Bruce whitied up the entire gull in the car on the way home. It was still pretty much whole and recognisable as a dead bird. If it smelt bad before, being mixed with Bruce's intestinal juices and regurgitated had not improved it.

Parking up outside her house, McCoist pressed her forehead against the steering wheel, closed her eyes. "*Shhhhhiiiiiit.* SHIT!" She punched the horn, hurt her knuckles. Did it again. And again.

There was a ripple of venetian blinds in Edith's window.

Fuck, fuck, fuck, fuck, fuck. What the fuck was she going to do? Devlin's "two ways" came into her head again. She started to cry and Bruce licked her face with his tongue, which had just consumed and unconsumed a rotting bird corpse.

Then her phone rang.

"I'm off this weekend, Gaz," her voice small, hopefully not too snively.

"Sorry, gaffer, but you need to hear this."

65

"HOW THE FUCK DID THIS HAPPEN?!" The outburst shocked the troops into silence. They were used to McCoist's occasionally spiky retorts but making the windowpanes tremble was not her normal style of leadership. There were a lot of detectives investigating their shoelaces.

The news had pulled in everyone on the MIT—even a few who had been at the pub and were reeking of lager, sweat and vape smoke, and would have to be told to fuck off again once the bollocking was complete and the duties were being doled out. Not that it was really anybody's fault—not anybody in the room anyway.

DI Griffiths stepped up to the chopping block. "Looks like a gang thing, gaffer—we're holding all involved and they've all got attachments to various young teams and even OCGs."

"I thought we were working on the premise that our bad guy was a hired hitman—outsider, no affiliations. Now he's a victim of a cross-party... *lynching*."

"No affiliation doesn't mean no enemies. It certainly means no protection."

McCoist grunted, conceding the point, her anxiety-fuelled eruption burning out. "And how did he come to be in the cafeteria with the rest of them anyway? I thought he was in solitary."

"He was. SPS are saying it must have been a mistake."

"Fucking right it was a mistake. A convenient one too. We'll need the guards questioned—not just the ones present at the time, all of them."

"Already on it, ma'am." Gaz, in a sweat-stained T-shirt branded with the word "Heroin" and ripped jeans, all but clicked his heels.

"I want bank statements looked at, employment records checked. I want family trees traced back to Genghis Fucking Khan—somebody owes someone something. Find out who and what."

She retreated to her office, considered a coffee, worried her heart couldn't take it and decided not to for now. Her phone rang—the other phone.

"These things happen, Bear," he said, and McCoist could picture the kindly smile at the other end, the glasses hanging from his neck, the wee tickle of the testicle to get comfortable. "Men who lead violent lives beget their own violent ends. Don't waste the overtime budget, eh?"

The line cut off.

Friday-night Radio 1 dance bangers pounded from the speakers as she raced off towards Bearsden in the north-west of the city limits—yet another leafy enclave of sandstone upper-class suburbia a stone's throw from one of Glasgow's many deprived ghettos. Bearsden was home to dentists and bankers and old money. And sheriffs.

A bad feeling bubbled in her gut, squeezing along with the bog-squelching beat of some mindless pill-popper robo-tune for bath-salt sniffers by Double Dunt vs Repetitive Strain Injury or some shite—*oontce oontce oontce oontce*.

She saw the blue lights as she approached the address.

"You said we needed to be patient, make decisions carefully. What happened to that?! What happened to the fucking long game?!"

"This will be best for everyone. Trust me. The fallout from charging Cresswell would have been too great, no way to know how we'd all weather the consequences. Better it all went neatly away."

"Neatly?! Two people have been murdered!" The heavy stink of the dead seagull and Bruce's vomit still lingered in the car, and McCoist felt she might just make her own addition to the bouquet, her stomach a greasy, queasy, overfull sack of fear and guilt and outrage.

"Actually, Sheriff Cresswell's death was by his own hand."

"You just gave him the rope."

"No, I simply explained what we knew and what the rest of his life might look like going forward. If anyone, it was you who supplied the rope."

"Fuck you."

"He was a bad man. He murdered a girl being held captive for sex. He had Carter Lennox and that young lad killed."

"Tim." What was left of the boy in the tub flickered into her imagination, followed by his mother and father, who would never get to know what had really happened. "Do you know for sure it was Cresswell? Did you test the evidence in the boxes?"

"Why ask, Bear? I'm sure, you're sure. Don't despair over a monster like him. Be glad. Justice has been done."

"He's not the only monster."

A chuckle buzzed in her ear. "I'll choose not to take that personally."

"And what about MacGillivary? Is he going to walk from all this? He was the one who told Cresswell that Lennox and Tim were onto him. They knew each other, old buddies, worked together on a book once—found it on Google."

"We'll keep an eye on him."

"And the others? The Shit List, the boxes of evidence—what have you done with it all?"

"Not for you to worry about." His voice had lost its sing-song Sunday-school-teacher friendliness, gone flat and featureless, the voice behind the façade. An order from the fucking Devil.

66

A glass of red stood untasted on the coffee table. Bruce's head in her lap went unclapped, his sad eyes rolling up to hers, imploring her. *Still angry about the gull?* his quizzical expression seemed to ask.

A headache was beginning to worm its tendrils through the soupy exhaustion in her brain but she couldn't move herself to either get some painkillers or go to bed. The telly played on without an audience. Her phone sat dead in her grip like a withered limb.

A message pinged. Personal, not work phone. Sender not recognised. Spam probably, but then the partial line of text shown in the caption on the lock screen pricked at her mind through the static. "Mark, Cameron and Theresa…" *What the fuck?* She opened it:

Mark, Cameron, and Theresa are in trouble.

There was a link below. Click a link on a message from an unknown sender? Aye, right, she wasn't her mother. But still, the text was alarming and—

Another popped up in the chat log:

Do NOT attempt to contact them. Do NOT attempt to contact anyone.

Then a map location—somewhere in the Gorbals, she could see the Citz pinned in the thumbnail—with a message below:

Proceed immediately. ALONE.

The fuck indeed? She wasn't tired any more. She sat rigid like a hunted animal, eyes, ears, nose wide and gulping in the surroundings for any sense of what was following them.

Clicked the link.

It opened a video feed. Murky verdigris of night vision. Centred: what looked like a container. No, steps going up to a door on its side. Windows. Not a container. A static caravan.

Her hand was shaking.

A grey shadow blotted out one of the glowing green windows, the light spilling out from within, the camera lens greedily sooking it up and amplifying it to a grotesque Hallowe'en decoration. A figure. It turned to face out towards the camera. Two piercing white pinpricks for eyes.

Mark pulled the curtain over.

67

McCoist lead-footed it towards the destination she'd been sent—satnav her co-pilot, David Coulthard admiring her cornering from the back seat. Focus of a laser-guided missile. The shakes only came back when the voice on her phone announced she'd arrived and she whipped to a stop with a sharp pain in her still-healing neck, brace forgotten.

The location was a derelict-looking tenement with boarded-up windows and blackened brick. She was wondering if she was in the right place when she noticed the man watching her from the car parked outside.

She approached, heart quivering, and the man got out. He was like an extension of the building—drab and grey, stubbled and grizzly. Seen better days. "This way," he said, dragging himself up the short flight of steps to the closed door, which he unlocked and held open for her. She had to squeeze past him to get inside—smell of cheap aftershave not hiding cigarettes, then mould from the cold, dark corridor within. "Go up to 3/1," he grunted, and closed the door behind her, left her alone.

She crabbed her way up the stairwell, footsteps loud on the worn-smooth concrete, checking the shadowy corners of the landings, nerves shrill in horror-film expectation of something jumping out at her.

The storm door to 3/1 was hanging open, the inner door unlocked. It opened into an empty, high-ceilinged hall, the last of the evening sun casting a gloomy green pall through the mildew-covered skylight. Male voices rumbled from behind a door. She was pulled towards it even as she wanted to turn and run.

She stepped into a living room. The empty fire grate with its grotty tiled surround and the mothy, floor-length curtains pulled shut let her know the room's purpose—it was otherwise stripped to the wood and plaster.

"DCI McCoist takes the silver."

Two men. Both suits. The one who had spoken was getting on, his face like an overboiled ham, eyes peeking out from flabby, hairy hollows. The other one was a gymfluencer—young, built, as handsome as Jesus Christ.

They stood behind a table with a laptop on it. Three chairs faced the screen. One occupied.

"Lottie…" She wouldn't look at her, was glaring straight ahead at what was on the screen:

Three windows open next to one another. A video feed on each. The first showed a plain-looking terraced house, council issue. The second focused on two windows on the side of a building—a flat? The third McCoist had already seen: Cath's caravan in Tyndrum, where Mark and the kids were staying for the weekend. The curtains were closed—no hint of what was going on inside. The only movement came from the leaves swaying on a tree between the camera and the caravan.

What the fuck do you think you're doing?! The words didn't come out. Caught in her throat along with her beating heart.

"Take a seat, lass," the old man continued.

She ignored him. "Lottie, are you all right? Are you hurt?"

Lottie kept her eyes locked straight ahead. 'That's Ari's flat," she said, her voice a husky monotone. "Gemma's there too. Ma fault. God, it's ma fault she's there." As if conjuring her, one of the windows in the second feed opened. A young woman—the older sister—leant against the sill, lit a cigarette, a third white pinprick of light forming an upside-down triangle with the eyes. Lottie whimpered. For a second, the girl looked straight down the lens as if she could see them sitting there watching her. She turned away again and Lottie keened like a kicked dog.

"Sit doon, missus," Jamieson said again.

"Fuck you," McCoist managed to squeak out, full of venom but no stinger.

The old man pulled a burner phone from his pocket. "Geez a wee wave, boays, will ye?"

The video feeds zoomed out and went topsy-turvy. The caravan, the flat and the house were each replaced by close-ups of faces hidden by balaclavas. Two in each window.

"Noo sit doon."

She did. Legs going from under her, stomach continuing to fall long after her arse had hit the seat.

He checked his watch. "As a awready promised Lottie here, yer faimly will be killt the night if ye don't gee me wit a want. Simple as that. Nae fuckin aboot. Av hud aboot enough ae that."

McCoist was trying, with difficulty, to slow her breathing, stop herself from tumbling into blind panic, get a hold on herself or the situation or anything at all. She almost asked him what it was he wanted, why he was doing this, but she stopped herself. Because she knew the answers already, knew who he was. And that would be fuckin aboot.

"Keys tae an empty locker. Ye hink am a fuckin mug? Ye could ae tried harder. Fuckin insultin, man." There was no theatrical sigh or shake of the head, no faux hurt on his face. Not a joke.

"Tell me where it is noo an al tell those men they can clock aff early. Nae tricks, nae games. Hud enough ae those, eh Lottie? Could ae hud this aw sortet an age ago waeoot any ae this pish. But nermind. Wit's done is done, so here we go: it's a simple, binary choice. Tell us or don't. Live or die. Easy."

"A telt ye a don't know," Lottie whined. For the first time she looked at McCoist and the accusation was written on her face. *You did this.*

Jamieson shushed her, checked his watch again. "Where is that useless prick? Wit is it wae these cunts? Tradies an delivry boays an aw them. Don't know the fuckin meanin ae 'immediately', just come alang whenever they fuckin please."

"Fuckin tell us aboot it," the glamorous assistant started, "av goat this fuckin gerdner who's sposed tae be puttin doon some astro fir ma maw but evry time he's meant tae be workin a get a call an..." He trailed off at the sight of his boss glowering at him.

Jamieson turned back to his audience. "A suggest ye use this time while we wait fir the fuckin wooden spoon tae huv a hink aboot that choice."

68

"Get oot ye dirty wee tramp!" Bell's maw had shrieked, throwing a slipper at his head. It missed and, grinning, he launched himself out Bell's bedroom via the window, landed on the roof of the lean-to below and then shinned down a drainpipe. Nat stuck her head out the window, her threats following him as he squeezed through a hole in the fence behind the garden shed—"Ye better no huv crushed ma bloody azzys ye speccy Bru bottle ye!"—and out into the alley which ran between the backs of the two terraces, a rutted trail in the muck where the bins were rolled back and forth each week, a treasure trove of old couches, burnt-out fridges and dead TVs.

That was the first time he'd been caught in Bell's room. He was fifteen. It happened many times after, until Bell's maw had largely accepted their relationship and was simply pleading with him to "Use the fuckin door!"

But he'd liked climbing up to her window. It was romantic. Bell made good use of it herself, sneaking out for an evening's tipple at the local play park after the sun had gone down.

That had been some time ago now.

The alley was much the same. Weans probably still loved going up and down it, pretending to be adventuring through the bush on a shortcut to wherever, seeing what there was to find abandoned there, like a pack of savage Wombles. Some of the fences were different—repaired, rebuilt, repainted, fitted with nails across the top to prevent pigeons roosting and housebreakers climbing—others had continued to rot, more moss than blistered paint on them. Nat's was one of the former but Chuck had come tooled up with a claw-tooth hammer to wrench out a few planks. Nat hated him anyway—or if she didn't then she certainly would after tonight—so what was a bit of broken fence between them?

The climb up the drainpipe was more taxing than he remembered. The drop below seemed more perilous too. He was above the neighbouring hedges and fences, exposed now. He hadn't seen anyone stationed in the alley, prayed none of Jamieson's goons had been planted in a neighbour's back bedroom or perched up the old telegraph pole as a lookout.

Of course it was Jamieson. They'd fucked him over and he'd found out. Maybe that polis had been bent after all, or maybe they underestimated his reach, or the three of them had just been complete numpties. Any and all made sense.

When the video first popped into his messages it had frozen him, sheer panic, nauseous horror, pinning him down. When he started to thaw his first instinct was to comply, follow the orders, the prodding pinpoint on the map, go wherever, do whatever, grovel, repent, throw himself in the shredder if it would make Jamieson leave Bell alone. Then he began to weigh the odds against him, check the form. Jamieson could kill Bell regardless of what Chuck did for him, no matter how he flagellated himself or let himself be tortured or even killed. Jamieson had that power, and there was no way he'd trust Chuck again. The best place for Chuck to be was by Bell's side. And the best place for Bell right now was as far from fucking Glesga as possible. He remembered the back way in, through the bin alley, and he began to come up with a plan.

There was never a shot too long for Chuck. *Fuckin eejit.*

The roof of the lean-to creaked worse than his back. This was where he'd tap on the window, and Bell would sneak a glance out, double-check her maw was downstairs with the telly on, before opening it up to let him in. He tried calling but Bell wouldn't answer. He knocked at the window. He sent a text. He needed to get off this fucking wall and inside the house. Now.

He was working the teeth of the hammer into the window frame when the curtain swooshed back, nearly causing him to fall. Bell, angry as he'd ever seen her, face like she might rip his fucking throat out with her teeth. "WIT THE—"

He held a finger over his lips then brought his palms together in prayer. He took his phone from his pocket and waved it, started to type. Fury turned to confusion as she read his message. She looked up to his face, wild and desperate, hand pressed against the dirty glass.

Getting Nat not to smash him over the head with a frying pan like a cartoon wifey took some doing. Bell had to intervene. "Wit the fuck is aw this, Stuart?"

"Al explain when we get oot."

"Yel explain right fuckin noo."

"We need tae get oot the hoose, get away."

"How? Where tae?"

"He's oan the fuckin drugs," Nat interjected.

"Maw!"

"Just look at the state ae him!"

"Wit?! Am no—look, fuckin forget it, we need tae get the fuck oot ae here. Come oan!"

Bell moved closer to her mother. "Yer scarin me."

He pressed his fists against his forehead, clenched his teeth. "Please!" he hissed. "There's nae time, they could brek in any minute."

"Brek in?! Who?!"

"Look, doll, am sorry, am so, so sorry. A fuckt up. Even worse than last time." His throat was hot and sore with choked tears, barbed words raking their way out. "There are men eftir me. Eftir you. They're ootside the noo, watchin the gaff."

Nat squealed. "Wit the actual fuck?" She went marching towards the bedroom door. Chuck dived in front, blocking her way, pushing his back against the door. "Don't go lookin oot the windae fir fucksake!"

Nat grabbed the collar of his T-shirt, snarled him in her glossy talons. "Don't *you* fuckin talk tae me like that ye wee shitebag. A always knew ye were fuckin trouble. A telt Bell no tae go back tae ye the last time. A fuckin telt her."

Bell was sniffling. "Maw. Please."

"A criminal. A waster. An *addict*. He'll only drag ye doon again, a says, even further the next time."

His eyes stung and he had to look away. He cast his eye around the darkened bedroom, mostly unchanged since Bell had moved out, except for some boxes and clutter being stored for sometime never. Dusty red cassette case of Gucci Rush and the DKNY apple among the detritus on the side table. A framed photo of Bell and her school pals at some disco, another at a music festival. The bed where they'd shagged for the first time—both of them losing their V plates together.

"Ye wur right, Natalie. Bell, she's right." He forced himself to meet Bell's eyes. He untangled himself from Nat and went to her. He reached for her; she let him. "Am sorry fir everythin av done. Ye didnae deserve any ae it. An now av put ye in danger. The last hing ad ever want tae dae." Tears flowed down his cheeks, Bell the same. "But a huv. Unforgivable, an al no ask ye tae. Aw a ask is that ye come wae me fir noo. Get somewhere safe."

"Then wit?" Her voice a thin whisper, sand blown over dunes.

"Al make it aw go away. Al no be yer problem any mare."

69

"Time's up." Jamieson pressed call. McCoist screamed for him to stop but—"Thunderbird Wan. Go."

"FAB," crackled the reply.

A figure stepped into the camera view from behind the shot and ran towards the door of the house, keeping himself low, something heavy-looking in one hand. The camera shook and followed, wobbling along behind. Up the path, it swooped to the left of the door. The man in the bally took the other side, chapping then withdrawing, crowbar at the ready to come down on top of whoever's noggin appeared to answer.

Nobody came.

He chapped harder.

So did McCoist's heart, which threatened to pound its way through her ribs and jitter across the floor like wind-up chattering teeth.

Lottie groaned.

"Open yer eyes," Jamieson commanded. "WATCH!"

The man on the screen chapped again. Still no answer.

"Pan in the fuckin windae," Jamieson growled into the phone.

The balaclava smashed his way in with his crowbar, the camera shaking so hard any visual sense of what was going on was lost. Then bright white light flooded the screen, overloading everything. Back in the old flat, Jamieson's jagged face was thrown into sharp relief by the intensity of it, a gnarled woodcut.

The night vision switched off. They were in a living room, so far, so beige. No people. They thrashed through a kitchen, a dining room…

Please, please, please, McCoist prayed.

Into the hall, storming up the stairs…

Please.

Bathroom. Shower curtain pulled back.

Please.

Bedroom one. Wardrobe opened, clothes torn aside. Under the bed…

Come on, for the love of Christ.

Bedroom two…

"Naebdy here, gaffer."

YES! McCoist started to shake, minor relief from the tension which held her piano-wire tight.

Marble gave his boss a nervous look.

"Get oot ae there," Jamieson said. If he was angry or deflated, it didn't show. McCoist almost wished he'd thrown a tantrum. The coolness was unnerving, bringing her pulse back up again. Her jaw hurt from clenching.

Jamieson turned his rotten, spoon-carved-tumshie face back on McCoist and Lottie. "Well then. That's that. Yer man Chuckie has just killt baith yer faimlies."

70

"Did a no mention it wis a collective decision? Wan fir aw an aw fir wan? Ye goat yersels intae this thegether, ye get yersels oot thegether. Nae chance ae that noo, but."

McCoist could barely hear him over Lottie's screaming. She sounded like she was giving birth. McCoist herself had slipped into a deep shock, her breath coming in wheezing gasps.

"He's fuckt it fir yer loved wans, but maybe yous could still come oot ae this alive." The phone was moving slowly towards his mouth.

Cam. Tess. Mark. Her mind scrabbled at their names but couldn't bring up their faces. No memories. Nothing could be dredged up, everything washed away by the frothing flood of panic which was shutting her down.

The sound of her own name brought her round a little.

"McCoist!" Lottie shrieked. "It wis McCoist. A geed her it aw. She's the wan who's taken it. Look, am sorry, a shouldnae huv lied, a should ae just geed ye it the first time ye asked, but…" Lottie's face was a slobbering mess of tears, mascara and snot. "Don't hurt ma weans. Please, Billy. No mine. It wis her!" She fell into a fit of sobbing. Jamieson approached, put the palm of his wrinkled hand against her cheek, teardrops catching on his thumb and running down towards his wrist like dew down a stalk of grass.

"Cheers, hen. But it's too late."

With an animal snarl, Lottie twisted her head and clamped her teeth down on his thumb, seasoned with her own tears.

Jamieson screeched, tried to pull away but Lottie had her teeth dug into him like Bruce with that bloody bird. McCoist dived for the phone.

The three of them sprawled on the buckled floorboards.

McCoist was on top, had both hands prying Jamieson's fingers from the phone, was ready to go in with the teeth herself when she took a polished wingtip to the face.

She rolled, scrambled back upright, blood running into her eye from a cut on her forehead. She faced the beautiful bodyguard who'd hoofed her, ready to make him much less pretty. But Jamieson pointed the phone at her like a gun. "Don't fuckin move."

She had to do something. She had to. *Do something. Do something. They're gonna fucking kill them, they're gonna*—"I know where it is. I can get you it. I can take you to the man who has it."

"Good. That's good. Sweet as a nut. Like a says, but, it's still too late tae save yer people. Wull talk eftir."

"No. Call them off or I'll say nothing."

"That right?" No smirk crossed Jamieson's crumbling face. Nothing at all on the outside, just pure malice burning in the caved-in pits of his eyes.

"You think I'll care what you do to me after I've watched my kids murdered?" She eeked the words out from herself, carving her guts up with a rusty, blunt knife. "The worst will have already happened. No. Call them off and I'll tell you. Otherwise, you'll never find it. You'll have to face Callaghan on equal ground. Fancy your chances?"

Jamieson, ever the businessman, weighed this up. "It's no a bad offer."

Hope and fear competed for first place. She was trading her family for Devlin. Jamieson would kill him for this. Or at least take the remaining testicle, have the full set. She could live with that. In this moment she was sure she could. "Give me clear evidence both my family and Lottie's are safe and I'll take you straight to him—"

"Temptin. But am a man ae ma word, see? An av awready made ye a promise."

"No!"

McCoist lunged at him—*GQ* henchman intercepted, holding her back.

"STOP!"

71

The voice came from the doorway: "Evrybdy play stick-in-the-mud or sad sack here gets a sunroof."

The shabby man who'd been watching outside was standing with his hands up. A double-barrelled hunting gun, sawn short like the wee man holding it, was pressed against the back of his head.

The man who had spoken was dressed in a silk shirt and high-waisted trousers, a suit jacket thrown over his shoulders: Ruraidh Callaghan. They were backed up by Ben Nevis. "Howsit goin, auld yin?" Callaghan continued, swaggering in. "Nice digs. Bit ae a fixer-upper but plenty ae potensh." He took the jacket off and folded it over his arm, had a casual gander at the laptop screen. "Wit's goin oan here then?"

"Nothin that concerns ye, lad. Leave noo an a willnae huv ye taken apart," Jamieson growled.

Callaghan laughed, loud and fake. "Aw, wid ye gee me the auld car keys an lug wrench trick? A love that story."

"Wit dye want?"

"A want ye tae tell yer men tae step doon."

"This has nothin tae dae wae ye—"

"Aye but it does. See, this is ma toon noo. Evryhin is tae dae wae me. Noo tell them."

"This willnae end well fir ye, son. Moan an see sense. Go oot the way ye came in."

"Call. Them. Aff."

Trav the gnome nudged the back of Roughcast's head with the barrels of the shotgun and he let out a whimper.

"If wur baith gonnae be playin in the same league, Billy, a hink we should start aff oan the good foot, naw? Yer a businessman eftir aw. An yev the experience tae know when yer ootgunned."

Even Jamieson couldn't keep the warring emotions inside him from his face this time, and he gurned and creaked and guttered until he finally pressed the button and said—McCoist closed her eyes, braced for impact—"It's aff, boays. Head oan hame."

The remaining video feeds on the screen flicked off.

McCoist let out a great, shuddering breath. The relief almost buckled her knees. Lottie mewed, still curled up on the floor.

"Gid man," Callaghan said. He reached around Jamieson's back and patted him on the shoulder.

Jamieson stared at Callaghan's hand resting there.

"An speakin ae startin oot oan the good foot, let's clear the air, chase the elephant oot the room," Callaghan continued.

The fire inside Jamieson's skull licked up into a white fury that threatened to melt what was left of his mouldy mug.

Callaghan squeezed in close. "A know it wis you who tipped aff the polis aboot Oban." The knife flashed out from under the folded jacket in Callaghan's other hand. It went into Jamieson's throat, who screamed and gargled blood. Callaghan held the old man tight as he sawed, in three jerking hacks, from one carotid to the other—severing trachea and oesophagus on his merry way, the blood lashing out in tremendous, rhythmic gouts—then dropped him to the floor.

The shotgun, point-blank to the back of Roughcast's head, tore a hole out through his face big enough to fit your arm in, pebble-dash spraying through the air. McCoist clapped her hands over her ears.

Marble threw his hands up in surrender as the gun turned on him. "Naw!"

"Hawd oan, Trav!" Callaghan called. "A fine-lookin specimen, this wan. Maybe we could find a use fir him?"

Marble nodded. "P-please."

"Bit ae meat oan him too," Nevis noted. "Can gee us a hawn movin these." He indicated the bodies, each marinating in an impressive amount of mess.

"*Gid* idea!" Callaghan beamed. His silk shirt was ruined. He looked around for somewhere to put down his bloody knife, decided the best place to store it was between Jamieson's ribs. "Man wis a legend... Ye build these guys up in yer heed an..." He gave a big, fake sigh then turned his attention to the hostages. "Nice tae see ye again, Ally. And this must be Lottie McGuinn. Never hud the pleasure, though a wis blessed tae huv a couple ae wee run-ins wae yer deed husband. He wis a pistol that yin." He crossed himself. "RIP."

Lottie dragged herself upright. She looked like she'd been on the ran-dan for a week. McCoist was woozy and off-balance from the ringing in her ears.

"Ye huv oor mutual pal Chuck tae thank fir aw this." He surveyed the bloodbath before them. "He called me, geed us the skinny, said it might be in ma interest tae tootle oan oer an see fir masel wit wis goin oan wae that sneaky auld bastart. Saved a couple ae damsels in distress while a wis at it, eh!"

"Eat ma chuff," Lottie spat, her voice a wreck.

Callaghan just laughed, a big showy, false thing it was—went perfectly with his straight, square, too-white rows of teeth. "Seriously though, we should sit doon an huv a proper chat once wur aw cleant up. Aye, Chief Inspector? Wan good deed deserves another." He gave her a beat and a smile to answer but ignored that she didn't. "Kwality! Right then, yous two head aff, yel be wantin tae go an see yer faimlies nae doot. Wuv goat a late wan here a reckon." He put his hands on his hips and shook his head, mugging to the audience, pantomime theatrics.

McCoist had passed through the weak-kneed terror, was now heaving full of simmering adrenaline, acid blood. *Who's this cunt now?* On to the next one and the next one. Paulo, Jamieson, Callaghan. Men who could only take more and more, never sated, never content. Her family were safe for the moment but for how much longer if she was in debt to a man like this? *Sit doon an huv a proper chat... Wan good deed deserves another...* Fuck that. Fuck it sideways with a cactus. Her toes were over the edge of the precipice, the maelstrom swirling below. She leapt.

The wee gnome didn't even see it—he was upright one second, the next doubled over gasping for breath. Sucker punched in the windpipe. McCoist got her hands on the bloody barrels of the shotgun and yanked. He stumbled and went arse over tit.

Callaghan turned his shock to laughter in a way that suggested a stripper had popped up out of his birthday cake. "Nice moves!" He threw a couple of shadow hooks. "But there are three, maybe four ae us an ye only huv wan shell left in that hing."

"One's all I need." She strode towards Callaghan until the barrels were almost touching his chin.

"Ah that's hot! Hot! Come oan! Aow, ah! Boays!"

"They can't help you. They touch either of us and I turn your head into a pinball machine." She visualised it—squeeze the trigger, feel the blast, the noise, the heat, the spray—remembered what it was like with McGuinn, snuffing someone out with all the effort of clicking a mouse. It would be so easy to do it again. Another notch on the belt for Dirty Ally. *What the fuck are you thinking?!* A rush of fear made her hand tremble on the already blood-slick grip of the gun, her finger on the trigger a high-wire act. A voice deep inside screamed for her to pull back.

He had a snake-laugh, all nasally hiss. "Then wit, ye gonnae fight them aw aff? Ad love tae see ye go a roond wae Big Ben, actually, hink that'd be worth the price ae the pay-per-view."

"Lottie," McCoist called, "who's still in Paulo's corner? Who's fighting for him? Who's out to take revenge? Who's still loyal?"

No answer came.

"They all went to you or Rogers or the next cunt. The dead man on the floor, whoever. Your boys will watch your brain fall out your arse and then they'll do fuck all. Corpses can't write pay cheques."

No laugh this time, no smile, no smarmy words.

"This is over. No sit-down. No wee chat. You want a favour? OK, I'll let you have your life. And some words of wisdom: you are alone in this."

McCoist backed towards the door, gun sweeping an arc across all of them. "Time to go, Lottie."

"Hawd oan." She walked over to Jamieson's corpse and put the heel of her shoe through his eye. "See ye."

Callaghan regained his composure and his grin and started applauding. "DCI McCoist, am very impressed indeed. The two ae yeez actually—absolute stars! Caw it even if ye want but a hink we'd make a *gid* team!"

She clattered down the stairs. Once she was on the bottom floor, McCoist broke the double-barrel open, pulled the unused shell from inside and pocketed it, tossed the gun and ran.

72

She blasted west out of the city, swinging around the airport, crossing the Clyde at the Erskine Bridge and heading along Great Western Road at manic speed for miles up towards the Trossachs, a rally all along the bonnie banks of Loch Lomond. She called Mark again and again but it went straight to voicemail. *Digital fucking detox! Stupid fucking cunt!*

She desperately needed to know they were OK. It was unbearable.

What if her children were dead?

What was the last thing she'd said to them?

Headlights scrolled white lines and her mind scrolled memories. Their faces as she left them that day after the hospital. A few terse text messages since then about some nonsense or other. The scrapbook flipped before her eyes. They were fast years, gone before you knew it, all the usual clichéd bullshit which was true.

McCoist genuinely tried to speak to God for the first time since she was a child. No answer on the dark road ahead.

She reached Tyndrum and turned off towards the caravan park, crawling along a path through woods and stopping just inside the entrance to the site. She'd been before when the kids were little, before the divorce, recalled a hive of screaming weans and drunk backpackers under a cloud of bastard midges, perpetual smell of burnt barbecued meat. She felt her way forward with her phone torch, scrabbling for hints of familiarity, any kind of touchstone her mind could dredge up to guide her.

She jumped as someone stepped out of a wooden wigwam on her right—just a bloke going for a smoke. *Christ, what if the balaclavas were still hanging around? Should have brought that gun. And have a shoot-out in the middle of a caravan park? Get a fucking grip, Rambo.*

She finally stumbled to a familiar-looking plot of static caravans, saw Mark's car parked next to one. The one she'd seen on the screen. There was a copse of trees opposite—the vantage point—which split the row of caravans from a handful of glamping tents on the other side. She headed towards it, keeping low, heart in mouth, looking like a prize fucking plum, the Grinch tiptoeing off to steal Christmas. It wasn't exactly the jungle but enough to hide two men in the dark. She wondered if they'd booked out one of the wee huts—if they'd decided to stay and enjoy the weekend now the kill was called off. Have a jolly instead.

The midges were even worse under the cover of the trees. They tickled her lips and nose; she blinked them out of her eyes. Her torch scanned grey bark, rustling vegetation.

Nothing else.

Elation burst inside her from a crack in a frozen pipe, gushing through her body. She ran to the door of the caravan, banging on it.

"It's me! It's me!"

Mark opened in his PJs. "What the—"

She pushed past him, inside, the caravan stuffy and smelling of sleep and the toilet. The kids were in their bunks, Tess looking up at the unhinged apparition, smashing into the caravan in the dead of night, Cam grunting and rolling over, teenage boy, the sleep of the dead.

She ran to them, dropped to her knees, shuddering with wild tears.

EPILOGUE

Devlin said they could do it without her, but she volunteered to be the bait. If it was going to happen, if she was going to be complicit, she needed to see it. The price she had to pay for the secrets she had decided to keep. "Good," he'd said, again ready to get the stickers out, or a lovely wee stamp for her progress chart. "It'll make things easier." He'd not exactly been thrilled about what had gone down with Jamieson, but he was partly (a fair fucking part) to blame so he took it on the chin. "An in with Callaghan may be useful then." He stopped short of saying "Good work". Which was fair, because it wasn't. Seemed like a long time since McCoist had done good work. Finding Lennox and poor Tim's killers had been completely overshadowed by the deaths and lies she was party to.

The victims' families would never know the truth. Even with the murderers dead and McCoist threatening a suitably terrified MacGillivary that she'd hound him to prison one day for his complicity, they would never have true justice. It was another cover-up.

Speaking out meant death or prison. She would accept neither without a fight. Decisions had been made that night, crying on her knees, clawing at her bairns, scaring them with her desperate love. She needed to be there for them. Always. She meant it this time. Penance would have to be paid another way.

And so she found herself by the Hope Sculpture in the early morning, grass glistening with the dew, steam rising from the paths as the sun climbed. Alone but for the man and his dog walking towards her. He unclipped the dog's lead, and Maisie bounded away towards Bruce, who was enjoying himself in the grass, snuffling for disgusting treats, launching himself back and forth in dizzying bursts of energy.

Slater hung the lead over his shoulders. The aggressive posturing of their last meeting was gone. "I'm glad you called," he said.

"Now we've both had time to cool down and think about it…" She trailed off. A flatbed council van with bin bags stuffed in the back turned the corner and crawled up the hill towards them.

"Aye. We both lost the heed a bit there." He turned at the sound of the van's engine and stepped off the path onto the grass. The van stopped by the nearby bin and a man jumped out the passenger seat to collect.

"Better if we come to some kind of arrangement, rather than dragging each other through the mud." McCoist moved out onto the grass too, circling slightly so Slater's back was to the van as it crawled past. And stopped.

"Even better if we just both forget about it, eh? Go back to how it was, before Findlay and all that shite. Right?"

"Right. Before Findlay. Before I found out about Melanie Coburn and the others. Before you told Billy Jamieson where he could find my family."

"What?"

"A couple of years ago, Melanie's husband hired a private investigator to find evidence to take you down. An investigator from Firestane. I checked." *There are already links between some of his "legitimate" private investigators and some of ours*—Devlin's words. "They made a deal with you instead.

You become one of their informants, they keep what they found to themselves."

"This is, this is fucking crazy, mental bullshit! The fuck are you on—"

"Who else knew about Tyndrum?!"

"I thought you came here to talk sense."

"I came here to say goodbye."

The men jumped out from under the bin bags.

The bedsit befitted a monk and for now that's how Chuck liked it. Reminded him of what he'd lost, what his gambling had cost him. Bell had gone back to the house once Chuck knew it was safe to do so. He was not welcome there.

Callaghan had let him know the result. "Gave the man some gills tae help him breathe under the water," he'd said. Who owed who in this situation was blurry. Chuck had photographed the evidence he'd pinched from Jamieson, which showed all the intel the old vulture had been gathering about certain shipping routes and the movements of a particular boat called the *Shippendale*. He'd exposed a dangerous rival for Callaghan. But Callaghan then getting rid of Jamieson was also good— very good—for Chuck. Either way, Chuck knew he was in no position to argue if Callaghan decided it was his turn to pick up the cheque. But he hadn't heard from him since and hoped it would stay that way.

Some new jobs had come in and Chuck filled his diary with the diligence of a man in recovery. He signed up to meetings again. He deleted the apps again. Even so, the ads could find you anywhere—a free go at this, a free hand at that, an extra tenner if you sign up, blah, blah, blah—so he decided to stay off his phone as much as possible beyond work calls. He kept the van's radio tuned to Classic FM and avoided any pub with a telly. So it was entirely by accident he found out Brentford had gone all the way to the cup final:

He was carrying a stack of paperwork out to his van from a pawnshop on Argyle Street when a guy in a red-and-white-striped jersey stumbled out of the pub next door and crashed into him. Rather than offering to help Chuck pick up the papers now littering the street, he grabbed hold of his shoulders and screamed "MOAN THE BEES!" into his face. It hit him like lightning.

The Great Accumulator... it was still on.

One match left.

He checked the app. (Hands sweating—took him two goes to get his PIN right.) The only one he hadn't deleted—of course he hadn't deleted that one. The amount he'd get if he cashed in now was substantial. Enough to make his money worries vanish for the foreseeable. Get a decent place, stabilise the business. His heart beat a conga. Euphoria lifted him out of body.

But if he held out, and Brentford won the final... Gold toilet seats and hunner-pound notes to wipe his arse with. Never have to work again. And Bell, Bell would—

But if they lost, he'd get nothing.

He already had nothing.

Be sensible, he told himself. Be smart. His thumb hovered over the phone.

"Make sure you get the chandelier in shot," the estate agent told the videographer.

"How could a bloody miss it? Is Buckingham Palace no lookin fir this?"

Lottie let them get on with it. Soon the place wouldn't be hers any more anyway. Maybe it already wasn't. That feeling of home, sanctuary, had left. Gemma was distraught. Ari delighted. She kept WhatsApping her listings for penthouse apartments in the west end. This alliance with her elder daughter felt at odds with the natural order, brittle, but it was nice to be closer to her for once. Hopefully Gemma would come around.

The doorbell rang. "Al gee ye a hunner quid an a nice rid van fir it!" the postie smiled, pointing a thumb at the FOR SALE sign at the bottom of the driveway.

"Hows aboot ye throw in yer bag an aw?"

"Ach, sorry hen, it's ma favourite wan, cannae be parted fae it." He handed her a board-backed envelope with "Do not bend" written on it and she waved him off.

She retreated to the office to open it, expecting it to be more tiresome legal bumf relating to the sales of the house and Ari's flat. She saw the letterhead of some lawyer's firm, as expected, but a name jumped out from the text, making her body stiffen: William Jamieson.

Since Jamieson's "disappearance", evidence had surfaced which implicated him in Paulo's death, apparently tying him to the two dead men who had supposedly been working for Colin. Good news for her sister and nephew, but Lottie hadn't bought a word of it. It stunk of manure and she could tell whose brand it was.

She remembered sitting in that chair, watching the screen, ill and hardly able to move, telling Jamieson it was McCoist who had fucked him over. It was McCoist's family who should suffer, not her own. Still, she had come through for Lottie after all that, throwing a bone for Colin. Why? To further shame her? To help? Hard to say, but if she could go the rest of her life without running into that fucking woman again she'd be happy. Still, maybe it would be a good thing to be on friendly terms with a DCI, considering what she and Luce were now cooking up...

The letter was from Jamieson's attorney, saying there were instructions that if anything happened to his client, this document was to be delivered to her. A note in Jamieson's scrawl read: "I am a man of my word. Here is the answer you seek."

Inside was a stack of rumpled loose-leaf papers, writing scribbled on all sides. And an empty bullet casing in a plastic sleeve.

Palms sweaty on the pages, Lottie leafed through, again and again. It was all about Paulo. His comings and goings to a car wash in the east end—the one where his life had been ended. His dealings—drugs, guns... women. A young woman stabbed to death by a "bigwig cowboy", the narrator helping to clear it up, Paulo covering it up, using the evidence as blackmail. The Shit List rearing its ugly head. It mentioned two polis. One called Croaker—dead at the scene, it was him who instigated the hit—and one referred to by a code: No. 9. It was No. 9 who had pulled the trigger.

Lottie put the papers down on the monstrous desk and spun round in the chair to face the wall, looking up at the signed 1997 RFC jersey hanging up in its frame:

McCOIST

9

ACKNOWLEDGEMENTS

Known associates who aided and abetted the creation of this book:

Lisa McSorley—I'd be lost without her, and I certainly wouldn't have achieved this dream. Our children Elliot and Nina keep my imagination growing.

Guerilla PR & marketing agent Marion McDougall (my mother), whose mugshot is up behind the counter at every bookshop in the country.

My family and friends.

Editor Daniel Seton, who is forced to ask the big questions, like "Does this pube joke actually make sense?", copy-editor Alex Middleton, who is a champion at "Scottish or typo?", and the amazing team at Pushkin Vertigo, who turned my scribblings into a book I can be very proud of.

Super-agent Emily MacDonald and her colleague Marilia Savvides, who also provided her help and services—I'm sorry for my Andy Murray-style celebration of good news.

kid-ethic, who created an amazing, eye-catching cover to give this baby its best shot at life.

Shredding technician and scuba-diving Renaissance man David Wilson, whose work tales sparked the idea for *Paperboy*, and who gave me the low-down on the shredding biz. His enthusiastic insights into if and how an industrial paper shredder could eat a man were invaluable and scary.

Steven Cahill and Stuart Gillies, who provided their advice and knowledge of police procedure—both have endured many silly questions sent at odd times of the day and their patient and detailed responses were extremely helpful. (Any mistakes are my own and at least some are deliberate.)

Habbie the Labbie provided the raw material for Bruce's disgusting adventures.

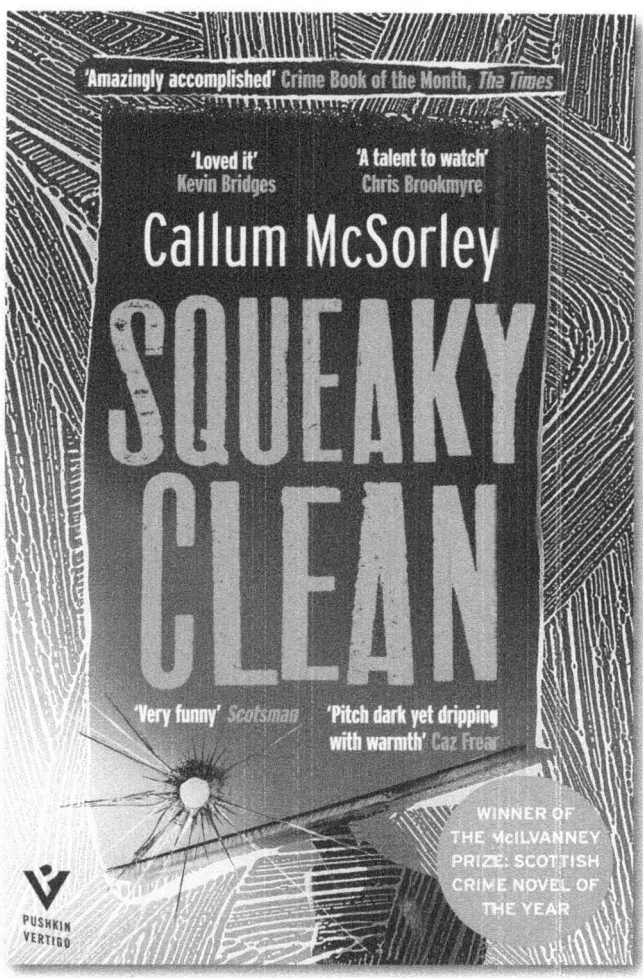